Odd Man Out

by Larry Clark

Scythe Publications, Inc.

A Division of Winston-Derek Publishers Group, Inc.

© 1996 by Larry Clark

All rights reserved. No part of this book may be reproduced in any form without written permission from the publishers, except by a reviewer who may quote brief passages in a review to be printed in a newspaper or magazine.

First printing

PUBLISHED BY SCYTHE PUBLICATIONS, INC.
A Division of Winston-Derek Publishers Group, Inc.
Nashville, Tennessee 37205

Library of Congress Catalog Card No: 93-61422
ISBN: 1-55523-669-3

Printed in the United States of America

To my sister, Catherine,
and nephew, Adam,
from whom I gleaned
the inspiration for this novel.

1

Anyone who knew Eunice particularly well would not have been surprised to see her wandering over the grounds of William H. Hilton Junior High School. It was something she did from time to time to reconnect with another period in her life. Sometimes it almost seemed like a previous lifetime—-like a Shirley MacLaine reincarnation recitation—- when she tried to juxtapose it with how she lived now.

She had once attended school at Hilton and graduated from there. That was in Virginia's preintegration days. It was William H. Hilton Senior High then. Integration had turned it into a junior high, with previously all white Brileyville retaining its senior high status and getting the tenth through twelfth graders among blacks as well as whites. That seems now to be the story in virtually every southern community.

A lot had changed since Eunice's high school days in the

sixties. Or perhaps not. Young caucasians should have been attending Hilton now, but as Eunice looked around, she saw no young white faces. That story she understood, too. A lot of the caucasian families had moved out after the desegregation process began. Three outlying counties absorbed the bulk of Brileyville's white flight from that period. Bedroom communities, some like to call such places.

Eunice lit a cigarette. She had not yet shaken that pernicious habit. A few times she had considered quitting but had not yet brought herself around to actually doing it. Now she sometimes remarked jocularly that she merely kept faith with the state of her birth and rearing. Virginia is one of the big tobacco growing states. The cancer inducing weed provides a solid employment base for much of that region. Of course, that the habit was a matter of faith wasn't exactly true. Eunice felt no great allegiance to tobacco, and in fact she was quite willing to admit that the world might be better off without it. She just happened to have a bad habit that she hadn't yet mustered the willpower to rid herself of.

The smoking habit had followed her through her days as a student at the all black Virginia Central University and then postgraduate studies at Ivy League Columbia and finally to Wall Street. The latter had been her operating base for more than twenty years. Her life in New York was very far removed from what she had grown up in. For a long time now, she had been acclimated to reasonably civil, if not always comfortable, communication with people from other ethnic groups. So much so that she even spent five years of that interim married to a white man. The marriage didn't work out, but she couldn't blame racial divisions for that. A few years later, she married a black man, from whom she now also was divorced. So she had come to wryly view herself as an equal opportunity failure in the marital process.

Eunice drew thoughtfully on her cigarette. She wasn't sure why her marriages hadn't worked out. She liked men, and her drives and crushes and fantasies had always been exclusively heterosexual. She still dated all kinds of men: some black, some white, occasionally a Hispanic or Asian. Sometimes she even had sex, which she generally liked well enough. Her enjoyment tended to depend on the man's performance level rather than his skin color, and over time she had come to rate black and white males as about equal. It seemed to break down only when she was married.

Eunice's thoughts diverted back to the school. It didn't really seem to have physically changed all that much from how it looked when she attended classes there. One new building extension had been added, but otherwise, it was pretty much as she remembered it.

It was late evening, and the first hints of darkness were starting to show. A slight chill in the air roused Eunice from her reverie and moved her to consider returning to her car and back to the relative warmth of her sister's home. She crushed her cigarette with her foot and started walking towards the school parking lot, where she had left her car.

As she turned the corner of the building, something made her look off to the side. Then she saw something strange—-an isolated basketball goal off to an angle from the building and a white boy shooting hoops at it.

The scene struck Eunice as singular when she remembered her own days there and how whites then were most conspicuous by their absence on these school grounds. Now here was one shooting baskets, a sport to which young blacks at times seem almost to have laid proprietary claim.

Then it struck Eunice that this young man seemed to be very good at the sport. He was shooting long jump shots, some appearing to be almost from professional range, and connecting consistently with them. At one juncture, she counted nine in a row he made.

After a while, the young man stopped throwing up the jumpers and started driving in for layups. His movements were quick and his ballhandling skillful. Eunice was impressed. She could almost picture a young Jerry West back in the early or middle fifties when he would have been a comparable age. This kid could shoot, slash, and dribble. He was talented.

The young man was totally oblivious to the middle-aged black woman watching him—-and to anything else. He appeared totally absorbed in a daydream of sorts, and his body was acting along with the drama. Eunice wondered if he imagined himself in a big game for an NCAA or NBA championship or perhaps to impress some young woman to whom he had taken a fancy. That motivation is certainly understandable for someone his age.

Eunice had been moving stealthily closer until now she stood at the edge of the rough court area. In a way, she now found herself as lost in this drama as the young man acting it out seemed to be.

The young man fell into the type some blacks call Very White. His hair was blond and his skin very fair, and even from a distance Eunice could detect the blue tint in his eyes. He looked to be about fourteen or fifteen, although Eunice understood that his particular type might often appear younger than the chronological age, particularly in the teens and early twenties. She didn't think he was much older than the fourteen or fifteen she had estimated—-not enough, certainly, to make some of those jump shots he was connecting on that much less remarkable.

The young man noticed her and suddenly stopped shooting. He showed an embarrassed grin. "I musta looked kinda silly," he muttered in an almost apologetic tone.

Eunice smiled warmly. "No, not at all. I was just thinking as I was watching you that Jerry West or Bob Cousy might have looked just like you at a comparable age."

The young man's knitted brow signaled that those two names from basketball lore might as well have been opera singers from a time long past. "Uh, I don't wanta sound ignorant, but I don't know who those two guys are," he responded in an almost choking tone.

Eunice nodded understandingly. "Sometimes when you get to be my age, you forget not everyone is going to remember the same things you do." She lit a cigarette. "Jerry West played on some pretty good Laker teams back before you were born. Bob Cousy played on some of the great Celtic teams of the fifties and sixties. I'd have thought you might have heard of them. They were kinda like the Larry Bird and John Stockton of their time."

"Bird'n Stockton I know 'bout," the young man said. He shrugged. "Way basketball's goin' any more, some people prob'ly think it didn't start 'til Michael Jordan came 'long."

Eunice laughed. "I suspect there's some truth in what you say." She drew on her cigarette and studied the young man. "You have remarkable shooting range and ballhandling skills for your age. I'd guess you play for the jayvee or junior high team."

The young man shook his head. "No, ma'am." His eyes rolled an unspoken appeal. "I went out for the team last fall, but Coach Stallings made it plain he didn't want me. I 'spect it's 'cause I don't get 'long too good with a couple of the black guys on the team. He said I'd be kinda a disruptive influence. So I quit an' saved him the trouble of cuttin' me. But that's not so bad. That means I can keep my part-time job after school an' on weekends an' kinda help out with the household 'spenses an' all. 'Sides, Mother's from Boston, an' she doesn't like basketball an' sports like that."

"Well, she might not like the sport itself, but she probably would appreciate the scholarship assistance it could bring you a couple of years down the road," Eunice mused. She drew on her cigarette. "I probably shouldn't be second-guessing your coach, but after watching you just now, I'd have to say if he can dismiss you that easily, the school must have one dynamite team."

The young man laughed. "If they do, they're keepin' it hid real good. I think they're two games over five hundred. That's not 'zackly dynamite."

Eunice shared the amusement. "No, it's not."

It was the young man's turn to study the black woman. "You must be from the school board or somethin'."

"Not quite." Eunice crushed her cigarette. "I grew up here, but I've lived in New York since 1967. I went to this school back when it was all black and a senior high."

"I've heard 'bout that time," the young man said through pursed lips. "Every once in a while, I hear somebody 'round these parts talkin' 'bout how it was a real dogfight when time came for integratin'."

"Two things I've always been grateful for," Eunice said. "That it finally happened, number one, and number two, that I was long gone by the time it did." She scanned the young man again and sensed a loneliness in him. "One of the tragic sidenotes is that a lot of the white people who used to live here decided to leave when the schools desegregated. I imagine it gets pretty lonesome for someone like yourself at times."

"I guess. It's somethin' I try to not think 'bout much," the young man said with a shrug. He tucked his basketball under his arm. "Nice meetin' you, but I think I oughta get on home. Mother's prob'ly havin' a hissy fit wonderin' where I'm at."

"I can give you a ride," Eunice offered.

"I just live a couple blocks 'way. It's prob'ly easier walkin'," the young man demurred.

"And better for you, too," Eunice said. She lit another cigarette. "By the way, I didn't catch your name."

"Hal. Hal McDonough," came the laconic revelation.

"Sounds very Irish," Eunice remarked.

The young man flashed a grin. "Yeah, both sides. My mother's maiden name was Dunleavy. 'Siderin' what she thinks 'bout my dad now, I 'spect there's times she wishes she was still named that 'steada McDonough."

A double name recognition flashed in Eunice's brain. "Boston! Dunleavy! There's a very well known banking family up there by that name."

Hal nodded. "Yeah. We're kin to them. Not that it does us any good. They're up there, an' me'n Mother're down here."

"What about your father?"

"He's down in Norfolk. He works for the shipyard down there. He damn near drove Mother crazy 'fore she finally 'vorced him. It's 'cause of him her family's cut her off'n all. He's kind of a pain in the you-know-what . . . pardon my french."

Eunice laughed. "I think I know the word you mean, and I'm not a prude." She drew on her cigarette. The young man was growing on her. "Uh, my name is Eunice Weller. I have a niece that goes to this school now. Shawna Hanson. I'd guess you to be just about her age."

"Yes, ma'am, she's in my class," Hal confirmed. He chuckled reminiscently. "She's prob'ly the prettiest girl in our class, but she seems to move to the beat of a different drummer."

"Shawna's definitely her own person. Much to my sister, her mother's, chagrin. She tends to take after me in that regard." Eunice smiled warmly. "That's probably not easy for someone your age to understand."

"I don't have a problem with it, but some of the other people in class do," Hal said with a shrug. "I don't have that much contact with her, so I can't really say. I know once in a while I hear some the black guys callin' her stuckup an' all. I 'spect that might be 'cause she doesn't seem in'rested in them."

Eunice broke into a hearty laugh. "I don't think you'll ever have to worry about Shawna setting her sights too low," she responded appreciatively.

2

Eunice was seated at her sister's dining table for the evening meal. Marian Hanson was probably a little more the natural homemaker of the two sisters, but not all that much so. Like Eunice, she tended to think of herself as a career woman: she had a nine to five job as a bank executive.

Unlike Eunice, Marian settled in the town of her birth and rearing and had remained married through the years to her college beau. Gerald Hanson owned a printing business in Brileyville, and the two together managed to provide a comfortable enough way of life for their daughter Shawna to grow up in. Marian and Eunice loved each other as sisters should, but as personalities, they often seemed at opposite poles. Church and traditional values were very important to Marian; Eunice, by contrast, tended to a morality whose only boundaries were doing right by or not bringing harm to other people. She seldom attended church, and she would hardly be likely to get upset if she found that her niece, whom she adored, had forsaken her virginity before marriage.

The two sisters differed markedly in their views on New York as well. By this juncture, Eunice couldn't even remotely consider living anywhere else for a protracted period. To Marian, one very brief New York visit every couple of years or so more than filled her quota.

Eunice sat on one side of the table, beside her niece Shawna. Shawna's personality would remind one much more of her aunt than her mother. Eunice often thought it was like looking at a younger version of herself in the mirror. Shawna loved New York—-the theater, opera, concerts, great out-of-the-way places to shop, the whole bit. Like Eunice, she tried to devour the city and milk it for all the cultural riches it offered at every opportunity.

Gerald Hanson sat at the head of the table. In traditional families, that was the patriarch's place. He was a nice looking man, even now when some visible hair loss had taken hold. He was not handsome exactly, and he certainly wasn't athletic, but his features exuded a certain kindly intelligence which Eunice found rather appealing.

"Care for some more of Marian's scalloped potatoes, Eunice?" Gerald asked. "I think that's my favorite dish in the whole wide world."

Eunice waved the potatoes off. "I agree they're delicious, Gerald, but I have to think about my waistline."

Shawna snorted. "Good grief Aunt Eunice, you got less reason to worry 'bout that 'un maybe any woman I know."

Eunice chuckled. It was true that she had held her figure rather well over the years. She and her sister had both started out slender. Marian wasn't really fat now, but she was showing a little more bulge than Eunice.

"Shawna does have a point, Eunice," Marian interjected.

"Maybe so," Eunice acceded with a shrug. She patted her niece on a cheek. "But I still feel it's a good idea not to overeat. Besides, with all the poverty and hunger and homelessness in this country, I think there's something cruelly insensitive about gorging yourself simply because you have the means to do it."

"On food I 'gree," Shawna said impishly. "But I hope you're not 'cludin' clothes an' stuff like that 'long with it."

"As you get older, my dear, I hope you'll come to realize that vanity should be kept at least a little bit in check, too," Eunice replied with a chuckle.

"I fear we may all be long dead and gone before Shawna finally comes to that realization, Eunice," Marian Hanson sighed.

"It's 'ppreciation for style, not vanity," Shawna told her aunt and mother with a grin.

That one drew a hearty laugh.

There was nothing evil about Shawna, but she could be thoughtless at times in a way that would have to be outgrown. She was exceptionally bright and pretty, and a lot of things came to her perhaps too easily for her own good. That could turn into a problem, but Eunice didn't expect it to. She always felt confident that Shawna's mental and emotional processes would grow to another level when the time came for that to happen. In the meantime, her youthful thoughtlessness was not without its amusing and even entertaining facets. One thing Eunice prided above all else was the inner assurance that Shawna would never be dull.

Eunice stretched and sipped the last of her coffee. "If you all will excuse me, I think I'd like to step out on the porch for a nicotine fix," she told her other family members. That was an acceptable compromise. Neither Marian nor Gerald smoked, and Shawna had shown no particular urge to take up the habit. Eunice wasn't forbidden to smoke in the house exactly, but her sister and brother-in-law made no secret of their preference that she not do so. No problem. She worked in an office setting that required her to go outside when she wanted to light up, so she was used to that. Besides, it helped her to cut down on the number of cigarettes she smoked. Even she had to admit that it was probably for the good.

Ah! That ineffably satisfying first puff!

As Eunice inhaled, the memory of her encounter with

young Hal earlier in the day came back to her. His account of how his coach didn't want to play him because he would be a disruptive influence bothered her. With the team's record, it didn't sound as if there was much to disrupt—even if he was a bad or no more than mediocre player. And she had a feeling that he was far above the latter. He had moves and a shooting range that seemed to her capable of carving a niche in any program for that age group in the entire country.

"Uh, oddest thing happened this afternoon," she said as she rejoined the other family members in the living room. "I was wandering around the Hilton school grounds . . ."

"Good grief, Aunt Eunice, I'd think someone that's gone as far as you'd wanta forget you ever went there, let 'lone back when it was still segregated," Shawna moaned.

Eunice heaved a sigh and patted her niece on a cheek. Her intended topic had been temporarily diverted. "Shawna, I think it's good never to forget where it is you came from," she said gently.

"As long as you also don't forget you don't want to go back," Marian Hanson supported her daughter.

"But it will always be important to someone," Eunice said. She made a quick trip to the kitchen to refill her coffee cup and came right back. "Anyway, that wasn't what I wanted to bring up. You interrupted me before I had a chance to get to what it was I was thinking about. There was this white boy, about Shawna's age. In fact, he told me he's in Shawna's class at school. He was shooting a basketball on an isolated court just behind the school administration building. I was watching him, and I got the feeling he might be pretty good. He was shooting jump shots, some from pretty far out, and he was making a lot of 'em, too. I counted nine in a row he made at one point. I'd guess he was shooting in the twenty to twenty-three foot range. And he seemed to have good ballhandling skills and all . . ."

"Well, if he can play that good, you know he's not on our team," Shawna remarked absently.

"I know." Eunice sipped some coffee and fought the craving for another cigarette. "He told me. He said he went out for the team, but the coach told him he'd be a disruptive influence..."

"If he can play, that could bruise some egos. I guess you could call that disruptive, if you wanta," Shawna said. Her head was buried in a book, and she was picking up only snatches of the conversation.

"Might be when he's out on the court alone, he looks pretty good, but when he gets in a game situation, that kinda falls apart," Gerald conjectured. "I used to feel pretty good about my game when I was shooting by myself, but that totally disappeared when I had somebody guarding me."

"I sensed something a little more than that, Gerald," Eunice mused. "I might be wrong, but I almost had the feeling that I could be looking at a young Jerry West if somebody bothered to work with the kid..."

"Who's Jerry West?" Shawna asked, again absently.

Eunice and Gerald laughed. Marian's attention was focused on a television news program, and she was totally oblivious to the conversation.

"Jerry West goes back about twenty, twenty-five years," Gerald provided the answer. "He might have been the best pure shooter to ever come along."

"He was good all around," Eunice said. "I'll never forget the few times I saw him tear up the Knicks in the Garden." She paused to sip some coffee. "As I was watching that kid today, I sorta thought that's how Jerry West might have looked at age fourteen or fifteen, in that jump shot of his and the moves and the whole bit. I just think somebody might be missing something if they don't try to bring that boy into the athletic program here."

Gerald shrugged. "Coaches have to make decisions all the time, Eunice. One of them is who plays and who gets cut. It comes down a lot of times to just a judgment call..."

"I can live with that if I feel it's done fairly," Eunice said.

"But just watching that kid today, I can't believe twelve other young men his age could possibly be so much better that he can't find a place on the roster—especially when the record's only a couple of games above five hundred. I can't get rid of the nagging thought that the coach might be refusing to play this boy simply because he isn't black. That smacks of the same thing we've taken whites to task for, justifiably, for doing to our people."

"If that's happening it's wrong, I agree, Eunice," Marian interjected absently. "But we don't know that."

"True, but I really think it ought to be looked into just to be sure," Eunice said. She turned to her brother-in-law. "Gerald, I remember you telling me you're good friends with the high school coach. Can't you talk to him and see what you can find out?"

"Yeah, but I don't know what good it'll do," Gerald said hesitantly. "He has no jurisdiction over the junior high. He can't tell the junior high coach who to play and who to cut."

"All I'm asking is that you talk to the coach, whats-his-name," Eunice appealed.

"Jerome Wimbush," Gerald said. He chuckled. "Okay, I'll talk to him first chance I get, but I don't know how much good it'll do."

"That's all I'm asking," Eunice said.

Shawna looked up from her book. "Just outta curiosity, Aunt Eunice, who's this boy you're talkin' 'bout?" she asked.

"He said his name was Hal MacSomething," Eunice said. "I always have a hard time keeping those Macs straight in my head. That's why I'm glad somebody back there in slavery times didn't stick an Irish or Scottish name on one of our family lines. I do remember he told me his mother was a Dunleavy, from the Boston banking family. That's a nice touch of pedigree..."

"But it's not worth much unless you can get your hands on some of that family money," Gerald remarked good-naturedly.

"Hal McDonough," Shawna said. She looked up from her book. "That's his name. I guess he's awright. I dunno. He's kinda quiet, keeps to himself pretty much. Some kids 'round school talk 'bout him like he might be a faggot . . . "

"Shawna, honey, that's a word I rather intensely deplore," Eunice interrupted. "I have a couple of good friends in New York who are homosexual. It's no more right for you to call them faggots than for white people to call us niggers."

Shawna waved defensively, heaved a loud sigh and closed her book. "I was just 'peatin' what I heard some the others say. I don't know he's that way myself. I think some people may make fun of him 'cause he's different. He seems nice 'nuff, couple of times I talked to him. He makes pretty good grades." She flashed a grin. "I don't 'member anything 'bout him ever gave me the 'pression he might be athletically gifted."

"Shawna, anbody from our ethnic background should instinctively understand why you shouldn't try to judge a book by its cover," Eunice reminded her niece.

3

Gerald Hanson's friendship with Jerome Wimbush went back some ten years, when the latter took over the head basketball coaching position at Brileyville High. Wimbush had played for Virginia Union back in the late sixties. He was a solid swingman, shooting guard/small forward, on the college level, but not good enough to play beyond that. When he graduated, he tried going into business, but over time he got the feeling that he was better suited to coaching. So he took a job with a junior high school in his hometown, and eventually the offer came for the Brileyville job which he held now. He had a feeling that he was there for the rest of his working life.

Wimbush's record over the years had been respectable, considering what he had to work with. Brileyville did not have a tradition of turning out great basketball players. As Wimbush often reminded various people, being black did not automatically make one a great athlete. He had coached a lot of athletically mediocre African Americans over that period, so he was willing to advance himself as an authority of sorts on the subject.

Wimbush and Gerald Hanson both liked to work out at the local recreation center, so that was where Hal McDonough's status finally was raised.

"My sister-in-law from New York was telling me about this white kid at the junior high she thought oughta be on the team there," Gerald said. "She was comparing him to Jerry West at that age. I don't know how valid that is, but she knows the game well enough so I'm not gonna totally discount her opinion . . . "

"Well, if I found a young Jerry West equivalent among any of our students, I'd definitely move Heaven and Hell to get him into a basketball uniform," Wimbush said.

"Uh, Eunice, that's my sister-in-law, she said the kid told her the coach over there wouldn't let him be on the team, called him a disruptive influence," Gerald said.

Wimbush shrugged. "Could be. We have problems with white kids at our school from time to time. They come up with some grievance. Usually it turns out they're just parroting something they picked up from their parents. Unfortunately, Jim Crow isn't dead, and some whites have a way of bringing him back even when they're not in the majority."

"It could be that, but Eunice thinks it might be a case of the coach not wanting to play him just because he's white," Gerald said. "She raised the point that it's no more right for him to be shut out unfairly than it was for whites to do that to our people, and I can't argue with that."

"Nor can I, if that's what's going on," Wimbush said. "But even if it is going on, I don't know how I could prove it, and even if I could prove it, I don't know what I could do about it." He patted his friend on a shoulder. "Gerald, Coach Stallings has a right to pick whoever he wants to play on his team. I understand the elimination process well enough from my own experience. I have twelve slots. If twenty guys come out for the team, that means eight are not going to make it. It's simple arithmetic. Some people are simply not as good at the sport as others. I would say this: If a young Jerry West or young Kevin McHale happened to come along, I'm pretty confident that one of the young African Americans currently on my team would be dumped. To me it comes down to finding the players that will help me win basketball games and, I hope, even a championship of some kind. If the kid you're talking about is that good and Coach Stallings didn't play him, I'd say Coach Stallings is being, at the very least, very foolish. Even so, I don't see where that in itself is an indictable offense. If it ever becomes one, we could all be in trouble at some point."

"Point well made," Gerald conceded with a chuckle. "I'm not saying I want Coach Stallings's head to roll or anything like that. But if this kid has that kinda talent, you could make sure he doesn't fall through the cracks."

"Yes, I suppose I could do that much," Wimbush agreed. His eyes rolled thoughtfully. "By the way, it would help if I knew the kid's name."

Gerald laughed. "You know, I can't even remember it now," he said. "Give me a couple minutes to call Eunice and get it from her."

Wimbush didn't visit the junior high school all that often, but he did come around enough so that he had no trouble finding the principal's office. Sandra Meacham was a middle-aged black woman with prematurely white hair and a pleasant smile. She had worked her way up through the Brileyville school system's ranks and gave every indication of regarding her current status as a dream fulfilled.

"Coach Wimbush, what brings you around here?" she greeted her visitor from the senior high.

"Hi, Mrs. Meacham," Wimbush returned the greeting. His lips pursed thoughtfully. "What can you tell me about a student in this school, a white boy, Hal McDonough?"

The question puzzled Mrs. Meacham. "Quiet kid. Good

student. He's usually on the honor roll. He's not in any kind of trouble, I hope."

"No," Wimbush assured her. "Nothing like that. It's just a friend of mine says his sister-in-law says she thinks Hal oughta be on the basketball team, but the coach wouldn't play him."

"I never knew Hal even considered playing any sport." Mrs. Meacham heaved a loud sigh. "His mother's a real pill. She's from Boston, and she's got a complex about a mile wide. Boy, that accent of hers, like she even looks down on the Kennedys. It's odd. She works as a secretary for an insurance company here in town, and you'd think by now she'd have evolved out of that, but she hasn't. It's kinda like the old thing I used to read about—-of aristocracy without money."

"She picked the wrong society and especially the wrong town if she hopes to carry that off," Wimbush said. His eyes rolled appealingly. "Any chance I can talk to Hal?"

"Certainly. I think this is his free period," Mrs. Meacham said. "Where should I tell him to meet you?"

"How about down in the gym?" Wimbush recommended.

Mrs. Meacham got one of the students to fetch Hal, and Wimbush headed for the gym to await his arrival.

Hal was discernably nonplussed as he entered the gym. "Uh, you wanted to see me?" he asked dubiously as he approached the area where Wimbush waited.

"Yes, I did, Hal," Wimbush said. He was balancing a basketball he had picked up from a nearby equipment box. "I've heard via the town grapevine you might be a pretty good player."

Hal shrugged. "I dunno who coulda told you that."

"Somebody noticed when you weren't watching, I understand," Wimbush said. He tossed the ball to Hal, fairly hard, to test the young man's reflexes. Hal caught it easily. "Let me see you take a shot."

Hal's head shook in bewilderment. "How come?"

"Just humor me," Wimbush prodded.

Hal shrugged, like someone with nothing to lose, and dribbled to a spot well behind the circle and released a jumper. The arc was beautiful and the aim true. The ball hit nothing but net.

"Not bad. Not bad at all," Wimbush remarked appreciatively.

"I do miss once in a while," Hal said. "If I'da missed that one, would that mean I'm a bad player?"

Wimbush laughed. "No." He retrieved the ball and tossed it back to Hal and moved closer. "Let's see what you can do with me guarding you."

Hal looked at the coach bemusedly. "You're kinda old for this, aren't you?"

"That probably depends on how good you are or might become," Wimbush said. He assumed a defensive stance in front of the young man.

"How come you're doin' this?" Hal asked hesitantly.

"Let's just say to satisfy my curiosity," Wimbush said. He crouched again. "C'mon, let's see if you can get the shot off with me or somebody else guarding you."

"I've never played on a team before," Hal protested.

"I'm aware of that, but if you can impress me, that may be about to change," Wimbush said.

Wimbush had no illusions about his own athletic ability or the fact that it had eroded. Still, he often did this with his own young players, and not many of them could get by him or get off a good shot with him in front of them. He was doing this now with Hal just to get some idea of whether the kid had any real quickness.

Hal shrugged and waited for the coach to resume his crouch. Then he faked with his head and upper body. Wimbush reacted and was caught momentarily off balance, and Hal quickly dribbled around him for an easy layup.

The coach was definitely impressed. The kid had the fastest first step he had ever seen in someone that age. No one he had ever coached showed anything even remotely resembling that sort of quickness with the dribble.

"Hey, no fair," he teased Hal. "You were supposed to try to get the jumper off."

"I think any basketball coach worth their salt'd figure I did the smart thing goin' 'round you for that layup," Hal replied with just the slightest trace of a satisfied grin.

Wimbush laughed and patted the young man on a shoulder. "Yes, he would, and so do I. C'mon, let's try it again."

Hal shrugged and took the basketball back behind the circle. Wimbush guarded him even more tightly this time, but the result was the same. Hal again dribbled past him for another layup, and this time he showed a nice twisting move for emphasis.

Wimbush suddenly had the feeling that he was looking at a young man with very special potential, the sort that could develop into greatness if properly nurtured. He couldn't help wondering if Wilbur Stallings, the junior high coach, had sensed as much himself and rejected it out of fear. Fear of what? The chuckles and inane joking that might go along with a white boy being the best player on the team? The resentment some of the young blacks under his tutelage might feel? Who knows?

"Where did you learn to handle the ball like that?" Wimbush asked Hal, almost in awe.

Hal shrugged. "I dunno. I like to watch the games on TV whenever Mother's not 'round. I kinda picked up on what some of those guys were doin', an' when I got somewheres by myself, I practiced it."

"Why didn't you get in games with other boys in your class?" Wimbush asked.

Hal gestured resignedly. "A couple times I tried it, but you got a couple of 'em wanta make it kinda like a rugby game or somethin' to get rid of me. So it was either leave or get in a fight. It seemed easier to just leave."

Wimbush pursed his lips thoughtfully. A part of him would have preferred to see the kid fight if need be for his rightful place among his peers, but he could understand why Hal didn't, too. Hal was slender, and while he was a gifted athlete, he might not be a match for a couple of the bulkier young men in a rough and tumble skirmish.

"I understand you did go out for the team here last fall," the coach finally pressed. "Any reason you know of why you weren't given a slot?"

Hal shook his head and threw up another long jumper that swished the net. "I scrimmaged a couple times, but the guys wouldn't throw the ball to me. Finally Coach Stallings told me I'd be a disruptive influence."

Wimbush laughed. "With their record, I don't know what you could possibly disrupt."

Hal shared in the amusement. "I'd figure the same thing. Watchin' those other guys out there, I got the feelin' I might be as good as any of 'em. But I can't do much if Coach won't play me an' the guys don't wanta throw the ball to me."

"That's certainly true," Wimbush conceded. He studied Hal momentarily. "I can't do anything about this year, but I certainly can do something when you come up to the senior high in the fall. Would you be interested in playing varsity ball next year?"

Hal was stunned. "You mean it?"

Wimbush smiled and nodded. "I do. Don't let it go to your head, but I think you just might have the most raw potential I've ever come across for a kid your age. If you're half as good as I think you are, you not only will be on my team, you'll be seeing a lot of action."

"Oh, yeah, I like the sound of that," Hal said. He took a deep breath. "But the guys that don't want me playin'? What 'bout them?"

"They'll have to deal with me," Wimbush promised. He patted Hal on a shoulder. "I do want to get you into some organized program so you won't be playing varsity ball cold turkey. What would you say if I could get you into the county rec league through the spring and then the city rec league summer program?"

"Why not the city now?" Hal asked in a bemused tone.

"Because I want a chance to work with you and help you polish your game, and if I did that now in the city with too many people around to pick up on what's going down, we might run into some resistance," Wimbush explained. "You have a lot of natural talent, but you also have some kinks that need to be worked out. I want to get you somewhere away from this setting so we can get that part out of the way in peace."

"Yeah, I guess I can see that," Hal conceded. He scratched his ear in embarrassment. "Uh, Coach, I hate bringin' this up, but I got a part-time job workin' at Mr. Pemberton's grocery store after school, an' I don't think Mother'd like it if I gave that up just to play basketball."

"Well, let me know what your hours are, and we'll work around it," Wimbush promised.

"One more thing," Hal appealed. "I'm all for doin' this, but I was wonderin' if I could get you to talk to Mother. If I bring it up, I think she'll shoot it right down."

Wimbush laughed and patted the young man on a shoulder. "Sure, I'll talk to her," he promised.

Before he left the junior high that day, Wimbush made a point of cornering the coach who dismissed Hal as a disruptive influence. Wilbur Stallings was about the same age as Wimbush and had been the junior high mentor for about the same number of years. It was well known that he had designs on Wimbush's job if and when the latter should move on. But to get it, he would have to do it without Wimbush's recommendation.

"Uh, you wanted to see me, Coach?" Stallings asked in a nonplussed tone as he entered an empty classroom Wimbush and Mrs. Meacham had designated for their meeting.

"Yes I did," Wimbush replied. He took a deep breath. "Coach Stallings, I understand Hal McDonough went out for your team and you made him feel unwelcome? Why?"

Stallings gestured helplessly. "I don't question you 'bout players you cut."

"I cut because in my honest judgment the ones I keep are better players," Wimbush said. "I've just been through a workout session with young McDonough. He has a really nice outside shooting touch and good ballhandling skills, and I don't think you have a player on your team that comes anywhere close to matching up with him in quickness. I can't understand why you wouldn't want him on your team. In your place, I'd certainly want him."

"He didn't fit in with my team concept," Stallings said nervously.

Wimbush groaned. "You're talking about a team concept that has you just one game over five hundred—-I do know about last night's loss on your home court. You have a player there that could help you win a lot more games than that practically just by himself."

"I'm tryna put a team together, not make superstars outta somebody," Stallings protested meekly.

"But some players are going to be superstars," Wimbush shot back. "Some just have that sort of transcendent ability that allows them to do things on a court others can't. When a player like that comes along, you don't want to waste him."

"How you know McDonough could be that good?" Stallings rebutted.

Wimbush emitted a choked laugh. "It just took me a few minutes with the ball in his hands to figure out that's a special talent. Let me ask you, if you got a young Kareem or a young Magic—-not them per se, but someone on that level and black—-in your program, would you dismiss them so casually?"

"You sayin' I'm against McDonough because he's white?" Stallings asked.

"I don't know. Was that a motivating factor?" Wimbush responded probingly.

"I never saw anything like what you're claiming in the young man," Stallings said. "Maybe I missed somethin' . . ."

"Or maybe you weren't looking for it," Wimbush said.

He heaved a loud sigh. "Let me pose this one to you. Say in a year or two, young McDonough emerges as one of the top players in the state, maybe has college scouts from all over looking at him. The sportswriters start getting interested in him. They research everything they can find out about him, and one of the things that comes up is the fact the coach in his junior high school wouldn't let him be on the team. Called him a potentially disruptive influence. And we're not talking about a team of championship caliber or anything of that sort. We're talking about a team that struggles just to break even. When all that comes out and you're approached with it, how will you answer?"

"You're kinda jumpin' the gun, aren't you?" Stallings came back defensively.

"Not really," Wimbush said. "If this kid is only half as good as I think he is, he will play varsity ball and excel. He'll move ahead of most of the guys you have on your team right now very quickly. He'll overshadow them. He'll probably have a spot in the starting lineup before any of them make it. Not because he's white and they're black, but because he's a damned talented young player who doesn't seem to have an attitude problem or chip on his shoulder that sometimes works against young men with that sort of ability. He'll help me win basketball games in ways those other young men couldn't even remotely hope to accomplish. He'll be the go-to guy in our offense, the one we'll want taking the shot when the game's on the line. And you're gonna be left with the nagging question of why you weren't helping with that young man's development when he was under your jurisdiction."

"All I can say, Coach, is I just handled the situation as I saw it," Stallings sighed. "I don't have anything against McDonough, but I just didn't think he fit in with what I was trying to put together."

"The team-organization concept also includes winning, and over the years your record doesn't indicate that you've been very good at that," Wimbush said.

"That's your opinion, I guess," Stallings murmured.

"I think it's the opinion of ninety percent of this community," Wimbush said with just a hint of a smirk. "At least ninety percent."

4

'Unkind fate' was an expression that often popped up in Kathleen McDonough's casual conversation. She didn't necessarily apply it to herself in every instance, but anyone who knew her well enough could sense that she always intended it that way. At this juncture, she was a beaten, hollow, embittered middle-aged woman. She had lost contact with what she felt should have been her natural place, or certainly a place in which she could have felt more comfortable and genuinely useful. So now she found herself in a Virginia locale just barely large enough to qualify as a city, stuck among a lot of blacks and a few semiliterate whites, working in a mundane job, maintaining a small apartment in a neighborhood she didn't really like and trying to rear a son amid influences that seemed to her vortex-like in their insistence on pulling him away from her.

So far, Kathleen McDonough had borne up under it—-or, more exactly, had learned to tolerate it. She hadn't always found it easy to do even that much. She briefly suffered a nervous breakdown when her son was seven years old. It turned out that she mostly staged that to gain a pretext that enabled her to get rid of a husband she had come to detest beyond expression. It was a marriage that should never have been in the first place. It wouldn't have if Kathleen McDonough hadn't decided to take some time off after her sophomore year at Harvard to go to New York's Greenwich Village. She had discovered through her time in boarding school and then while at the university that she had a better than average flair for writing, in both verse and prose. In those early days, too, she was somewhat more Bohemian than one knowing her casually now could imagine she ever might have been. While in New York, she met Charles McDonough. A mutual attraction formed, although now Kathleen McDonough seemed to have lost virtually all memory of herself ever feeling anything.

Charles McDonough at that time was a bluff, ruggedly handsome young man from Nebraska. He attended Creighton University for a couple of years—until he and a roommate were booted out after being caught with liquor in the dorm. He was fascinated by Kathleen McDonough's Bostonian aura, and she enjoyed the rare novelty of a handsome man's attentions . . . albeit briefly. The latter soon wore off, but not before she found herself pregnant with Hal.

Charles McDonough was intelligent enough, even intellectual to a point. But as Kathleen McDonough discovered to her eventual chagrin, it was mostly a plaything to him, something to bring out to humiliate some less gifted but more earnest sort but not to be applied in any useful way. His most remarkable characteristic was a tendency to criticize and try to deflate the image of anyone he perceived as wielding power or influence. That followed no ideological pattern; he seemed to feel contempt for liberals and conservatives and moderates about equally. That constantly got him into trouble with his numerous employers, almost all of whom initially liked him and wanted to give him a chance. If he had ever bothered to develop a sense for accommodation or compromise, or at least learn how not to go out of his way to offend people in authority, he probably could have risen to great (or at least respectable) heights in any one of several professions or vocations he might have chosen. But some inscrutable inner demon—-or moral sensibility, he probably would have called it—-wouldn't let him. So he kept getting fired (or let go, as the polite term goes) from one job after another, in New York, New Jersey, Delaware, Pennsylvania, West Virginia and finally Brileyville, Virginia. All this while dragging an emotionally fragile woman and an infant son with him.

To her credit, Kathleen McDonough in a lot of ways was not a bad mother. In Hal's more reflective moments, he often admitted as much. She worked and scrimped to make as much of their small home as humanly possible. She meant well always, but a lot of times she was simply out of touch with the reality around her.

That understanding of Kathleen McDonough came to Jerome Wimbush from confidences imparted to him by Hal. The coach felt that he had to try to fathom those forces that made Kathleen McDonough tick before he approached her. The more he gained from Hal, the more he sensed in her almost a split personality.

Wimbush normally was not given to crying, but he felt almost moved to tears as he listened to Hal's account of his early life. That combined with the difficult social situation he had been thrust into made it all the more remarkable that he wasn't antisocial at this juncture. A cruel twist of fortune had put Hal in this place. The smallest turn the other way would have had him growing up in opulent Boston surroundings among mostly well-to-do white youngsters. There, his athletic gifts, if anyone had bothered to give him a chance to display them, would have surfaced at a much earlier period. They probably would have been directed towards tennis or perhaps soccer; basketball and football are not sports normally embraced by the upper social stratum. Hal would have been a very good tennis player; Wimbush had no doubt of that. His size and build made him much more ideally suited to that sport than basketball. He was exceptionally quick, both of hand and foot; he might well develop in the manner of a John McEnroe and right now have dreams, well within his power to realize eventually, of playing on Wimbledon's famed Centre Court.

Now here he was in Brileyville, directed towards basketball. Wimbush entertained no illusions; some of the young African American males would resent being upstaged by a white boy. He would have some defiant African American egos to bring back into line if Hal turned into anywhere close to as good a player as he envisaged. Hal would probably catch a lot more of the abuse when the coach wasn't around to keep the peace.

"You ever thought about the fact that if you were in Boston now, you might be playing tennis instead of contemplating basketball?" he asked Hal once just out of curiosity.

Hal shrugged. "Not really. But then I guess if I was there, I prob'ly wouldn't be thinkin' much 'bout what I'd be missin' not bein' here."

Wimbush laughed. "Of course, there is a difference. Being here, you still know something about where Boston is. If you were in Boston, you probably wouldn't know or care if this place existed." He studied Hal momentarily. "You're a natural athlete. I don't want you getting swell-headed on me or anything, but you do seem to be. I can't help wondering where that came from."

"Well, far's I know, I don't have any African 'merican blood in me," Hal said with a grin.

Wimbush laughed again.

"My dad played semi-pro baseball," Hal went on. "He wasn't good 'nuff to play in the Majors, but I guess you gotta have some 'bility to play semi-pro."

"It probably means you're better than average," Wimbush conceded.

"My mother told me, too, my grandfather won a pretty big tennis tournament up in the Boston area a couple times when he was young," Hal said. "You didn't have the money in the sport then like you do now, so he prob'ly didn't feel any great need to push himself like McEnroe or Agassi or some those guys. But whatever I got in athletic 'bility coulda come from him, too, I guess. I know one thing: It didn't come from Mother."

"Your mother's not athletic, I gather," Wimbush probed.

"She doesn't think of herself as athletic, so I guess that 'mounts to the same thing," Hal reasoned. He laughed. "Course, 'til you came 'long, I never thought I might be. When the other guys don't want you playin' with 'em an' all, you kinda get to thinkin' maybe it's 'cause you're no good."

Wimbush nodded and pursed his lips understandingly.

Wimbush hadn't thought about it before, but he had seen Kathleen McDonough numerous times before over the years. They shopped for groceries in the same supermarket, so their paths had crossed several times there. He also had seen her waiting with her arms full for a bus to carry her home from those shopping excursions. If he had known her better, he would have offered her a ride; as it was, he surmised—-correctly, as it turns out—-that she would have interpreted such a gesture the wrong way. She wouldn't understand that he was happily married to a black woman more attractive than she in his eyes and that the offer could possibly have been made with no ulterior motive. She would have difficulty divesting herself of the notion that he might want to initiate sexual involvement, even though she was a woman few men, black or white, would find particularly desirable.

One other tidbit Wimbush gleaned from Hal was that Kathleen McDonough liked blacks, but only to a certain point. There was something peculiarly maternalistic in her feelings. She sometimes confided to her son genuinely fond memories she held of black servants in her parents' Boston household. She expressed much less kindly assessments of them as teachers, executives, et al. A certain social consciousness instilled in her long ago refused to let her accept that many from that racial group might well scale to such heights legitimately.

The thought struck Wimbush that he probably could penetrate her defenses more easily if he was caucasian. If he had a caucasian assistant, he might have sent that person to talk to her. But he didn't, so he had to make the sales pitch himself. Talk reasonably, he told himself, and don't lose your temper. Make your point and, when she tries to puncture it, come up with a measured, convincing argument in its defense. Stand your ground, but don't come off sounding belligerent.

Kathleen McDonough by this juncture had taken on a bloated look. Wimbush learned from Hal that this was in large part due to a bladder problem. At an earlier period in her life, she might have been judged moderately attractive. Her features reminded Wimbush slightly of Katharine Hepburn. Her hair now was a kind of fading (almost a bleached looking) red; the whitening process was taking a gradual toll. Hal could remember when the red had been much brighter. Wimbush supposed that she might never go totally gray, the way most other people eventually do, but the red would become progressively less pronounced over time.

"I hope you don't mind if I smoke," Kathleen McDonough said as the two adults were seated in her living room. Then she lit up in a casual manner that suggested indifference to how Wimbush felt.

Actually, Wimbush did mind. He had never smoked himself, and he didn't really like being in closed quarters with people who did. But it was her home; he couldn't call the shots there. "I always say if people want to kill themselves that way, it's their health," he reasoned.

Kathleen McDonough drew insouciantly on her cigarette. "What could you possibly want to talk to me about Harold, Mr. Wimbush? He doesn't even go to your school yet."

"Well, he will be going there in the fall, Mrs. McDonough," Wimbush reminded. He paused momentarily to gather his thoughts. "I don't know if Hal—-Harold—-has talked to you about it, but I think he's interested in playing basketball . . . "

Kathleen McDonough shook her head. "Harold gets a lot of crazy ideas, Mr. Wimbush. I'm surprised someone like you would take him seriously."

"Uh, Mrs. McDonough, I have worked with Hal—-Harold—-a little bit, and I think I can tell you with assurance he is an unusually talented athlete," Wimbush countered.

Kathleen McDonough smiled patronizingly. "No offense, Mr. Wimbush, but if he had that sort of talent, I think it's safe to say that someone else would have noticed it by now."

"Not necessarily. Not if someone wasn't really looking for it."

"You can hardly expect someone to look for basketball talent in a boy like Harold. I think he's going to wind up well short of seven feet tall. And I hope you don't take this wrong, Mr. Wimbush, but he's the wrong color."

"You don't have to be black to play basketball, Mrs. McDonough. Have you ever heard of Larry Bird? Jerry West? Kevin McHale? John Stockton?"

"I know almost nothing about basketball, Mr. Wimbush, and I wouldn't be unhappy to know even less than that. No offense, but it's not the sort of world I want for my son."

Wimbush saw his opening. "But it can open up other worlds that you might want for him. If Hal—-Harold—-turns out to be as good as I think he will be, and he keeps his grades up, he should be able to write his own ticket as far as what college he winds up going to."

Kathleen McDonough had just crushed one cigarette, and Wimbush noted that she almost immediately was lighting another. "I find that very hard to believe, Mr. Wimbush."

"Believe it, Mrs. McDonough. What college would you

want your son to go to? Duke? Stanford? Princeton? Those schools offer basketball scholarships."

"Well, I went to Harvard myself, for two years."

"Harvard has basketball, too. He could go there, although I'm not sure I'd recommend it personally. I think he'd be better off going to a school with a legitimate shot at winning a national championship."

"Are you sure it's my son you're talking about? My son has blond hair and blue eyes, and he's in the ninth grade. He's not a young man, as I believe some of your people are fond of calling it, of color."

Wimbush laughed. "The young man I'm talking about is blond and has blue eyes and is not of color. Uh, I'd like your permission to work with him, get him into the county recreation league program so he can gain some experience and then into the city summer league program. He needs that for his development. He has the talent, but he has a lot to learn."

"What if it turns out that he's not as good as you think he is, but it goes to his head and he starts neglecting his studies?" Kathleen McDonough murmured.

"If I see his grades start to slip noticeably, I'll help you crack down on him," Wimbush promised. "As for the other, well, I can't guarantee you with absolute certainty that he'll be a superstar. But sometimes you have to test the water just to find out for sure. If you don't test the water, you could be missing out on a great opportunity."

"I suppose there's some truth in that," Kathleen McDonough conceded.

5

So Wimbush was able to begin the development process with Hal. He worked with the young man individually at first, pointing out such little but important things as how to position the feet and hands, avoid taking that extra step that could draw a walking call, spot up, play defense, et cetera. A lot of it can be boring to someone Hal's age, and at first the coach halfway expected the young man to go into a sulking fit. But that never happened. Now that Hal had his first opportunity to excel at something, a gnawing hunger had set in. His incredible physical ability combined with this newly found voracity to create almost a sponge-like absorption.

A white supremacist might have pointed to that as a sign of superior intellectual prowess or will, but Wimbush saw it a little differently. Hal certainly wasn't stupid, but he wasn't necessarily brighter than a lot of the other young men in that setting either. He simply was more driven at this point because of how he had been put down and deprived earlier, and nature or God or whatever had given him a better running piece of machinery than average to work with.

Eventually, Wimbush was able to get Hal into some of the county rec league games. Over the years, he had developed a contact out there: a thirtyish white man with prematurely thinning hair and a shoulder stoop, named Rick Stallard. By day, Rick worked for a worldwide help-the-children organization with an office in Richmond—about an hour's drive away. His evenings and weekends were spent working with the county rec league programs in the seasonal sports. He had been best at baseball, and overall, that and softball remained his first love. But he liked the other sports well enough too, and was more than willing to help them along.

Rick had always seen his role as helping add another dimension to a young person's social development. He had never seen a really outstanding young athlete in the budding stages and, frankly, had come to expect that he never would. He vaguely realized that such creatures have to spring up from somewhere, and the possibility (like buying a winning lottery ticket) theoretically always existed that at some point it would happen in his backyard. But it wasn't something he wasted a great deal of time looking for. He agreed to let Hal McDonough into the program simply as a favor to a longtime friend. He didn't expect much beyond that to come out of it. So he was genuinely surprised to find a bona fide phenom on the floor.

"My God, Jerome, where'd you get that kid?" he asked Wimbush in almost a shocked tone.

"Practically in my backyard," Wimbush said with a shrug. "He's lived in Brileyville for six or seven years now, but he's been kinda out of the flow. He goes to the junior high school there. Can you believe it? The coach wouldn't even play him."

"Well, I can tell you this much: You wouldn't find anyone out here missin' a talent like that," Rick said. He watched as Hal made a juke move and easily went around a black defender. "If it gets back to the coaches at one of our high schools out here, you might find somebody beatin' a path to his parents' door tryna get them to move out here."

"Parent," Wimbush corrected. "He's being raised by his mother. His parents are divorced." He smiled knowingly. "His mother doesn't drive. Hal told me she's scared to death to get behind the wheel of a car. One advantage to her living in Brileyville is that it is possible to catch a bus or cab there. Granted, the service isn't very good, but it does get her to and from work every day. So unless your coaches have someone that's willing to provide chauffeur service twice a day for fifty or seventy-five cents, not to mention affordable living accommodations, I don't think your people'll be able to steal him away from me."

"Even so, I wouldn't put it past one of 'em to try," Rick said with a chuckle. His eyes opened wide as Hal drained a really long three-pointer. "God, that kid's got so much talent. How could anyone miss it? In Chicago or New York, he'd have been in programs like this for years."

"Sometimes if you don't think to look for something, you can miss it, Rick," Wimbush said. He patted the white man on a shoulder. "You're right. That kid's talent hits you in the face practically. And unless something goes awry, I've got him for the next three years. And if one of your coaches out here wants to try to steal him away from me, he'd better hope he follows the book to the letter."

"Well, if they're gonna find out about it, it'll be from someone other than me," Rick assured him.

Wimbush took notes during the games and scrimmages Hal participated in and then later, when the two were alone on a private court in the coach's back yard, critiqued the young man's performance.

"You're gonna make mistakes," he told Hal. "I'm not worried about that. I just want you to make sure you learn from those mistakes."

"Well, yeah, I understand that, Coach, but I have a hard time figurin' out what's wrong with takin' the dribble through four guys when I wound up makin' the layup," Hal protested mildly.

"Against good defensive pressure, you're not going to be able to do that," Wimbush said. "You try that maneuver against good teams, somebody's going to draw you into a charging call or tie you up or get you turned around so somebody else can steal the ball away from you on the blindside. You're a good ballhandler, and you don't want to get in the habit of giving up your dribble too soon, but when you go in and find four guys in front of you, your first instinct should always be to look for the open man."

"Closest open man was Jerry, an' that turkey couldn't score a basket if the goal was as big as the James River an' somebody was holdin' him directly over it in a helicopter," Hal groused.

"That's not the point," Wimbush said. He patted Hal on a shoulder. "Jerry will never be a very good basketball player, that's true. He might not be able to make that shot. But you need to look to him just to get in the habit of doing it. Think of him as McHale, the Chief, Kareem, somebody like that, somebody that can get the ball in the hoop. Don't think of those four guys in front of you as chumps you can have for lunch whenever you want. Think of them as the Detroit Pistons."

Hal laughed. "Forgive me, Coach, but I don't see anything out there 'minds me of Isiah, Dumars, or Rodman."

Wimbush laughed too. He realized that his analogy had been a little farfetched. "It's your work ethic I'm thinking about, not the caliber of player you're going up against now. You need to know how to do all the right things before you go up against the better teams and players so you won't go making dumb mistakes."

He patted Hal on a shoulder again. About this time, his wife Velma was coming out of the house with a pitcher of lemonade and two glasses on a tray.

"Looks like you two gentlemen could use a thirst-quencher 'long about now," Velma Wimbush said. She set the tray on a table near courtside.

Wimbush agreed. "I think we've covered as much as we need to for today," he said. He nudged Hal over to the table, took one glass of the lemonade his wife had just poured and handed the other one to Hal.

Hal swallowed some lemonade. It was good, and his body was letting him know it was grateful to be absorbing it. "Thanks, Miz Wimbush," he said.

"Don't mention it, Hal," Velma Wimbush replied with a smile and a kiss for her husband. "I've had to put up with this man for twenty years, so I know how rough he can be."

"Don't let her kid you, Hal. Around here, she's the boss," Wimbush said with a twinkle.

Just then, the phone rang in the kitchen. "I'll get it," Wimbush volunteered.

He departed, and Hal was left momentarily alone with his wife.

"You know, Jerome is really excited about being able to work with you like this," Velma Wimbush said with a warm smile.

Hal laughed. "Maybe so, but sometimes the way he drives me and gets on me when I screw up, I awmost think he's tryna kill me or somethin'."

Velma Wimbush patted him on a hand. "I can assure you he isn't. He just sees a lot of potential in you, and he's trying to help you develop that to the fullest."

"I guess that's true," Hal said. He sipped some lemonade and flashed a grin. "Course it may take a few years 'fore I come to fully 'ppreciate it."

"I wouldn't be at all surprised," Velma Wimbush said with a warm smile.

Warm always seemed to be the operative word when describing Velma Wimbush. Hal thought she might be the most genuinely nice person he had ever met. She wasn't beautiful in appearance exactly; she tended to an almost square look in her figure, with a round face that gave the impression of being almost flat in front. But she wasn't fat, she carried herself well, and she had very big, expressive, almost embracing eyes. Hal found her peculiarly attractive in her way; and the thought wryly crossed his mind a time or two that if he was twenty years older or so, he might even find her sexy.

Her husband came back out. "It was your mother. She wants you home right away," he told Hal. He heaved a loud sigh. "God, how that woman can talk. Can't she answer anything with a simple yes or no or just a one sentence explanation?"

Hal flashed a grin to Velma Wimbush. "Now there's one I've had more 'sperience with," he said.

6

By the time school let out for the summer, Hal had absorbed almost three months of Wimbush's drill sessions, including an exercise regimen set up by the coach. "You haven't played on the organized level much yet, so the one area you need to work on is your stamina," Wimbush told him. "We don't want you running out of gas down the stretch in big games."

Hal had no problem accepting that. He was new enough to his status as a genuine athletic talent that he hadn't yet learned how to take anything for granted. If he had evolved in the same manner as his classmates and was one of them now, he might be more cocksure and less willing to accept instruction. After all, he would certainly be established by now as the best player in that group by far. He might have developed what is commonly referred to as an attitude.

It did bother him that a vital part of what he had the potential to develop into had been overlooked for so long. But when he thought about it seriously, he felt obligated to take some of the blame for that himself. He might not now be so much an outsider in his own peer group if he had made more of an effort to ingratiate himself with others of a comparable age. It might have helped if some of the others had reached out to him more, and some of them might have done so if they thought he needed or would be receptive to such a gesture. His classmates were not, for the most part, bad or cruel young people. They just had their own agenda and never stopped to think that this lonely, strange looking white boy might want to be a part of it.

Wimbush understood much of this. It wasn't something he and Hal talked about at great length. Hal hadn't yet got to the point of feeling comfortable with opening himself up that much. Even so, Wimbush understood enough about the teen psyche to realize that young people in that age group need to feel a part of some peer group society. Failure to find that is bound to leave a great void.

"A lot of very bright new worlds may very well be opening up to you very soon," he remarked to Hal on one occasion. "I'm sure as they begin opening up, you're going to be reminded more and more of what you've been deprived of over the last several years. I hope you temper any feelings you might harbor of wanting to lord it over some people that you feel snubbed you or to get back at someone you remember as having hurt you."

Hal rubbed his eyes noncommitally. Amorphous outlines of such thoughts had been coursing through his brain of late. It was almost as if the coach had been reading his mind.

"If you have those thoughts and/or feelings, I think it would be hard for anyone acquainted with the circumstances to blame you," Wimbush went on. He patted Hal on a shoulder. "But for your own sake, I would urge you to put them aside—-try to wipe the slate clean—-and focus on where you want to go, not on whom you want to exact revenge. If you get wrapped up in some revenge seeking course, you're going to wind up hurting yourself more than anyone else. If you focus on where you want to go, everyone eventually will have to respect you at least, and the other things—-like friends, girlfriends, whatnot—-will come in due course. You're at an age where it's not easy to wait for what you see as your due. I understand that. But for your own sake, you should take it one day, one step, at a time. Believe me, it moves faster than you might imagine."

"Well, I'll try, Coach," Hal promised. He flashed a grin. "Course now, couple guys I might wanta just take down a peg or two. I think I owe 'em."

"Just do what you know you have to do and don't worry about them," Wimbush said. He chuckled and patted Hal on the shoulder. "If I find you getting a wild hair to go after somebody, don't be surprised if I call you down on it."

"You call me down on everything else. How come you think that's gonna 'prise me?" Hal responded with a laugh.

Wimbush got Hal on a summer rec league team made up of county youngsters and a couple of guys who attended out of town military academies. Some of Hal's Hilton classmates would be on another team. Hal knew all the latter in passing. Wesley Thigpen, the biggest, would play center. Lonnie Hairston and Earl Wilson were the forwards. Melvin Peebles and Thurlow Carter played point and offguard respectively.

Hal had to wonder which of that five he eventually would bump out of a starting position. Thurlow seemed most likely. He was smaller and less skilled than Melvin. Hal's natural position was guard, and by now he had every confidence that neither Melvin nor Thurlow was in his class.

He almost wished it could be Melvin. Melvin had picked on him a lot in the early school years and had beaten him up several times. Even now, Melvin was prone to throw sneering taunts his way and to call him such names as sissy or faggot for no discernible reason other than to be a nuisance. A couple of people had assured Hal that Melvin was really not a bad young man and would in time grow out of it, but that did little to salve the wounds. He felt that he owed Melvin a hurting in return and was a little impatient to repay it.

He appealed once to Wimbush to get him on the team with his classmates, but the coach refused. "I put you on the team with them, they might refuse to throw you the ball, and then, now that you're getting pretty frisky, you might decide to hog it when you do get your hands on it, and we've got a real mess," he told the young man sternly. "This way, if you hold your own playing against them, they're going to have to respect your ability and accept the fact that you will be part of the team."

"Course when they go up, they're gonna have to 'pete 'gainst juniors an' seniors," Hal reminded. "S'posin' I get a startin' position 'fore any of them do?"

"That could happen. In fact, I wouldn't be surprised if it does," Wimbush said. He patted Hal on a shoulder. "But this way, they'll know darned well it's because you can play, not because you're a teacher's pet or anything of that sort."

"Melvin's the one I always had the most trouble with," Hal murmured. "He's always mouthin' off to me an' callin' me names an' whatnot. A lotta that I'm gettin' real tired of."

"Well, when crunch time comes, if young Mr. Peebles has a problem with your being on the team, you leave him to me," Wimbush said.

Hal nodded and voiced assent, but that was halfhearted at best. He really hoped Melvin would give him an opening to dish out some humiliation.

The way the schedules were drawn up, Hal's team wouldn't be playing the Hilton contingent for another couple of weeks. As a team unit, the Hilton players were probably the best in the field. Hal had a feeling already that he might be the best individual player, but he didn't have much in the way of help. One of the academy players, a white boy from Fork Union, was passably skillful. Otherwise, his team seemed more like a crew gathered to film a slapstick comedy.

As it turned out, a lot of the other teams in the field were not particularly good either. So through the first three games, Hal almost singlehandedly was able to produce victory for his own squad. On three or four occasions, he drew a mild rebuke from Wimbush by dribbling through three or four opposing players at a time for easy baskets or pulling up on the fast break to drill a trey. But he was scoring more points than anyone else and playing tenacious defense, and he compiled a lot of assists and would have had many more if his teammates could hang onto the ball with consistency.

The Hilton team had been winning, too, and on the eve of their game, both were unbeaten.

Hal's Hilton classmates were vaguely aware of what was going on. A couple of times, Wesley Thigpen and Lonnie Hairston came by and said hello and congratulated him on what they heard was a good game for him. They probably thought he looked good only because he had been going up against white boys and blacks who played like they were white. But those two didn't wish him ill. They were nice enough to him most of the time. They didn't go out of their way to be friends with him, but they didn't seem to dislike him either.

Melvin Peebles was another story. At this juncture, he was still inclined to bully, and he still regarded Hal as a vulnerable target.

"Hah! You think 'cause you score some points 'gainst them chumps, it mean you can play," Melvin snorted to Hal after the latter's team had won its third game.

"I dunno," Hal said with a shrug and started to walk away. He basically wanted a confrontation with Melvin, but Wimbush had urged him to avoid that, and he was trying to honor the coach's dictum.

Melvin clasped him by a shoulder. "'Morrow night I'm gonna clean you fuckin' clock," he grunted.

Hal shrugged. "If you do it, you do it."

"You don't really think you can hang in with me, do you?" Melvin pressed with that bullying smile.

"Well, I'm gonna show up anyways," Hal said.

Later, Hal told Wimbush about his encounter with Melvin, not so much to get Melvin in trouble as to get across the message that he had taken about as much as he intended to from that young man.

"It's not like I'm tattlin' on him or anything, but he's been pickin' on me since we were in the third grade," Hal said. "I been tryna steer clear of him. But I go out there an' do pretty good 'gainst him on the court, he might wanta turn it into a rumble to get even."

"I'll take care of Melvin. You just go out and play basketball," Wimbush said. "If you outperform him and he doesn't like it, that's going to be his problem, not yours."

"What am I 'pposed to do if he comes after me, though?" Hal appealed.

"Try not to let him catch you alone or with no one around except three or four of his rowdy friends," Wimbush said. "If he tries anything while I'm there, I'll take care of it. You just tend to what you know you have to do."

"Yes, sir," Hal sighed.

As gametime neared, the two teams massed on the court. "Man, I'm gonna clean you so bad, you gonna wanna go out an' buy you a dress an' go hang out with the fags for real," Melvin taunted.

A couple of Hal's teammates laughed. Hal shrugged and bit his lower lip to contain some rising anger he felt. "I guess we'll find out soon 'nuff," he said.

"What's that you say?" Melvin growled.

"I guess we'll find out soon 'nuff," Hal repeated.

The whistle blew, cutting off Melvin's intended sharp rejoinder. The teams got in a circle. Melvin attached himself to Hal. That suited Hal just fine.

The center on Hal's team was about Wesley's height, but he couldn't jump. So Wesley controlled the tap. Lonnie Hairston got the ball and flipped it to Melvin.

Fun time. Melvin took two dribbles before Hal moved in, swiped the ball from him and raced downcourt for an easy deuce.

"Maybe you're the one oughta be gettin' fitted for that dress," Hal taunted as he passed Melvin on his way back to his defensive position.

Melvin glared at him menacingly.

The inbounds pass this time went to Thurlow Carter. Hal let Thurlow bring the ball up the court. He felt nothing personal against Thurlow. Thurlow threw the ball into Wesley, who easily scored over the opposing center.

Hal took the inbounds pass and dribbled downcourt. Melvin fronted him and tried to pay him back for the steal he had just made. Hal responded with a juke move that got Melvin off balance, then a behind-the-back dribble that left Melvin standing flatfooted and able only to watch as he created a three-on-one situation and an easy basket for a teammate.

Melvin's teammates were starting to take a fresh look at Hal. Some other people gathered on the sidelines cheered wildly as the white boy showed Melvin up. Hal was not the only person in that age group who disliked Melvin.

"You better play off him, Melvin. That dude's quick's a cat," Hal heard Wesley exhorting solicitously.

"Fuck. I can handle him an' three more like him," Melvin grunted.

Oh, yeah? Hal thought to himself.

The next time Hal had the ball, Melvin played him a little more loosely. Hal dribbled tauntingly for about ten seconds or so and then faked with his upper body as if to go around Melvin. Melvin backed up as if moved by springs, and Hal calmly drilled a three-pointer.

Laughter accompanied the cheering as the two teams headed back upcourt.

Melvin's eyes were flashing. He didn't like being humiliated, especially by this white boy whose very masculinity he so many times had questioned. And Hal, in turn, was ready to drive the nail in even deeper. Thurlow could dribble all day, and he made no attempt to steal the ball. But as soon as the ball touched Melvin's hands, he pounced like a tiger. He wanted to teach Melvin a lesson.

"I think somebody gettin' some payback," he heard Lonnie remark to Wesley at one point.

"I think that boy 'longed on our team last year, an' somebody fucked up not pickin' him," Wesley muttered.

Wimbush sensed what was happening and called Hal over. "Stop trying to humiliate Melvin," he told the young man angrily. "That's an order."

"Where the fuck was everybody when he was comin' down on me all the time?" Hal snapped back.

Wimbush grasped his shoulders. "Look, you got a raw deal, and somebody should have been watching out for you. But that doesn't give you license to just try to humiliate Melvin now. You're a better player than he is. You know it, I know it, and I expect deep down he knows it, too."

Hal shrugged. "I guess I proved whatever I needed to," he said. He exhaled sharply and flashed a grin. "I couldn't resist it. If anybody asked for it, it was him."

"That's true. Now exorcise that demon and just focus on playing basketball," the coach said.

Wimbush chuckled softly to himself as Hal headed back onto the court. The young man's competitive spirit may have been misdirected, but it was not a bad thing for him to display. That, even more than his natural athletic ability, would determine how good a player he eventually would become.

The Hilton players for the most part had turned quite respectful. "Man, I think I'll be glad to be playin' with you 'steada 'gainst you when we get to high school," Wesley remarked to him in passing. At another juncture, Thurlow Carter told him humbly: "I 'spect if you was 'round last year an' Coach Stallings'd been smart 'nuff to play you, I'da been sittin' the bench." Lonnie Hairston patted him on the back once when he made a difficult twisting layup. Earl Wilson said once, after he drilled a trey: "Man, you got some range on that jumper."

Only Melvin seemed unwilling to give him his due. A

sullen, almost defiant, look seemed frozen on Melvin's visage. That bespoke a smoldering hatred not destined to go away anytime soon.

"I think you're making believers out of most of your future teammates," Wimbush told Hal during one timeout.

Hal shrugged. "Wesley, Lonnie, Thurlow an' Earl been sayin' nice things. But Melvin still seems kinda in a snit."

"He'll get over it," Wimbush said. "Melvin's had it kinda rough. His father was an alcoholic, and he beat him a lot. And I understand he has an older brother that's homosexual."

"Shit, if I had that, I wouldn't be callin' anybody faggot," Hal grunted.

"A lot of it's defensive with Melvin," Wimbush said. He patted Hal on a shoulder. "You don't need to prove anything to Melvin. Just let him work it out his own way."

"O.K., long's he doesn't try provokin' anything with me," Hal agreed.

What neither Hal nor Wimbush figured on was the extent of Melvin's anger. That didn't become apparent until a few minutes later when Hal was driving to the basket and had to cut past Melvin. As he made his move, Melvin countered by hooking him around the neck and sending him crashing face down to the asphalt.

An eerie silence ensued. Hal lay motionless on the court, and some blood could be seen trickling from the side of his face. Wimbush rushed over to him. The coach was angry with Melvin, but that was put momentarily on hold; he didn't want his future star player's promising career nipped before it really got started.

He turned Hal on his back. Finally Hal stirred and moved his arms and legs ever so slightly, just enough to indicate that he wasn't paralyzed. Wimbush heaved a huge sigh of relief.

Hal shook his head and forced a grin. "I didn't know we were 'pposed to be playin' football," he moaned.

A collective sigh of relief was heard. Everyone gathered

around the young man seemed glad to see that he wasn't seriously hurt. Only Melvin, who was off to the side, appeared dispassionate.

"Neither did I," Wimbush said. He sat Hal up and noticed a gash over one eye from which blood was oozing. He pulled a handkerchief from his pocket and pressed it over the gash to stem the bleeding. "I think we'd better get you to a doctor to make sure you're all right."

Hal nodded. He didn't feel seriously injured, but he was groggy and hardly inclined to argue the point in that moment.

Wimbush got one of the rec league workers to drive Hal to the city hospital. Then he sought out young Mr. Peebles.

"Melvin, if I ever catch you pulling a stunt like that again, you're going to wish you'd never been born," he told the young man angrily.

"Huh? Wha' you talkin' 'bout? That were a accident," Melvin defended himself.

The defiant tone angered Wimbush that much more. "That was no accident, and you know it," the coach told him sharply. "You deliberately tried to hurt that boy. Did it ever occur to you that you might have injured him permanently?"

"Well, if he can't take it, maybe he don't 'long out here," Melvin shot back.

"You're the one that seems to have the problem of not being able to take it," Wimbush snapped. He grasped Melvin's shoulders brusquely. "You'd better start adjusting right now. That boy can play, and right now he's easily good enough to play on your team or any team in your age group in the country. If you get rid of that attitude you've been showing, you and he could be teammates eventually. But if you pull another stunt like what I just saw, you damn sure won't play for any team I have anything to do with. And you can take that to the bank."

"Shit! How come you makin' such a fuss over that lily-white faggot?" Melvin groused.

Wimbush was steaming now. He had all he could do to refrain from smacking Melvin hard across the mouth. "He can't help being white any more than you or I can help being black," came the tight-lipped response. "As for the other, I have no reason to believe he's that way and neither do you. You start throwing accusations like that around, you'd better be ready to back them up."

Melvin responded with a cold shrug.

"If I hear you throwing out something like that about Hal with no proof ever again, I'm really going to come down on you," Wimbush said sternly. He got right in Melvin's face. "Do I make myself clear?"

"Yeah," Melvin said with another cold shrug.

Wimbush let it go for the moment. He knew that he hadn't really penetrated Melvin, but belaboring the point accomplished nothing either.

"Don't forget, I'm going to be keeping an eye on you," Wimbush told Melvin as a parting shot.

Then he turned and walked away. He could almost see Melvin's middle finger salute from the back of his head. He knew that whatever Melvin might be scheming wouldn't be implemented where he could see it. That might require his keeping a closer watch on Hal or arranging matters so that Hal wouldn't be left alone someplace where Melvin and some of his friends might isolate and try to hurt him. If it came to a fair fight, he had a feeling now that Hal might win. Hal was a much better athlete than Melvin, and he was starting to show a scrappiness out on the basketball court that could transfer over fairly well to hand-to-hand combat. But if Melvin just wanted to hurt Hal, he wouldn't worry about being fair.

It didn't bother Wimbush so much that Melvin extended him little respect personally. Adolescents since time immemorial have had to outgrow that proclivity in their dealings with older people. But the vicious, mean spirited way in which Melvin had taken Hal down did concern him. That was uncalled for. He might have forgiven it more easily if Melvin had shown some remorse. But he sensed none of that. He wondered if Melvin would have felt any genuine regret if Hal had been killed or paralyzed for life.

He found the rec league worker who had taken Hal to the hospital. "Hal Okay?" he asked solicitously.

"Yeah. He had to get a couple stitches over the eye, but Doc says no reason he shouldn't be back playin' ball within a couple days," the rec league worker said. He chuckled. "Darnest kid I ever saw. He wanted to come right back out here an' play some more."

Wimbush laughed. "Yeah, he's a pretty gritty kid," the coach agreed.

7

Hal was back ready to play the very next day, a fact which amazed everyone around. Some heavy wrapping and a lot of soreness over the cut eye were the sole vestiges of the previous day's now infamous encounter he had with Melvin. He felt physically fine and emotionally ready to go at it again as quickly as possible.

"You know, you don't have to rush it," Wimbush told him. "I'd easily understand it if you wanted to take a couple of days off to give that eye a chance to heal."

"No way. I wanta play," Hal responded.

The opponent this time was from Cedar Grove Academy, just outside the Brileyville city limits. Cedar Grove was a Catholic school whose ethnic balance was about ninety-eight percent white. Most of the youngsters who went there were from well-to-do families or at least families with enough money to make a good pretense to that status. That didn't necessarily exclude blacks, although the unspoken preference was for having as few of the latter group around as possible. Some young blacks did go to Cedar Grove, and the summer team's best player happened to be an African American named Wayne.

Wayne's father was an Army major stationed at nearby Fort Lee. He was there because his father could afford to enroll him and because both parents wanted to be very sure that he didn't graduate from high school speaking in street slang or scoring low on his college board exams. The same was pretty much true for all the other blacks at Cedar Grove. Blacks are no less cognizant than whites that the public school systems are falling short in educating their children.

Wayne was assigned to guard Hal. By now, every team in the summer league had figured out that Hal probably was the best player in the entire program and the one who had to be stopped. Wayne was a grade ahead of Hal in school and about a year older, and his coach reasoned that he might at least be able to neutralize the white boy. The plan quickly backfired. Wayne was no match for Hal on either side of the ball, and the Cedar Grove unit was forced back into a zone and a slow-down offense to try to keep the outcome respectable. Hal's team wound up winning by twelve points. Hal scored twenty-six and could easily have doubled that if he hadn't followed Wimbush's directive and spent a lot of time setting up his teammates for shots.

Unlike Melvin, Wayne accepted the defeat graciously. He recognized that he had just gone up against a superior opponent and was quick to acknowledge it.

"You're some player," he told Hal sincerely. "I sure wish we could have you on our team at Cedar Grove next year."

Hal laughed. "My mother'd like to get me there, too, or someplace like it." He patted Wayne on a shoulder. "Nice game."

The Cedar Grove coach also was impressed with Hal. "Boy, if I had that kid, I might have a shot of winnin' the state Catholic League championship," he remarked enviously to Wimbush.

Wimbush chuckled. "Well, I know what it costs to go to Cedar Grove, and I know his mother can't afford to send him there, so you're outta luck."

"Well, we do offer scholarship assistance," the Cedar Grove coach said.

"Yeah, but not enough to cover all the expenses the boy's mother would have to meet," Wimbush said. He patted the Cedar Grove coach on the back. "If you guys want to try to get him away from me, go ahead. But I warn you: I know the Virginia High School League rulebook inside and out. If I catch you in one violation, I'll have you before the board faster than you can spit."

The Cedar Grove coach shrugged and turned away. He sensed that Wimbush wasn't boasting idly.

"No hard feelings, I hope," Wimbush said.   The Cedar Grove coach laughed. "Naw. In your place, I'd do the same thing," he replied.

Hal, courtesy of Wimbush, now had a part-time job at the rec center. He took care of the swimming pool and performed general cleanup work around that area. Previously he worked three hours a day at minimum wage in a small grocery store. This job paid a little more than that, along with providing more hours and access to the indoor facilities (the basketball court, most notably) when the center wasn't open to the public.

His other basketball-playing classmates—-Wesley, Lonnie, Earl and Thurlow—came around fairly often, and all talked to him in a genuinely friendly manner nowadays. They were loosening up with him, as was he with them, to the point of joking and good-natured banter. Melvin was the only notable absentee. Hal understood that Melvin still seemed to feel no remorse for the incident on the basketball court that sent him to the hospital. Melvin was in no hurry to forgive and forget. What Hal might have done that required foregiveness was locked away in the inscrutable recesses of Melvin's mind, but that didn't make it any less real.

"I know Melvin been pretty close to Coach Stallings last couple years," Wesley confided one day. "He kinda look on Coach Stallings as his daddy. Now you come 'long, an' suddenly folks start sayin' Coach Stallings look like a first-class fool 'cause he didn't pick up on how good you are, and that get Melvin in a huff."

"Well, I can't say I'm any great fan of Coach Stallings," Hal said with a shrug. "I'll let him go, but if folks wanta say he made an ass out of himself in not playin' me, I'm not gonna pretend that makes me unhappy."

"I can see that. I 'spect everybody 'round see that but Melvin," Thurlow interjected. "He think somehow you to blame, like if you wasn't here wouldn't none of this be comin' back on Stallings now."

"Fuck, man, you think I asked to be stuck here, made a freak show for y'all all those years an' for Melvin to beat up on 'cause he was bigger?" Hal snapped. "Goddamn, nothin' 'gainst y'all, but I got stuck here every bit as much as any of y'all did, an' I didn't have anybody standin' up for me 'cept maybe my mother, and shit she's off in the ozone layer half the time."

Wesley gestured to Hal to calm down. "You're right," he conceded. "Somebody say whitey, an' you the only white boy we can get at. It kinda fuck you up when it come to gettin' girls'n whatnot, too, I 'magine."

"Well, I 'spect it would be easier if we had some white girls 'round that didn't look like somethin' beat on with an ugly stick," Hal sighed. He thought about his most recent outburst and shook his head and chuckled sheepishly. "I don't feel anything 'gainst you guys, really. I'm willin' to make peace with Melvin even. But he better not pull anything like he did out on the basketball court that day."

"Well, Wimbush already give him the word on that," Earl Wilson said.

"Well, I'm not hidin' 'hind Wimbush," Hal said firmly. "I don't wanta fight Melvin, but if he pushes me too far, I got no choice."

"Well, you better be careful if it come to that," Wesley said. "You quicker'n Melvin an' a better athlete an' all, but he know a lotta dirty tricks, an' he ain't shy 'bout usin' any of 'em."

"Well, if he starts doin' that, I'm not gonna be shy 'bout doin' it back," Hal said.

8

For a couple of weeks, Hal had a feeling that a fight with Melvin might be inevitable, so he began preparing himself for it. The rec center had a weight room and a punching bag, and when no one was around, Hal put both to good use. He also picked up a book on boxing techniques from the public library. He studied the various instructions for positioning his feet, throwing a jab and counterpunching; and when no one was around, he practiced all that as best he could assimilate it. It might not help him much if Melvin cracked him over the head with a crowbar before he knew what was happening. But as long as he was on his feet and had Melvin in front of him, he at least had something to fall back on.

Hal's next face-to-face encounter with Melvin was scheduled for a day when Wimbush wouldn't be on hand to supervise matters. Wimbush had to be out of town. A favorite niece was getting married, and one can't very well miss something like that. Wimbush hadn't forgotten the Melvin problem, and he took steps to have that covered.

"I told Mike Combs to keep an eye on things in case Melvin wants to start something," the coach told Hal before he was ready to leave. "Whatever happens, don't get suckered into a fight with Melvin."

"What if Melvin gets me cornered somewheres that I got no choice?" Hal countered.

"Avoid that. I don't know who could win between you and Melvin if the fight was fair, but what little I know about Melvin leaves me with the feeling it wouldn't be fair, and you don't know enough to fight dirty the way someone like Melvin can," Wimbush told him, gently but firmly. He patted Hal reassuringly on a shoulder. "If you get in a fight with him, you're losing on two fronts. It's not worth it."

"Well, I'm not gonna be lookin' for it, but I'm not gonna let him push me 'round either," Hal said softly.

"Look, if anything starts, let Mike handle it, you hear me?" Wimbush exhorted.

"Okay," Hal agreed.

Mike Combs was a heavyset black man who had been in charge of rec league youth activities as far back as most Brileyville residents could recall. He had played football once and still conveyed an aura of strength that one hesitated in challenging. Hal knew events with Melvin would be kept under control as long as Mike was around, but Mike couldn't be everywhere. At some point, Melvin might be able to isolate him and force him into a fight. As long as it was kept fair, he didn't feel bad about his chances. The unfair part was another story.

Hal chuckled. His mother had spotted the boxing book while she was cleaning his room one day. "What are you doing with a book on pugilism?" she asked him in a nonplussed tone.

"It's one I've had 'round for a while," Hal lied. "I was gonna do a book report on it, but I wound up doin' it on *The Great Gatsby*. I've had this book 'round for a while an' just never got 'round to turnin' it back in."

"Oh," his mother said with a shrug. She chuckled and

set the book back on a table. "Well, I'm not the greatest Fitzgerald fan in the world, but I must say that's a step up from boxing."

"My teacher thought so too. She gave me an A," Hal said.

His mother, of course, could have caught him in the lie simply by opening the back of the book and seeing the dates stamped there. But for all her intelligence, she was not a very curious person; and, besides, her son hadn't lied to her (or been caught in it) enough so that she felt any reason to doubt his word. Hal was relieved when she left the room, and he made a point of getting that book back to the library very soon thereafter.

The day had arrived for the rematch with Hal's Hilton classmates. It was an encounter Hal felt obligated to go all out for. It would, of course, decide the summer league championship in that age group; and besides, he had a message to get across to Melvin that he was not backing down. If that led to a fight, so be it, but he wanted Melvin off his back once and for all.

"Well, I see you ain't got Wimbush 'round for you to hide behind," Melvin said with a sneer as the two teams lined up for the opening tap.

"We're just playin' basketball. What I got to hide from?" Hal responded insouciantly.

Hal made his point quickly. Melvin's team got the opening tip, but Hal stepped into a passing lane, picked off a pass intended for Lonnie and raced the length of the court for an easy layup. On the Hilton team's next possession, he trapped Thurlow behind the time line for a ten second call. On top of those two plays, he had the range on his jumper. So in the early going, Hal's team was in the lead twenty-three to eight, with nineteen of the points scored by Hal personally.

Then Melvin had the ball. Hal moved over and trapped him in a corner. He was expecting a five second whistle. But before that came, Melvin lashed out with a forearm and hit Hal flush in the face.

For a moment or so, Hal's head spun crazily. He moved his hand up to his nose and felt the stickiness of his blood oozing out. Mike Combs rushed out onto the court. "You're outta this game right now, Peebles," he roared at Melvin.

"Huh? Wha' I do?" Melvin responded in feigned innocence.

"You know fuckin' one hunret percent what you done," Wesley interjected. "Ain't no call for that shit, Melvin."

Melvin glared in semi shock at the larger black youth, whom he long had regarded as a friend. "How come you takin' his side?"

"It ain't a question of takin' anybody's side. It's a question of what's right an' wrong, an' you was wrong," Lonnie threw in his two cents worth.

"Outta here," Mike Combs followed with a forefinger stuck menacingly just a couple of inches from Melvin's face. "You get off this court right now or I'm gonna throw you off."

Melvin shrugged. However tough he might have thought he was, he knew Mike was no one to mess with. He started to walk off the court. But he did stop as he passed Hal. "You dead meat, white boy," he muttered.

"I'm fuckin' scared to death," Hal shot back sarcastically. If Melvin wanted a fight, he was ready.

"You think you such hot shit, meet me down behind the junior high back near the woods after the game," Melvin said coldly.

"Peebles, I'm telling you for the last time: Get your black ass off this court or I'm coming after you," Mike growled.

"I'll be there. If you ain't a chickenshit motherfucker, you'll be too," Melvin told Hal with a smirk as he was departing.

One of Hal's teammates sighed in bewilderment as he watched Melvin head off up an embankment. "God, what's he got 'gainst you?" he asked Hal solicitously.

"Gettin' his clock cleaned by a white boy, I guess," Hal said with a shrug.

Mike Combs came over. "You all right, Hal?" he inquired solicitously. He checked the nose which by now had stopped bleeding. Hal had stemmed the blood flow with a portion of his t-shirt.

Hal put his hand to his nose. The pain had gone, and nothing felt broken. "Yeah, let's play ball," he said.

Hal was a little less possessed with Melvin gone, but his team had a large enough lead, and he was able to do just enough to protect it easily. His team won by fifteen points, which put the two squads in a tie for the season's championship. But the players on the other team decided to be gracious.

"We've agreed we're giving the championship to your team 'cause you mighta won the first game if Melvin wouldn'ta knocked you out the way he did," Mike Combs told Hal.

"It's only fair," Wesley chimed in. He laughed. "'Sides, you really oughta be playin' for us anyways, so it ain't like we really lost nothin'."

"'Cept next time you gonna be on the A team 'steada the B," Earl Wilson told Hal. He rumpled the latter's tangled blond hair.

"Well, that's settled," Mike said. He gathered up the basketballs, put them in a bag and departed.

"Hey, you ain't gonna go meetin' Melvin, I hope," Wesley appealed to Hal.

"I don't see any way out of it," Hal reasoned. "If I don't, I'm always gonna have to be lookin' over my shoulder for him. He ain't gonna let it 'lone . . . "

"You don't gotta worry 'bout Melvin," Wesley said. He draped an arm over Hal's shoulders. "Far's I'm 'cerned, if he want a piece of you, he gotta come through me."

"He gotta come through three or four of us. He don't want that," Lonnie said.

"You don't know Melvin like I do," Thurlow Carter said.

"You may be a better athlete'n him'n all, but you don't know one tenth the dirty tricks he can do."

Hal was touched. It felt good to have this bunch expressing concern for him and making offers that sounded very much like friendship. But he still had a matter of honor to resolve. "I hear what y'all sayin' an' I 'ppreciate it, guys, but I gotta show Melvin he better stop pushin' me 'round," he said.

"Well, if you gonna be that hardheaded, least you can do is let us come 'long an' make sure Melvin don't go grabbin' no equalizers or nothin'," Earl Wilson said.

Hal shrugged. If they wanted to come along, why not? At least they could help keep the fight fair.

So the group trekked to the area behind the school to meet Melvin. It turned out that Melvin also had a group there. Hal recognized some of them as having been in his class or the class above a year or so earlier. They had dropped out, and he had heard rumors that a couple of them might be selling drugs or working for pimps or running numbers. Brileyville wasn't notorious for its crime, but it did have an underworld of sorts.

"I thought you was 'pposed to be comin' 'lone," Melvin remarked to Hal.

"You ain't 'lone," Hal reminded him.

Wesley turned menacingly to Melvin's companions. "We just come 'long to make sure none y'all 'cide to go makin' this a four-on-one dance or somethin' like that."

"It'll be just me'n him, don't worry," Melvin said. He glared at Hal. "'Cept maybe he gonna need somebody to help carry him out."

"Well, you wanna try me 'steada Hal, we can always go that route, too," Wesley offered.

"My quarrel with him, not you," Melvin said. He knew he wanted no part of Wesley. He had tried the big fellow before and been humbled.

"I'm gonna tell you right now, too, Melvin, this the last time you gonna come down on this boy," Lonnie interrupted.

"He ain't did nothin' to you, an' far's I'm 'cerned, if he say he wanna walk 'way from this fight right now, he can do it with his head high an' my blessin's. But win, lose or draw, you ain't gonna mess with him no more. You catch my drift?"

"You can try comin' through me on that one, too," Wesley said. He tossed glances at Melvin's companions to let them know they were included in the invitation.

Hal's hands raised appealingly. "If we're gonna do this, let's do it an' get it over with."

"Y'all stay out of it," Wesley warned Melvin's companions one last time.

No argument there. They were not the nicest bunch around, but the prospect of taking on Wesley, Lonnie and Earl kept them firmly in check.

A circle formed for the two combatants, as much to shield what was going on from someone who might happen to look down from a nearby embankment as anything else. Melvin took his shirt off and threw it on a clump of bushes. Hal did likewise and started loosening his shoulders and waiting for Melvin to make the first move.

He expected a punch, but Melvin fooled him by ducking down, grabbing him by the waist and wrestling him to the ground. The hold wasn't very secure, however, and Hal managed to wriggle free and get back to his feet. He knew Melvin was a little bulkier than he and probably a little stronger as well. He didn't want it to turn into a wrestling match.

As Hal retreated to get his balance, Melvin caught him with a roundhouse right to the side of his face. It hurt just enough to start his adrenalin flow.

Hal remembered what he had learned from the book and his private sparring sessions and began utilizing it. He got on his toes and started moving and throwing flicking jabs and caught Melvin with a couple of the latter blows that hit the bridge of the nose. It snapped Melvin's head back and drew some blood.

Now Hal realized that he could hurt Melvin, and that raised his confidence level enormously. Melvin threw a couple of wild punches that he easily evaded, and now he just started pumping that jab out and following it up with occasional straight rights. A boxing purist might have concluded that he was getting more arm than body into the punches, but they were taking a visible toll on Melvin, snapping his head back repeatedly and making his face puffy and putting him on the defensive.

This had gone on for some three or four minutes, and Hal's arms were starting to get tired. Wimbush's remark about stamina flashed through his brain fleetingly, and for the first time he was grateful for that exercise regimen. Even so, he was coming to the end of his endurance level; he didn't think he could keep this up much longer. He kept hoping that Melvin would throw up his hands and say enough, as virtually any sensible person would. After all, as tired as he was of throwing the punches, Melvin had to be even more so of catching them. But still Melvin kept coming on and throwing punches, and finally one caught Hal on the mouth and split his upper lip.

Hal didn't lose his poise, but a sense of anger and desperation started taking hold. He had been peppering Melvin with relatively light, short punches that were taking a toll but not likely to score a quick knockout. And it looked like he might need a knockout. That meant having to put more into his punches. So he waited until Melvin had committed with a left and came over it with a hard right with as much of his shoulder and body weight behind it as he could figure out how to muster.

It caught Melvin flush on the mouth, and a tooth came flying out. The punch wouldn't remind anyone of Rocky Marciano or George Foreman, but it had enough to drive Melvin backwards. Hal followed up this advantage by throwing a barrage of punches. Some missed, but several connected, too. Melvin was driven across the field until finally he went down—-probably more from fatigue and the punch accumulation than Hal's power—-and his hands went up in what looked like a surrender signal.

Hal felt a great surge of relief. It was over. He didn't want to gloat over Melvin's fallen body or turn tables and start picking on the black youth in the same manner he had been victimized. He just wanted to get away, get something cold to drink, rest a while, heal his own wounds.

He turned for a second to walk away and heard Wesley yell: "Look out, Hal."

He turned back around just in time to catch Melvin's right hand on the side of his face. The blow didn't land full-force, and Hal fell on his back more from the impetus of Melvin's rush than the punch itself. Melvin dived on top of him, grabbed him by the neck and tried to reach a rock to hit him with.

Wesley's foot was on top of Melvin's hand the very second it had hold of the rock. "We ain't gonna have none of that," the bigger young man growled.

Melvin was momentarily distracted, and that was enough to enable Hal to wriggle out of his grasp and get to his feet. Now he wanted blood. He waited until Wesley had backed away and Melvin was up, then bore in with both fists flailing wildly. The arms no longer felt tired as he threw punch after punch, at Melvin's face and any other body part he could hit. He felt Melvin's body go limp under his onslaught, and still he kept throwing punch after punch after punch. Melvin finally sagged to the ground, totally unable to fight back any longer, and still Hal kept punching, wildly, insanely, as if some demon had taken over.

Then he felt Wesley and Lonnie grabbing him and pulling him away from Melvin. "Stop, man, you gonna kill him," Wesley was shouting to him.

Wesley's tone of urgency reawakened him. He really had lost control. Melvin was lying almost inert on his stomach, with only some barely audible moaning to confirm that he was still alive. Hal shook his head and ran his hands over his face, as much to bring himself back to some sense of reality as anything else. He knew that he didn't really want to kill Melvin, although for several moments that demon that had taken hold of him wiped that totally from his mind. If his two friends hadn't grabbed him, he might well have kept punching until Melvin was dead.

"You awright?" Wesley asked Hal solicitously.

Hal exhaled sharply. "I guess so," he said with a headshake. He took a deep breath. "I'm glad this is over."

A couple of Melvin's companions examined the fallen youth. "We better get him to a hospital," one of them said.

A sinking feeling suddenly hit Hal when he heard hospital. He didn't want Melvin to wind up permanently disabled either. Somehow the rationalization that Melvin had started it seemed a little hollow in that moment.

He felt relief when Melvin was finally pulled to his feet and actually walked a couple of steps. The companions helped him to a car. Melvin glanced at Hal fleetingly as they passed, but Hal couldn't detect what message those eyes might be trying to convey.

Wesley scanned Hal and noticed that the split lip he had sustained was still bleeding. "You oughta go see a doc, too," he recommended.

"Just long's Melvin doesn't wake up an' 'cide he wants to fight some more," Hal murmured. For the first time, he realized that the lip was bleeding and it hurt. He tore off a section of his t-shirt to stop the blood.

Wesley laughed and slapped him on the back. "I 'spect it be a long time 'fore Melvin want any part of you," he said.

Hal liked the sound of that. He didn't care if Melvin didn't want to be friends with him—-indeed, if Melvin decided to dislike him intensely, however irrational the reason behind it—-but he didn't want to be bullied or picked on or called a faggot or sissy or any other such undesirable name ever again. He hoped he had put that problem behind him for good, although he was not totally confident of it. Melvin had a quality reminiscent almost of Jason from the *Friday the 13th* movies; he was down and seemingly beaten thoroughly, and all at once he was back up wanting to fight again. Hal was almost afraid the same thing might happen at the hospital.

He got a ride to the hospital with Lonnie's older brother, who had a car. He vaguely knew Vernon Hairston. Vernon now worked for a factory just outside Brileyville. He briefly had a scholarship to play basketball at Virginia State but left after he came to the conclusion that he would spend his entire four years there on the bench. Some young men would at least parlay the scholarship into a degree, but Vernon didn't particularly like attending classes. Without the sport, college had scant allure for him.

"I heard Melvin kinda pushed you into that fight," Vernon remarked solicitously as he drove Hal to the hospital.

"Yeah," Hal said. He heaved a sigh. "I think 'bout it, I prob'ly shoulda backed out. I had a chance. Lonnie an' Wesley an' the others said they'd back me..."

"Sometimes you gotta stand up, just to let dudes like Melvin know they's certain lines they better not cross," Vernon said with a shrug. He laughed. "I hear Melvin kinda shook up 'cause you showed him up playin' basketball."

Hal chuckled to himself. "That was part of it. He used to pick on me back in the early grades. He beat me up two or three times. Last couple years he's kinda 'nored me, but I guess he still had me pegged as this sissy white kid, a real chump an' all..."

"Well, I don't think after today anybody 'round here gonna be callin' you sissy no more noways," Vernon assured him good-naturedly.

As Hal pretty much suspected, he was not seriously injured. The gash over his eye hadn't been reopened, and the lip didn't require stitches. A bandaid and some salve did the job.

"If this is the worst that ever happens to you, I imagine you can expect a good long life," the black doctor who examined him said.

"What 'bout Melvin? He gonna be awright?" Hal asked.

"Oh, yeah," the doctor said. He put the bandaids and salve he had pulled down for Hal back in a nearby cabinet. "He will be a little sore for a while. And he's got a broken rib, but I think that'll heal soon enough."

"Broken rib?" Hal responded in surprise.

"Yep," the doctor confirmed. He squeezed Hal's right bicep. "Evidently you have a little more strength in you than you thought or someone just looking at you might expect you to have."

"I never thought 'bout it," Hal said with a shrug. He heaved a sigh. "But I am glad Melvin's gonna be awright."

"I am, too, as much for your sake as his," the doctor said.

Hal left that wing of the hospital and took the stairs down to the main floor. He didn't remember ever hitting Melvin in the ribs, but he must have. All this must have happened over two or three minutes when he was swinging away at Melvin, but he really had no memory of it. That scared him a little. He didn't like the idea of himself possessed in that manner.

He got to the main floor and started to leave and was startled to see Melvin standing at the entrance. He could see the taped rib through Melvin's shirt.

Melvin glanced at him uneasily, and he looked at Melvin in a similar manner. He didn't know what to say, and he sensed that Melvin felt the same.

"Hey, I hope you're not gonna be wantin' to fight me any more, certainly not today anyway," he finally said. "I think I've had 'bout as much of this for one day as I can handle."

Melvin responded with a chagrined headshake. "Me, too," he murmured.

"Sorry 'bout the broken rib," Hal said with a gesture of sincerity.

"I axed for it," Melvin said with a shrug. He looked at Hal incredulously. "Man, where the fuck you come from? It's awmost like I'm just meetin' somebody I never knowed before."

"Well, I guess a lot 'bout myself I never knew before either 'til a few weeks 'go," Hal said. He chuckled. "It's awmost like I'm seein' a different person, too."

9

Hal wasn't inclined to make a big deal out of beating Melvin in that fight, but some other people were. For weeks after the fight, people were making comments to him about it, calling him names like Slugger and Rocky and in general keeping alive an incident he would have preferred to see speedily forgotten. But one of the penalties imposed by adolescence is a tendency for people to define a person before the person has a chance to do that for himself or herself. Hal felt a little embarrassed by all this attention, but he couldn't think of any graceful way to avoid it.

He had to deal with his own mother, of course. When he got home with his face a little puffy and his lip bandaged, her face contorted in horror. "What happened to you?" she asked through her moue.

"I got tripped up goin' for a basket an' busted my lip," Hal lied. "It's not bad. I'll be okay."

"I have a hard time understanding how someone reputedly so athletically gifted can keep falling down as often as you do," his mother sighed.

Hal chuckled to himself whenever he thought about that latter remark. His mother still had a hard time assimilating his newly found status as an athlete. It was so new that he wasn't always sure he believed it himself, but he was adjusting to it. His mother seemed to have difficulty doing even that much.

One memorable encounter he had came when he was heading home one evening after working at the rec center. He was waiting for a bus when two black guys he recognized as part of Melvin's rooting section for the now infamous fight approached. He tensed momentarily; he almost feared that they might try to even the score for their friend.

"Hey, man, you ever thought 'bout takin' up boxin'?" one of the two guys asked.

Hal was thoroughly taken aback. "What?"

"No, I mean it, man," the black guy said. "I got a cousin that manages fighters, an' he's always talkin' 'bout how a good white fighter could be a real gold mine. I 'magine he wouldn't mind checkin' you out, if you in'rested."

Hal's head shook bemusedly. "You're kiddin', of course."

"No," the black guy assured him. "I seen the way you handled Melvin. I told him 'bout that, an' he sounded real in'rested."

"Fightin' Melvin ain't 'zackly like fightin' some those other guys," Hal reminded him. "I dunno. I kinda think I'd rather stick with basketball."

"Well, you change you mind, let me know," the black guy said.

"Yeah, O.K.," Hal responded.

Hal rather hoped that word of the fight wouldn't get back to Wimbush, but he had a feeling that it was too much to expect. It was.

"I told you specifically to stay away from Melvin," Wimbush reminded him.

"He kept pushin' for the fight," Hal defended himself. "An' then he threw out the place he was gonna be an' dared me to meet him there. He didn't give me any choice."

"You could have ignored that, just gone about your business until I got back into town," the coach said.

"I figured if I didn't settle things once for all, I might have him breathin' down my neck 'til doomsday," Hal sighed. "Least this way, it's over."

"Yes, it does seem to be, and I suppose that's for the good," Wimbush conceded with a shrug. He grasped Hal's shoulders. "But in the future, young man, if you run into a situation like that, you let me take care of it, you hear?"

"Well, I don't 'spect anything like that from Melvin anyway," Hal murmured.

Wimbush chuckled. "No. I understand Melvin's a much sadder and wiser young man these days."

Hal flashed a reminiscent grin. "Couple guys he hangs out with came up to me other night as I was leavin' the rec center. Turns out one of 'em's got a cousin that handles fighters. Said his cousin'd be in'rested in takin' me on."

"The fact that you can beat Melvin in a fight doesn't mean you oughta be considering a career in boxing," Wimbush said. "I hope you're not seriously pondering such a move."

"Naw, I told him I thought I'd stick with basketball," Hal said. He chuckled. "He threw out a line 'bout a white fighter bein' a hot item."

"I'm sure that's true if a good white fighter happened to come along," Wimbush said. He patted Hal on a shoulder. "You're a gifted athlete, and you could probably excel in any one of several sports you set your mind on. But I'm not sure boxing would be one of them. That's a rough game, and unless you can get to the very top, it doesn't offer much in the way of returns. I'd advise almost any young man with your kind of natural athletic ability to stick with one of the mainstream sports. At least those offer you the means to chart a pretty good future for yourself." He patted Hal on the shoulder again. "And I hope the fact that you proved you can beat Melvin doesn't get you thinking of yourself as some sort of tough guy."

Hal laughed. "Not hardly." He ran a finger over the split lip. The bandage had come off, but a scab was still visible and it hurt. "If I learned nothin' else from that 'sperience, I learned fightin's too rough even if you win."

Wimbush laughed. "You got that one dead on the mark," he agreed.

Melvin indeed had undergone a personality metamorphosis. It wasn't as if he was ready to join Mother Teresa or the Peace Corps or something of that sort, but a nicer, more thoughtful human being was emerging. The thought occurred to Hal that the nicer Melvin might have been there all along but had been afraid to come out until now.

"I'm glad Wesley stepped on my hand 'fore I could hit you with that rock," he told Hal in a peculiarly humble tone a couple of weeks later when their paths finally crossed again. "Funny. When you was just wailin' 'way at me an' all the strength seemed to be gone outta my body, I was awmost wishin' you was gonna kill me. It 'ccurred to me wouldn't none of this be happenin' if I wouldn'ta acted like such a asshole, an' I really felt like I'd be better off dead."

"Yeah, but I'd have to live with it," Hal said. He slapped Melvin on the back. "I 'spect then I was thinkin' 'bout killin' you, but I think 'bout it now I'm glad I didn't."

The backslap aggravated Melvin's still very sore ribcage and caused him to wince. "Uh, be gentle," he appealed to Hal. "That hurt."

Hal nodded. "Sorry. I forgot 'bout that."

"I'd like to forget 'bout it, but I 'spect it won't be 'til after this pain go 'way," Melvin murmured.

10

That summer provided a lot of pivotal moments for Hal, but probably none as memorable as an encounter he had one day with Charmaine Jackson. Charmaine was two years ahead of him in school and the best player on the high school girls basketball team. Hal knew that much about her, but beyond that had had virtually no contact with her. She was black and taller than most of the guys around school and about average in looks—-not really ugly but not very striking either. Hal was cleaning out the rec center swimming pool one evening after he thought everyone had left when Charmaine came by and started looking at him curiously.

"I hear you 'pposed to be a hotshot player now," she remarked to him in almost a sneering tone.

Hal shrugged. "I dunno." He resumed working.

"Shit, you can't even beat me," Charmaine said.

Hal didn't know how to respond to that one. "If you say so," he said finally.

"C'mon, I'll take you on right now," Charmaine challenged him.

"I got work to do," Hal groaned. He didn't appreciate being pushed into a corner with something that to him seemed so ridiculous.

"Fuck you. You scared I'll clean your clock," Charmaine pressed.

"You wanta think that, go 'head," Hal said vacantly. He continued working.

"Oh, c'mon, play me." Charmaine's tone now sounded more like a plea.

Hal chuckled. He recalled a Neil Diamond song his mother sometimes liked to listen to. "What? You, the words or the tune?" he responded.

"Don't get smartass with me, chump," Charmaine shot back. She was not a Neil Diamond fan and so missed the humorous twist that Hal thought he was throwing in.

"C'mon, Charmaine, what the fuck I wanta play you for?" Hal moaned. His primary attention was still on the work he was trying to get finished. "You just a girl."

Wrong thing to say. Charmaine was instantly in his face. "Yeah, a girl that can whup your ass any day," she growled.

Hal sensed that he had hit a wrong chord. "Look, I'm not in'rested in tryna prove somethin', an' I don't wanta get in a fight with you, Charmaine. Just let me get back to work, please," he appealed to her.

"Not 'til you play me. If you don't take me on, you a chickenshit mothuhfuckuh," Charmaine told him with a shrug.

Hal shrugged back. She was persistent, and he wasn't going to get rid of her without either beating her up or taking her on in some one-on-one. "If it'll get rid of you, okay, but don't 'spect any mercy," he finally yielded.

"You gonna be one cryin' for mercy," Charmaine said.

Hal found a basketball in a shed-like building near the pool. "After you," he said with a gesture to Charmaine.

"Well, least you ain't throwin' no French out or nothin',"

Charmaine remarked as she moved into step with him heading towards the basketball courts.

"It's apres vous, if you wanta know the French," Hal said. He started dribbling the basketball as the two walked along.

"If I beat you, you ain't gonna be no hotshot no more, y'know," Charmaine told him teasingly.

"Well, I guess that'll just mean I wasn't a hotshot in the first place," Hal said with a shrug. He chuckled. "How come you want a game so bad?"

"Just curious," Charmaine said.

They got to the court, and Hal tossed the ball to Charmaine. "Make-it, take-it all right? Say to eleven?" he asked her.

"Yeah, but when we get to 'leven, don't you go cryin' foul an' wantin' it to go to twenty-one," Charmaine said. She tossed the ball back to him.

"If I'm losin' when we get to 'leven, I'll hang it up," Hal promised. He tossed the ball back to Charmaine. "You go first."

"You do that, you might not get to touch the ball," Charmaine said.

"Well, that just means I can get back to work that much quicker," Hal reasoned.

Hal didn't think Charmaine could beat him. He heard about a couple of times she had thrown out similar challenges to some varsity boys' team players and been beaten. But until he showed her one way or the other, she wasn't going away.

Charmaine faked and began her dribble. Hal moved with the feint and quickly swiped the ball from her and scored on a layup. He took it out and dribbled back in and around Charmaine just enough to get free for a long jump shot, which he made.

"I won't even bother to drive," he said as he took the ball back out again.

He hit two more long jumpers, each time making moves

around Charmaine and easily getting himself free. Finally Charmaine raised her hands in surrender. She realized that she was no match for this white boy—at least when it came to playing basketball.

"Didn't you mama tell you you was 'pposed to take it easy on girls?" she remarked to him with a teasing grin.

Hal laughed. "It was you wantin' this, not me," he reminded her.

Charmaine nodded, heaved a sigh and sat down on a nearby bench. Hal had some extra change, so he got two soft drinks from a nearby machine, gave one to her and sat down on the grass in front of her and began sipping on the other.

"Thanks," Charmaine said. She took a swallow from the drink and scanned Hal with interest. "You gonna be like one them gunfighters in a ol' western movie. Everybody gonna wanna be tryin' you out."

"Least they're not likely to be carryin' real guns," Hal said with a grin.

Charmaine chuckled. "Better hope the wrong one don't come 'long. You got some that might tote a gun if one's 'vailable." She took another swallow from her drink. "I heard 'bout the fight you had with Melvin. It's all over town by now."

"Yeah, I know," Hal said through a grimace. "I'm tryna forget 'bout it, and everybody else keeps wantin' to bring it up. Me'n Melvin've made peace. I wisht people 'ud let it die."

"It'll take a while," Charmaine said. She studied Hal. "You kinda a curiousity to most folks I know. Ain't too many white boys 'round here can play basketball an' stand up for theirself in a fight like you done."

Hal shrugged. "Most of 'em don't have to. They're off at Cedar Grove or someplace like that, 'way from where they get thrown into situations like that."

Charmaine nodded. "Maybe if more white folks had to scrape 'long like you, they might understand a little better 'bout where we comin' from." She sipped some of her drink. "I guess it have been kinda rough on you, ain't it?"

"I dunno," Hal said. He chuckled. "Not easy to think 'bout a social life when you're 'bout the only white 'round, an' the black girls either don't seem in'rested in guys at all. Or if they are, it's just the brothers."

"You got a few white girls 'round," Charmaine reminded him.

Hal winced. "Yeah, an' they're all homely, too."

Charmaine laughed. "Beggars can't be choosers."

Hal heaved a sigh. "I guess you're right. Somewhere 'long the line I might have to suck it up an' maybe start datin' one of them or somethin'. Course couple them even seem to prefer black guys. I might just be stuck out in the cold 'til I get to college or somethin'."

"Well, way you play basketball, I 'spect somethin'll pick up for you 'fore you know it," Charmaine said. She grinned impishly. "Course you know it ain't outta the question for a black girl to go out with you if you ax her nice 'nuff."

Hal shrugged. "Couple black girls in my class I wouldn't mind askin' out. Course one of 'em's kinda in the clouds somewhere. I don't think she likes anybody in our school or this town."

"I know who you talkin' 'bout," Charmaine mused. "That Hanson girl. Couple the guys I know kinda tried hittin' on her. They came 'way talkin' 'bout how she could kill a hard-on in a hurry."

Hal laughed. "I met her aunt once, few months 'go. She went to school at Hilton back when it was still segregated 'round here an' Hilton was still a high school. She made a remark 'bout Shawna not bein' the type to set her sights too low."

"Well, where she's comin' from, that might 'sclude most of the human race," Charmaine said.

Hal chuckled appreciatively. "Maybe. I gotta 'mit, though, she is pretty. The thought of tappin' that has crossed my mind a couple times."

"Shit, just play it cool an' keep playin' basketball good, an' you'll get somethin' twice as good as her, whether it's white or black," Charmaine told him warmly.

"Yeah, but I don't wanta have to wait forever for it," Hal said.

"You won't," Charmaine said in an assuring tone.

11

Harry Moore had been coaching the Brileyville High football team for twenty-plus years and had recorded the school's only state championship in any sport. He once played for Alabama under Bear Bryant, and he seemed to think of football as a good ninety percent of life. He was white and generally fit the redneck stereotype in his social philosophy, but on a personal level he got along well with most of the African Americans he knew. In fact, his stoutest vocal defenders included many of the black players he had coached over the years. Somehow he could communicate with them on a level that defied liberal scrutiny.

At the very least, everyone around the Brileyville school scene respected Moore. His teams over the years had been consistent winners. The range had been anywhere from seven to eleven victories per season, but only once over the span of his years there did one of his teams actually wind up with a losing record.

Part of that success was owed to a network the coach

had around the school that could ferret out the best male athletic talent and direct it into his program. That included young men coming up from the junior high. That was how the coach learned about Hal McDonough.

A black assistant who helped out at the rec center from time to time heard about Hal and checked him out in a game against some of the older players. In Hal he saw quickness, great hands, acceleration, toughness: all the ingredients that go into a really good wideout, running back, or safety. He quickly relayed his thoughts on this young man to the head coach, who felt obligated to check all this out firsthand.

Moore liked what he saw. Hal's slightness of frame bothered him a little, but some time in the weight room could bulk him up. And as much of a fundamentalist as he was at heart—-blocking and tackling being the two concepts he stressed the most—he appreciated the dimension the quickness of someone like Hal could add to a football team. And those incredible hands could be a tremendous asset in a passing game. And the kid seemed more than tough enough, his size considered.

"I told you he's quick," the black assistant said as he saw the head coach's eyes light up. "They tell me he's fast, too. Like he might have sprinter's speed."

"Oh, yes. I think Clifford would like havin' someone like that to throw deep, too," Moore mused. "Only problem is, how will Clifford feel 'bout throwin' to a white boy?"

"Clifford don't care if he's purple if he can get open an' hang onto the ball," the assistant said with a chuckle.

Moore responded with a smiling nod. "I think somebody musta been feedin' that guy watermelon." He slapped the assistant on the back. "No offense, I hope."

None was taken. The black assistant was accustomed to Moore's stereotypical humor. "Well, could be he got that fast by stickin' his tongue up some girl's twot," was the joking response.

Moore laughed. "If that was all it took, I'da been able to

outrun Bob Hayes or John Carlos or any of those guys."

Hal was swigging some liquid from a Gatorade bottle when the two coaches approached. "Hi, I'm Harry Moore," the head coach introduced himself. "I coach football at the high school."

Hal knew who Moore was, but that was about it. He was a little puzzled over why the coach seemingly wanted to talk to him.

A taller, slender young black man came by. "Nice game, Hal," he remarked to the latter with a pat on the back. "See you tomorrow."

"Yeah, good game, Ernest," Hal responded.

Ernest played center for the varsity basketball team. Moore was only vaguely aware of that. As far as he was concerned, any student who didn't play football was either a girl or didn't count.

"I understand you're coming up to the high school in September," he said to Hal after Ernest had departed.

"Yes sir," Hal confirmed. He wondered where all this was leading.

"I'd like to have you come out for the football team," Moore told him bluntly.

That caught Hal totally by surprise. "I don't think I'm big 'nuff for football," he murmured. He shook his head in bewilderment. He had difficulty ingesting what he had just heard. "'Sides I'm kinda committed to playin' basketball for Coach Wimbush. He kinda helped me get started, an' I feel like I owe it to him."

"You wouldn't be the first guy to play both football an' basketball in the same year," Moore argued. He scanned Hal's frame. It was slender, but he detected a bone structure that indicated fair room for filling out. "And if you play for me, I'll guarantee we'll beef you up."

Hal was still nonplussed. "But why? You got all kinda guys bigger'n me 'vailable. How come you're in'rested in me?"

"'Cause you're a helluvan athletic talent," Moore

answered matter-of-factly. "You have the quickest reflexes I've seen in a young man in a long time. I don't know if I ever seen anybody with your natural athletic ability."

Ego massaging is a good way of reaching the juvenile psyche, and Hal wasn't immune. But football was a pretty big stretch. "I've never played football before. Lotta the other guys you got comin' up played Little League'n all . . ."

"The kind of athletic ability you have can overcome a lot of things, 'cludin' lack of experience," Moore said. He put a toothpick in his mouth and drew on it as if it were a cigarette. "What you need to know you can pick up in a pretty short period of time. After that, it's heart an' guts an' instinct, an' I got a feelin' you got your share an' then some of all three."

Hal bit his upper lip thoughtfully. "I wouldn't mind tryin', but I'd feel kinda like a traitor to Coach Wimbush, 'specially if I break an arm or leg or somethin . . ."

"Guys get their legs broke playin' basketball, too," the coach reminded. He slapped Hal on the back. "All I'm askin' is you come out for the team. You try a few practices, an' if it don't work out, you can quit. Who knows? Maybe you won't be good 'nuff to make the team."

Hal shrugged. That sounded like the easiest way out of this situation for him. "Well, like I just said, I wouldn't mind tryin', but I think somebody other'n me's gonna have to do the sell job on my mother," he responded. "It was hard 'nuff gettin' her to go 'long with me playin' basketball. I 'spect she's really gonna think football's too rough."

"I'll talk to your mother," Moore assured him. "If I can get her to let you play, will you come out for the team?"

Hal chuckled. "Sure, why not?" he agreed.

Harry Moore thought he had seen a lot of the world. He had been to college on a football scholarship, served his country in the post-Korea/pre-Vietnam Army as an officer and had traveled fairly extensively. He had met and worked with a lot of different types of people. He was rough in his manner but far from stupid and actually fairly sophisticated in viewing humankind in general.

None of that prepared him for his meeting with Kathleen McDonough.

Hal's mother wasn't the first Boston reared person he had ever met, but this was the first time he had ever been exposed to so pronounced a Beantown accent. His first mental reaction was to marvel that Hal wasn't walking around in knee britches like Little Lord Fauntleroy.

"I've already semi agreed to let Harold play basketball, Mr. Moore, and now I'm starting to have second thoughts about that," Kathleen McDonough said as they sat in her living room. "He comes home with stitches over one eye, apparently from a fall. Then I see him come in with his face bruised and swollen and his lip split open. If he can get that playing basketball, I shudder to think what playing football would do to him."

The 'Harold', especially the tone in which it was pronounced, had Moore struggling to stifle a giggle. "Don't you want your son to develop into a man, Mrs. McDonough?" he queried.

"I think the gender placement process was taken care of while Harold was in the fetal stages," Kathleen McDonough responded coldly. She lit a cigarette. "As nearly as I can determine, Mr. Moore, my son is not homosexual, and as far as I'm concerned, that's as much of a man as he needs to become. Frankly, I'm not so sure that's a blessing. I don't think I'd like to see another version of his father foisted on some unsuspecting future generation."

"I hope you're not sayin' you want to see your son turn queer," the coach countered in a bemused tone.

"I think the ideal would be if he turns out to be asexual, Mr. Moore." Kathleen McDonough drew thoughtfully on her cigarette. "I've agreed to let Harold play basketball because it could be a way for him to get a scholarship to one of the better institutions of higher learning. I am not in the financial position to send him to a better school myself, thanks in large measure to his father, and so many of the other aid programs seem designed more to help colored people than anyone else. If it weren't for that, I don't think I'd want him playing any sport at all."

"Uh, the scholarship 'ssistance you're talkin' 'bout: He can get that through football, too," Moore said.

"If he doesn't get killed first," Kathleen McDonough rebutted. "Mr. Moore, I've heard from several sources that my son is what I think some people like to call a gifted athlete, and I suppose that may be true, although I have to wonder how someone reputed to be so graceful can fall down so much. But I can also see that he totally lacks the bulky frame a young man needs to play your sport. I don't know a whole lot about football, Mr. Moore, but of that much I am aware."

"We have weight programs, Mrs. McDonough," the coach persisted. "Mrs. McDonough, ma'am, it's high school football. We're not talking about the pros and him goin' up 'gainst three hundred pound guys an' whatnot. Your boy's on the slim side, but he's not that much smaller'n the other guys out there. An' he wouldn't be the smallest guy I've ever had playin' for me."

Kathleen McDonough crushed one cigarette and lit another. "I think I liked it a lot better when he seemed like just a nice, quiet boy who did reasonably well in his classes," she murmured.

Moore laughed. "'Ventually you may come to 'ppreciate the fact he isn't. If he can mix classwork an' sports, that makes him a better-rounded person."

"I think that's overrated, too, pretty much like I think sex and sexuality are," Kathleen McDonough said with a shrug and a drag from her cigarette.

"When I see somebody smokin', it kinda brings back an ol' hunger in me," Moore remarked with amusement. "I used to be a two-pack-a-day man 'til I had a heart attack three years ago. Doctor told me I better quit or start makin' funeral 'rrangements, so I quit. Sometimes I almost think I mighta made the wrong choice."

That struck a chord. Smokers, current and former, speak a common language. "I can sympathize with you in that regard," Kathleen McDonough said.

"I think you owe it to your son to at least let him give it a try," Moore swung back to his main topic. "It won't kill him. I think I can pretty much guarantee you that. And it could help open some doors."

Kathleen McDonough heaved a sigh. "If Harold wants to play, I won't try to stop him," she relented.

Moore pulled some forms from a briefcase he had with him. "I'm gonna have to get your signature on a couple of these before I leave," he said.

12

One of Harry Moore's favorite anecdotes in coming months was Kathleen McDonough's *'I think the ideal would be if he turns out to be asexual.'* He repeated it in variations for the benefit of friends, family and coworkers and even came up with a comical imitation of that unique accent which frequently drew hearty laughter.

Hal was no less amused than anyone else. He almost wished he could have witnessed the exchange between his excessively refined mother and the rough hewn football coach. The thought crossed his mind that those two, with some fictionalized twists, would make a great movie or television comedy match—-with better looking people playing the respective parts, of course.

"I don't wanta see you lose your nuts," the coach told Hal just before his first practice session. "That's what gives football players the juice to excel. Sometimes when you're in the trenches an' the goin' gets real tough, just bein' able to think 'bout that nice piece of pussy you got lined up or you'd like to get lined up can drive you as much as anything."

Hal laughed. "I'll try to 'member that, Coach," he said.

"It strikes me you don't seem all that abnormal 'siderin'," Moore said. "I don't mean to throw a slam on your mom or anything, but I can't help wonderin' how you got to this age without bein' dressed in knee-britches."

"That was a tough fight," Hal admitted with a grin and a headshake.

"I can imagine," the coach said. He patted Hal on the shoulder. "Well, let's get out there. You better start gettin' used to gettin' hit right now."

If Hal had a choice for position, he might have picked quarterback. He had a relatively strong arm and could throw the football long and accurately. That along with probably the team's most mobile body might have guaranteed him the position in most other seasons. But Brileyville had a returning man behind the center, Clifford Jenkins, who earned all-region honors the previous year, so that position was out. Some thought was given to making Hal a running back or a corner or safety on defense. But when Hal consistently beat everyone in the practice sprints easily, Clifford lobbied personally to get this white boy at flanker.

"Ain't no way I'm lettin' them get you 'hind the line or playin' defense," Clifford confided to Hal with an arm draped over his shoulder. "You gonna help me light up them scoreboards this year."

Clifford was one of those ebullient personalities it was almost impossible not to like. He was always smiling or laughing and was in general a thoroughly nice young man. He and Hal hit it off immediately.

Clifford was three or four inches taller than Hal and had a really strong arm. He could zip the ball downfield in a manner that might remind one of Jim Kelly, Dan Marino, or John Elway. In fact, Marino was his favorite among the NFL quarterbacks, and he often joked to Hal about how they were destined to become the next Marino-to-Duper combination, with the skin tones reversed.

Football practice was rough, certainly rougher than anything Hal had ever gone through in his young life. For several days, he felt severe pain in parts of his body that he never imagined existing before. The thought crossed his mind once or twice to quit, but it was harder for him to work up nerve to do that than just to bear up under it. Besides, he got enough encouragement from his coaching staff and some of his teammates to keep him going.

His mother didn't go away through any part of this. He frequently had to endure snide remarks from her whenever he was at home. One evening after a particularly tough practice in which he took a couple of vicious hits, he came home walking noticeably more stiffly than normal. His mother took note of this and appealed to him: "Don't you think it's time you gave up this foolishness?" She crushed the cigarette she had been smoking. "I think one sport is certainly enough for any young person to handle in a year."

Hal agreed at heart and had resolved within himself to so limit himself in the future, but not this year. "I promised I'd give it a fair shake, and if I quit now I'd be goin' back on my word," he responded.

Kathleen McDonough shook her head, sighed loudly and lit another cigarette. "It pains me to think I might have reared my son to be a masochist," she murmured.

Gradually, Hal got into the flow of his new sport and even found himself starting to like it. He was getting to the point where he could take being tackled hard and piled on after he caught a ball downfield without any lingering pain or stiffness.

That didn't mean, of course, that he had suddenly developed an immunity to pain. Once when he and Clifford hooked up on a down-and-in pattern, a big linebacker named Wilbur gave him an especially hard pop. He wasn't hurt seriously, but he was a little slow getting up.

"Hey, I thought we were 'pposed to be on the same team," he remarked to Wilbur.

"Shit, you my mother an' you try comin' in this territory,

you gonna get hammered," Wilbur said. He flashed a grin and patted Hal on the back. "Get used to it. You gonna have a lotta guys slammin' into you 'fore you done. An' don't look for no mercy from the white boys we run into. Some them gonna be meaner'n a lot of the brothers."

Hal winced.

Wilbur noticed and laughed. "It come with the territory, man," he said with another backpat. "This ain't a patty-cake sport."

Had Wimbush been on hand, Hal might have avoided the football recruiting process. Unfortunately, Wimbush had to be out of town for a few weeks visiting various family members. When he got back, he found his prize player in the middle of football practice. He was more concerned than angry.

"Don't you know how easy it is to get hurt in that sport, to break an arm or a leg or something?" the coach posed to Hal.

"People get hurt playin' basketball, too," Hal rebutted. "Uh, Coach, I'm not turnin' on you or anything. It's just that Coach Moore came to me an' put the bug in my ear 'bout goin' out for football."

Wimbush heaved a sigh. He knew roughly the sequence of events without having to be told. "Harry Moore found out you're a good athlete, and he decided he wanted you on his team . . ."

"He's not easy to say no to," Hal reminded.

"You don't have to tell me. I've seen him operate dozens of times," Wimbush said with a shrug. He shook his head. "He probably had you questioning your own manhood and sexuality and everything else before you finally said yes."

Hal laughed. "Kinda, yeah," he agreed.

"Well, I won't try to stop you," Wimbush said. He patted Hal on a shoulder. "I just hope and pray I'll have you in one piece for basketball season."

"I'll be okay, Coach," Hal promised.

"I hope you're not going to try to tell me you can guarantee that," Wimbush said.

Hal chuckled. "No, I guess I can't guarantee it," he conceded.

13

About this time, the Cedar Grove athletic director was gathering intelligence of sorts on this new basketball phenom about to burst onto the public high school scene. Edgar Trainham had never before gone after a Brileyville player. The fact that most of the Brileyville players over the years had been black had something to do with it, although that wouldn't have mattered very much if one of them had happened to be good enough to arouse his interest. None had. He wouldn't argue the point that the best five players Brileyville had over that period were better than Cedar Grove's top five, but the difference wasn't enough to make him want to go out of his way to lure any of those to his school.

Now all at once he had a double treat: a player that good and white to boot. He felt almost as if he had died and gone to Heaven.

Trainham sensed that he would find a receptive ear in the young man's mother. He did his homework and found that, if anything, her social attitudes were more elitist than those of the average white Brileyville parents who were sending their offspring to his institution. The thought did strike him a time or two that such attitudes and motivations were not wholly rational, but he had an athletic program to run. If he could play on those to bring in the most gifted athlete that area had seen in his memory, his stock would rise dramatically among the school's hierarchy.

Trainham's experience over the years included some time coaching, and he had met a fair number of college recruiters along the way. Invariably, they all seemed to agree that the most successful among them were the ones who mastered best the art of working on the young phenom's mother. That didn't usually include getting her into bed, although at some point the latter may have happened, too. But chances are that if and when it did, the mother in question was less sexually unappealing than Kathleen McDonough.

Trainham researched as much as he could on the Brileyville-based McDonoughs. He talked to some people who knew of the home situation and were willing to impart some of that knowledge to him. Then he paid a call on Hal McDonough's mother at her place of work and invited her to have lunch with him.

Kathleen McDonough had no prior notion of what Trainham was trying to do, but she liked the fact that he was from a private school and seemed interested in her son. So she accepted.

"The reason I wanted to talk to you, Mrs. McDonough, is because we'd like to have your son Harold in our basketball program, and we are in position to offer you some scholarship assistance to enable you to enroll him in Cedar Grove," Trainham said.

"What kind of assistance?" Kathleen McDonough asked. She lit a cigarette.

Trainham didn't smoke and didn't like being around people who did. But this was a special situation, and he was willing to endure a little more than he otherwise might. "Money for books, some of the tuition costs, that sort of thing," he said. "I can't give you exact details right now. If the wrong thing got out to the public school folks, they might raise a stink."

Kathleen McDonough nodded. She understood that much.

"I can tell you I'm in a position to help you out a whole lot," Trainham went on. "I know your circumstances are a little straitened right now, and coming up with money to meet expenses with Harold in our school on what you make would seem impossible."

"If it weren't impossible, Mr. Trainham, I would have had Harold in a school like that long ago," Kathleen McDonough said.

"I understand," Trainham said with a nod. He smiled and exhaled sharply. "I can't funnel money to you per se or slip it to you under the table. For starters, I don't personally have that kind of money. But I do have connections. And I know a lot of people with money who would like to see someone like young Harold in our basketball program. A bug in the right ear and a job paying two or three times what you're pulling in right now could be yours before you know it."

Kathleen McDonough nodded thoughtfully. She liked what she was hearing.

"I'm not going to sugarcoat it, Mrs. McDonough," Trainham went on. "The fact that your son is a gifted athlete is primarily why we're interested in him. He's a good student, too, of course."

"But that wouldn't carry much weight just by itself," Kathleen McDonough mused. She lit a second cigarette from the one she had been smoking before she crushed it.

"No, and I suppose that's a tragedy of sorts, but you have to deal with life as it is, not as it should be," Trainham said.

"That's a lesson I think I've learned fairly well by now,

Mr. Trainham," Kathleen McDonough said. She drew on her cigarette and studied the Cedar Grove athletic director. "Why my son specifically? There must be other gifted athletes, as you call them, in the area."

"I think you sell your son very short, Mrs. McDonough," Trainham said. Her smoke was starting to irritate him. "He's what's referred to in athletic recruiting circles as a genuine blue chipper. By the time he's ready to graduate from high school, he'll have offers from virtually every major college and university in the country. He'll probably be one of the twenty-five or fifty premier high school players in the country. He is that good. He can help our program substantially, . . . perhaps lead us to a state championship. That in turn could lure some other prospects to our school: kids now going to schools like Fork Union, Oak Hill, Benedictine, Masanutten, schools like that. He can give us tremendous exposure, both across the state and nationally. I admit it: self interest does enter into the equation. But you and your son stand to gain a lot out of it, too. Your son especially. He'll be in a predominantly white school environment, without the distractions that might at some point cause him to slip in his grades."

"I like the thought of him in the predominantly white school environment," Kathleen McDonough mused. "I have nothing against colored people personally, but I think my son would be better off among more of his own kind."

"I take it you're interested," Trainham probed.

"Yes, you take it correctly," Kathleen McDonough confirmed.

"We can't finalize anything, of course, until you've talked to your son and we know for sure he's interested," Trainham said.

"Oh, he'll enroll there, whether he thinks he's interested or not," Kathleen McDonough said.

"Well, I suppose I'll be talking to you very soon," Trainham said. He handed Kathleen McDonough a business card and got up and extended his hand for a shake. "The number where I can be reached is on that card. Call me as soon as you have everything under control."

"I will," Kathleen McDonough promised with a smile as she shook the proffered hand.

As Edgar Trainham left the restaurant, the main thought that struck him was that he was glad to be getting away from all that smoke.

Hal was taken aback when his mother broached the notion of his attending Cedar Grove later that evening. "Why?" he protested. "I'm gettin' settled into things at Brileyville pretty good right now. I don't wanta go to Cedar Grove."

"It's not a question of whether you want to go or not, Harold," his mother shot back. "Harold, listen to me. This is a wonderful opportunity for you. You have a chance to go to a really fine school . . . "

"Mother, all that place is is a segregation camp, and everybody knows that," Hal groaned. "It's set up for rich white kids that don't wanta go to school with blacks. Or their parents don't want them to anyway. A lotta people sendin' their kids to that school can't really 'fford it either. They're way over their heads in debt and just barely makin' ends meet . . . "

"I'm not defending the motives of everyone who sends his or her child to that school," Kathleen McDonough rebutted. "It's not a perfect world. And when I hear you come in here saying something like getting settled into things pretty good, I know for sure I need to get you to a place where English is spoken properly and you won't be picking up so many bad grammatical habits."

"Okay, settlin' in pretty well," Hal sighed. "Mother, I know grammar pretty well. I make mostly A's in English. It's just not somethin' I feel like I gotta be on guard 'bout every moment. Least I didn't feel that way 'til just now."

"And dropping the G in your gerunds and participles," Kathleen McDonough said. "And I gotta instead of I have to or I must. I could go on and on. Harold, your spoken grammar is atrocious, and I have a feeling the young people by whom you're surrounded have a great deal to do with that."

"Mother, I 'spect . . . I imagine . . . if you look closely 'nuff, you're gonna find a lotta the kids at Cedar Grove don't use the best grammar 'round either," Hal sighed.

"Around," Kathleen McDonough interjected. "And stop protesting, Harold. As the saying goes, it's a done deal. You are going to Cedar Grove."

Hal protested meekly for a little while longer, but he realized that he would not sway his mother away from her stand. So he decided to take his appeal to another court. He opted first for Wimbush. If Wimbush couldn't or wouldn't help him, he would go to Harry Moore. He knew Moore was happy with how he was progressing in football practice with the season opener just a couple of weeks away and probably would pull out some heavy artillery to keep his prize new recruit in the program.

Wimbush may have been a little miffed by his decision to play football, but he was no more ready than Harry Moore would be to lose him to Cedar Grove. "I heard Edgar Trainham's been asking around about you, but I wasn't sure he was ready to go this far," the basketball coach mused. "Boy, they're not kidding when they say news gets around fast in this town."

"Coach, I don't wanta go to Cedar Grove," Hal appealed. "Maybe a year or so 'go, when things were kinda draggin' for me, I wouldn't mind. But now it's kinda lookin' up. I found I can play basketball pretty good, and Clifford and I been hookin' up on some good pass plays, an' I'm gettin' 'long with everybody, an' I just feel like I'd be kinda out in the cold somewheres like Cedar Grove."

Wimbush heaved an understanding sigh. "You certainly would be a shot in the arm to their basketball program, but aside from that you'd probably have more difficulty fitting in there than you've had here. You haven't been insulated enough or had enough training in how to be a snob to function easily in that sort of social environment."

"Anything you can do to stop Mother?" Hal appealed. "She's hellbent I'm goin' there." He laughed. "She waits 'til after I get used to takin' pops in football practice. She didn't even have the courtesy to bring it up back when I was so sore I could hardly walk."

"Edgar Trainham's the architect of this, not your mother," Wimbush said with a sympathetic shoulder-pat. He paused momentarily to collect his thoughts and then heaved a loud sigh. "I've got a couple of ideas. Just hold tight, and I'll get back to you."

Edgar Trainham did, indeed, have a lot of contacts throughout the state, but so did Wimbush. Wimbush placed a couple of calls to people he knew in strategic state offices and got some pressure put on Trainham. Then he talked to a few black businessmen, including Gerald Hanson, about tossing out threats to white counterparts who might be thinking of providing the sort of employment to Kathleen McDonough that could enable her to meet expenses comfortably while Hal attended Cedar Grove.

"What's the big deal 'bout keepin' one white boy?" one of the black businessmen asked while Wimbush was making his appeal. "Shit, if they don't wanta be here, who wants 'em?"

"This boy's content with being here right now, William," Wimbush responded. "It's his mother. I'd say if nothing else, we would like to keep him here because he's a pretty damned good little basketball player. He's the kind of player that might help us have a shot at winning a state championship or at least getting to the state championship round. The school hasn't done that in forty years and certainly not since desegregation."

"Yeah, I been hearin' some good things 'bout him on the basketball court," William said, with some interest starting to surface in his voice. "Course you wasn't able to keep him 'way from Harry Moore. How you know he ain't gonna get too banged up playin' football to do you any good in basketball?"

Wimbush laughed. "I don't." He patted William on the shoulder. "But I do know if that happens, Cedar Grove will lose interest in him, too."

William laughed. "Serve them right."

Wimbush appreciated the humor, too. "Well, if I can't stop this move, that means he won't be playing football, and you know damned well Harry Moore isn't going to take this lying down," he said. "I think the kid belongs in the basketball program more than football, and when and if he decides to settle on just one sport, it could put me at a distinct disadvantage if it turns out Harry Moore's the one he feels grateful to for keeping him out of Cedar Grove."

"Yeah, see what you mean," William responded with an understanding nod.

A day or so after that, Edgar Trainham received a luncheon invitation by phone from one of the well-to-do parties he was counting on to help finance his venture.

"I don't really think I can go through with this, Edgar," the white businessman told him over lunch.

"But you promised," Trainham protested.

"I know," the white businessman admitted. "But I've been getting some heat put on me the last couple of days. Seems the Brileyville coaching staff—I don't know if it's the basketball or football coach—-they've been getting the word out, and I've been getting calls from some of my black clients threatenin' to cut off business with my company if I give that boy's mother a cushy job so she can send him to that school."

"But Arnie, think of the prestige, the exposure a kid like that can bring to the school," Trainham pleaded.

"I'm sorry, Edgar, truly," Arnie said with a lugubrious headshake.

"Arnie, it's your school. You went there. So did your two boys," Trainham pleaded.

"I have to live with these people and do business with them," Arnie rationalized. "It would be different if the boy really wanted to go there. But I don't think he does. And it's too much to put on a kid to force him into a situation where he's not comfortable just to boost the athletic image of our school. The school's gotten along just fine without much of an athletic image before. Why do we have to bend the rules to get one now?"

"Sports is the defining image in the American culture," Trainham reasoned.

"In New York, L.A. or Chicago maybe, but not necessarily here," Arnie rebutted. "I admit it would be nice if we could get a kid like that in our basketball program. If he's as good as I hear he is, he might help us win the state championship. But it's not worth risking an all out cultural war that might split our already fractured community even more."

So when Trainham and Kathleen McDonough finally sat down in Trainham's office to talk again, Trainham had far less to offer than he envisaged beforehand.

"I can secure some scholarship money, Mrs. McDonough, but the job I mentioned, that seems to be out," he said in an apologetic tone. "It seems that some people from the Brileyville school community have been putting the word out to some of the people I was counting on to assist me."

"I'm not surprised," Kathleen McDonough murmured. She lit a cigarette.

"Mrs. McDonough, please, I do wish you wouldn't smoke in my office," Trainham moaned.

Kathleen McDonough looked at him through hurt eyes and crushed her cigarette. She had a feeling that her son would not be attending Cedar Grove . . . ever.

Later, she communicated as much to Hal when he came home from football practice. "Well, looks like you get your wish," she sighed. "The deal Mr. Trainham spoke of has gone totally out the window, as they say. Seems as if someone from your school—-I wouldn't be surprised if it was that colored basketball coach of whom you seem to think so highly—-has been exerting influence to keep white people with means from spending money so you can go to that school. And, quite frankly, I can't afford to send you there on the salary I draw." She lit a cigarette. "That man had the effrontery to tell me he didn't want me smoking in his office. Before it didn't matter. He let me smoke as much as I wanted. But then when he couldn't get somebody to subsidize you, it was you bother me, don't go away angry, just go away."

"I'm sorry you got shot down. I guess that was pretty rough," Hal said, with genuine sympathy.

"People only want you for what they feel that they can get out of you. I've always basically known that," Kathleen McDonough said. She drew on her cigarette and studied her son. "Did you put anyone up to this?"

"No," Hal lied. He heaved a sigh. "I mentioned it to Coach Wimbush you were thinkin' 'bout sendin' me there, but that's it."

Kathleen McDonough's lips pursed. She wasn't sure if she believed him, but it probably didn't matter any more, so she let it go.

14

Everyone close to the football scene knew that Hal would be good, but there was some question of how quickly he would develop. In the first game, it seemed as if it might take some time. Early on, he dropped a couple of easy passes. Nerves had taken hold.

"Hey, you wasn't droppin' them in practice," Clifford reminded him when they came back to the huddle.

"Yeah, I know," Hal sighed. "I guess that's what they call first game jitters."

"Well, I'm gonna keep goin' to you, so you better work 'em out," Clifford told him sternly.

A couple of plays later, Clifford called a fly pattern for Hal. He could see that the corner defending against Hal wasn't very fast, and it occurred to him that a long pass play might be the best way to get Hal into the flow. Some players need something easy; Hal might fall into a reverse category. In any case, it worked. The play ended sixty yards downfield with Hal spiking the ball in the end zone and the

Brileyville partisans cheering wildly. The jitters were gone.

"Awright, Baby, now we got the peppah-n'-salt dynamite workin' for real," Clifford greeted the white boy in the end zone with a hug.

Hal caught two more long touchdown passes before that Friday night was over and set up yet another with a forty-yard run on an end-around. Brileyville won the game over Hempstone, the defending district champion, forty-one to thirteen. Hempstone no longer was favored to repeat as champion, and Brileyville had a new athletic hero to cheer for.

The Wednesday that followed the first game, Hal was coming out of French class. He was discovering, if he ever had any contrary illusions, that athletic heroism only carries over so far. The backslaps and high-fives from his male peers and the respectful, almost flirtatious smiles from females who before seemed barely to note his existence didn't alter the fact that to the teachers and school administrators, he was just another student.

He vaguely noticed Shawna Hanson moving into step with him as he walked down the school corridor. He didn't think anything about it. She was a student there, too, and had a class to go to the same as he. The hallway was crowded with students and teachers, and virtually everyone had someone beside him or her at any given moment.

"I'd figure by now the coaches'd be lookin' for a way to keep you outta classes," Shawna finally quipped.

Hal was taken aback. Over the seven years he had been in classes with Shawna, he couldn't recall her ever saying anything directly to him.

"I mean by you playin' football. I thought they'd wanta lighten your classroom load so you could spend more time on practice," Shawna followed with a grin.

Hal shrugged. "They might, but my mother's got other ideas. She wouldn't be 'pressed if I scored a hundred touchdowns. An' she's the one I gotta go home to an' face every night."

Shawna laughed. "Good for her." She studied Hal impishly. "I don't know if you're 'ware of it or not, but the main reason you shot up to sports hero from bein' class wallflower so quick is 'cause of my Aunt Eunice."

That was the first time Hal had thought about his sudden twist in fortunes from a cause and effect perspective.

"She told my daddy, and he talked to Coach Wimbush, and that's how come he dropped 'round at Hilton to see you an' all the rest," Shawna went on. She flashed another grin. "My daddy's been keepin' tabs on you. 'Bout every night over dinner, he's bringin' your name up in conversation. An' Aunt Eunice calls from time to time to ask 'bout how you're doin'."

"I never thought 'bout it 'til just now, but I 'member she came 'round when I was shootin' baskets an' we talked a while," Hal said. "She seemed like a real nice lady."

"She is a real nice lady," Shawna said. She tossed a challenging look Hal's way. "An' however big you get to be, I hope you never forget how much of it you owe to her. Lotta people 'round kinda wanted to keep you down. She didn't wanna let 'em. That's how come you're where you're at right now."

"Well, now I know, I definitely won't forget," Hal said. He gestured in appeal. "Uh, next time you talk to your aunt, tell her I said thanks."

"I will," Shawna said. She smiled and turned into a classroom. "I got history this period."

"I got English down the hall," Hal said.

So their paths diverged temporarily.

Shawna was a very attractive young woman, slender and pretty in the way of a fashion model or movie actress. It occurred to Hal that he could get very interested in her very quickly if he had any reason to suppose that she might requite that feeling. He didn't, of course. He might be an athletic hero, but socially he really wasn't a part of, or had any feeling of belonging to, any of the various groups around the school. That included the few whites who attended there. His limited experience with them left him at least as disenchanted as he had been with the blacks. He didn't like hearing words like nigger thrown out frequently when no blacks were around to challenge those whites, so he didn't try to associate much with them either.

Shawna also was a bit of a loner, but that was mostly her choice. She probably would have been the most popular girl among the boys in his class if she didn't make a point of letting all of them know they couldn't measure up to what she wanted in a man. If they couldn't, Hal didn't think he could either, so he didn't spend a great deal of time fantasizing about a relationship with her.

He did chuckle once or twice to himself over how livid his mother would turn if she found out that he had a black girlfriend. For this period, that was about the extent of his thoughts on Shawna.

A couple of non-athletic caucasian male students tried to grab on to a piece of his celebrity. "Awright, do it for the white boys," one of them remarked to him in the school cafeteria during lunch.

Charmaine Jackson, who was sitting nearby, stood up and got in that white boy's face. "He do it for the team, he do it for the school, he do it for hisself even, but that's it," she said angrily. "You want somethin' done for the white boys, you do it you'self. Don't go buggin' him."

"What's bitin' you?" the white boy murmured in response.

"You gonna be wonderin' what cracked you thick skull you don't leave this boy 'lone an' let him finish his lunch," Charmaine shot back.

The two white boys didn't want to challenge Charmaine. They had at least the good sense to recognize that as a losing proposition no matter which way a real fight with her might go. So they departed.

"Thanks, Charmaine," Hal said with sincerity. He wouldn't have been as belligerent about it as the black girl was, but she expressed roughly what he felt.

"Think nothin' of it," Charmaine said. She sat down on the other side of the table facing him. "You gonna run into all kinda chumps like that gonna try'n leech on you now you showin' some real stuff. I hope you got good sense 'nuff to not let 'em."

Hal nodded. "I think whenever it happens, I'm gonna call on you to get rid of 'em," he said.

Charmaine laughed. "Well, you ain't always gonna have me 'round, so you better start learnin' to shove 'em 'way you'self."

"I'll keep that in mind," Hal promised.

Brileyville's home opener was the Friday night of that week against Warrenton Central. Warrenton knew about what Hal and Clifford had done against Hempstone, but that was generally brushed aside as an aberration. Clifford made the visitors pay dearly for that thought. Before the night was over, he and Hal had hooked up on four touchdown passes and numerous other completions. He compiled some very Marino-like numbers, including almost four hundred yards passing. Brileyville won by a whopping sixty-two to eighteen.

Clifford gave Hal a huge bear hug in the winners' locker room after it was all over. "We really stuck it to 'em," he exulted.

"Yeah, we sure did," Hal cheered back. He shook his head and grinned. "I couldn't believe they just kept playin' that one guy on me."

"Me either, but I figured they gonna give me that, I'm gonna beat 'em to death with it," Clifford screamed for the benefit of all his teammates. He flashed a huge grin and hugged Hal again. "Me'n you, we gonna be rewritin' some records before this year's out, Baby."

"Just win games," Harry Moore interjected.

"Don't worry, Coach, we gonna do that, too," Clifford promised.

Hal took his shower and put on clean clothes and headed

out of the gym area. He was figuring on cadging a ride home with one of the coaches. He had to go outside to arrange that.

He felt good. A few aches and bruises from the game lingered, but his body by now had adjusted so that those didn't bother him much. Really, the sweet memory of his four touchdown night rendered those almost nonexistent in his mind.

Just then, he was jolted out of his reverie by the sight of Shawna with her parents and aunt standing near the hallway exit.

He vaguely recognized Gerald and Marian Hanson. He had seen them in school for some function or other periodically over the years. A couple of times, he remembered even exchanging words with them, although nothing of a memorable nature. Of course, the memory of Eunice was somewhat more vivid.

"I had to make sure this athletic phenom I've been hearing so much about really was the same young man I met on that basketball court several months ago," Eunice greeted him with a warm smile.

Hal's head shook bemusedly. "Shawna told me you were the one got all this started," he murmured.

At that moment, Clifford was coming down the hall with his arm around a fairly pretty black girl Hal recognized from the senior class. He turned to the Hansons and Eunice. "Y'all take care of this boy. He's my main man."

Hal chuckled as Clifford and his date faded from sight.

"I take it that's one of your teammates," Eunice remarked to Hal.

"Yes, ma'am, our quarterback," Hal verified. He flashed a grin. "He was the one layin' it out there so good tonight. All I had to do was hang on."

"I always cringe when I hear young black men using those hip expressions like *my main man* with such animation," Eunice sighed. She cast an appealing glance Hal's way. "I hope you don't feel a compulsion to pick up such expressions. They sound bad enough coming from blacks, God knows, but when whites start picking them up, it really sounds ridiculous."

Hal laughed. "My mother'd cut me off in a heartbeat if she heard me talkin' like that. I don't think you need to worry."

"Uh, Eunice, if we're going to the restaurant, I think we'd better get started," Gerald Hanson interjected.

"Yes, I suppose we should," Eunice agreed. She started to slip a light jacket on. Then another thought struck her. "Has anyone thought to invite Hal?"

Hal's hands raised defensively. "Uh, thanks, but I really oughta be gettin' home," he replied. The invitation was appealing in providing some potential for ingratiation room with Shawna, but he didn't want to look or sound like a beggar.

"Why don't you call your mama an' tell her some folks 'vited you out to dinner after the game?" Shawna recommended. She chuckled. "You don't have to tell her the invitation came from folks of color."

"I don't see where there should be any problem," Eunice appealed to her brother-in-law. "We certainly have enough room for one more."

"Well, if Hal's mother doesn't object, I suppose it's all right," Marian Hanson said. She chuckled. "It's not often we have a genuine athletic hero in our midst."

"I have no problem," her husband said.

"There you have it," Eunice told Hal. "I'm sure an athletic young man like yourself who's just finished playing a game is bound to be hungry."

That was certainly true. "It sounds nice, but I'm not sure I should," Hal replied, more from a sense of obligation than what he really wanted to do.

"I think we're the best judge of that," Eunice said. She grasped Hal's shoulders gently. "Come on. We'd love to have you. I'm dying to hear about what's happened to you since the last time we talked back at Hilton that day."

"I can loan you a quarter if you need money to call your mama," Shawna volunteered.

Hal reached in his trousers pocket and pulled out some change. "I got some money. That's not what I'm worried 'bout."

"You're not 'shamed to be seen with people of color, I hope," Shawna teased.

Hal chuckled. "If I was that, I picked the wrong school an' town to be in." He turned to Eunice appealingly. "You sure it's awright?"

"I don't think we'd have extended the invitation if it wasn't," Eunice assured him warmly.

Hal shrugged. "Well, I'll call Mother then."

"If you have problems, I'll talk to her," Eunice offered.

Hal's mother was predictably dubious. She might have kept him on the phone for the better part of the night detailing the life story of every person in the party if Eunice hadn't interceded. Eunice had the kind of professional-sounding telephone voice that could reach a Kathleen McDonough. She didn't sound black to the average white ear. And she was used to business dealings in which she had to break down a prospective client's sales resistance, so she soon dispelled any lingering doubts Hal's mother might have entertained and convinced her that her son was in good hands.

"Boy that mama of yours really must be some kind of suspicious woman," Shawna remarked to Hal as the group headed to the car.

Hal laughed. "You don't know the half of it."

"Well, if I had a son, I'd want to know all about the people he was out with, too," Marian Hanson defended the absent white woman's motives.

"But maybe there's such a thing as being too suspicious," Eunice said.

"All I know is we coulda starved to death waitin' for that woman to make up her mind," Shawna groused.

In the car, Hal found himself on one side in the back.

Eunice sat in the center and Shawna on the other side. Gerald and Marian Hanson were seated up front.

"What you were saying about that *my main man* remark, Eunice," Gerald brought up. "Now that I think about it, it occurs to me if I were a quarterback and some young man had just caught four of my passes for spectacular crowd pleasing touchdowns, I think I might be calling him my main man too."

Hal chuckled. "Well, maybe I oughta call Warrenton's defensive coordinator my main man. He just kept that one guy on me. That let me get open all night, an' all Clifford had to do was just lay the ball out there for me to run under."

"I did wonder why someone didn't switch over and try to double-team you," Eunice mused.

"They prob'ly just figured it's only a white boy. He can't really be very fast," Shawna teased.

Hal laughed. "Maybe. But prob'ly it comes down to them only havin' one defensive formation. They don't see passin' offenses much in this district. So somebody comes up with one, they don't know how to 'just to it."

"When I saw you out on the playground, it struck me that you looked pretty quick," Eunice remarked to Hal. "But you're downright fast. You were just running away from that other boy tonight."

Hal chuckled. "It was prob'ly more a case of him not bein' so fast as me bein' so fast."

"I don't know," Eunice said. She eyed Hal with interest. "I've followed football and basketball pretty much my entire adult life, and I think I know genuine speed when I see it. I'd say you've got a fair amount of it."

Hal shrugged. "I can outrun all the guys on our team, but I don't know if that means much. At some place like Florida State, I'd prob'ly be just middle of the pack."

"Middle of the pack at Florida State puts you at the top of the heap a lot of other places," Eunice told him with a smile and cheek pat. "By the way, what happened to basketball?

That's not out now, I hope."

"You can thank Coach Moore for him bein' on the football team," Shawna volunteered. "He saw Hal playin' basketball an' figured he'd be good in football, too. So he got on his case 'bout him bein' a candyass an' maybe even a fag if he didn't play football. Played on his macho insecurities."

Hal grimaced. "That's 'bout it," he agreed with a nod to Eunice. "He bugged me 'bout comin' out for football. I finally told him if he could get my mother to let me, I'd do it. I didn't figure he had a snowball's chance in that hot place of pullin' it off, but somehow he was able to talk her into it. Seems like everybody can talk her into stuff 'cept me."

"Mothers know about con jobs from their children by instinct," Marian Hanson said with a fleeting glance back at her own daughter. "She wouldn't be doing her job well if she didn't put you on the spot more."

"I think maybe sometimes there's such a thing as doin' the job too good," Hal muttered.

"Here, here," Shawna endorsed.

"I hope basketball isn't out for you now that you're rising to football stardom," Eunice remarked to Hal. "Doing well on the high school scene is one thing. But on a higher level, I think your lack of size might work against you."

"I think basketball's still my favorite," Hal said. He laughed. "An' I think I like playin' for Coach Wimbush better'n Coach Moore. He's not always makin' everything a question of your manhood like Coach Moore does."

Eunice laughed. "Sounds like he realizes there's only so much about your manhood you should have to prove. Good for him. Too many men seem to have a problem with proving their masculinity."

"Well, an' plus you don't have those two hundred and fifty pound monsters ready to break every bone in your body when they can zero in on you," Hal said.

"You seem to take it pretty well," Gerald Hanson interjected. "I noticed you took some pretty hard licks out there tonight, and you seemed to get right back up easily enough."

Hal laughed. "'Lieve it or not, I got hit harder in practice 'un in a game so far. We got this big linebacker who really popped me once when I caught a pass from Clifford on a down-and-in. I 'member as I was gettin' up I kinda joked to him 'bout us bein' on the same team, an' he came back with a line 'bout how he'd hit his own mother if she came into that zone."

"Sounds like that young man has a true football soul," Gerald Hanson mused.

"Sounds to me like he's a psychopath," Shawna murmured.

"I think anybody playin' his position an' likin' it's gotta be kinda psycho," Hal said with a chuckle.

They got to the restaurant and found a table for five. It was a buffet eat-all-you-want-for-$5.95 establishment. They got their food, Gerald Hanson picked up the tab, and soon they were seated.

By now, Hal was a certifiably public figure in Brileyville, and the restaurant was full of people who had just come from the game. So several customers passing the Hanson table made a point of congratulating him on the great game he had just played. Some no doubt wondered what he was doing sitting at a table with an African American family, but they kept any questions or comments on that to themselves.

"I'm s'prised one of 'em doesn't ask for your autograph," Shawna commented wryly to Hal at one point.

Hal shrugged. "I think people only do that in New York an' Hollywood."

"Well, I'm no expert, but I'd say you have the kind of athletic ability that could get you to one of those two cities," Eunice said. She scanned Hal warmly. "It gets even worse when people start seeing you a lot on TV."

"I get to that point, I guess I'll just stay home," Hal said with a chuckle. "I hope I find a girl that knows how to cook."

"Well, I know one right off the bat. Her name's Budget Gourmet," Shawna threw in impishly.

That one drew a hearty laugh from everyone at the table, including Hal.

The restaurant didn't have waiters and waitresses as such, but it did have some people—mostly very young—cleaning the tables after the customers vacated them. One such young black woman was visibly stricken by the sight of the very Nordic looking young man seated with a table full of people of obviously African descent. She didn't follow the Brileyville sports scene, so she was unaware of Hal's celebrity status. But she was fascinated by the obvious contrast between him and his dinner companions.

"I know you ain't a member of this family," she finally remarked to him with a nervous smile.

Hal was groping for a response. Then Eunice interceded. "Did you ever see that story in the National Enquirer about the woman who had the alien's baby?" she asked in a deadpan tone.

"What?" the young woman responded in bewilderment.

"You know, the one had the alien's baby. The guy from outer space," Shawna interjected. She picked up on the joke quickly and decided to do her part in moving it along.

"Uh, yeah, I 'member seein' it in the grocery store once when I was shoppin'," the young woman said hesitantly.

"Well, I'm that woman," Eunice said. "This young man is my son."

Hal bit his lower lip to stifle a giggle.

"That's the truth," Shawna told the young woman with a perfectly straight face. She glanced at Hal and grinned slightly for his benefit.

"It couldn't be. Even if it was, the baby'd be only 'bout a year, maybe two years old," the young woman murmured.

"The young people on the planet this young man's father comes from age much more rapidly than people on earth do," Eunice said. "The fact is, this young man is only about fourteen months old."

"Ah, you pullin' my leg," the young woman said. She tried to smile.

"No she isn't," Shawna supported her aunt. She patted

Hal on a shoulder. "He just started learnin' how to talk two weeks 'go. Say somethin', Hal."

"Da, da," Hal joined the practical joke.

"He look like just a regular ol' white boy to me," the young woman murmured.

"He would because that's what his father looks like," Eunice said. She patted Hal on a cheek. "The genes of the Trogonipheron males are much more powerful than earth genes. That's how white people came into being on this planet in the first place. Trogonipheron males came down and mated with black females and produced a line consistent with the rest of humanity except for the lighter hair and skin color, and then they moved them to Europe which wasn't inhabited then to allow that line to evolve. They're coming back now because the white line has grown weaker in recent years. This young man when he reaches maturity will be able to outrun and outjump Michael Jordan."

"You people crazy," the young woman said with a headshake and thin smile. She departed, still shaking her head, probably not entirely convinced that Eunice wasn't telling the truth.

Everyone at the table started cracking up as soon as the young woman was gone.

"Eunice, that was a cruel thing to do to that poor girl," Marian Hanson scolded her sister between giggles.

"The sad thought that struck me is that I think she might have halfway believed it," Gerald Hanson said.

"I don't think you're gonna see her on any list for a Rhodes Scholarship anytime soon," Shawna remarked.

Hal laughed. "Somethin' tells me she never even made it all the way through high school."

"Well, she obviously has enough of a sharp eye to figure out Hal's not likely to have any genetic connection to the rest of us at the table," Eunice said. She patted Hal on a shoulder.

"Oh, I dunno. I've read 'bout blacks that look white 'nuff to pass for bein' white," Hal said. "Maybe I'm one of those. I could always pass myself off as that anyways."

"I don't think they usually look quite as white as you do, Hal," Gerald Hanson told him with amusement.

"Well, yeah, I guess I do look pretty white," Hal conceded. "I hope y'all don't hold it 'gainst me."

"If we held it 'gainst you, we wouldn't be sittin' here with you, silly," Shawna told him with a grin.

15

One concern that struck both Eunice and Marian after that night was a feeling that Shawna might be starting to show the seminal stage of a crush on Hal. It wasn't so much anything Shawna said or did; in that regard, she was perfectly innocent. But she was looking at Hal in a way that signaled a certain interest that might lead to something more serious over time. That worried the two sisters a little, and they talked about it briefly on one or two occasions when Shawna wasn't around to hear them.

Marian's concern was from the standpoint of family and ethnic unity and religion. She felt nothing against white people per se, but she didn't think blacks should be mating with them. To her, it was a kind of divine structure somehow violated when individuals from the two groups crossed the line. Eunice took a slightly differing view. She didn't see anything wrong particularly in such line crossing, but circumstances would in time be pulling Hal into another world in which Shawna might not fit easily or comfortably. Sooner or later, that would include ample opportunity for companionship with white females, a luxury he hadn't enjoyed to speak of to this point, and that could transform his personality drastically. She wasn't sure how well he or Shawna would handle that sort of situation.

Then the Boston specter struck her. Hal wouldn't be in this position now if he had been able to grow up in that Massachusetts metropolis where his mother was spawned. A slightly luckier turn here or there, or absent one or two of the unluckier turns his mother had gone through, and he might well be in Boston now, established, accepted, socially well-adjusted with a girlfriend and a feeling of security and a confidence in dealing with his peers. He had some of that now by dint of his remarkable athletic ability, but the social part was still lacking. Assuming that he was normally heterosexual, and Eunice had no reason to suspect otherwise, he would want and should have a girlfriend in his life. As matters stood now, Shawna would seem a prize catch if he ever picked up on the feeling that she might be interested. It occurred to Eunice that she might want to try to help him find an available and attractive option before nature of that sort took hold too firmly for anyone to put reins on it.

As it turned out, Eunice had a Dunleavy contact in New York: a first cousin to Kathleen McDonough. Willard Dunleavy came from a poorer side of the family and now worked as a lawyer for a firm on Park Avenue. Poorer, in Willard's case, didn't mean poverty stricken; it was just that his family had to count their dollar assets in the hundreds of thousands instead of a few million, as Kathleen McDonough's father could do. Willard could have remained in Boston and generally pursued a life of idleness and dissolution had he so chosen. He was homosexual, but that would not have been terribly unacceptable if he had been willing to keep his relationships private and occasionally escort a woman to some function to keep the gossip mongering set at bay. Willard refused to do that, however, and the family, while not totally disowning him, made it clear to him that they did not want him in their proximity where that lifestyle could reflect on their other members. So he headed off to New York and parlayed the Harvard law degree he had managed to obtain into a relatively lucrative practice.

Eunice had known Willard for several years and had a few business dealings that passed through him and/or his law firm. They were not close friends in the sense of socializing together frequently, but they did like each other quite well and enjoyed the times they were able to see and talk to one another. So Willard wasn't really surprised to get a call from Eunice one day near the noon hour.

"Eunice, wonderful to hear from you," he greeted her in what some people would take to be a Kennedyesque accent.

"Willard, I was hoping we could have lunch," Eunice said. "It involves a kind of forgotten part of your family."

"Ouch. The most forgotten part of my family is yours truly, and you know how I detest talking about myself, dear lady," Willard responded.

Eunice laughed. "You're not the only forgotten part of it, I can assure you. I'll explain further when we get together, okay?"

"Boy, this does sound juicy," Willard said. "It doesn't involve someone else whose behavior might be said to border on the scandalous, does it?"

"No, nothing quite that exciting, I'm afraid," Eunice answered with a chuckle.

"Well, my life's been pretty dull lately, so I suppose that's too much to ask for," Willard said insouciantly. "Where do you suggest we meet?"

"Tavern on the Green okay?" Eunice suggested.

"Their drinks are as good and potent as any other establishment's," Willard acceded. "What time? Say one-thirty?"

"One-thirty sounds ideal," Eunice said.

Willard was younger than his cousin Kathleen, by a good dozen years or so. That put him, by Eunice's reckoning, probably in his early thirties. He bore a marked resemblance to Hal, with blond hair and blue eyes and similarly angular features. His hair was starting to show signs of thinning now. Eunice hoped that Hal would be luckier some fifteen or so years into the future when he was approaching that same age. She also hoped that he would remain more sexually mainstream. She had nothing against homosexuals as people and indeed even had some homosexual friends, but she understood how complicated that bent can be in almost every segment of American society.

Willard was in the restaurant and already seated when Eunice arrived. "Eunice, so lovely to see you again," he greeted her. He pulled out a chair for her to sit down. "Most people from a Boston family, if it got back to the family that a scion was seen in a prominent establishment with a black woman, they would probably feel scandalized. In my case, however, they might be elated that it was with a woman of any kind."

Eunice laughed. She started to light a cigarette and quickly remembered the no smoking rule that recently had been implemented and put the cigarette back in its pack. "I keep forgetting," she sighed. "The smoking lamp is no longer lit in these establishments."

"Naughty, naughty," Willard said good-naturedly. He sipped some wine.

A waiter came by and took their orders.

"Anytime someone mentions my family, it naturally piques my curiousity," Willard said after the waiter had departed.

"You have a cousin. Kathleen I think her name is," Eunice said. "How well do you remember her?"

Willard laughed. "The one member of the Dunleavy family even more of a black sheep than yours truly." He sipped some more wine and shrugged. "Actually, I remember Kathleen quite fondly. She was the one person among all my cousins and/or siblings who treated me as if my existence had some value. I wasn't very old when I last saw her. Six or seven, as I recall. She was at Harvard. Then I heard she dropped out and went to Greenwich Village. Then I heard she married this brute of a man from out in the midwest somewhere. Charles Something-or-other. And then I heard old Harland, her pater, disowned or disclaimed or whatever you do when you cut off all relationship with someone. I think it had something to do with her breaking faith with the old Mother Church. Kennedys may do that with some impunity, but it's strictly verboten among Dunleavys."

"That may explain why Kennedys become Democrats and your family tends to vote Republican . . ."

"True. Kennedys go into politics. We buy politicians. I say *we*, I mean the family. I'm no longer a part of that. I buy booze, maybe even sex from time to time, but I let others worry about buying politicians."

"It seems to me if I wanted to buy a politician, I'd try to get more for my money than they seem to manage."

"Ah, dear Eunice, you are so right. Last election when it was Bush versus Dukakis, I found the prospects of either man winning so depressing I think I stayed drunk for the whole week of the election."

"You must have some rather understanding bosses to allow you to do that. I don't think I could get away with it even if I wanted to."

"I suppose. A lot of my cases can be put on the back burner rather easily. I just call in and say I'm sick. Which may not be all that far from the truth. My God, Eunice, do you have any notion how painful a hangover can be?"

Eunice laughed. "I've had a couple of them myself. Yes, I'm aware they're rather painful."

"Um, yes. But we were talking about my cousin Kathleen. She married this schmuck, Charles Whatshisface . . ."

"McDonough. That's the name her son goes by now."

"Ummm, yes. I remembered it as an Irish name, but evidently too shanty for old Harland to endure."

"It turns out too shanty for her to endure, too. She's since divorced him."

"Well, the Mother Church frowns on that, too. Unless you're a Kennedy, of course. Kennedys seem to get away with things the rest of us poor well-to-do mortals aren't able to."

"They become Democrats. That excuses a whole litany of evils."

"Yes, but they seem to have more fun. Most of my lovers have professed themselves to be Democrats, if they acknowledged any political affiliation at all. A couple of them have even been married, although I'll not bore you with the details on any of that."

"Oh, I don't think I'd find it boring," Eunice said with amusement.

"You wouldn't, but that's because you have a sense of humor and a soul, dear lady," Willard said affectionately. He sipped some wine and paused as their food was being put on the table. "Apropos Kathleen, however. You mentioned a son. He's not homosexual, I trust. I think one of us is enough for any family to be cursed with for any one generation."

"No, nothing like that. Or at least I haven't picked up on any signals that might lead me to suspect he's that way," Eunice said. She bit into some of her food. "They're living in Virginia now."

"It's fitting in a way, I suppose. The two colonies settled first. Kathleen seemed to have a love for historical significance."

"I think this time it was more chance than choice that brought her to Virginia. She wound up in Brileyville, the city I told you about where I grew up and where I still have family."

"She must love that. A vanilla chip in a bowl of chocolate milk."

"I think she's chafing under it actually. But really it's her son I'm worried about. I have a niece who's in his class at school. He's emerging into a top football star, and I think he's going to be an even better basketball player, and I think my niece may be developing an interest in him that some people might see as, shall we say, complicated."

"Uh, yes, some would see it that way. I suspect it would be even more true in a southern state like Virginia. One advantage to being of my persuasion is you're already looked on as a pervert, so you can cross ethnic lines in picking lovers without upsetting anyone any more unduly."

"I never thought about it quite that way, but I suppose you have a point."

"I never have a point, dear lady. I recognize life for the inane entity it truly is and merely speak my observations. But the young man? Does he show signs of requiting your niece's? . . . Uh, . . . I think the word you used was interest."

Eunice heaved a sigh. "I think the danger exists that he might. That in itself doesn't bother me. If they wanted to date, go together, whatnot, that in itself is not a problem. But the social forces they could run into could be a problem."

Willard shrugged. "True." He bit into some of his food and washed it down with some wine. "But how can I help? As I see it, all I have to offer is sympathy. You can get that a lot of places. This world is full of professional sympathizers. Some of them are much more skillful than I at sympathizing."

Eunice laughed. "I'll have to remember that." She sipped some wine and chewed some more of her lunch. "I thought possibly if he could be reconnected to his Boston relatives . . . "

"I wouldn't wish that off on the most despicable person in this world," Willard interrupted.

"Hear me out," Eunice pleaded. "If he could be reconnected to his Boston relatives, get into a social setting with a lot of attractive and interesting white girls, that might naturally wean him and Shawna, my niece, away from any tendency they might feel to begin a relationship . . . "

"Eunice, you don't know that world like I do," Willard said. "It's cold. It's elitist. It's a world of aura, and you have to be reared in it to pick it up. My cousin's son—I'd like to say my nephew, but I don't think he quite qualifies as that —-has not been a part of that world. He hasn't picked up that aura. He couldn't fit in, even if he wanted to. And if he has as much going for him as I hope he has and you seem to think he might, he wouldn't want to. I don't want to, and I think that would be true even if my sexual preference was for women."

"Still, Willard, isn't it worth a try?" Eunice appealed. "He's been cut off from much of his natural family. Shouldn't he at least have a chance to get acquainted with them?"

Willard heaved a sigh. "If you insist, I'll talk to Uncle Harland and get back with you. I wouldn't expect too much if I were you, however. I don't exactly wield the most influence with anyone in that family, and my guess is they're not going to want anything to do with the young man. The fact that he's athletic and plays sports they tend to look down on probably will work against him. It's not like in the movies where the dashing hero who can inject new life into the family line is warmly embraced by most. They don't want new life. They're kinda like Dracula, preferring to remain in a kind of suspended status halfway between life and death."

"You're probably right. I realize that," Eunice said. "Still I'd like to see what can be worked out, if anything. It could help the young man. Or if nothing else, it can give him a glimpse into something he can know for sure he doesn't want to be a part of."

"That would be my hope for him," Willard said. He patted Eunice's hand. "I'll talk to Uncle Harland and get back to you. I think you're wasting your time, but that's part of the life experience, too."

Eunice laughed. "That's how we learn, Willard," she responded.

16

Willard may have been personna non grata to the rest of his family, but most of its members at least would speak to him. That included his Uncle Harland, Hal's maternal grandfather. He explained the situation to Uncle Harland, including Eunice's interest in Hal's welfare, and the venerable Dunleavy patriarch agreed to talk to Eunice if she wanted to drive (or fly) up to Boston.

"I talked to Uncle Harland last night, and he said he would be willing to listen to what you might have to say," Willard communicated to Eunice by phone at the earliest opportunity.

"Did he sound encouraging?" Eunice asked.

"I think the operative word is blase," Willard answered with a chuckle. "As I told you earlier, passion and excitement are not emotions you're very likely to see from anyone in that clan."

"Well, it never hurts to check it out anyway," Eunice said. She fiddled with a cigarette she planned to take outside the office and smoke. "Thanks, Willard."

"The least I can do for you, dear lady," Willard said insouciantly.

A couple of days later, Eunice drove to Boston. The trip was roughly the same distance from New York as when she visited her old hometown in Virginia. It took her a while to adjust to that fact. In her mind, Boston always seemed so much closer to New York—-geographically as well as philosophically—-than did any Virginia point. She didn't realize how expansive a region the northeast was until she actually moved up there. Even now, the reality seemed somehow skewed at times.

The drive took about eight hours. That was roughly how much time she spent on the road when she went home to Brileyville. She always drove. It made more sense. She had no problem with flying, but the time to and from the airports and the imposition on her sister and brother-in-law considered, she could get there about as fast by car. Not to mention how it left her more in control of events. If she wanted to go somewhere, she didn't have to wait until it was convenient for someone to drive her there.

She had been to Boston several times over the years, but this would be her first actual visit to Beacon Hill. Previously, she had taken in the historic sites and nightspots and occasionally a Red Sox or Celtics game. She liked Boston rather well, from what she had seen of the city. She understood that many of her fellow blacks didn't like it and, indeed, were inclined to see it as more racist than much (if not all) of the south. She supposed there was some truth in that, although she personally hadn't seen it. She tended to go to the places where one is not turned away regardless of color if one has the money or credit card to meet the cost of admission. At this point in her life, she could manage that easily enough.

Harland Dunleavy surprised her. From Willard's description, she rather expected to see a shriveled, stooped little old man with one foot firmly in the grave. But instead he turned out to be quite a handsome, distinguished looking elderly man, still vibrant and athletic in his movements. She was especially struck by his very thick head of wavy white hair. If, as she had heard, the male hair gene is passed on through the mother, that bode well for Hal thirty or forty years into the future.

"I'm sorry to keep you waiting, Mrs. Weller," Harland Dunleavy greeted her in the study of his expansive home to which a servant had directed her. "Or is it Ms.? I never know any more."

"Technically, it's Mrs.," Eunice said with a shrug. "It was the last name of my most recent husband." She flashed a smile. "My maiden name is Heatwole. That's why I'm in no hurry to change back to it."

"Well, last names at birth are not our choice to make," Dunleavy said. He poured himself a drink. "Would you like a glass of wine or a beer?"

"No, thank you, Mr. Dunleavy," Eunice responded.

Dunleavy stirred his drink and sat down facing her. "My nephew tells me you have some news of a grandson of mine."

"Yes sir," Eunice verified. She had braced herself not to smoke, but when she saw Harland Dunleavy put a match to a cigar, she interpreted this as permission to light up herself. "Your daughter Kathleen . . . "

"Kathleen has not been my daughter for a number of years," Dunleavy interrupted curtly.

"Well, you did sire her, Mr. Dunleavy. She is the product of your seed," Eunice reminded him in a similarly sharp tone. She drew on her cigarette for emphasis.

"Yes, that's true," Dunleavy conceded. He sipped on his cocktail. "So she had a son."

"He is of your blood, Mr. Dunleavy," Eunice said. "I don't know the details of your split with your daughter or who's right and wrong in that or any of the rest of it. But the young man is an innocent party in all of it . . . "

"Excuse me, Mrs. Weller, but what personal interest do

you have in any of this?" Dunleavy cut her off.

"Excuse me?" Eunice replied. The question took her aback.

"I mean, what do you stand to gain by it?" Dunleavy expanded. "You come all the way up here to make a case for a young man who I suppose is my grandson by blood but whom I've never met. I find it hard to believe that you do it with absolutely no personal gain for yourself in mind."

That remark angered Eunice. She had all she could do to refrain from lashing out at the elderly man. "Mr. Dunleavy, I assure you that I stand to gain nothing out of coming here personally," she said firmly. She drew deeply on her cigarette. "The young man has been cut off from his blood relations. I was hoping that something could be worked out so that he could meet you and his grandmother and his cousins and uncles and aunts. That's all. I have no intention of trying to milk your family for money or anything else. The young man in question, Hal, is my sole concern."

"If you say so," Dunleavy said insouciantly. He puffed on his cigar and stared vacantly at some spot beyond Eunice. "Is the young man living in poverty or something of that sort?"

"No, of course not," Eunice groaned. She shook her head to bring herself back under control. "Well, the family circumstances are a little straitened, but he and his mother are getting by fairly well."

"Well, then, what's the problem?" Dunleavy asked.

Eunice took a deep breath. The thought struck her in that moment that some woman merited pity for being married to this man. "There is no problem, Mr. Dunleavy," she said, just a hint of the irritation she felt creeping into her voice. "I just thought it would be a nice thing for the young man to get to know some of his relatives."

"I think the young man should be able to speak on his own behalf," Dunleavy said. He puffed on his cigar and sipped from his cocktail. "I don't get the feeling that the young man is interested in getting to know any of us. And his mother certainly is not welcome in this house."

"It might be to your benefit to get to know him, Mr. Dunleavy," Eunice shifted her appeal. "He's really quite a remarkable young man. He's a quite gifted athlete, in fact. I understand he may take after you in that regard."

"I played some tennis and polo. I never played football or any of those sports that seem to be so popular," Dunleavy said in a blase tone.

"He plays football right now, and I have a feeling he's going to be an even more exceptional basketball player," Eunice said proudly. "And he's quite a nice looking young man. I think if you had a chance to see him up close, you'd be very proud."

"I have a family full of nice looking grandchildren and great-grandchildren and nieces and nephews," Dunleavy said with an expansive wave. "Mrs. Weller, I don't need to go out in the hinterlands looking for the progeny of lost family sheep. I have more than enough right here to give me a full, warm feeling."

"Yes, but try to consider the young man, Mr. Dunleavy," Eunice pleaded. "None of what happened between you and your daughter is his fault . . . "

"That's not the point, Mrs. Weller," Dunleavy cut her off again. "If that young man were brought into this family setting right now, all you would accomplish is arousing resentment and hard feelings among his various cousins and other relatives. And I, frankly, don't see that the young man would fit in among us. I'm sure he hasn't the polish or the manners or the social graces that would enable him to move easily in our society. And, frankly, I don't think he would want to fit in."

Eunice heaved a sigh. "I think it's your loss and your family's loss more than it is his," she said peevishly.

"Well, if that's your opinion, you're entitled to it," Dunleavy said with a shrug.

Eunice heaved another sigh and got up. "I'm sorry to have taken up your time, Mr. Dunleavy," she said.

"I'm sorry you wound up wasting so much of your own, Mrs. Weller," Dunleavy replied coldly.

When Eunice got back to New York, she called Willard and arranged to meet him at a restaurant in the Village. She knew it to be a spot with a reputation for being frequented by homosexuals. That didn't bother her. At least she didn't have to worry about being hit on there.

"Well, I gather that you struck out with my venerable uncle," Willard said.

"That is one impossible man," Eunice sighed.

Willard laughed. "I think I tried to tell you as much."

"Yes, you did," Eunice conceded with a nod. She sipped on a drink. "I didn't think it was possible for anyone to be so cold where a blood relationship is concerned."

"Uncle Harland lives by a code that defies all explanations of family ties you're accustomed to," Willard said. "Or several codes. I haven't figured out which. Someday I might get interested enough to try. Or I may not. It probably isn't very important. I think the line from the good book goes: This, too, shall pass. They strut and fret their hour upon the stage and then are heard no more. Really, if you stop and think about it, young Hal is probably better off without any connection to that part of the family. Those athletic gifts you seem to sense in him give him a shot at a life and an identity that he can form himself. With that bunch, he would always have to be fighting against whatever label they decided to put on him."

"I suppose you're right," Eunice conceded.

"Plus he has some life, and they would bore him dreadfully," Willard said.

"They are pretty boring, if old Harland is any indication," Eunice said.

"He's the most alive of the lot unfortunately," Willard sighed.

"That's scary," Eunice said through a moue.

"And that leaves you back to where you were before:

The possibility that nature might decide to take its own peculiar course with your niece and my first cousin once removed," Willard said.

"Yes, I am back to that point," Eunice agreed.

"Well, it may just come down to the cold, hard basic fact of your having to learn to live with it if it actually happens," Willard said. He patted Eunice on a hand. "I can't even really offer much in the way of sympathy on that one. I don't see where it would necessarily be a bad thing."

"Well, if it comes to that point, I think I can learn to live with it," Eunice said. She sipped on her drink and chuckled. "But I have a feeling my sister might have a great deal more difficulty doing so."

17

Shawna and Hal were in the same grade, and both were in the college-bound academic program, but they only took one class together. That was French, in the morning. Since that night at the restaurant, their contact had been virtually non-existent. A couple of times they did say good morning or hello to one another, but that was the extent of it. If Eunice had been privy to this, she would have felt foolish for expressing her concerns about the two to Willard.

Their contact might have remained casual and detached for some time longer if Eunice hadn't called one night and confided to her sister details of her meeting with Harland Dunleavy. Marian Hanson in turn expressed concern over the dinner table. The entire family, Shawna included, sympathized with Hal in the situation, but they were in no position to do anything about it.

"I just don't understand how you can just cut somebody outta your life like that," Shawna mused. "Heck, if I found out I had a cousin or an older brother or sister I didn't know anything 'bout before, I'd wanta meet that person."

"Normal people would," her mother said sympathetically. "But evidently those relatives of Hal's don't fit into the category of what we would see as normal."

"They live by a different set of rules," Gerald Hanson said. "There have been times when I've envied them for the money they have and whatnot. But when I hear about something like this, I find myself very grateful that I did not come through a family like that."

"I'd say Hal's better off without 'em," Shawna said.

"I think I would agree," her mother responded.

As Eunice had surmised, a fascination of sorts for Hal was evolving in Shawna. It wasn't a crush as such. Certainly Shawna didn't think of it as that. But it was starting to occur to her that he wasn't unattractive, and he was on his way to establishing himself as the school's premier male athlete, and he made good grades and seemed aware enough of what was going on in the world to keep up with a conversation—-and, to top it all off, he had a legitimate pedigree. Granted, it wasn't a pedigree that he could parlay into anything substantial now, but if he had been able to grow up in those surroundings, Shawna could easily imagine him now with more polish, dash and sophistication. It also occurred to her that in such surroundings, he no doubt would have a lot of silly white girls harboring genuine crushes on him.

She accosted Hal after French class the following morning. "My Aunt Eunice met your granddaddy," she told him.

Hal was taken by surprise. "What?" he exclaimed.

"Your granddaddy," Shawna repeated. "Aunt Eunice met your granddaddy. You do have one, you know."

"I prob'ly got two of 'em, 'ssumin' the one out in Nebraska's still 'live," Hal said. He studied Shawna. He still had difficulty ingesting this new information. "I 'spect it was the one in Boston she met."

"Yep," Shawna confirmed. She grinned and patted him on an arm. "Well, gotta get to history class. See you later."

Hal finally caught up with Shawna again at lunchtime in

the school cafeteria. "You really knocked me for a loop back there," he said. He set his books on a table and sat down across from her. "What your aunt find out?"

Shawna shrugged. "What makes you think she found out anything?"

"Well, way you brought it up made it sound like it might be kinda 'portant," Hal sighed.

"Well, if you must know, she found out your granddaddy doesn't want any part of you," Shawna said. She flashed a grin. "Not that I blame him."

"Nothin' I can do 'bout that," Hal said with a shrug. "I 'spect it's got more to do with Mother 'un me. I hope it does anyhow. Since he never met me, I don't know how he could hold anything against me."

Shawna realized that her last remark had been more cutting than was necessary and heaved a sigh. "Well, for what it's worth, Aunt Eunice doesn't think very highly of him, and she told us she thinks you're better off without him in your life." She studied Hal impishly. "Y'know, a little better luck 'long the way, you could be in some fancy prep school like Choate right now."

"What's Choate?" That was almost like a foreign language to Hal.

Shawna laughed. "You come from a family that takes goin' to a school like that as natural as the rest of us do takin' a drink of water, an' you gotta ask me what it is. You oughta be 'shamed of yourself." She cast a mock scolding glance his way. "It's an exclusive prep school up in New England. I'd figure your mama'da made sure you knew that much anyway. It's where the rich kids from the snooty New England families go to get ready for Harvard and Yale and schools like that."

"Mother doesn't talk much 'bout that life now, so I got spared that one," Hal murmured. He sipped some soda from a can he had carried into the cafeteria. "So that's where I might be goin' now if I was livin' up there."

"For a young man from a line with that sort of breedin',

you're remarkably slovenly in your manners," Shawna said. She was teasing, but her tone didn't always make it sound that way. She eyed his drink. "If you were a gentleman, you'd inquire if I would like one."

That one took Hal noticeably aback, too. "Well, excusez moi," he said. "Miss Hanson, would you care for a drink?"

"Yes, thank you, a Coke if you please," Shawna answered with accent appropriately affected.

So Hal got her a Coca-Cola from a nearby drink machine. "You do know, of course, if you got in the habit of havin' me fetch you drinks in that tone of voice, sooner or later I might have to tell you where to stick it," he said as he handed the soda to her.

"For the sake of your manhood, I would certainly hope so." Shawna sipped some soda and eyed Hal impishly. "You know you also got a fag uncle."

Hal almost choked. "What?"

"He lives up in New York and works for some law firm on Park Avenue," Shawna said. "Evidently, he's a real flamer. Aunt Eunice says he's been kinda ostracized from the rest of the Dunleavy family 'cause of that."

Hal shook his head. "Well, way Mother talks 'bout that part of the family, I guess I'm not s'prised." It was his turn to study Shawna. "Any reason your aunt felt this compulsion to go checkin' on my relatives?"

"She just thought she might be doin' you a favor," Shawna said with a shrug. She sipped some soda. "Aunt Eunice is like that. She realizes you don't have to be black to be poor, isolated and kinda stuck 'way from people that could help you. I 'spect she prob'ly wanted to help you get someplace with a lotta white girls. I heard her'n Mama talkin' one night like they were worried you'n I might someday get too friendly."

That prospect sounded rather appealing to Hal, but he wasn't ready to open up too much of himself to Shawna's cutting wit. "Well, I wouldn't mind havin' a few more white girls 'round to choose from," he mused. "Ones we got here are kinda on the homely side."

"Beggars can't be choosers," Shawna said teasingly.

"That's how come I'd like to up the ante," Hal said. He flashed a grin and sipped thoughtfully on his soda. "A fag uncle. How'd that pop up?"

"He just likes boys," Shawna said. "You know, they say things like that get passed through the genetic line."

"I hope you're not suggestin' I'm that way," Hal defended himself.

"I dunno. Are you?" Shawna responded impishly.

Hal heaved a sigh. "Look, without goin' into all the particulars, I can tell you honestly and truthfully my urges have all been for girls. If I'm that way, I'd be more 'prised 'un anybody 'round."

"Those urges? They for anybody I know?" Shawna asked with a probing grin.

"No way I'm tellin' you. It'd be all over school," Hal shot back.

Shawna shrugged. "Well, I was just tryna be helpful." She eyed Hal teasingly. "Some people 'round think you might have a crush on me."

Hal almost choked. "If I did, you think I'm gonna tell you an' give you an open shot at puttin' me down? No way, Jose!"

"Jose's a boy's name," Shawna reminded with nose crinkling. "I hope that's not a Freudian slip."

Hal shook his head in exasperation. "I could always throw in 'bout me bein' a pretty good athlete, which oughta say somethin' for my manhood, but I got a feelin' you'd figure out a way to shoot that down, too."

"You find good athletes that're gay, too," Shawna said insouciantly.

"Well, if you wanta find out how normal I am for sure, we can always slip out behind some buildin' somewheres an' I'll be happy to show you," Hal responded in a challenging tone.

"In your dreams, white boy," Shawna told him with just the thinnest trace of a smile showing.

18

The football season had passed the midpoint, and Hal was on a record breaking roll. He had scored at least two touchdowns in every game and had compiled some impressive yardage statistics. These stats were due, in large measure, to the fact that he and Clifford had come up with patterns that some of the other teams weren't used to defending and were only just now starting to figure out how to stop.

Then came game six, against Blanchard, and for the first time Hal learned what it felt like to be stymied. The Blanchard coach had induced what the other mentors evidently overlooked: that Hal wasn't likely to be kept in check with single coverage. So on this night, every time Hal went out on a pattern he had two and three defenders around him. When he tried to go long, he found himself sandwiched between at least one cornerback and the safety. He caught a few passes, but on each reception he was gang-tackled viciously. So as the first half wound down, he was without a touchdown for the first time in the season.

It wasn't disaster time, to be sure. Blanchard had little in the way of an offense; and Clifford, when he found his beloved passing game grounded, had the presence of mind to go to his running game and tight end, Wes Ferrell, and Brileyville went into halftime with a seven point lead.

"They layin' for us, my man," Clifford remarked to Hal as the two headed for the locker room. He draped an arm over the white boy's shoulders. "Look like this could be one night me'n you ain't gonna be lightin' it up like a pinball machine."

"I can live with that, but they're bangin' the shit outta me even when I'm nowheres near the ball," Hal moaned.

Clifford laughed. "That's 'cause they know what you can do once you got a step on somebody. Take it as a compliment, my man."

"I'll 'member that if I find myself in traction tomorrow," Hal said with a chuckle.

Brileyville received the second half kickoff. Harry Moore instructed Clifford to stick with the running game and short passes to Wes and just use Hal as a decoy for the time being. That ended in a touchdown drive covering seventy-two yards and eating up almost seven minutes, which provided the Falcons (Brileyville's nickname) some breathing room. So now Blanchard had to go back to playing against the run. That finally gave Hal some room in the secondary, and early in the fourth quarter he hauled in a long scoring pass from Clifford to help put the game away.

During the game, Hal also sprained his ankle. The coaching staff had taped it up sufficiently so that he could play through the pain, but as he left the locker room after his shower, the ankle definitely hurt and he was noticeably limping. Clifford and his senior girlfriend, Shalimaine, walked partway down the hall with him.

"Better take it easy on that ankle next couple days," Clifford said with genuine solicitude. "I want you at full speed next Friday."

Hal grimaced and nodded. He wanted that, too.

"Uh, sometime you oughta get you a date and hit the town with Shalimaine and me," Clifford said. "What 'bout that pretty sister I see you talkin' to in the lunchroom sometimes?"

Hal laughed. "She's a ball-buster, man." He gestured for emphasis. "Not that I'd mind necessarily. She's pretty 'nuff for sure. But I don't think she's ready to let me or anybody else get that close."

"Ah, you might be s'prised," Clifford said. He slapped Hal on a shoulder. "I bet you worked it right, you'd have a shot at it. You a bonafide athletic hero, my man. That's kinda like money in the bank. You just gotta go draw out some cash once in a while."

"Better be careful throwin' words like that 'round," Shalimaine warned her boyfriend.

Hal laughed. "Well, an' even if I could break through with her, then I got my mother I gotta worry 'bout."

Clifford nodded. He knew a little about Hal's home life. "Yeah, kinda make me glad sometimes I'm not white," he said.

Hal flashed a grin and slapped Clifford on a shoulder. "Thanks for the offer anyhow. See ya later, Shalimaine."

"Goodnight, Hal," Shalimaine said pleasantly. "Take care of that ankle."

"Yeah, I need you at full speed next week," Clifford reminded him anew as he and Shalimaine headed out a side door.

Hal continued limping towards his exit. Suddenly Wimbush emerged from a classroom. He winced as he saw Hal's condition.

"I've had nightmares about seeing you like that," the basketball coach said.

"Those nightmares you get are no match for the real pain," Hal groaned. He shook his head and flashed a pained smile. "It's just a sprain. If I take it easy, it oughta be gone in a couple days."

Wimbush nodded. "Yeah, it might help to put some ice on it when you get home." He scanned the young man. "You did take a pounding tonight. I guess any worries anyone might have about your toughness oughta be erased."

Hal grimaced. "I think Shawna Hanson would call it masochistic. She likes to throw words like that 'round."

Wimbush laughed. "It's probably not inappropriate. I do like football, but mostly when I can watch it on TV from my living room. I get a little uneasy when I see the guys I'm counting on for my basketball team out there taking those kinds of shots."

"Well, knock on wood, I figure I oughta be in one piece for basketball season," Hal said. "I'm more'n halfway through football season, an' if the worst I get is an ankle sprain, well, that puts me 'head of the game."

"Don't speak too soon," Wimbush cautioned him with a shoulder pat. "You're still one of the smaller guys out there, and it only takes one good hit to break something. You don't want to jinx yourself by bragging."

"Good point." Hal winced as he tried to move around on his sore ankle and the pain shot up through his leg into his upper body. "Uh, I think next year I wanta go with just one sport. You think you can work somethin' out that can help me get outta football without havin' to go through that candyass lecture bit from Coach Moore?"

Wimbush chuckled. "Well, it just so happens if things work out, I might be able to get you into a basketball camp in August when the football team'll be practicing." He patted Hal on a shoulder. "I'd prefer it if you ducked football, too."

"I like Coach Moore'n all, an' I like playin' football, too," Hal said. "But playin' two sports like that back to back is kind of a drain. I'd like to stick with just basketball, but I don't wanta go through the drill 'bout maybe bein' a fag or somethin' just 'cause I 'cide not to play football."

"I understand very well, and I'll see what we can work out," Wimbush said with a knowing smile and another shoulder pat. "By the way, I can give you a ride home if you need it."

"Thanks Coach, but Coach Moore's got his van out front, an' I was gonna go home with him," Hal said. "I do 'ppreciate the offer, though."

"Any time," Wimbush said sincerely.

Wimbush headed up the hallway and Hal limped towards the exit. Just then, Shawna and a black girlfriend Hal recognized as Trina Jefferson came in the doorway he was about to exit by.

"I hope you're not lookin' for sympathy," Shawna said with a grin as she noticed his limp.

"If I was, you're 'bout the last person I can think of I'd be likely to get it from," Hal said through a grimace.

Trina laughed. "Hi Hal," she said.

"Hey Trina," Hal responded. Trina wasn't very pretty, but she was genuinely nice. Hal recalled her as one of the few black students in his class who used to talk to him in more than a perfunctory manner back in his pre-athletic days.

"Trina and I thought we'd go out for a burger an' fries," Shawna said. "Trina's got her mama's car tonight. If you behave yourself, we might be willin' to let you ride 'long."

"Well, I 'ppreciate the offer, but I was gonna ride home with Coach Moore," Hal said. "He's got his minivan outside."

"You mean you'd pass up the chance to ride 'long with two beautiful women to be in a van with a bunch of sweaty guys," Shawna teased.

Hal heaved a sigh. He had to admit that the thought of riding with Shawna and Trina was a lot more appealing. "Well, if the offer's good, why not?" he reasoned. "Let me tell Coach Moore."

So he told the coach, and a few minutes later he was in the back seat of Trina's mother's car. The two girls sat up front. He stretched the leg with the sore ankle to give it some rest.

"You only got one touchdown tonight. You must be slippin'," Shawna teased.

"More like they finally figured out what me'n Clifford been doin' an' how to stop it," Hal said. He studied the two girls momentarily. "I didn't think you two liked football all that much. I'm kinda 'prised to see you at the game."

"It was Shawna's idea," Trina said.

"Sometimes one needs to see how the male animal is in their most primitive element," Shawna said insouciantly. "'Sides, I had to check to see if you really are all that good. Tonight you weren't."

"Well, when you got anywheres from two to five guys 'round you every step you take, it's hard to look good," Hal defended himself.

"C'mon, Shawna, give Hal a break," Trina appealed. She glanced back at Hal solicitously. "The leg hurt real bad?"

"The ankle. It hurts like billyhell, but they say it oughta go 'way in a couple days," Hal said.

"Well, you gonna play that sport, you gotta 'spect some pain," Shawna told him with a teasing grin.

"Yeah, I guess you're right." Hal chuckled. "Coach Moore says it's like life. You're not really into the flow 'til you feel some pain."

"I think Coach Moore carries the pain part a little farther than most sensible people see as healthy," Shawna said with amusement.

They got to the burger joint and had a pleasant half an hour or so talking and eating and drinking sodas. A few of their peers stopped by their table, including Melvin, Wesley, and Thurlow Carter.

"Well, look like your social life kinda picked up," Thurlow remarked to Hal with an appreciative scan of the latter's two female companions.

"How would you know 'bout social life?" Shawna grunted indifferently.

Thurlow's teeth clenched. He wanted to come back with something comparably cutting.

Hal sensed as much and knew that Thurlow was no match for Shawna when it came to repartee. "They took pity on an injured man," he said, pointing to his taped ankle.

"I bet Wimbush'd have a hissy-fit he seen you like that," Wesley said with a chuckle.

Hal nodded soberly. "He awready has, but he knows the score. It ain't like I'm tryna 'splain it to my mother or somethin'."

The three young men laughed. Then they slapped Hal on a shoulder and headed to the counter to place their orders. They acknowledged Trina warmly enough, but their nods to Shawna were perfunctory at best. She was probably the least popular girl among the males in Hal's class, more for her attitude than looks.

That didn't bother Shawna in the least. "In your place, I'd hate to play basketball if for no other reason 'un havin' prolonged 'ssociation with that bunch," she said with a shrug.

"Oh, they're not bad guys once you get used to 'em," Hal said. He flashed a grin. "And don't throw out some line 'bout them bein' fags or somethin'. They prob'ly hate fags worse'n I do."

"I'm not s'prised. Ignorance tends to make people hate what they don't understand," Shawna said.

"What's this 'bout fags?" Trina interjected.

Her totally baffled look stirred Hal to laughter. "Shawna found out through her aunt I got a fag uncle in New York. She's been givin' me a hard time 'bout it, like it bein' maybe in the family genes or somethin'. I told her one way for sure I could prove I'm not one, but she won't take me up on it."

"Even if I did, it might just mean you're a bi," Shawna said with a teasing grin.

Hal shook his head and heaved a loud sigh. "Sounds like I'm not gonna win with her no matter what I do," he remarked to Trina.

"Trina laughed and patted him on an arm. "The best way to win is don't worry too much 'bout it," she advised.

Hal was unusually late, even for a Friday night after a game. So when he came through the door and saw his mother sitting up, he expected a lecture. He was scratching through his brain for a good lie, or at least a slant on the truth she might accept, when he noticed a wistful smile seemingly frozen on her face. She looked far, far away in that moment.

"Uh, sorry I'm late, Mother," he greeted her hesitantly.

"You'll never guess in a million years who called tonight," his mother responded, in a tone that sounded connected to some other sphere and consideration.

That was certainly true. "I dunno. Who?" Hal responded with a bemused shrug.

"My cousin Willard. I think that makes him your cousin, too," Kathleen McDonough said with rare enthusiasm—almost youthfulness. "He's not your uncle exactly. The age difference might lead some people to think of him as such, but I think he's what's referred to as a first cousin once-removed. Anyway, he said he heard about us from some woman named Eunice Weller."

Hal chuckled. The Eunice specter seemed to be popping up every time he turned around. "Yeah, I told you 'bout her. She's the one got the ball rollin' for me to play basketball. Her niece is in my grade at school."

"Oh, yes, the colored woman. I knew I didn't know her, so I didn't know what connection she might have to the family. Anyway, you could have knocked me over with a feather when Willard called. Last time I saw him, he was only six or seven years old. I was enrolled in Harvard at the time," Kathleen McDonough reminisced. "I had no idea he would even remember who I was except possibly from the second hand information he got from others in the family, most of which would be unflattering thanks to your father."

Hal shrugged. He had heard her account of how she became estranged from her Boston family enough to be tired of it. By now the reason for it no longer struck him as very important.

"It appears that Willard and I have in common the fact that we both have been banished from the family," Kathleen McDonough went on.

"Well, what Shawna tells me 'bout what her aunt says, I 'spect in his case it's on 'ccount of him bein' a fag," Hal said.

"Fag? Oh, yes. That's the euphemism you young people use for homosexual," Kathleen McDonough said.

Hal shrugged. "I don't think it's just young people. I think they get called that by people of pretty much all ages."

Kathleen McDonough shrugged and lit a cigarette. "Well, I'm not really surprised. He sounded rather effeminate on the phone, and I vaguely recall how he used to scandalize his family at an early age by insisting on wearing girls' clothes."

Hal laughed. "Sounds like he really got started early."

"It's not something you should be laughing at, Dear," his mother told him sternly. "Anyway, he said he plans to try to come down and spend a couple of days in Brileyville over the Christmas holiday."

Hal wasn't sure he liked that idea. "Uh, I hope you make it clear to him I don't want him tryin' anything with me," he said with a gesture for emphasis.

"I'm sure he has the good sense and grace to keep any aberrations of that sort away from the family," Kathleen McDonough said. She studied her son momentarily. "I'm a little perturbed by all the times you mention this girl Shawna. There isn't something going on between the two of you, I hope."

"Not likely," Hal said. "I couldn't break through to her even if I was in'rested." He chuckled. "I think she's holdin' out for some guy that's super smart and goin' to Harvard or Yale or someplace like that."

"She sounds very sensible, which I very much appreciate," Kathleen McDonough murmured. "I get cold shivers at the thought of your wanting to run off with some Nubian wench. I like colored people well enough in their place, but one thing I definitely draw the line on is the possibility of some little pickaninny calling me grandma."

"I can't run off with her if she doesn't want to go," Hal reasoned. He kissed his mother on a cheek. "I'm tired. I think I'm goin' to bed."

"Goodnight, Dear," his mother replied.

Hal long since had learned the virtue of retreat when his mother got on her soapbox.

19

Hal's most memorable touchdown reception came the following week on what started out as a simple ten yard down-and-out pattern. He caught the ball and immediately had three defenders surrounding him, one with a firm grip on his shoulders. He shook free from the grip, somehow eluded the other two and got to the middle of the field and ran for another fifteen yards until four more defenders zeroed in on him. Somehow he got away from that group and dashed back to the sideline and raced downfield for another fifteen yards until he hit another human cluster. He wove his way somehow through that bunch and ran back to the middle of the field, where he found some more would-be tacklers. He squirted free from this group, too, and finally got a block that sprang him to where he could get back to the sideline and dash the rest of the way downfield to the end zone.

"Awright, Baby, ESPN highlight films," Clifford exulted as he hugged Hal after the six points were on the board.

"That's one you know folks 'round here gonna be talkin' up awhile."

Hal's head shook in disbelief. "Man, I thought they had me 'bout four or five times back there. I don't know how I got loose."

He went on to catch two more touchdown passes from Clifford that night, and Brileyville won the game easily. But as Clifford predicted, that one play was what most people around school were talking about on Monday.

"Everywhere I turn, I hear people talkin' 'bout that run you made," Shawna remarked as she and Trina sat across from him in the lunchroom.

"You don't watch out, somebody gonna be givin' you a nickname like crazylegs or dancin'-feet," Trina chimed in with a grin.

Hal laughed. "It was a good run, I guess, but I hope nobody's lookin' for 'nother one any time soon. Actually, I gotta 'mit I got kinda lucky on that one."

"Listen to him tryna make us think he's modest," Shawna teased.

"Well, he did kinda make his own luck there, too," Trina reminded her friend appreciatively.

"When you score a seventy yard touchdown on a play set up to gain ten, you gotta figure the defense got a little bit slack," Hal said with a shrug. "One guy had me right by the shoulders, and 'nother two guys had grips on me an' didn't hang on, so I coulda been a cooked goose way back upfield. Prob'ly shoulda been. So I'm not gonna beat myself on the chest too much." He grinned impishly. "Well, maybe a little bit. If somebody wants to call me a hero, I'm not gonna stop 'em."

The two girls smacked him on an arm good-naturedly.

A little while later, Hal ran into Wimbush in the gym. "At our coaches' meeting this morning, I thought Harry Moore would never shut up about that run you made on that short pass play," the basketball coach confided with a grin.

Hal chuckled. "Yeah, I been gettin' a lotta flak on that,

too. Course, like I keep tellin' people, you don't make that kinda run on that kinda play without bein' a little bit lucky an' havin' somebody out there in the secondary gettin' a little bit slack."

"True, but you couldn't have pulled it off if you didn't have some pretty fair athletic ability," Wimbush said. His mind drifted momentarily, and he chuckled. "You know what Coach Moore had the gall to ask me? Had I been feeding you watermelon?"

That struck Hal as weird. "What?"

"I think it's the old line whites used to like to throw up about blacks having an abnormal affinity for watermelon, and I don't think Coach Moore ever quite outgrew it," Wimbush said with a shrug. "He might have the idea that's what makes some of us so fast. It never did a whole lot for me."

"I like watermelon okay, but I don't think it's got anything to do with how fast you are," Hal said. He flashed a grin. "Course if somebody can prove different to me, I'll eat all of it I can get my hands on."

"Wouldn't we all?" Wimbush agreed with a chuckle.

The next game was away, at Piney Grove High School. At this juncture, the Falcons were seven and zero and evidently on their way to winning the regular season district championship. They had already beaten Hempstone, the only team with any reasonable chance of catching them. They could clinch the title just by winning two of their final regular season games. Strange things sometimes happen in sports, of course, but it didn't seem likely that they would lose any of those three games. Certainly they didn't figure to lose to Piney Grove, the district's last-place team.

Harry Moore made sure no complacency took hold among his players. "I hope y'all ain't figurin' you got this game in the bag awready, 'cause if you are, I can tell you right now this team could sneak up on y'all," he told the players just before they were to take the field.

No response. The Falcons understood and were ready to play solid football.

"This team you're playin' tonight, their record is kinda misleadin'," the coach went on. "They been in almost all their games. They had a touchdown lead on Hempstone in the third quarter an' were drivin', an' then they lost a couple fumbles an' Hempstone went on to win. But don't think they're gonna lay down an' play dead for y'all. They know they can't do much to salvage their own season, but they can do a lot to mess y'all's up."

Again silence. That went without saying.

"Awright, let's go out an' kick some ass," the coach finally exhorted his charges.

'*Kick ass*' arose in a discordantly enthusiastic chorus as the players grabbed their helmets and raced out onto the field to do battle.

Brileyville won the coin toss and elected to receive, and on the third play from scrimmage Clifford and Hal hooked up on a fifty-eight yard touchdown pass.

"We off'n runnin', Baby," Clifford told his favorite receiver with a huge grin.

They definitely were. By halftime they had clicked for four touchdowns, three of them covering more than fifty yards. Another came by an interception runback and yet another by a short-yardage running play that capped an eighty yard drive. With one extra point missed, the score at halftime was forty-one to nothing.

"Well, I guess y'all can take it easy the second half," Moore told his charges in the locker room. "We don't need to run up the score. Just as long as they don't get close 'nuff to give me heart palpitations, I'm satisfied."

Moore figured on leaving the first team in until early in the fourth quarter and then letting the substitutes finish out the game. He might have put the subs in earlier, but his bench strength was limited, and there was always the possibility of Piney Grove getting a couple of quick scores and momentum. Such a turnaround wasn't unheard of. Probably the forty-one points was too much for Piney Grove to overcome, but Moore liked the numbers better with eight minutes to play than sixteen.

"You don't have to light it up any more," he told Clifford after the Brileyville defense forced Piney Grove to punt on the first possession and the offense was taking the field. "Keep it on the ground."

Clifford followed the coach's directive. He conducted a seventy-three yard drive which ate up most of the rest of the third quarter and added another touchdown to the Falcons' lead.

Piney Grove managed one first down on its next possession, but that was all. Another punt and the Falcons were on the move again. This time, however, the drive temporarily stalled. Two penalties created a third-and-long situation for Clifford. A running play wasn't likely to pick up the yardage needed for a first down. So Clifford decided to go to Hal downfield. He just wanted to keep the drive alive and eat up some clock. Piney Grove expected pass and had Hal covered, but Hal eluded the two defenders assigned to him and got open for the first down reception. He started to pivot, trying to break free for some more yardage. But just as soon as he turned, he was gang-tackled by about half the Piney Grove defense. This wasn't unusual. He had been gang-tackled numerous times before. But this time, as he lay underneath the massive human pile, he felt one additional body diving on and heard a snapping sound. A searing pain that suddenly tore through his entire body signaled to him that it came from his right leg.

The pile cleared, and Hal remained immobilized on the field, his face contorted in pain. A loose feeling in the leg left him with the feeling that it was broken.

"Oh, God, man, I shoulda just called a runnin' play an' then had us punt," Clifford was moaning.

Then a first-aid team was rushing onto the field to get Hal on a stretcher and to an area hospital. One of the rescue squad members confirmed that the leg was broken.

"I think that's all for that kid this season," Hal heard one of the medics say.

"A real shame," another responded. "He's a helluva ballplayer. I don't think I ever saw a white boy can run like him."

Then he was put in an ambulance and rushed to the hospital. He wasn't sedated, so he had to suffer through the pain the entire ride.

One medic noticed his facial contortions. "Looks like it hurts pretty bad," he said sympathetically.

Hal winced and nodded.

"We'll be at the hospital in a few minutes," the medic said. "Just hang on. You're not gonna die."

In that moment, Hal wasn't sure if that was a good or bad prospect.

They finally got to the hospital. A doctor set his leg and put a cast on it. By this point, much of the pain had subsided, but now he had to endure a rather annoying itching under the cast.

"Way you ran over our boys tonight, somebody might think me a traitor for treatin' you," a Piney Grove doctor remarked pleasantly as he set the leg. "You oughta be thankful I take my Hippocratic Oath seriously."

Hal had never heard of the Hippocratic Oath, but he had a feeling that it wasn't to be confused with hypocritic.

"Shame somethin' like this has to happen to such a fine young athlete as yourself," the doctor mused. "I sometimes marvel the way y'all bang each other 'round out there that I don't find myself havin' to treat more of these."

"Yes, sir," Hal agreed through a grimace.

"This should hold you 'til you get back to Brileyville and can check with your own doctor there," the treating physician told him. "You'll walk again, but I think it's safe to say you won't be playin' any more football this season."

"What 'bout the playoffs if we get that far?" Hal asked.

"Not 'less you figure on playin' in the Super Bowl," the doctor said.

Hal's face contorted in disappointment. He knew the

Super Bowl wouldn't be played until late January. By then, his own team, win or lose, would be long finished with its playoff games.

"You oughta be back in full stride by late January, early February, but not much if any before then," the doctor said.

Hal groaned. "Boy, that's gonna cut into my basketball season bigtime."

The doctor shrugged. "Can't be helped." He patted Hal on the shoulder. "Don't take it personally, but if you're anywhere near as good at basketball as you are football, our team'll be gettin' a break. I think we play you first week or so in December."

Hal sighed in frustration. That was not an easy pill for him to be forced to swallow.

20

Hal didn't adjust easily to his cast-and-crutches ensemble. The physical discomfort was bad enough, but on top of that he had to deal with the continual commentary and commiseration from those around him. It began with the balefully stunned glance from his mother when he lumbered through the apartment door.

"Good God! What happened to you?" she asked.

"Broken leg," Hal mumbled.

"I knew I should never have let you play that sport," Kathleen McDonough groused. "You're not big enough."

"Mother, bigger guys get broken legs, too," Hal tried to reason with her.

"I should have told that coach no right off the bat and ended it right there, and then this wouldn't have happened," Kathleen McDonough grunted.

"Too late to worry 'bout that now," Hal said. He kissed his mother on a cheek. "I think I'm goin' to bed now."

On Monday, he ran into Shawna in the school corridor

between classes. "Well, what's this? The big macho football hero made unmacho?" she greeted him with a teasing grin.

Hal grimaced. "You think you could handle some two hun'ret and fifty pound dude crashin' down on you after 'bout six other people already got you down?"

Their conversation was put on hold as the two went to their respective classes. Shawna caught up with him again at lunchtime.

"I wasn't really makin' fun of you," she told him in a semi apologetic tone. "I know a broken leg isn't somethin' to make light of."

"Better to laugh 'un cry as they say," Hal replied. He flashed a grin. "But couldn't you think of a better word 'un unmacho?"

Shawna chuckled. She was relieved to see that he hadn't lost his sense of humor. "It hurt much? The leg, I mean."

Hal shrugged. "It did at first. Now it's mostly just the itch. That's 'bout to drive me nuts."

"You were kinda temptin' fate, weren't you, lettin' that Piney Grove doctor set your leg?" Shawna pressed impishly.

Hal laughed. "He was talkin' 'bout how I oughta be grateful for him bein' faithful to his Hippocratic Oath. I don't know what that is 'sackly, but I guess it's not like bein' a hypocrite."

"It goes back to Hippocrates and the ancient Greeks. He's 'sidered the father of modern medicine," Shawna said. "This gonna mess you up for basketball much?"

"I'll lose a couple months anyhow," Hal sighed. "That's 'til I get the cast off. Then I'm gonna be rusty. I'll be lucky to be back up to speed by tournament time."

"It's gotta be frustratin'," Shawna said sympathetically.

"Yeah," Hal agreed.

A little later, Hal saw Wimbush. The basketball coach didn't seem surprised by the cast. Hal figured he probably had already been informed on what happened.

"Well, I understand it'll be at least a couple of months before I'll be able to count on you," Wimbush said. "For basketball, I mean."

Hal nodded. "I hope it doesn't mean I'm off the team."

Wimbush heaved a sigh. "It should." He patted Hal on a shoulder. "But I'll keep a spot open for you. I hope you're back up to speed in time to help us down the stretch. But please, please, please, don't break anything else for a while."

Hal laughed. "I'll try not to," he promised.

Basketball practice had started. Hal looked in on it a couple of times and quickly left when he found watching without being a part of it too frustrating.

On one occasion, the senior point guard, Elmore Davison, stopped him. "I'll be glad when you off them crutches so I don't have to hear everybody talkin' 'bout how you gonna take the point guard job 'way from me," Elmore said. "Then we can prove whatever need to be proved on the floor."

"You don't want that any more'n I do, Elmore," Hal assured him.

"Ain't nothin' 'gainst you," Elmore said with a shoulder-pat for assurance. "I know you real good, an' you might take the job 'way from me. But if you gonna do it, I'd rather it be on the floor 'un through the school gossip mills."

"Me too, Elmore," Hal assured him.

"You'll be the man, ain't no doubt 'bout it, an' it may come this season, but if you do it, you gonna have to earn it," Elmore said.

"I wouldn't want it any other way," Hal replied.

By this point, Hal was generally well-liked by the other students. That included especially the football and basketball players. But he had a few detractors, too. He overheard a couple of them grousing in the school cafeteria because Wimbush was keeping a slot open for him.

"How come they gotta have him on the team if he ain't gonna be able to play?" one of them was asking.

"You gotta ax Wimbush 'bout that," someone else replied.

"Shit, he wasn't white, he wouldn't get shit," the first young man grunted. He wasn't aware that Hal was listening, but he probably wouldn't have cared even if he had known.

Charmaine Jackson stood up. "That's 'bout 'nuff of your shit," she told the first young man angrily. "That boy can play, an' he earned his stripes bigtime. I'll tell you, when that cast come off, he'll eat your ass 'live an' three more like you. So shut you trap an' let the rest of us finish eatin'."

The young man was stunned into silence, and none of his friends dared to challenge Charmaine. A little while later, when the young man and his friends had departed, Hal dragged himself over to her table. "Thanks, Charmaine," he said.

Charmaine shrugged. "He got a big mouth. Don't worry 'bout him. The other guys know how good you are."

Football season wasn't quite over. Hal found out at play-off time that he had been named first team all-district at wideout and second team all-region. Some, including Harry Moore, complained about the latter; they felt that Hal should have been named first team on that squad as well. Moore even went so far as to declare him the best receiver in the state. But those votes, once in, are irreversible. Whether Hal deserved first team all-region or not, he wasn't going to get it. Not this year anyway.

He had an open invitation to attend the remaining games, of which he took full advantage. That included the regional game against a team from northern Virginia that ended the Falcons season. The northern Virginia team was able to put pressure on the line to stop the Brileyville offense cold and move the ball well enough to put three touchdowns on the board by halftime.

"Man, I wish we had you out there," Clifford moaned to Hal just before the second half was to start.

"I wish I was out there, too," Hal sighed.

"Man, every time I think 'bout that dumb pass that got you leg broke, I just wanna kick myself," Clifford murmured.

Hal patted him on the back. "Hey, don't beat yourself to death over it. In your place, I'da done the same."

"But we didn't need the first down," Clifford moaned.

"Well yeah, I guess that's true, but you don't wanta get in the habit of not tryin' either," Hal said.

The final score was twenty-seven to three. As the game clock wound down in the fourth quarter, and it was painfully obvious that the Falcons would lose, Harry Moore wandered over to where Hal was leaning on his crutches.

"Don't look good, does it?" the coach muttered.

Hal shook his head. "'Fraid not," he agreed.

"When we lost you for the season, I kinda knew the enda the line wasn't far off," Moore said with a shrug. "With you out there, they've always gotta keep a couple guys loose to watch you. We don't have nobody else to give us that dimension. So with you out, they can stack the line an' take the runnin' game an' tight end 'way from us, an' we spend the whole night goin' three-an'- out."

"Runnin' game's good, but any more I think you gotta be able to throw the ball," Hal agreed.

Moore nodded, slapped him on a shoulder and headed back to the bench to watch the clock run out along with his visibly disappointed players.

The basketball season opener came a week after the football team's regional loss. Hal was working at the rec center that night. His hours were flexible, and he could have gone to the game if he wanted to, but somehow he was unable to bring himself around to it. The thought of sitting in the stands watching the game and not being able to play was more than he wanted to bear. Besides, he rationalized, he could always use the extra money.

Then Shawna and Trina came by. "We're goin' to the basketball game, an' we thought you might wanna come 'long," Shawna invited.

Hal heaved a sigh. He had been stacking some boxes, which wasn't easy with his leg in a cast. "I think I gotta pass on that one," he said.

"How come? 'Cause you can't stand watchin' the other

guys out there playin' with your leg all wrapped up in plaster?" Shawna teased.

Hal chuckled. "Yeah, I guess that 'bout sums it up."

"Well, you gotta figure if you're gonna be a really good player, sometimes it helps to stop an' watch an' maybe pick up some ideas 'bout how you can improve your game." Shawna flashed an impish grin. "'Sides, how often do you get a chance to go somewhere with two beautiful women?"

That was a more cogent argument than the first point. "Awright, if you don't mind havin' a cripple ridin' 'long with you," Hal relented with a shrug.

So he wound up in the back seat of Trina's mother's car again. He chuckled as he recalled the previous time. "Be kinda nice if someday I can ride in this thing without havin' somethin' wrong with my leg," he said.

"Well, least in basketball you don't have to worry 'bout somebody tacklin' you," Trina said good-naturedly.

"Not legally anyhow," Hal conceded. He flashed a grin. "Course you do get some guys that play the game kinda rough."

When they arrived at the school gym, Trina and Shawna found seats among the Brileyville fans and Hal drifted down to where the teams were warming up. Melvin and Wesley greeted him. They were on the team, although not yet starting. Both figured to be first-stringers the following season.

"Gotta be kinda rough for you," Wesley remarked to Hal sympathetically. "I 'spect you'da been startin' if this wouldn'ta happened." He motioned to Hal's cast.

"A chance, I guess," Hal mused. He glanced over to where Elmore was shooting jumpers. "Elmore let me know if I want his job, I'm gonna have to earn it."

"With your talent, that won't be too hard," Melvin said.

It still seemed odd to hear words like that coming from Melvin. Still vivid in Hal's memory was how hard Melvin had fought to keep him down when he was starting to emerge as a legitimate player.

"I see Melvin bein' a little bit nicer to you since that time you beat him up," Trina remarked as Hal returned to his seat with the two girls in the stands.

"I think Melvin's a different person now, for real," Hal said with a shrug.

"I 'spect it's 'cause he finally figured out he don't want no part of you any more," Trina said with a grin.

"Well, if he wanted revenge for the fight, I'm 'bout as vulnerable now as I'm ever gonna be," Hal reasoned. "He didn't act like he wanted that, so I gotta 'ssume he's a better human bein' now."

"Well, human might be givin' him a little bit too much credit," Shawna said. She patted Hal on the shoulder. "You're prob'ly gonna be movin' in faster company before too much longer. I'd figure you'd be lookin' for better quality people 'un Melvin Peebles an' Wesley Thigpen to be 'ssociatin' with."

That sounded strange, almost surreal, coming from Shawna. "I got 'nother two years of playin' on the same team as them," Hal reasoned. "'Sides, they're not such bad guys. Maybe I'll be able to get a scholarship to a better college'n whatnot, an' I might even have a shot at playin' pro ball someday. But that doesn't mean I should look down on them or 'fuse to 'ssociate with 'em."

"You're more tolerant 'un I'd be in your place," Shawna said with a grin. "I think they're both a couple of bozos."

Hal didn't have a very sophisticated understanding of perception differences among African Americans. He had come to sense, however, a feeling of mutual antipathy that existed between Shawna and some of the black males in their age group. Shawna was intellectual and tended to look at life in terms of substance and productive potential; grades and a superior way of expressing her thoughts came easily to her, and she tended to have no use for people who in her mind failed to measure up to certain standards she held. The basketball players, Melvin especially, regarded her as stuck up. Each view had a certain validity; each also was comparably distorted. Some day in the future, after all parties had spent some time in adulthood, they might come to understand one another much better. But until then, this schism wouldn't go away.

After the game, Trina proposed going to a burger joint for a sandwich and some fries. "Okay, I'll treat," Hal offered.

"You don't have to," Trina told him.

"Well, with you chaufferin' me 'round, I figure that's the least I can do," Hal said.

"Well, if he's gonna be a gentleman, don't discourage him Trina," Shawna said with a grin.

Trina relented, and they spent the next half an hour or so eating and drinking sodas and having a good time.

Trina dropped Shawna off first. Shawna had a big test coming up and wanted to study some for it before she went to bed. Besides, her home was closer.

As Hal rode home with Trina, he was surprised when she asked: "When you an' Shawna gonna finally get together?"

"What?" Hal asked in a shocked tone.

"You know you got a crush on her," Trina told him impishly. "An' I 'spect if she's honest 'bout it, she's got one on you, too."

Hal laughed. "Well, I'm not gonna deny it on my part. I guess I do, although I'm not gonna lay myself but just so bare for her to take potshots."

"She wouldn't take them potshots if she didn't like you," Trina said. "If she didn't like you, she'd just ignore you, like she do with Melvin an' Lonnie Hairston an' them other guys."

"Shawna's a pretty girl," Hal finally said. "She can have a lotta guys. She could prob'ly have Melvin an' Lonnie eatin' outta her hands if she didn't go outta her way to make 'em feel like their 'zistence doesn't mean much."

"Ain't no 'ccountin' for taste," Trina said. She grinned impishly. "I'm tellin' you, that girl got a crush on you big-time. She may not know it, but she do."

Hal laughed. "If she doesn't know it, how come you do?"

"Oh, I know," Trina said in a mysterious tone that made her seem to possess some special insight. "Trust me, I know."

"Course you know I go rushin' anything with her, I'm gonna get shot down," Hal said.

"Oh, I know that too," Trina said. She was by now in his block, and she pulled up in front of the apartment complex in which he lived. Then she patted him affectionately on the cheek. "You gonna have to do some pretty nifty jugglin', but it's there for you if you want it bad 'nuff."

"Well, some the brothers like to talk 'bout racial solidarity," Hal said. He took a deep breath. "Sounds like you're almost goin' 'gainst that."

"It's not always wrong to cross the line," Trina said. She squeezed Hal's hand as he was getting out of the car. "Race ain't always gonna be the be all n' end all in who you wind up with. Maybe someday I'll hit it off with a white boy, an' I don't want somebody tellin' me I got no right to marry him 'cause I'm 'pposed to live up to somebody else's idea of what bein' black's 'pposed to mean. I don't want it to mean I can't have white friends or trust no white folks or nothin' like that."

"Well, prob'ly a lotta white folks you shouldn't trust, but I hope I'm not one," Hal said. He squeezed her hand back and motioned to the floor on which he and his mother lived. "I can think of one white woman right off the bat I'll have hell with if I ever do get anything goin' with Shawna."

"That's one you gonna have to handle on you own," Trina told him with a grin.

21

When Hal came home one late December evening and saw a stranger in the house, he had a feeling that it was his mother's cousin paying his promised holiday visit. Actually, that wasn't difficult to deduce. He understood that Willard, in age, was at about midpoint between himself and his mother. Besides, Willard resembled him a little. Their height, weight, eye and hair color, and facial structures were about the same.

"Harold, I'd like for you to meet my cousin Willard," Kathleen McDonough introduced the two. "I suppose he's your cousin too, although it wouldn't be inappropriate for you to call him Uncle Willard."

"Just Willard will be fine," the visitor said. He approached Hal with his hand extended. "How are you, Harold?"

Hal felt a little uneasy as he shook the proffered hand. He had to free his arm from a crutch to accomplish that physical function. "Fine, sir," he said. It occurred to him that

Willard's hand felt soft and almost cold in his own. He wondered if that was standard for people of Willard's sexual bent. "I guess you're the first member of the family outside of Mother an' my dad I ever met."

"We won't mention that other person, Dear," his mother told him archly.

Willard studied the crutches and the leg still encased in plaster. "Eunice told me about your football injury," he remarked. "Shame it has to cut into your basketball season, too."

"Nothin' I can do 'bout it now. But least there's a place on the team for me when I finally get this thing off," Hal said with a shrug.

"Even so, I envy you, dear boy," Harold told him in a tone of sincerity.

Hal laughed. "You envy me walkin' 'round with a broken leg?"

"My walking around, Dear," his mother corrected his grammar. She turned to his cousin. "Harold picks up these sloppy speech habits from the other students where he goes to school."

"You don't have to be on guard with your speech habits every moment, Kathleen," Willard defended the younger man. "I'm sure Harold will be quite capable of using correct grammar when he's in a situation where that's necessary."

"Well, I do make A's in English," Hal threw in as a reminder.

"Yes, he does," his mother confirmed. She laughed and lit a cigarette. "He makes quite good grades actually. I wonder how sometimes. I haven't heard that he's been caught doctoring his report card or anything of that sort, so I have to presume that the grades are legitimate, but I also have to wonder why his speech habits are so colloquial."

Willard laughed. "He speaks a whole lot like the people around him do." He patted Hal on a shoulder. "I wasn't envying your broken leg, dear boy. It was your athletic ability and, I suppose, general masculine aura that struck me.

Oh, how I used to wish I could be like that to please my dear old pater."

"Pater? I guess that means your dad," Hal said.

Willard and Hal's mother laughed over that one.

"It's Latin, Dear," his mother told him. "One doesn't grow up in a Dunleavy household without being exposed extensively to that classic language."

"Classic meaning dead," Willard confided to Hal with a twinkle. "It's not like classic rock 'n' roll, where it's only ten or twenty years old."

Hal laughed. He had a feeling that he was going to like Willard. The cousin's homosexuality still bothered him a little, but as long as no advances were made to him directly, he supposed he could live with it.

Hal's mother prepared the evening meal, and they ate and talked for a while. Hal was fascinated by the stories Willard and his mother exchanged on their respective Greenwich Village days. The way they talked about New York brought it to life for him in a way he had never imagined before. He was particularly happy to see his mother brought out of herself for a change. He had a feeling that under different circumstances, she might be a fairly enjoyable person to know. She always seemed out of place in the setting he knew anyway, and he supposed that explained much of the dour, almost bitter turn her personality had taken. He often thought his father had done her a great disservice by removing her so forcibly from the world in which she truly belonged.

Then he saw the clock on the wall and realized that he had some studying to do. "Well, if y'all'll 'scuse me, I got a big English test comin' up," he said as he rose. He glanced Willard's way and laughed. "I wanta keep gettin' those A's. Otherwise, I'm gonna hear 'bout it from Mother."

"I can't stop him from using that ugly y'all," Kathleen McDonough sighed. She looked at Willard and smiled warmly. "I remember that as the first prospect I dreaded when his father decided that we were going to move to a southern state. And, sure enough, my worst fears have been realized."

"Well, there are worse things in life than saying y'all," Willard replied pleasantly.

So Hal went to his room to study, and Willard and his mother continued talking well into the night.

Studying was no problem for Hal. His mother got him in the habit of doing it early on, and it stuck. It became more important as he contemplated going to college. His grades were always good; he had long been near the top of his class. A couple of the other students, Shawna included, were slightly ahead of him, but he might have a shot at valedictorian or salutatorian if one of them slipped. He was fairly smart as young people go; he had scored well on the IQ tests when he was in the early grades. But he didn't really see his grades as necessarily proving him to be that much brighter than some of the other students. It was simply that when test time rolled around, he knew the material better than most of them.

At one point, he felt his mouth going dry, so he eased out to the kitchen to get a glass of milk.

"Well, how's the English coming along, young man?" Willard asked him.

"Okay, I guess," Hal said with a shrug. He got the milk from the refrigerator. "I couldn't help hearin' y'all talk 'bout New York. It sounds different 'un the way I hear a lotta people talkin' 'bout it. They talk 'bout the dirt an' crime an' all."

"Oh, you'll find plenty of that, too," Willard told him with a chuckle. "But there are other sides to the Big Apple. Where else can you go to see first-run Broadway plays or see them even before they make it to Broadway? Or go to the best opera house in the world to hear Pavarotti, Domingo, Kathleen Battle, Leontyne Price, people like that in person? If you like good jazz, you can find any number of nightspots that offer the best you're likely to find anywhere. And the food! Whatever mood your palate is in, there's an establishment close by with cuisine to satisfy it."

"There's this black girl in my class, Shawna Hanson, that talks 'bout New York kinda like you do. I think you know her aunt," Hal remarked to Willard.

"Harold has a bad habit of bringing this girl's name up a lot, which sometimes concerns me," Kathleen McDonough confided to her cousin. "I have no trouble with colored people per se, but I definitely have trouble with seeing their young and white juveniles thrown together so indiscriminately."

"Well, look at it this way, Kathleen: Even in a worst case scenario, he's showing an interest in girls which, you have to admit, is better than if he showed an interest in boys," Willard said in a jocular tone.

"I'm not so sure," Kathleen McDonough sighed.

"I keep tryna tell Mother nothin's goin' on 'tween Shawna'n I, but she won't listen," Hal appealed to Willard.

"Between Shawna and me," Kathleen McDonough corrected him in an exasperated tone. She sighed and lit a cigarette.

"Between Shawna and me," Hal took the correction. He swallowed his milk and put the glass in the sink. "Well, gotta get back to the books."

He went back to his room and resumed studying. He had his door slightly ajar, and, at one juncture, he heard Willard say he needed to get back to the hotel before Bruce got anxious and had the police out looking for him. He supposed Bruce to be Willard's boyfriend. He chuckled to himself. He had never met anyone who was homosexual before this night—or anyone he knew to be that way at least. He had heard other people talking about isolated instances involving a person they might have met who displayed that bent. Melvin Peebles once confided to him that he had an older brother who was an avowed homosexual. It didn't seem to rub off anywhere—or so Hal gleaned from Melvin's case anyway. As nearly as he could judge, Melvin was as straight as anyone else he knew.

Hal long had accepted, intellectually if not emotionally,

that it existed as a condition in some humans, and it probably wasn't something those people could help. He had come to accept—more recently by prodding from Shawna, who was much more understanding than her use of such words as faggot might indicate—that it was not necessarily something to be hated or feared. But he wasn't quite ready to accept that people of that orientation were equal to heterosexuals. He didn't know quite how to resolve that issue, of course. He didn't think he wanted it done by booting Willard out of the law firm he worked for and filling the position with a heterosexual male or female. Probably just better to leave it alone, he reasoned.

He heard his mother excuse herself to use the bathroom. A moment or so later, Willard was standing in his bedroom doorway. For a moment or so, he tensed up. He hoped that Willard wasn't planning to make a homosexual advance on him.

"I just wanted to say goodnight," Willard said pleasantly. "Eunice is always calling you Hal. Is that what your friends at school call you?"

"Yes sir," Hal confirmed. He felt a great surge of relief that Willard evidently was not working up to an advance. "I prefer Hal. I just can't get Mother in the habit of callin' me that."

"Your mother has become a bit stiff in her advancing years," Willard conceded. He flashed a smile. "Okay, it's Hal. When Kathleen's around, of course, I might call you Harold just to keep her pacified, but I know it's Hal."

"Thanks, Uncle Willard," Hal said with a chuckle.

Kathleen McDonough emerged from the bathroom, and Willard headed out to say his farewell. After Hal heard him leave and the door close in confirmation, he headed out to the kitchen for another glass of milk. His mother sat at the table smoking a cigarette, with a faraway glaze over her eyes.

"He seems like a nice guy," Hal said.

"Yes," his mother agreed. She drew pensively on her

cigarette and sipped some coffee. "It was amazing talking about Greenwich Village like that with him. I had almost forgotten how wonderful a place Greenwich Village could be."

"Sounds like it," Hal murmured. He sat down facing her. "I don't think I ever saw your face light up like it was while Willard was here."

"Well, Dear, I'm sorry, but I've had to feed you and put a roof over your head in one of the dreariest hellholes God ever saw fit to disgrace this planet with," Kathleen McDonough snapped.

"I wasn't criticizin' you. I was just sayin' how different you were," Hal defended himself with a gesture. He sipped some milk. "I heard him talkin' 'bout somebody named Bruce. I guess that's his boyfriend."

"I think the word they use now is companion," Kathleen McDonough said with a shrug. She sipped some coffee. "But, yes, it amounts to the same thing. He told me he was homosexual before you came home. That's the main sore point between himself and his father. It always has been. His father's attitude has always been pretty much like I imagine those young men with whom you play basketball and football feel. They see it as something shameful and dirty. They don't stop to consider that it just might be a condition someone can't help having, like a birth defect or something similar."

"I wasn't knockin' Willard," Hal said defensively. "I mean, hell, whatever turns 'em on an' all that. It's none of my business. I was just askin'."

"Well, by now you should be starting to understand that not all questions have simple yes and no answers," Kathleen McDonough told her son arcanely.

"I met my fag uncle last night," Hal confided to Shawna over lunch the next day. "He came down from New York to visit Mother."

"Well, he try anything?" Shawna asked with an impish grin.

"Nah." Hal thought about it a moment and chuckled. "I was studyin' in my bedroom, an' just before he was gettin' ready to leave, he came to the doorway to say goodnight. I was scared for a moment there he might try somethin', an' I was ready to deck him or somethin' if he did."

"You'd have a little trouble managin' that with your broken leg, I would think," Shawna said.

Hal grimaced. "Uh, yeah."

"You know, of course, he mighta wanted to look in just to see if you were undressed," Shawna teased.

"With my mother 'round. No way I'm gonna be undressed," Hal reasoned. He bit into some of his lunch. "He seems like an okay guy, even if he is a fag."

"A lot of 'em are decent people if you just bother to get to know 'em as people," Shawna said. She eyed Hal impishly. "Course the fact that you can talk 'bout thinkin' 'bout deckin' him prob'ly shows you need some social cultivation."

"'Member, I didn't get to go to one of those hifalutin schools like Choate to learn that higher intellectual way of dealin' with people," Hal said insouciantly. He studied Shawna momentarily. "Thought just hit me. What if you met some girl that turned out to be a dyke, an' she suddenly came on to you? What would you do?"

"I'd knock the shit outta her," Shawna said. She watched until Hal's eyes dilated and then laughed and patted him on a cheek.

22

Willard only stayed a few days, but he crammed a lot of activity into them. He started it by renting a car and driving Kathleen and Hal to Colonial Williamsburg. Surprisingly, Hal enjoyed the trip. He found that he had a natural fascination with and curiousity about events and people from periods before he was born. He was veritably awestricken by all the Revolutionary War reminders dotting the Williamsburg landscape.

"It's kinda staggerin' when you think 'bout Patrick Henry, George Washington, Thomas Jefferson, James Madison an' all those guys hangin' out here," he remarked at one point.

"Well Dear, when one grows up in Boston and is constantly reminded of Samuel and John Adams and Thomas Paine, it doesn't strike one as all that impressive," his mother said curtly.

"Kathleen, the boy didn't have the advantage—or as I see it, the disadvantage—of a Bostonian rearing, so I think he may be excused for expressing his enthusiasm," Willard said. He turned to Hal and winked. "Bostonians tend to deify their own Revolutionary War gods and forget that other states, among them Virginia, contributed to the cause."

"I think Virginians are just as bad about it, and to make matters worse, they do it by saying y'all a lot," Kathleen McDonough groused. "Bostonians have their shortcomings, granted, but at least they express themselves properly."

Willard and Hal shared a chuckle.

Eunice had also come down for the holiday, and she and Shawna joined Willard and Hal one evening for dinner. Kathleen McDonough begged out; she didn't like gatherings, especially when a couple of the parties were of a differing pigmentation.

Willard and Shawna turned out to be the true soulmates on that occasion. Shawna had a deeply rooted love for New York's cultural offerings, and Willard shared her enthusiasm. They spent a good portion of the evening talking about the opera, Broadway, the Village, the great out of the way shops in lower Manhattan and whatever else happened to pop into their heads.

"I think if I was tryna make time with Shawna, I'd be kinda jealous," Hal remarked in a jocular tone to Eunice when the two were out of earshot.

Eunice chuckled. "Shawna loves New York. She's found a soulmate in Willard, and she's feasting on it. She takes after me in that regard. Her mother, in contrast, hates the place. When she and Gerald visit, it's like pulling teeth to get her to go out."

"I sorta got that feelin' from talkin' to Shawna," Hal said. He gestured to change the subject. "I was born there, but I don't know anything 'bout the place. I was less'n two when my dad 'cided to pull up stakes an' leave. So all I got to go on is what I hear from other people, an' a lot of it's not good."

"Both sides have a great deal of validity," Eunice said. "Shawna may think differently some day if and when she's ever raped or mugged up there or put in a position of having to try to get by on very little money. But that she'll have to find out for herself when the time comes. For now, far be it from me to deny her or any other young person their dreams." She patted Hal warmly on a cheek. "The best and worst of both your lives lies ahead. Go for it."

"Well, my dream's to play in the NBA someday," Hal said.

"I don't know, but I think it may be within your power to realize it," Eunice said.

A little later, Willard went to get his rental car, and Hal, Shawna, and Eunice waited outside in front of the restaurant for him.

"Your uncle's a neat guy," Shawna told Hal. She chuckled. "Course with him, it's kinda like talkin' to 'nother girl in a way."

Hal shared her amusement. "Mother told me when he was little he used to like to dress up in girls' clothes," he recalled. "You got a thing for good clothes. Maybe the two of y'all oughta get together an' swap outfits."

"You two are terrible," Eunice said, while at the same time stifling a giggle of her own.

"Well, I might, but I don't think we wear the same size," Shawna said.

Hal's traveling companion, Bruce, never actually visited the family, but he hung in almost spectral manner over the times Willard came around. A couple of times Hal's mother asked about him and wondered aloud why Willard didn't invite him over for dinner. Kathleen McDonough was not liberal by most standards, but she could be surprisingly sympathetic to homosexuals, especially now that she knew her favorite cousin was one. The first time Willard made up an excuse for Bruce's absence. The second, he finally admitted that he purposely kept Bruce away because of a history his lover had exhibited with an affinity for really young men. He nodded in Hal's direction to indicate that his cousin's son might easily stir Bruce's passions. Hal was quite glad when this revelation was aired that Bruce was being kept away. Kathleen McDonough conceded, as well, that all parties concerned probably were better off with Bruce not around.

Then one day Willard sent Bruce packing. It turned out that Bruce, in his lover's absence, had a tendency to hit the lounges and bars looking for young men. He tried the lounge in the hotel where he and Willard were lodged and happened to pick on the wrong target. The young man in question, evidently an attractive Nordic type, of the sort Bruce favored, laid Bruce out. In so doing, he also broke a number of lounge items. Willard wound up picking up the tab for the damage when both the young man and Bruce refused to pay, but with the understanding that Bruce would leave town. Bruce had no problem on that score. Small places like Brileyville did little for him if he couldn't find the male companionship he craved.

Willard told the story to Hal, with the understanding that the young man would not in turn relate it to his mother. Hal had no problem with that. He understood all too well how easily his mother could be moved to overreact. He also found himself cracking up with laughter to hear Willard's colorful description of what took place.

"Sounds like Bruce really has a problem," he said.

"I'd say," Willard agreed. "I guess I'm kind of a flamer myself really, but I'm nothing like Bruce is. At least I try to keep it in my apartment and pretty much private. He goes to bathhouses, the really sleazy gay bars, you name it. And I also have a hard time getting him to use the raincoat when we do it . . . "

"Raincoat?" Hal interrupted.

Willard laughed. "Condom. That's what a lot of people call it. Used to be rubber, prophylactic. Now it's raincoat. A little slang never hurt anyone."

Hal chuckled. "Well, yeah, I figured that's what it prob'ly meant." He studied Willard. "Uh, my own feelin' is I wouldn't wanta do it with a girl without one of those if I didn't know her or where she's been. I'm not tryna tell you how to live your life, but I think if I were you, I'd be thinkin' 'bout dumpin' Bruce permanently. He sounds like a prime candidate to get AIDS from."

Willard nodded and heaved a sigh. "I've thought about that. Of course, he is dynamite in the sack. I don't know if I could replace that easily. But I may have to try." He patted Hal on a shoulder. "And you're wise to think that way about any girlfriends you may have in the future. Persons of my persuasion are not the only ones around getting that deadly disease."

"Yeah, so I hear," Hal said.

On Willard's last night in Brileyville, he treated the two families to dinner in the hotel dining room. It was the first time Kathleen McDonough had been brought face to face with the Hansons and Eunice and vice versa. Hal's mother far and away was the most unwilling member of that gathering. Willard was forced to ply every resource at his command before he finally persuaded her to come along.

When she saw Shawna, she felt even more uneasy. "I get these cold shivers when I hear Harold bringing that girl's name up so often in conversation," she confided to her cousin. "But when I see her up close, I get downright terror-stricken."

Willard laughed. "Why, Kathleen?"

"Look at her," Kathleen McDonough said. Then she thought about to whom the directive was delivered and gestured helplessly. "Well, maybe you wouldn't understand."

"I can see she's a pretty girl, dear cousin," Willard said soothingly.

"Yes, and Harold has a history of exhibiting crazy hormonally driven impulses, and seeing him in that sort of proximity to a girl who looks like her strikes me as somehow akin to pouring gasoline on a fire," Kathleen McDonough murmured.

Willard patted her on a shoulder. "Your son is a very level-headed young man, Kathleen."

"I'm not sure how level-headed any young man might be around a girl who looks like that one does, and Harold is scarier in that regard than a lot of other young men I can think of," Kathleen McDonough sighed.

"Well, from what I can judge, he's not likely to turn out to be of my persuasion," Willard reasoned. "You should be thankful for that, at least."

"I'm not so sure," Kathleen McDonough said. She flashed a wan smile. "I don't want him to be homosexual, but I do wish more white girls were around to divert his attention away from that one." She motioned to Shawna.

Willard took a deep breath. "I agree that might make matters less complicated. But even in a worst case scenario, I don't see where you have that much to worry about. Besides being very attractive, she's quite intelligent. Frankly, I think if you ever bothered to sit down and talk to her, you might find the two of you have remarkably much in common."

Kathleen McDonough shrugged. "But I don't want to see some little half breed coming up to me at some future date and calling me grandma."

Willard chuckled. "You might be surprised, if that ever happens, just how cute that little tyke might suddenly become in your eyes," he said. Again he patted his cousin on a shoulder. "Relax, Kathleen, the worst thing you can do is worry yourself to death over your son. As nearly as I can judge, he and Shawna are still quite detached and at most just friends. And they both have more than enough other interests to keep their respective lives away from each other."

"I hope you're right," Kathleen McDonough muttered.

A little later, Kathleen McDonough felt the urge for a cigarette. Willard had reserved a non-smoking table, so she had to go out into the hotel lobby to light up. She had taken her second draw when Eunice came out to join her.

"Kinda rough on us smokers these days, isn't it?" Eunice greeted her. She also lit up.

Kathleen McDonough nodded. "I love my cousin dearly, but I have to wonder what possessed him to book a no-smoking table."

Eunice chuckled. "Most of the people in the party don't smoke. And I happen to have it on good authority that at least two members of that group absolutely detest cigarette smoke. I'm referring to my sister and her husband. Whenever I'm around their place, I have to step outside if I want to light up. Well, I'll take that back slightly. I probably don't have to, but they kinda leave the message hanging out ever so subtly that they prefer it that way."

"It's turning into a strange world," Kathleen McDonough said with a shrug. She looked inside the restaurant and spotted Hal and Shawna talking semi animatedly about something. "Doesn't it bother you to see your niece and my son conversing so casually?"

Eunice almost choked. "Why?" She glanced inside the restaurant and shrugged. "When I left the table, they were talking about the doctor that set Hal's leg. It was quite innocent really. If there was any romantic interchange anywhere in it, I certainly missed it, and I think my much more uptight sister did too."

Kathleen McDonough exhaled sharply. "But aren't you concerned about what something like that might lead to?"

Eunice cleared her throat. "I talk to people every day in a friendly manner, and when work ends, I go my way and they go theirs. I don't see that it's automatically destined to go anywhere. And if it does, well, I guess we'll all just have to learn to live with it."

"I thought your people were every bit as much against that sort of cross socializing as mine," Kathleen McDonough said.

Eunice's brow furrowed. "Mrs. McDonough, I was married once to a white man, so I'm probably not as sympathetic to your point of view as some other African Americans I know might be. On the other hand, I've also been married to and divorced from a black man, so I might be a good one to talk to if you want to tear apart the institution of marriage. Beyond that, all I can say is you're less likely to get the worst if you don't go looking for it."

Kathleen McDonough gestured bemusedly. "You mean you wouldn't try to stop it if you felt that something was developing between those two?"

Again, Eunice found herself almost choking. "I might offer advice to one or the other of them. It does occur to me that they probably will fare better if their future lives go in different directions. But out and out try to stop it? No, of course not."

"I don't think I could be quite that casual about it," Kathleen McDonough said.

"If it comes to that point, you may have no choice," Eunice replied. "Let me again emphasize: I hope it doesn't. But that's not something I have any control over, nor do I want to try to exert any control over it, and if you're wise, you'll take a similar approach."

"I'd feel a lot more comfortable if Harold wasn't so compulsive at times," Kathleen McDonough sighed.

Eunice laughed. "He's a normal young man, Mrs. McDonough, and that's complicated by him being a gifted athlete. I'd think you should be glad he's compulsive, as you call it. That's part of being alive."

"But I'm not sure it's always conducive to a long life," Kathleen McDonough said with a resigned gesture.

"But it might help him find fulfillment," Eunice reasoned. "If I had to choose between a short interesting life and a long mundane one, I'd pick the short interesting one in a heartbeat."

"Of course interesting and reckless often get confused," Kathleen McDonough said. "I see a lot of his father in him."

"Well, I never met his father, so I don't know if that's good or bad," Eunice reasoned.

23

As Willard came and went, so did the holiday season and the old year. By early January, Hal was able to have the cast taken off and lay the crutches aside. That didn't mean that he was ready to step into a starter's role or even a viable reserve slot on the basketball team. The leg had to be worked back up to strength, and Hal had to work on getting his quickness, timing, and shooting touch back.

Wimbush didn't rush him. The team was in the midst of a sub-par season; it had lost five of its first nine games. Wimbush never had a losing season before and didn't like the prospect of suffering one now, but the thought occurred to him that it might well be something every coach has to go through and it just happened to be his turn. He could see some wisdom in working Hal into the flow to get him ready for the next season, but he didn't want to risk reinjuring the leg before it was fully healed.

He put Hal on a special exercise regimen and began phasing him into the team's practice sessions. Early on, that was a little awkward for the young man. The leg still felt stiff, and Hal had nothing even closely resembling his normal mobility.

"Don't worry about it. You'll get it back soon enough," the coach told him in a solacing tone.

"Yeah, but it seems like it's gonna take forever," Hal grumbled.

Wimbush laughed. "At your age, two days can seem like forever," he said.

Hal nodded soberly. He knew that Wimbush was describing his mood rather accurately.

He continued his daily workouts when he wasn't in school or at his part-time job. For the next couple of weeks or so, he was a familiar sight in the afternoons, clad in sweats and running around the school track. That included a few very cold days, when temperature highs never got out of the twenties. He didn't have any especial affinity to extreme cold, but he did find that if he focused on his workout and put everything else out of his mind, he could get through it well enough.

On one of the really cold days, Shawna and Trina came by. They weren't particularly concerned about putting anything out of mind in that moment, so they both were bundled up like Eskimos. It had struck Hal on more than one occasion that Shawna looked particularly sexy in some of her sweater and boots ensembles.

"Kinda silly, isn't it, runnin' 'round like you're doin' on a day that's this cold?" Shawna greeted him.

Hal stopped and tried to catch his breath. "I never thought 'bout it bein' cold 'til you just mentioned it."

"Well, if you need somebody to tell you it's cold, you got problems the best teacher in the world ain't gonna be able to help you with," Trina said through chattering teeth. Both Hal and Shawna laughed.

"Didn't your mama ever tell you that you can catch your death of cold workin' up a sweat on a day like this?" Shawna teased him.

Hal shrugged and tugged at his sweatsuit. "This is insulated. It keeps out the cold pretty good. An' I been poppin' a lotta vitamin C. Knock on wood, I hope that keeps me from catchin' pneumonia."

"Well, Trina'n I're goin' inside where it's warm, which is a better way of not catchin' pneumonia," Shawna said with a grin.

The two girls waved as they headed back to the main school building. Hal waved back and resumed working out. He fairly salivated as he watched Shawna from the rear. Somewhere along the line, he knew he would have to make a move on her. By this juncture, she had his inexperienced libido churning insanely. Even so, rushing something with her would probably blow his chances forever. He probably didn't want to wait too long either, and he might at some point have to guess on the time for making his move, but right now certainly didn't seem right. Besides, he had to worry about getting himself back up to speed for basketball.

That did start coming. He found the leg feeling stronger, and again the quickness, probably his single greatest asset, was there. He was matched against Elmore in practice, and Elmore couldn't stay with him. Plus, he was finding the range on his jump shot. He felt as if he was close to being ready to assume a major contributing role on the team.

"Yeah, I think you just 'bout there," Ernest Farlow, the team captain and center, told him after one practice.

Ernest had a huge smile that might remind one of Magic Johnson. He was a skinny six feet and six inches and had already been recruited and signed by Ferrum College. He wasn't nearly strong enough to play any inside position for a major college, nor were his ballhandling skills adequate for guard. But everyone around seemed to feel that he could play small college ball well enough. As Hal was discovering, too, Ernest was a really nice young man. It was almost like the rapport he enjoyed with Clifford Jenkins when he played football.

"How's the leg comin' 'long?" Ernest asked him.

"I don't feel the soreness any more, and most of the stiffness seems to be pretty much gone," Hal answered.

Ernest flashed that magnificent smile. "I 'spect Elmore be really cringin' to hear you say that. Way you been blowin' by him in practice, he prob'ly don't wanna hear you can get even quicker."

Hal laughed.

24

Once each regular season, Brileyville played an intersectional game against Winslow from the Southern Leaf District. The two schools had met a couple of times in regional tournament play. In recent years, the series had become rather lopsided, with Winslow winning seventeen games straight, eleven of which were against Wimbush-coached teams.

That might have been more embarrassing if Winslow hadn't established itself as one of Virginia's premier high school programs: the legendary status developed over twenty-some years under a coach named Phil Laughinhouse. Three state championships, twelve district titles, and nine regional crowns more than testified to Laughinhouse's ability to coach. In virtually any conversation over who was the state's best in that profession, his name was certain to come up. Wimbush was among his peers tipping the hat to him as top man.

Laughinhouse was at least as renowned for a womanizing

bent he had exhibited over the years. Over time, stories of his conquests made the rounds through all parts of the state and even a little beyond. No doubt some of the stories were embellished for effect, but none seemed to qualify as pure fiction. It was almost certain that Laughinhouse did stray from his wife from time to time. Why she stuck with him through it all is probably at least as interesting a story in its own right if all the facts were on the table. Unfortunately, those facts were known only by the two people involved and perhaps one or two others very close to the situation. No one in that group was communicating them to the outside world.

One Laughinhouse story of a less flattering nature had to do with a time he was caught in a compromising position with an underage Winslow cheerleader. A matter of public record was that such a charge had been made and a hearing held. This had occurred some seventeen years earlier, when Laughinhouse was still in his twenties. Newspaper accounts of the incident indicate that the Winslow community was fairly evenly divided between a faction calling for his summary dismissal and another wanting to retain him because he was an established winner. The fact that only a year earlier he won the first of his state championships probably had a lot to do with the final decision not to dismiss him. Winners tend to get the benefit of the doubt almost everywhere long before it's extended to also-rans or losers.

Hal picked up snippets of the Laughinhouse legend from some of his teammates and an assistant coach. Ernest especially found it fascinating.

"What I got trouble figurin' out is how come his wife sticks with him if he plays 'round like that," Hal remarked to Ernest as they were warming up before the game.

Ernest laughed. "Maybe he's such a stud she figure she ain't gonna do no better. An' since he don't play 'round with nothin' but girls, she ain't likely to catch a dose of the Big A. Or maybe she just don't know. Or maybe she got somethin' goin' on the side. I hear you white folks get kinda kinky sometimes."

"I'm prob'ly less of a 'thority on what white folks do 'un you," Hal said with a shrug. He looked across the floor to where Laughinhouse stood, gazing across the floor almost like one might picture Plato or Aristotle doing. "You think he really fucked that cheerleader?"

Ernest flashed that Magic smile. "You figure at the time he was still pretty young. You get one them cheerleaders lookin' pretty foxy an' like she might be eighteen or older, you think you wouldn't in his place?"

Hal nodded and pursed his lips thoughtfully. He could understand how a vibrant young man might at least be tempted in such circumstances. What Shawna was stirring in his own libido gave him ample insight into what other heterosexual boys and men experience within themselves. He glanced across at Laughinhouse again and understood how such attraction might be mutual. Laughinhouse was still a handsome man, tall and lean with ample black hair still worn long and hanging over his forehead. That would have been much more pronounced when he was younger, and it wasn't difficult to imagine some impressionable teenage girl with a body developed beyond her emotional and intellectual maturity letting him know that she was available.

"Some guys prob'ly get more pussy 'un others 'cause girls make theirself more 'vailable," Ernest said, almost as if he had been reading Hal's thoughts. "Could be Laughinhouse is one of them guys."

Hal shrugged. He couldn't argue that point.

The game got underway with Hal on the bench. This one, though played on Brileyville's court, soon began following a familiar pattern. Winslow took control early and methodically built a fourteen point lead by halftime. To make matters worse, Elmore had picked up three fouls.

"Looks like I might be playing you a little more tonight than I figured on," Wimbush told Hal in the lockerroom. "You think you're up to it?"

"I been ready," Hal said.

Wimbush smiled and patted him on a shoulder. "I don't want you doing too much out there. I don't like to throw in the towel, but I'm getting the distinct feeling that we're not going to win this one. But it is a good way to get you some game experience."

"I think I been ready for it at least a week now," Hal replied.

"Yes, you're coming around," Wimbush conceded. He heaved a sigh. "But I'm still a little worried about the leg. I want to be sure it's going to hold up before I go throwing you full tilt at some other team. So take it easy out there, okay?"

"I hope you're not tellin' me if I got a shot I shouldn't take it," Hal said.

Wimbush shook his head. "No, but I don't want you forcing anything. You'll run the offense, bring the ball up, look for Ernest and Sammy inside."

"We been doin' that all game, an' they been clobberin' us," Hal reminded the coach.

"I realize that Hal, but we might just have to accept they're a better team than we are," Wimbush sighed. "Just do what I say, okay?"

"Sure," Hal acquiesced with a nod.

Winslow got the ball to start the second half and scored quickly to go up by sixteen. Hal took the inbounds pass and dribbled upcourt. A Winslow defender moved in front of him and quickly backed off; he recognized that as token pressure to slow his progress to the ten-second line. He got the ball into the frontcourt and set up behind the circle and prepared to work Wimbush's offense. Then it struck him— he didn't have a defender within five or six feet of him. This team was giving him a shot, the three-pointer, with which when unguarded he was deadly. He thought about the promise he had made to Wimbush to work the ball into Ernest and Sammy Williams, the team's power forward. Then it hit him again that if a team was foolish enough to give him any kind of shot like that, he would be a bigger fool not to take it. So he set and jumped and watched as the ball rose in a beautiful arc and hit nothing but the bottom of the net.

For the first time since the opening tap, there were sounds of some cheering in the Brileyville stands.

Winslow had a salt-and-pepper backcourt tandem, and an even larger cheer went up a few seconds later when Hal trapped the black half of it behind the time line and drew a ten-second call. He vaguely heard Laughinhouse yelling at the white guard to stay back and help out when the ball was being brought upcourt.

Hal again got the inbounds pass and dribbled into the Winslow zone. This time the black guard came out to guard him. That was no problem. Hal sensed that he was quicker than the Winslow guard and used this advantage to get around him and set up for another trey that again swished through. Now the Brileyville section really was starting to rock.

This time the white Winslow guard did stay back, and the black guard passed over Hal to him which got the ball into the frontcourt and the pattern offense. But the white center, who up until now had dominated Ernest inside, fumbled the pass out of bounds. Hal again got the ball, dribbled upcourt, slashed into the middle and drew the white center out to guard him and passed easily to Ernest for an easy dunk. For the first time in quite a while, the Winslow lead had been cut to single digits, and pandemonium was breaking out among Brileyville's partisans.

Laughinhouse called time out. "Where in hell did that boy come from?" Hal could hear the Winslow coach groaning as he headed back to his own bench.

"Hey, I thought I told you to take it easy," Wimbush told Hal with just the thinnest trace of a smile showing.

"You also told me to take my shots when I had 'em," Hal reminded him. He flashed a grin. "You know I can hit that three-pointer. If they're gonna give it to me, I'd be a damn fool not to take it."

Wimbush heaved a sigh and nodded. "I should take you out right now, but because of you we've got some momentum going, and I hate to give that up," he said through pursed lips. He patted Hal on the back.

Winslow got a basket after the timeout, a turnaround in the lane from one of the forwards that put the visiting team back up by ten. The inbounds pass again came to Hal, and this time both Winslow guards came up to trap him. It didn't work. Hal was a good natural ballhandler, with more than ample dexterity in both hands. He dribbled through the two with what to him felt like almost ridiculous ease and got the ball into the front court and set himself up for yet another trey. Now the rocking and chanting in the Brileyville stands sounded almost like a crescendo.

The two teams traded baskets on the next couple of posssession changes, and then Hal took over again. He caught the white guard in a corner, stripped him of the ball and bounce-passed an easy assist to Sammy Williams for a running layup. Then he challenged the white boy in the backcourt and rattled him into throwing the ball over the black guard's head and out of bounds. On the inbounds play, he drove the lane, made a nifty in-air move that turned the Winslow center around and fed Ernest for another easy two.

The third quarter was winding down, and the seemingly hopeless sixteen-point deficit of seven and half minutes or so earlier had been cut to four.

"I knew probably by this time next year, I'd be telling the team to get the ball in Hal's hands as much as possible, but I didn't expect to be doing it quite this soon," Wimbush told his team with a headshake. He took a deep breath and exhaled sharply. "He's making it happen. Might as well stick with it."

No one protested. Elmore was back in, but he was playing off-guard. Like all the other team members, he was almost awestricken by the performance Hal was giving.

Hal lost his hot hand for a brief span early in the fourth

quarter. He missed two jumpers, one from just a couple of feet from the basket, and Winslow built the lead back to nine with six minutes remaining. But then Hal redeemed himself by swiping the ball from a forward underneath the Winslow basket and sinking a twisting layup and drawing a foul call. He completed the three-point play to cut the deficit to six. Then he forced the black guard to dribble the ball off his foot and out of bounds. A moment later, he worked himself free from another attempted double-team and drilled another trey to cut it to three.

The two teams traded baskets on the next two possession changes, and then Hal worked free for another three-pointer that tied the score. The Brileyville stands were really rocking now.

Laughinhouse called another time out. "Goddamn, how come I never knew about this boy?" he was groaning as the teams headed to their respective benches. Ernest flashed a grin Hal's way when he heard that and draped an arm over the white boy's shoulders.

"The way you guys came back, I can't say enough," Wimbush told his players. "Even if we don't win this one, I'm damned proud of you."

Winslow regained the lead briefly with about three minutes remaining. On the Falcons' next possession, Hal again beat the double-team and found an open Brileyville player underneath with a lookaway pass that again tied the score. Then on Winslow's next possession, he swiped the ball from the black guard and raced almost the length of the floor to give the Falcons their very first lead of the night. A minute and a half showed on the clock, and the Brileyville gym rocked almost as if caught in an earthquake.

Laughinhouse called another timeout, his team's last. The game definitely had got away from him. Wimbush, on the other hand, appeared the soul of calm as he gathered his troops around him. He was only just now sensing this as a game he could win, so he hadn't really had a chance to get nervous. "Play tight D, and when you get the ball again use up as much of the clock as possible," was all he said.

Brileyville, or Hal, didn't challenge in the backcourt, and this proved to be a mistake. Winslow was able to set up in its halfcourt offense and get a three-point play from the center. This also drew the dreaded fifth foul on Ernest. Wesley would have to play the final fifty seconds at center.

"I think I hope you take the shot down there," Wesley whispered to Hal as he came out onto the court.

"If you got a better shot, I'm gonna be lookin' for you," Hal alerted him. It occurred to him that this must have sounded like something Clifford would have told him during football season.

It turned out that Hal got the shot. He dribbled upcourt, penetrated into the lane, spun deftly around the white center and laid the ball up softly with his left hand to put the Falcons back in front.

"Awright," Wesley cheered and exchanged a high-five with Hal as the two headed back to play defense.

Laughinhouse was hoping to run the clock down and try to win the game at the buzzer, but this time Hal didn't back off. He saw the white guard telegraphing a cross-court pass and stepped into the lane and intercepted it. He spotted Wesley racing back upcourt and led him with a football pass that was converted into a slam dunk. The Falcons had a three-point lead with just ten seconds showing, and their partisans were cheering insanely.

Wimbush called time out—he had a couple to spare.

"The only way they can tie the game is by hitting a three-point shot, unless one of you is dumb enough to foul somebody. Don't even breathe on anybody," he told his team. "Hal, you pick up the black guy in the backcourt, make him use up some time. I don't want him taking the three-point shot, and he'll have to give the ball up with you guarding him. The rest of you stay back, and if they throw the ball to somebody underneath, let that person take the shot. They can't beat us with a two, and they have no more timeouts. We've got this one. Just be careful not to let it get away."

Hal challenged the black guard and forced him to throw to his caucasian backcourt mate. The latter wound up taking a desperation shot from about forty feet out which clanged off the backboard nowhere near the goal. The horn sounded ending the game, and the Falcons had a historic and very memorable victory.

Pandemonium broke out everywhere on the Brileyville side, from both fans and players, as the game ended. Everyone seemed to be trying to grab and hug Hal—his teammates, students, former students, his coach, and finally Shawna and Trina, who had been among the faithful yelling themselves hoarse in the stands.

"Baby, you were beautiful out there tonight," Shawna was telling him.

"Yeah, you sure was. I never yelled so loud in my whole life," Trina agreed.

Those two got pushed aside in the rush of other people reaching for Hal. A couple of sportswriters moved in to get a quote from him.

"I was just in the flow," he told them before others swept them and him in different directions.

"Man, when you missed them two shots early in the fourth quarter, I thought you was coolin' off, but you was just gettin' you second wind," Ernest exulted as he squeezed into the human mass to hug Hal himself.

Hal scratched his head and grinned broadly. "It was just there for me tonight," he said. He felt good. He had shown what he was capable of producing. And above all, he just had the body of the girl of his dreams pressed against him. It was like being elevated from Purgatory into Heaven.

The pandemonium finally subsided, and Hal was able to get into the locker room to take a shower and change clothes. Elmore intercepted him as he was preparing to head back out into the gym.

"Good game . . . no, great game," Elmore told him sincerely. "You pulled our fat outta the fire big time tonight."

"Lucky, I guess," Hal said. He realized that from this

night's performance, he was probably pushing Elmore down into a secondary role. He was sensitive to the fact that it couldn't possibly leave Elmore with a good feeling.

"No, it was more than luck," Elmore conceded. "When I seen you in the second half, I could tell I was lookin' at somethin' real special. You gonna be the best player this school ever had, ain't no doubt 'bout that."

Hal sensed the truth in that. Of course, it wasn't necessarily something to brag about. The school didn't have a history of great players. "Maybe, but I gotta do it first," he said.

"Oh, you will," Elmore told him. He chuckled. "An' you know how come? 'Cause you got a hunger in you eyes. That prob'ly got a lot to do with how come some brothers been so good at them white schools. Now you come here an' you get put down, an' you gonna play good 'cause deep down you always gonna be tryna get back at somebody. I can see it in the way you play, an' I can see it in you eyes."

"You make it sound almost like I'm crazy," Hal said.

Elmore laughed. "In a way you are," he agreed. He slapped Hal on the back. "But it's a good kinda crazy. I wish I had it. An' I wouldn't mind havin' you first step to go 'long with it."

"I might lose it, but it ain't mine to give 'way," Hal responded with a grin.

Hal then headed out to the gym to look for his coach. Wimbush had been giving him and a couple of the other players rides home from the games. Until he could get his own car, he had to depend on that.

"Don't you think you oughta be playin' for us?" a raspy-sounding male voice suddenly interrupted his reverie.

Hal turned around and found himself face to face with Phil Laughinhouse. The question confused him for a moment. Then he looked past the coach and saw several white Winslow players and realized that their coach was making a joke about the two teams' respective racial compositions. He chuckled belatedly.

"I couldn't let you get out of here without at least

congratulating you," Laughinhouse said. "You really did a job on my boys tonight."

"I hope you're not lookin' for me to 'pologize," Hal quipped back.

Laughinhouse chuckled. "No. The object is to win. You did it better than we did tonight." He studied Hal momentarily. "They tell me you're just a sophomore."

"Yes sir," Hal confirmed.

"You hit us like a whirlwind tonight," Laughinhouse said in a serious tone. "Right at the end, I couldn't even bawl my players out any more. Purvis, my point guard, was telling me he's probably gonna be seeing you in his sleep for weeks to come."

Hal laughed. "Tell him it's better dreamin' 'bout girls."

Laughinhouse flashed a grin. "I'm sure he'll appreciate hearing that." He studied Hal momentarily. "It's been at least twenty-five years since I've seen a white boy that could handle the ball, shoot and play defense like you. Where'd you learn all that?"

Hal shrugged. "Nowheres special. I don't guess anyway. I've lived in Brileyville since the third grade. I used to practice a lot when I was 'lone. Most of it just seemed to come natural."

"Yes, you definitely are a natural talent," Laughinhouse conceded with genuine admiration. He shrugged. "When I played high school and college ball, I would have given my eye teeth for one third of your natural ability. I got by, but not in the way I expect you're going to."

"Somebody told me you played at Bridgewater," Hal said. He couldn't recall if he picked that up from Ernest or Wimbush or someone else affiliated with his own team.

"Yeah," Laughinhouse said with a nod. He shook his head and chuckled. "I imagine by the time you get ready to graduate, a school like Bridgewater won't even be able to dream about getting a player of your caliber."

Wimbush was coming around the corner just then looking for Hal. "I hope you're not trying to lure my player away from me, Coach Laughinhouse," he remarked jocularly.

"I was just telling him by rights he should be playing on my team, considering we're more evenly mixed racially," Laughinhouse said with a broad grin.

"I think Virginia High School League rules state that it's where the student lives," Wimbush joked back. "I don't think ethnic composition has anything to do with it."

"Well, can't blame a guy for tryin'," Laughinhouse said. He flashed another grin and patted Hal on a shoulder. "We'll be running into each other again, next time at my place."

"Well, it could always happen in the regionals," Hal said.

The effrontery in that remark struck both coaches as amusing. At that point in the season, Brileyville still had a losing record.

"You keep playin' like you did tonight, I wouldn't be surprised," Laughinhouse said. He again patted Hal on a shoulder and nodded to Wimbush. "See ya later, Jerome. Enjoy your victory. You earned it."

"I was due. I lost eleven straight to you," Wimbush said. "Take care, Phil."

Hal and Wimbush watched as Laughinhouse rejoined his own players, and they all headed out to the team bus.

"Sounds like you'n Laughinhouse're pretty good friends," Hal remarked.

Wimbush nodded. "Oh, yeah. We try to beat each other. I'm glad I beat him tonight, but it's not a personal thing. Phil Laughinhouse has the best basketball mind I've ever run into."

"Kinda odd hearin' you talk like that 'bout him an' hearin' some the other guys talkin' 'bout all the times he's out chasin' floozies'n whatnot," Hal mused.

Wimbush shrugged. "A lot of that gets blown out of proportion. I'm not saying there's no truth in any of it, but I'm sure Phil doesn't spend as much time doing that sort of thing as some people like to say he does. You don't win three state championships by bed hopping."

Hal laughed. "No, you sure don't."

Wimbush turned him around. "You know, young man, you did kinda go against my directive tonight," the coach said.

"I figured since we won the game, you'd forgive me," Hal reasoned.

Wimbush nodded and patted him gently on both shoulders. "I had a feeling last summer that you would be my best player. But it is a shock to see it happening so soon."

"Well, I hope you're not askin' me to slow down to meet some timetable," Hal replied.

Wimbush chuckled and shook his head. "No, but I still have to pinch myself from time to time to make sure I'm not seeing things. You made us a better team out there tonight. You did it with scoring and setting up other players and defense, but you also did it even when you weren't doing any of those things. I've never had a player that could do that before, and it takes a while to adjust."

"Sounds almost like tellin' Cindy Crawford or Kim Basinger not to be pretty," Hal reasoned.

Wimbush laughed and patted him on a shoulder. "You're right, it does." He shook his head. "You know you scored twenty-three points. In three full seasons, most of that time as a starter, that's ten more than Elmore's scored for an entire game."

That took Hal momentarily aback.

"Twenty-three times two is forty-six," Wimbush went on. He heaved an incredulous sigh. "That's staggering."

Hal shrugged. "They were givin' me the shots."

Wimbush shook his head. "They gave you two shots. The rest you did yourself. I was swept along in it like everybody else. Tonight I almost felt like a fan."

Hal gestured bemusedly. He didn't know how to respond.

"I'm pretty sure if we salvage anything out of this season, you're the guy that's gonna have to provide most of the spark," Wimbush went on. He patted Hal on a shoulder. "You'll be getting a lot more playing time now. But it is the last year for Elmore and Dwayne, and I hope you don't object if I continue to let them start the games."

Hal shrugged. "No, I guess not." He thought about it a moment and laughed. "I can be like McHale, the best sixth man maybe."

Wimbush laughed. "Well, you and Kevin McHale are not exactly the same type of player, but I guess there is a parallel," he conceded.

25

A Star bursts upon the Falcons appeared as lead headline on the following morning's Brileyville Courier-Gazette sports front. Hal was now a genuine celebrity. A game story and sidebar devoted more attention to him than to the game itself or the remarkable comeback the team had made against a foe it hadn't beaten in fifteen seasons. Both coaches were quoted extensively, and each had glowing things to say about this remarkable sophomore who appeared on the verge of taking Brileyville basketball to a whole new dimension.

He was getting attention from all over. Other students constantly surrounded him in the school corridors and lauded his performance and in general tried to experience vicariously some of the special aura they now seemed to see him as exuding. Some of the prettier girls from the junior and senior classes—who before seemed hardly to notice that he existed and could probably have cared less—were now smiling at him and flirting with their eyes and hinting at an interest that might be pursued to a higher plane. Before, the only young females who seemed to show any interest in him were a couple of homely white girls in his own grade who were totally incapable of arousing any sort of passion in him.

All this was pretty heady stuff, and he was enjoying it. But he didn't get carried away by it. He realized that one game could be quickly forgotten if he didn't continue to perform well. Instinctively, he also sensed how quickly those feminine smiles could turn into frowns. Really, the only feminine smile he wanted fixed on him that seriously was Shawna's. But he might have to go through a period of having other girls lavish attention and compliments on him before she would look at him that way. So he didn't want to lose that just yet.

In games that followed, he came off the bench and generally led the team in scoring, assists and steals. His quickness both of foot and hand made him about as good on the defensive end as the offensive. His coach quickly realized that he could also play a stopper's role if a player on the opposing team started showing a hot hand. He was very good at that. Sometimes he felt a little odd about being assigned to guard a black player who averaged in double figures. He had watched enough basketball on television to understand that usually it worked the other way around. But to date he had encountered no one he couldn't at least slow down considerably. He was beginning to get the feeling that he might be the quickest high school player in his area, white or black.

He got his points and assists too, of course, and he was doing that consistently and seeming to improve ever so gradually. That didn't mean that he was incapable of a bad night. He had one which by standards he set for himself was horrible: A three for nineteen shooting performance in a home loss to Hempstone. He was visibly disconsolate and very down on himself as he walked, head down, off the court after that game finally ended.

Wimbush caught up with him. "Hey, don't worry. You're gonna have those kinda games. Everybody does," he tried to cheer the young man up.

"Shit, I stunk the place up tonight," Hal grumbled.

"True, but you're also capable of lighting it up," Wimbush told him with a shoulder pat. He turned his new star player around. "You had a bad game. Don't take that to mean you should stop shooting and doing the other things you quite often do so well. The only people that never have bad games are the people that never do anything out there. You can't miss a shot if you don't take it, but you can't make it either."

Hal didn't feel that much better immediately, but he did work his way out of his depression in a short period. He led all scorers for both teams in seven of the Falcons' nine remaining regular season games and continued racking up good totals in assists and steals.

Others remarked on his defense. A couple of Courier-Gazette stories focused on how he gave Brileyville that added dimension with his ball-hawking and tenacity. Even some of his teammates told him as much from time to time.

"You oughta always let you defense kinda set the tone for you," Ernest advised him on one occasion. "You got a great shot, but it ain't always gonna go down. Sometimes you gonna have you dry spells. But you got the 'vantage of real quick hands'n feet. If you usin' them on defense like you oughta, you'll work outta you shootin' slumps a lot quicker."

Hal took that advice to heart and found that it seemed to work. He liked having the three-pointer and didn't mind taking it, but those shots seemed to fall a lot more consistently for him when he didn't have to depend on them. A good steal that he could convert into a layup or assist often proved to be the spark that brought the rest of his game along.

He continued to sit on the bench for the games' opening taps, while Elmore and Dwayne Lockerman, the team's off-guard, started. But Wimbush was sending him in after a couple of minutes or so, and the bulk of the ballhandling and setting up of the offense fell on him. And for the most part, he was up to the responsibility. He was only a sophomore, and he would have his bad games, but he was the best player and most of the time outperformed everyone else on the floor. His teammates understood this; and, if anyone resented it, that feeling was never expressed openly.

"It do feel kinda funny, me startin' an' then you comin' off the bench an' rackin' up the big stats," Elmore remarked to him once.

"I'm not doin' it to show you up, if that's what you're worryin' 'bout," Hal assured Elmore.

Elmore chuckled. "I know you ain't." He patted Hal on a shoulder. "I know Wimbush think he's doin' me'n Dwayne a favor by lettin' us start, but shit, we both know you the best player out there."

Hal shrugged. He didn't mind hearing someone compliment him in that way, but sometimes he did feel a little embarrassed by it. "Doesn't matter to me," he responded with a shrug. "You see guys in the NBA comin' off the bench all the time an' leadin' the team in scorin'. Some guys prob'ly play better comin' off the bench. Maybe I'm one of 'em."

Elmore grinned. "Well, next year with what's comin' back, you definitely gonna be a starter, so you better start gettin' used to it," he said.

Hal hadn't stopped thinking of Shawna or having periodic romantic or erotic dreams (of both the day and night variety) with her as a central player. But basketball and his newfound celebrity status, along with school and his part-time job, occupied his mind to the exclusion of virtually everything else for a time. So he was a little startled when he sat down in the school cafeteria to eat lunch one noon and heard: "If I didn't know better, I might almost think you been 'voidin' me."

He turned and found himself facing Shawna. It felt odd because a little while earlier he had been daydreaming about her.

He shook his head. "I haven't been 'voidin' you, least not on purpose. I just been kinda preoccupied with other things."

"Yes, I know." Shawna flashed a grin. "I saw the *New Star Bursts* headline in the paper. It's always a little bit sickenin' when journalists try to be poets."

She sat down across the table facing him and rested her chin on a cupped hand.

Hal laughed. "I never thought 'bout it as tryin' to be a poet, but I guess you got a point," he said. He bit into some of his lunch.

"I hope you haven't forgotten how much of this newfound celebrity status you got you owe to my family," Shawna reminded him.

"No, I haven't forgotten it," Hal said. He gestured helplessly. "I don't know how I can find time to say thanks as much as I oughta, but that doesn't mean I'm ungrateful."

"Well, I'm glad to hear that," Shawna said. She flashed an impish grin. "An' I just thought you'd like to know Aunt Eunice is comin' down this weekend, an' she plans to make a point of seein' you play Saturday night."

Hal almost choked. "I kinda wisht you wouldn'ta told me that," he sighed. "For your aunt, I'd like to put on my very best performance of the year. Bad thing 'bout it: If I know she's up there, I might find myself thinkin' 'bout it too much an' start messin' up."

"Don't think 'bout it then," Shawna advised. "Just look at it like 'nother game." She tweaked his nose playfully. "An' figure you mess up, you gonna have me to answer to come Monday mornin'."

26

Saturday night came, and Shawna and Eunice were in the Brileyville stands for the home game against Blanchard. Blanchard was a respectable opponent—ranked higher in the district than the Falcons at this juncture in fact. Plus, Brileyville had lost to Blanchard earlier in the season.

Eunice was a little puzzled when Hal didn't come out with the starting team. "If he's been doing so well, I'd figure he'd certainly be starting," she remarked to her niece.

Shawna patted her aunt comfortingly on an arm. "It's a courtesy thing to Elmore an' Dwayne," she replied. "They're seniors, an' they been starters for the last two years." She flashed a grin. "Don't worry. I 'spect you'll see Hal goin' in pretty quick."

Hal had noticed Eunice in the stands earlier and tried to put it out of his mind. He understood that he owed her a lot, and a good game on this night when she made a special effort to see him play would be at least partial repayment. But if he dwelled on it too much, he could find himself badly off form, so he tried to put it out of his mind and concentrate on just playing basketball.

A loud cheer erupted from the Brileyville stands a couple of minutes later when Wimbush sent Hal in. That preponderantly African American gathering had emotionally adopted this white boy almost as one of its own.

"Sounds like Hal's rather popular here now," Eunice remarked to Shawna with a smile.

Shawna chuckled and nodded. "They 'ppreciate the lift he's given the basketball team," she said.

Hal had semi-joked about wanting to play his best game of the season for Eunice's benefit, but it wasn't something he necessarily expected. He was still relatively inexperienced, but he had learned that the so-called zone would not be with him every night. He could play well enough so that he would get a fair number of points, assists and steals even when he wasn't in the zone, but he would have to work a little harder for them.

Surprisingly, this did turn out to be a zone night for him. He started out by hitting five three-pointers in a row and wound up breaking the school scoring record that had stood for almost twenty years. The final stat sheet showed him with thirty-four points, eleven assists, six steals and nine rebounds. And more importantly, he led Brileyville to an eighteen point triumph.

He was a little surprised to hear that he had broken the record. It had occurred to him that he probably would do so eventually, but he didn't expect it to happen quite this soon.

"Man, I can't believe it! A school record!" Ernest screamed with an incredulous headshake in the lockerroom. He flashed that Magic smile. "'Fore you done, only the Lord know how many times you gonna be doin' it."

Hal shrugged, almost in embarrassment. "I guess anybody could do it you take 'nuff shots," he said.

Ernest shook his head and slapped him on a shoulder. "No way, my man, not like you was doin' it. Some them three-pointers you was hittin' gotta be comin' from 'bout NBA range."

Hal chuckled. "I guess I was figurin' the further back I got, less likely somebody was gonna be in my face."

Ernest again flashed that magnificent smile and draped an arm over his shoulders. "When you in a zone like you was tonight, ain't nobody gonna be stoppin' you, least not on this level," he assured Hal.

That much by now Hal knew to be true. He could work himself open for good shots, the kind he was capable of making at any time, against anyone assigned to guard him—at least up to this point. He had a couple of bad and so-so nights, but that was more because of himself than any defender. If he wasn't shooting well on a given night, the other team might not have to worry about guarding him. If he was shooting well, it didn't matter who was in front of him.

He dressed and headed out into the gym area. He expected to find Eunice and Shawna waiting for him there. Along the way, he was mobbed by several students and assorted other people, congratulating him on a great game and praising and thanking him alternately for the tremendous boost he had suddenly given the Brileyville basketball program.

Weaving through a double-team suddenly struck him as a snap compared to this.

He finally found Eunice and Shawna.

"I was wonderin' if I was ever gonna make it through that mob," he remarked to Eunice with a grin.

"Well, you'd better get used to it, young man," Eunice said. She chuckled warmly. "I think your celebrity status in this school is only just beginning."

"Showoff," Shawna said to him with a teasing grin. "You broke the school record just to 'press Aunt Eunice."

Hal laughed. "Believe it or not, I didn't even know what the school record was. I been close to it a couple times. I got twenty-nine points last week 'gainst Rockwell." He glanced appealingly at Eunice. "Course, if I gotta do it, I'm glad it was on a night when you were here to see it. I do kinda owe you. I haven't forgotten it."

"All I did was just put a bug in someone's ear. The rest you seem to have pretty much taken care of by yourself," Eunice said. She scanned Hal and smiled. "You were moving quite a bit better out there tonight than the last time I saw you."

Hal grimaced. He hadn't forgotten the cast and crutches period. "Yeah, I'd say a little bit." He heaved a sigh. "Shawna was kinda jokin' with me how I oughta have my best game on 'ccount of you comin' tonight, but I wasn't really 'spectin' it. In fact, I was kinda halfway scared I might really mess up just 'cause of that. So I just kinda tried to blot it outta my mind."

"That's a good way to approach it," Eunice said appreciatively. She studied Hal momentarily and assumed a mock critical pose. "You did miss a free throw tonight. You need to work on that part of your game."

Hal almost choked. "I went to the line four times an' got three of 'em. That's seventy-five percent. You find a lotta guys in the NBA not doin' that."

"Well, now that you put it that way, you have a point," Eunice conceded. She shook her head and chuckled. "With the range you were showing on that jump shot, I don't think it's gonna do anybody any good to try to push you out away from the basket."

"I was jokin' with Ernest our center a few minutes 'go 'bout goin' out that far 'cause nobody'll think to come out to guard me," Hal said. He flashed a grin. "Actually, I think I shoot better when somebody is guardin' me. I get better rhythm when I'm on the move. I can shoot standin' still, too, I guess, but I just like it when I gotta juke an' pivot a little bit."

"You're a player," Eunice said. She hugged Hal. "Good players always think that way. Somebody like Steve Alford of Indiana or Steve Kerr of Arizona will always need someone to set picks and whatnot for them. Eventually, you'll have to learn how to avail yourself of those, too. But you'll also be able to get your points and assists on your own, which they can't really do very well."

Hal laughed. "Yeah, I think I've heard couple the guys callin' that white-boys ball."

Shawna almost choked. "Who suddenly put kinks in your hair?"

Hal and Eunice laughed.

"Well, yeah, I'm a white boy, but I like to think I'm not 'zackly typical," Hal defended his remark.

"Well, you certainly play a different brand of basketball than what I'm used to seeing from white boys," Eunice conceded.

"Uh, let's get outta here an' get somethin' to eat. I'm starvin'," Shawna murmured.

Hal and Eunice chuckled.

"Uh, you're welcome to come along with us," Eunice told Hal.

"Uh, you sure?" Hal responded hesitantly.

Shawna grabbed him by the arm. "Aw, c'mon, drop that false modesty pose an' let's get outta here." She flashed an impish grin. "Less you got some sort of fixation with the site of your big glory night."

Hal almost choked. "No, not hardly. I figure I'll be seein' a lot more of this place before I'm through."

"And I imagine this won't be the only time he'll be setting a new school scoring record," Eunice told her niece.

"Well, they say I'm 'pposed to get better as a junior an' senior, so if I don't I'm in trouble," Hal agreed.

"Ah, shuddup an' let's get outta here," Shawna responded.

So the three headed out to the parking lot to Eunice's car. Eunice and Shawna sat up front. Hal stretched out on the expansive back seat.

"I am happy to see after I put myself out on a limb for you that you haven't turned out to be a bust," Eunice told Hal once she had her car moving.

Hal nodded. "Me too." He heaved a sigh. "I can't help

wonderin' sometimes what goes through Coach Stallings' head at the junior high. I guess he's heard 'bout what I been doin' lately. He had a chance to play me an' 'fused to. I wonder how he's justifyin' that right now."

"I hope for your sake you don't spend a lot of time feeling bitterness against him," Eunice said. "Not that it wouldn't be understandable to some degree. You probably wouldn't be human if you didn't feel at least some tendency in that direction. But right now, things seem to be looking up for you, and I think harboring such feelings would be seriously counterproductive."

"Yeah, I kinda 'gree," Hal said with a shrug. He laughed. "Course if I was him, I think I might be thinkin' 'long 'bout now how it mighta helped me win a few more games."

"He'll probably be answering to this community for not playing you for a very long time," Eunice said. She glanced back and smiled warmly. "I'm sure a lot of people are not going to let him forget it. I don't think I'd waste a second thinking about him, if I were you."

"'Sides, it's not like you got turned down for the lead in the school musical an' now you're a big Broadway star," Shawna said impishly.

Good point.

The conversation shifted as Eunice drove along, Hal mostly just listened. His right hand was resting on a point near the car's console, and at a certain odd point it struck him that Shawna's left hand was just a few inches away. He wrestled within himself for a couple of moments on whether he wanted to reach over and clasp it. Very briefly, he felt a fear—mixing panic and embarrassment—over the consequences of such a move. Shawna might suddenly lash out and start upbraiding him unmercifully and cause her aunt and everyone else close to the scene to regard him as an insensitive brute and want nothing more to do with him thenceforth. But another side of his nature also was evolving, the one that told him he had to take the shot if he hoped to make it. The latter was growing more and more dominant, and in this instance it finally prevailed. He reached over and deftly interlaced fingers with Shawna.

The initial physical contact sent shock waves coursing through his entire body. Part of that was erotic; another part no doubt was apprehension over Shawna's response. Shawna looked back at him briefly, almost blankly, and then resumed talking to her aunt. They were discussing a couple of Broadway shows at the time and an opera Eunice recently had seen at the Met with Luciano Pavarotti and Kathleen Battle. But Shawna made no attempt to remove her hand. It was almost as if she was unaware that Hal was holding it.

Hal knew she wasn't unaware, of course. Shawna was as smart as anyone he knew. What he didn't know was what she might be thinking in those moments.

Eunice stopped by a mall pharmacy. "I have to get a pack of cigarettes," she told the two young people. "I'll be right back out."

So she departed, and Hal was left with Shawna's hand still in his own.

Shawna looked down at the two clasped hands and then back at Hal. "How come you're holdin' my hand?" she asked, with no trace of emotion or humor showing.

Hal was hardpressed to respond. "Uh, is that your hand?" he finally came back weakly.

"What you think it was? You were playin' with yourself?" Shawna's response came in a sarcastic sounding tone.

Hal shrugged. He had a feeling almost akin to someone just realizing that he or she had bet on the wrong horse. "Well, I figured I had to make a move 'ventually, an' now just seemed to be a good time," he finally said, in an almost apologetic tone. He removed his hand. "I guess I was wrong. I'm sorry."

"Well, I hope 'cause you're gettin' to be a big sports star an' all, you don't think that gives you license to go hittin' on every girl 'round," Shawna said.

"I said I was sorry," Hal reminded her. He took a deep breath. "Awright, I kinda had a crush on you. I don't think it's a crime."

"No, but sometimes you gotta figure the person you got the crush on isn't always gonna feel that way 'bout you," Shawna said. Absolutely no tone of humor or sympathy was detectable. "Whatever man winds up in my life is gonna have to be somebody pretty intellectual."

"Well, I don't know 'bout intellectual, but I do make pretty good grades," Hal defended himself. "I make A's in courses like English, an' I did even better'n you did in French."

The latter was true. Both got A's in the course, but Hal was a few points higher on the grade scoring.

"Well, it's more'n just grades an' all," Shawna said. She sighed wistfully. "Some sophistication's gotta come in there somewhere, too. You're kinda lackin' in that department."

"Well, excusez moi," Hal shot back sarcastically. "It's kinda hard to be sophisticated when you live in a rinky-dink town like this and go to a rinky-dink school like we go to."

Eunice returned and cut off their conversation. For Hal, that was a merciful intercession. He was steaming inside now. And hurt. Not that he disputed what Shawna said. He wasn't yet all that sophisticated, and he probably wouldn't become so for a long time if ever at all. Even so, he did find something a little cold in how she phrased it. He could take being shot down, but he wouldn't have minded if she had done it a little more gently.

But he was still friends with Eunice, and they conversed rather animatedly once the trio got to the restaurant. They were seated at a round table, with Hal between the two females. He was vaguely conscious of Shawna on one side of him, but he was trying to put her out of his mind. He felt a little foolish for having wanted her in the first place, and it occurred to him that now that he knew for sure he couldn't have her, he was probably better off. Some of the other girls in school, including a couple of other rather attractive black girls, had tossed out signals as if they might be interested. Why not pursue one of those possibilities?

And then he felt Shawna's hand slipping into his.

This really threw Hal for a loop. He glanced out of the corner of an eye at her and picked up no reaction. But her hand was there, and this time she had initiated the contact. Now he felt his penis starting to get hard, and he hated himself for not being able to control that. He wondered if Shawna was playing some kind of game with him. If so, he didn't want to be a pawn. But he didn't remove the hand either. Might as well play the hand (no pun intended) out, he reasoned.

Eunice excused herself to use the restroom and smoke a cigarette. That left the two young people alone with hands still clasped.

Hal finally turned to face Shawna. "I didn't suddenly get sophisticated in the last half an hour or so," he said gelidly.

Shawna smiled almost apologetically. "I guess when I think 'bout it, I'm not gonna find anybody real sophisticated 'round here," she said. Her eyes rolled appealingly. "I think I could be a pretty good actress if I set my mind to it. Don't you?"

Hal almost choked. But he had to admit to himself that she was probably right. Certainly if what she had put on a little while ago was an act, it had him more than convinced.

"You'd been gettin' kinda impetuous, an' I figured you needed to be knocked down a peg," Shawna told him with an arcane smile.

"Well, you wanta be careful how you go 'bout doin' that to people. It can backfire," Hal said. He glanced down at the two clasped hands. "I better warn you, you're playin' with dynamite here. You got no idea what's churnin' in me right now."

"What makes you think somethin' isn't churnin' inside me, too?" Shawna asked him challengingly. She moved her head up and lightly brushed his mouth with a kiss. "Men aren't the only ones feelin' that sorta thing, you know."

"No, but they seem easier to figure out," Hal murmured. Eunice returned, and that conversation was put on hold.

27

For the first time in his young life, Hal had a genuine girlfriend. As he found out later, Shawna had a crush on him almost as long as he had one on her. It was almost like the chicken and egg question as to who felt what before the other, but for some time the two passions had been building up. Now they were on the verge of exploding.

Discretion was followed, of course. They were both practical enough to understand that they had no choice. If their respective homefronts found out that they were seeing each other in this manner, a lot of forces would quickly come together to try to pry them apart. That wasn't something they wanted to have to deal with at this juncture.

They would have to deal with those forces eventually, of course. They recognized that much. If their relationship was ever to progress to a higher plane, they would have to go through some disapproving people—most notably two sets of parents. But for now, they were content to savor the feeling of just being boyfriend and girlfriend and exploring each other and dreaming about the possibilities that alone had to offer.

Even that part wasn't exactly easy. At school, they tried to make a point of not hanging over each other in public and flaunting their in-love status as so many other young unmixed couples are wont to do. But they did touch and hold hands and kiss when they thought no one was watching, and they did not always guess accurately on the latter. And the certain way they had now of looking at each other —dotingly, adoringly—was not going unnoticed. Not everyone in their peer group necessarily disapproved, but enough did so that they would not totally escape confrontation.

Hal was cornered in the hallway one afternoon by some young black men. A couple of them he recognized as being in his class; the others were assorted juniors and seniors. "You think 'cause you a hotshot athlete'n all, or 'pposed to be, that give you license to go 'round chasin' after one of our women?" the group's leader, a junior whom Hal vaguely knew as Reginald, pressed him.

"I wasn't chasin' after anybody, I was 'ware of," Hal defended himself. "If you're talkin' 'bout me'n Shawna, we got a right to walk 'round together an' talk an' whatnot, same's you got with anybody else in this school."

That didn't pacify anyone in that group; and, indeed, Hal might have been in for an unpleasant interlude if Clifford Jenkins, his old football playing mate, hadn't happened along.

"Hey, y'all ain't hasslin' my main man here, is you?" he greeted the black group.

"Hey man, he ain't got no right to be chasin' 'round after no sister," another member of the group spoke up.

"Shit, man, you'd be cryin' rights louder'n anybody 'round if you had a chance at some white pussy an' a buncha rednecks told you that you better leave it 'lone, an' you fuckin' know it," Clifford shot back angrily. He draped an arm over Hal's skinnier shoulders. "Now you got two bad dudes here. I happen to know this boy can fight, an' I don't think any one of y'all wanna try him one-on-one. You want anything else right now, you gonna have to come through both of us."

So much for that confrontation. The young men may have liked the odds if they could just gang up on Hal, but Clifford thrown into the equation was a little more than they wanted to deal with. They didn't stop grumbling, but they did go speedily away.

"Thanks Clifford," Hal said as he watched the last of the group disappear through a door. "I think they kinda had thoughts of gangin' up on me an' beatin' the shit outta me. I prob'ly couldn'ta stopped 'em, but I was thinkin' 'bout which one I was gonna take out before I went."

"Shit, they ain't nothin'," Clifford said. He flashed a grin and patted Hal on the back. "Well, I hear you finally got 'round to makin' it with that pretty sister you was hangin' out with durin' football season."

"Well, makin' it doesn't mean I'm gettin' any pussy," Hal said. He flashed a grin. "I 'spect she's gonna try to keep the lid on that for a while longer."

"Well, you keep pressin' up 'gainst it long 'nuff, sooner or later you'll get it in," Clifford assured him with a good-natured shoulder pat. "I been followin' you on the hardwood, by the way. Seem like you kinda makin' a real big splash there."

"Yeah, pretty good," Hal said. He chuckled. "Least there I can kinda control things a little bit better'n in the other areas."

"Don't worry," Clifford told him with another reassuring shoulder pat. "You get into trouble an' you need any help, you just let me know, okay?"

"I may take you up on that," Hal said.

That was the only time Hal actually came close to being physically threatened. A couple of other times, he was verbally attacked by some African American in the school who wanted to recite a history of what whites had done to blacks over the centuries, beginning with their abuse of women.

Implicit in that seemed to be some thought that whites were incapable of anything other than the most brutish motives and that it was not possible for a caucasian man to feel anything for a dark-skinned woman other than as an object to be exploited. A couple of times he was cornered by white students who somehow saw it as treasonous for him to be so attracted to a black girl. But aside from that, most of the other students and teachers seemed to feel that what he was doing was harmless enough. Or if they didn't, they kept the thoughts to themselves, which suited him just as well.

Oddly, his most touching confrontation was of a friendly sort with a couple of his own teammates, who didn't think Shawna was good enough for him.

"Man, that girl's poison," Melvin told him one day. "She's a ballbuster, pure an' simple. She's gonna eat you 'live, you ain't careful."

"She's out in la-la land somewheres," Lonnie agreed. He patted Hal on a shoulder. "Shit, man, you can do a lot better'n her, trust me. You like black womens, it ain't no skin off my nose. But you damn sure can do a lot better'n her."

Hal shrugged. He was touched by the genuine concern the two young black men were expressing for him, but he had a more positive view of Shawna. "I kinda see her different," he said.

"That's 'cause you ain't had nobody else before, an' she just happened to be there," Melvin said. "Shit, Hal, you want I can fix you up with somethin'. I know least two sisters dyin' to go out with you, an' you won't have to put up with no bullshit from them."

"Well, maybe later, but not right now," Hal demurred with a shoulder pat to Melvin to convey his appreciation for the offer.

It occurred to Hal as he and the other two went their separate ways that Shawna could at times behave in a manner that a lot of males would find irritating. He hadn't forgotten how she put him down when they were in Eunice's car. A lot of other young men wouldn't put up with something like that, and he wasn't sure they necessarily would be wrong. He wasn't sure what it said for or against him that he did forgive Shawna. He was now seeing another more substantial side to her that some of those young men might appreciate if they had a view of her from that light. Of course, some of them probably wouldn't hang around long enough to determine if such a side existed, so that consideration was largely moot.

Some John Lennon lyrics came to mind: Christ, you know it ain't easy . . . / You know how hard it can be . . . / Way things are goin' . . . / They're gonna crucify me . . . "

It was doubly tough on Shawna. A kind of code has evolved in some black circles that decrees fraternizing in a romantic or sexual way with whites as racial betrayal. Brileyville wasn't as full of that as some other communities, but it wasn't totally lacking in it either. And the full force of what it did have seemed to come swirling down around Shawna.

To her credit, Shawna bore up under it well enough. She was never one to follow some dictum from a crowd, and she tended to harden in that resolve as she grew older. So the fact that someone didn't like something she was doing never in itself particularly bothered her. Mostly she just found herself increasingly annoyed by some people's insistence on belaboring the point.

An example came one day when a black female civics teacher asked her to step into her office for a private consultation.

"Uh, Shawna, I suppose you might say it's none of my business, but I can't help feeling concerned about you and that McDonough boy apparently getting so cozy," the teacher said.

"You're right 'bout the part of it bein' none of your business," Shawna said with a bored shrug. She picked up her books and started for the door.

"Uh, hear me out, please," the teacher said.

"Miz Hammer, you don't like it. Half the people in this school don't like it. Well, y'all don't have to like it," Shawna sighed and reached for the door.

"What I'm trying to say is in times like this, there's really more of a need for black women and black men to be trying to rediscover each other," the teacher said.

Shawna snorted. "Miz Hammer, I'm not tryna discover or rediscover anything right now. It's not like I'm thinkin' 'bout gettin' married or anything. An' when I do, it's gonna be to who I want to do it with, not who y'all wanna tell me to do it with. I know what you're tryna say, I been hearin' it 'til it's up to the gills, an' I'm not gonna change myself 'round just to satisfy any of y'all. So put that in your pipe an' smoke it."

"Uh, Shawna, there's no need for you to get belligerent," Mrs. Hammer appealed.

"Well, there's no need for you to be tryna tell me how to live my life either, so there," Shawna responded and exited.

On another occasion, Shawna was accosted in the hallway by a black girl from the junior class. She recognized the girl as being named Sabrina but otherwise hadn't had any contact with her. "Hah! I notice ain't none your color rubbin' 'way," Sabrina said in a sneering tone.

"I didn't know it was 'pposed to," Shawna said with a bored tone and tried to walk past Sabrina. "If you'll 'scuse me, I got a class I gotta get to . . . "

Sabrina moved around and blocked her path. "Yeah, I bet you thinkin' he gonna marry you an' y'all gonna live in some nice lilywhite suburb somewheres..."

"I wasn't thinkin' anything of the sort," Shawna said as she moved around Sabrina again.

"Yeah, he be all candy'n roses for now just so's he can get 'tween you little pink slit," Sabrina pressed. "But you just wait'll he get a scholarship to some lilywhite college with all kinda white chicks 'round an' see what happen. He be droppin' you like Listerine on bad breath."

"Oh, go 'way, you ignorant bitch," Shawna moaned.

"Who you callin' a ig'orant bitch?" Sabrina screamed. She struck a more menacing pose in front of Shawna this time. "Who you think you are to be talkin' to me like that, little miss prissypants?"

"Somebody gonna knock the shit outta you if you don't get outta my face," Shawna roared back. She was angry and more than willing now to duke it out with this officious interloper.

Just then, a white male teacher emerged from a nearby classroom. "What's goin' on out here?" he barked.

"Uh, nothin' sir," Shawna said. She tossed an angry glance Sabrina's way as a warning.

"Nothin'," Sabrina muttered.

"I'm tryna teach a class, an' I'd 'ppreciate y'all takin' whatever grievance you got somewhere else," the teacher said.

"Yes, sir," Shawna agreed. She headed back up the hallway and noticed that Sabrina took another direction. She didn't mind that so much. She could do without a fight with Sabrina. She just wanted to be left alone.

A little later, she ran into Trina in the school cafeteria. "Girlfriend, I don't know what you done, but Sabrina's madder'n a wet hen," Trina told her. "She was talkin' 'bout how you was callin' her a ig'orant bitch'n all an' how she want a piece of you some kinda bad."

"Well, if she really wants a piece of me, I'm not that hard to find," Shawna said with a bored shrug. She set her books on a table and found a seat.

"She hasslin' you 'bout Hal?" Trina asked solicitously.

Shawna nodded. "That doesn't bother me. I don't care if they like it or not. A lotta things I don't like, but I don't feel duty bound to go puttin' my two cents worth in."

"Well, they kinda look at it from four hundred years of bein' 'sploited by the white man, an' they're kinda tryna get back at the white man in a way," Trina said.

Shawna snorted. "By what? Hasslin' Hal'n I? We weren't even 'round when most of that was goin' on. Least not in the bodies we got now anyways. An' you don't go back a couple centuries to try to justify meddlin' in somebody else's business now."

Trina motioned for calm. "I didn't say they was right. I just said that's how they felt," she clarified. She shook her head. "I 'dore Hal. Actually, I kinda envy you. When I first figured out he had a crush on you, I was kinda jealous."

"I'm sorry," Shawna sighed. She patted her friend on an arm. "I'm not tryna take anything out on you, believe me."

"I understand," Trina said in a comforting tone.

Brileyville, like many schools around the country, had a wooded area nearby and a path for the young people to walk through or hold hands or whatever. If one looked closely enough, a stray used condom here or there provided evidence of another kind of activity that one might stumble onto if one picked the wrong time to take a stroll there. Hal and Shawna now were availing themselves of the path as much as possible, but they weren't yet doing anything that might involve dropping a used condom somewhere. That certainly might come in time, but if and when it did, they both figured on finding a more suitable place for it. Somehow the thought of doing it on the cold ground didn't strike them as very appealing.

"You know how complicated you're makin' my life," Shawna murmured as the two walked along holding hands. Her head rested on Hal's shoulder.

"I been gettin' some static too," Hal said with a shrug.

"Yeah, but you don't have anybody preachin' to you 'bout betrayin' your race or whatnot," Shawna sighed.

"Well, that's not 'pletely true," Hal said. He turned around just enough to brush Shawna's mouth with a kiss. "Couple rednecks from the senior class kinda got on my case other day. They were talkin' 'bout how I'm tryna prove somethin'. I don't think I am. I don't know what I'm 'pposed to be provin' if I am."

Shawna chuckled and wrapped her arms around him.

"Ol' Miz Hammer from our civics class gave me a big lecture on how black women an' black men oughta be reachin' out more to each other today. I dunno why they should reach out more today 'un any other time, but she seems to think they should. She was kinda preachin' to me, an' I told her it was none of her business. I don't think she liked that."

"Well, I guess somethin' like us you gotta figure you're gonna get some flak," Hal said. He kissed the top of Shawna's head. "But you kinda find out who your real friends are, too. Some brothers were hasslin' me, an' Clifford Jenkins came 'long an' let 'em know if they wanted to keep it up, they had two bad dudes they were gonna have to deal with. I don't think they liked the change in the odds too much, so they split."

"Well, only thing I found out like that, I think, is Trina 'mitted she kinda had a crush on you once," Shawna said. She grinned impishly. "I bet you never even noticed."

"I knew one white girl in our class kinda did, but she was so homely I think if she was the only woman in the world, I'd take that vow the Catholic priests an' nuns take."

"Celibacy," Shawna told him in a mock scolding tone. She nuzzled his neck. "I 'clare, Mr. McDonough, for someone that comes from a pedigreed line an' that 'cludes bein' Catholic, you're awfully ignorant."

Hal chuckled appreciatively. "Ernest, on the basketball team, was talkin' to me 'bout the kinky sex things white folks like to do, an' I told him he prob'ly knows more 'bout what white folks do 'un I do. I don't know if that's true 'sackly, but he couldn't possibly know much less. I guess I should know more 'bout bein' Catholic. Mother drags me to that 'piscopal church 'cross town every Sunday, an' they're kinda like Catholics 'cept their rectors are 'llowed to get married an' have sex. It's just not somethin' I ever paid a whole lotta 'ttention to. I figure if I didn't have Mother breathin' down my neck, I wouldn't bother to go to church at all, so I don't really feel any need to go learnin' 'bout their whole process an' whatnot."

"Religion's 'portant to me mostly just in how it 'ffects other people," Shawna agreed with a shrug. She smiled wistfully. "I know it has a lot to do with 'pinions people form an' the kinda lifestyles they set for themselves an' whatnot, but it's not somethin' I really feel a need to be part of. I'm not knockin' it, an' I do believe there's a God, but I don't see how bein' part of some group's gonna bring you closer to Him or Her or It."

"I believe there's a God too, but I'm kinda like you in that regard," Hal said. His arm went around Shawna's shoulders. "Maybe someday I'll feel a need to look for Him or Her or It, an' that'll lead me to some church, but right now I'm not hung up on it." He kissed Shawna's ear. "By the way, what's this I hear 'bout you'n Sabrina Ellis almost dukin' it out in the school hallway?"

Shawna winced. "Somehow I knew that was gonna get back to you'n everybody else 'round." She buried her head in Hal's chest. "She wanted to get nasty, an' I got nasty back an' called her an ignorant bitch, an' then she started makin' noises like she wanted to fight. That's okay by me. I'll give her a knuckle sandwich in a heartbeat if she pushes anything with me. It's kinda like you were with Melvin Peebles last summer. Sometimes you just have to stand your ground."

Hal laughed and kissed her.

About this time, Trina started dating a young black man from one of the county schools named Derek. Derek was almost Hal's exact reverse; he had a history that some might see as white. His father had a degree from Duke and worked as a stock broker with a Richmond based firm that had a Wall Street connection, and his mother had grown up in a mostly white Washington suburb and attended William and Mary College. Derek's father was as anti-city as many, if not most, white people are, and so he didn't hesitate one moment in looking to the county to make his home. So Derek grew up attending mostly white schools and probably would have had some trouble adjusting to a setting such as Hal was now used to.

Derek, of course, had a car. He was a responsible enough young man, and his parents could afford to buy him one, so they did so. It was a rather sporty little model, which contrasted a little with Derek's basic personality. He tended to be quiet and reserved, and he generally dressed rather conservatively.

Hal liked Trina quite well, but he wasn't exactly sure why Derek seemed so smitten with her. It had occurred to him that Trina had nice buttocks, but everything else about her was at best ordinary. And Derek was a fairly nice looking guy. He wasn't a Mr. America or anything like that, but he probably ranked ahead of Trina on their respective looks scales.

"I thought 'bout maybe tryna date a couple the white girls out there," Derek confided when Hal posed the question to him once in private. "But, man, you talk 'bout a hassle. What you gotta go through with their folks is unbelievable. An' then you're gonna have your redneck elements right there in the school practically ready to lynch you on the spot. An' I didn't meet anybody in the school that turned me on 'nuff to make me wanta go through that, like you've done with Shawna, I guess."

"But why Trina?" Hal asked. He gestured reassuringly. "I'm not knockin' it. I love Trina. She's been a great friend to me, an' that 'cludes a time when I was really down. An' I can see how come you might wanta check out the sisters here in town. But you got a lotta pretty foxy ones 'round our school, an' I 'spect guy like you comin' 'round in a nice sporty car'n all 'd kinda draw their interest."

Derek chuckled. "I dunno. Just somethin' 'bout Trina turned me on. I don't know how else to 'splain it. She's funny an' a real trip to be 'round."

Hal nodded. He could see how Trina might be perceived that way. He also had a feeling that whoever wound up with her for a wife might well be getting one terrific lady.

He just hoped for Trina's sake that the guy who wound up with her was smart and sensitive enough to appreciate her.

Hal didn't really remember it, but he and Derek had met once before: the previous summer during the rec league basketball season. Derek reminded Shawna and Trina of that fact once when the four were together on a doubledate.

"They told me to guard this character," he said. He motioned to show that he meant Hal. "So I figured it oughta be easy, him bein' a white boy'n all. Yeah, easy. Whoosh! Next thing I know, he's by me faster'n I can blink."

"Oh, he's pretty fast out there," Shawna said. She glanced affectionately at her boyfriend. "He's kinda fast in some other ways, too."

Hal shrugged. "I think it's kinda like when they talk 'bout altitude 'justment when you're flyin'. You see so many slow white boys, you find one that can move at all, it kinda shocks you so much you can't move."

Derek laughed. "Don't let him kid you. This guy's a player," he told the two girls.

"Yeah, we hear it 'round school a lot," Trina said. She grinned and punched Hal playfully on an arm to let him know she was only kidding.

Hal imagined that word of his new involvement with Shawna had leaked back to his coach, but he didn't know it for sure until Wimbush called him aside after practice one afternoon. "Why do you insist on continually complicating my life?" the coach moaned.

That caught Hal completely by surprise.

"What have I done?" he asked in a hesitating tone. "I haven't broken up anything recently, an' I thought I been playin' some pretty good basketball."

"You have. That's not what I'm talking about," Wimbush said. He took a deep breath. "I keep getting these reports, rumors, whathaveyou, on you and Shawna Hanson."

"We're good friends. So what?" Hal reasoned.

"From what I've been hearing, your relationship has

progressed well beyond good friends, as you call it," Wimbush said probingly.

Hal shrugged. "Maybe a little bit, but it's not like we're havin' sex in the hallways or anything. In fact, I'm sorry to disappoint you, but so far we haven't had sex anywhere. Not that I wouldn't like to, but . . ."

"Well, holding hands and exhibiting affectionate behavior can be almost as damaging in some people's eyes," Wimbush said. He patted Hal on a shoulder. "This puts me in an awkward position. You know, Shawna's father and I are close friends."

"Yeah, I was 'ware of that," Hal said.

"I feel kinda awkward being privy to something like this and knowing he isn't," Wimbush said. He patted Hal again on the shoulder. "Hal, what you and Shawna do in your spare time is your own business. I'm not trying to make it mine. And if the two of you have certain feelings for one another, well, I can live with that, too. A good friend of mine from my college days is now married to a white woman, so I understand that passions and love do cross color lines. But I think to avoid these awkward situations, you should tell your respective parents so that people like yours truly don't get caught in the middle."

"We plan to," Hal said. His lips pursed thoughtfully. "It's just not easy workin' up to it. I know my mother's gonna flip her lid, an' Shawna's mother won't take it much better."

"I know Marian Hanson fairly well, and I got a pretty good read on your mother the one time I talked to her, so I understand where you're coming from," Wimbush conceded. "Even so, they have to know. You may have to deal with it."

"There's no may 'bout it. We will," Hal murmured.

"Yes, I'm sure it'll be hard, but it has to be done," Wimbush said. He clasped both of Hal's shoulders. "You'll always have a special place in my heart, and I think the world of Shawna, and I am willing to go to bat for you, but not behind anybody's back."

Hal nodded. He accepted Wimbush's point as valid.

28

Somehow through all that was happening in his life at this juncture, Hal also found time to play basketball. He hadn't broken his school scoring record again as of yet, but he was for the most part performing quite well, providing points, assists, steals and even a fair number of rebounds. He got his first triple double in an intersectional game against a team from Richmond, which the Falcons won, and on another occasion just barely missed a quadruple with nine steals and eight rebounds to go along with twenty-six points and fourteen assists.

The triple double may have been the school's first ever. The first statistics of that sort weren't compiled until the early seventies, so no one knew for sure who might have done what before then. It was generally agreed, however, that Hal might very well turn out to be the best player the school ever had from any era and probably would end up with records that might never be broken before he was through.

Brileyville had ended the season on a high note, with four straight victories, including two away games. That preserved Wimbush's personal string of no losing seasons, but it did little to help the team's final position in the standings. So when district tournament time came around, Brileyville would be seeded fifth in an eight team field.

One advantage in that was that the first round opponent was Dunston, which finished fourth. A disadvantage was in the tournament being played on Dunston's home floor. The two teams had played twice previously, with Dunston the victor both times. But that was in the BH (before Hal) period, so the Falcons' mood going into this meeting was more upbeat.

"Go out and play like you're capable of playing, and I think you can beat this team on this floor or any other," Wimbush told his charges.

Hal had what for him was a fairly average good night: Twenty-eight points, nine assists, a half-dozen steals and seven rebounds. He even blocked one shot as Brileyville won by twelve.

The white Dunston coach was gracious in defeat. "I think that McDonough kid's definitely pushin' your team to a whole 'nother level," he remarked to Wimbush after it was over.

"Long's I can keep him healthy, I think you're right," Wimbush said. He glanced affectionately over to where Hal and the other team members were celebrating their triumph. "He played football last fall and broke his leg. It took a while before we got him back up to speed."

"Well, from where I'm standing, maybe the leg mended just one game too soon," the Dunston coach said. He flashed a smile. Then he glanced over and noticed a couple of sportswriters moving in to talk to Hal. "You know, with a kid like that, you're going to find sportswriters and college recruiters around your school a lot. I hope you're emotionally up to dealing with that."

"If he helps me win as many games as I think he might,

I'll make myself ready for just about anything," Wimbush replied.

Oddly, one of the people in the stands for the game was Wilbur Stallings. Stallings still coached the junior high, even though much of the Brileyville community was starting to take a more critical look at him for not playing Hal McDonough when he had gone to school there.

Hal sincerely tried to forgive and forget, but when he saw Stallings in tight lipped silence leaving the Dunston gym, a demon took hold and moved him to rub something in. So he circled around a crowd and cut Stallings's path off. "How ya doin', Coach Stallings?" he greeted the junior high coach.

"Hello, McDonough. Nice game," Stallings said tersely and eased around Hal and continued towards the exit.

Hal didn't really want to let Stallings off the hook quite so easily, but he wasn't prepared while still in uniform to venture out into the chilly night air either. So he started back towards his own locker room.

Ernest had noticed what went on and confronted him. "You tryna rub somethin' in on ol' Stallings 'cause he didn't play you when you was at the junior high?" the taller young man asked.

Hal shrugged. "Not really." He paused and noticed Ernest's dubious look and amended his response. "Maybe a little bit. I can't help makin' him wanta think 'bout it in case he 'cides to cut somebody else that might be good 'nuff to play outta a chance to be on the team."

Ernest draped an arm over his shoulder. "I 'spect he's awready been gettin' a whole lotta heat on 'ccount of him not playin' you when you was over there, an' take it to the bank, he's gonna be catchin' a hun'ert times that much—a thousand times maybe—'fore it's all said and done. Next year, when you on the all-state team an' maybe all-'merican, it's gonna come back on him. An' then you sign with one of the top programs, that'll be like a whole 'nother slap in the face. An' then maybe you make the college all-'merican team an' get drafted by the pros, an' then maybe you make the all-NBA team. An' then fifteen years, twenty years down the road, folks makin' a big deal outta you comin' back to speak to the local Jaycees' banquet or the Chamber of Commerce or whatever, an' he gotta sit in there an' listen to you an' still havin' folks mindin' him how he 'fused to play you. You got the aces, my man. Don't blow it by tryna get back at him. He ain't worth it."

Hal nodded acquiescently. He knew deep down that Ernest was right.

The following night, the Falcons beat Piney Grove by fifteen points and gained the championship finale and an automatic berth in the regional tournament. That was because Hempstone, their title game opponent, had already gained one of the district's two allotted slots by winning the regular season championship. So really, all the Brileyville players had to do was show up for the game.

No one among the Falcons was thinking that way, of course.

"We lost to this team twice this year, but we've been playing well enough of late so I think we can beat 'em now," Wimbush told the team just before the game. "It's true, we've got a regional berth locked up. We're going to get a low seeding in the regional whether we win or lose tonight. Hempstone will be seeded higher. They deserve it because they had a better season. I'm not worried about the seeding. I'm concerned about us and our sense of pride and commitment. I personally don't want to backdoor into anything. I much prefer us proving on the court that we deserve that regional berth. So go out and give it your best shot."

The players all felt the same way. That was especially true for Hal, who still smarted from by far his worst performance of the season against that same Hempstone team. The one comforting thought he took away from that humiliating experience was that no Hempstone player stopped him or seemed capable of doing so. He just performed below par. He wanted revenge.

He got the latter in spades. Again he set a school record, this time hitting for thirty-seven points. That included seven of nine shots from the three point range. He complemented that sparkling display with thirteen assists and eleven rebounds for a triple-double. He had seven steals to go along with all that, which had the stat guys whistling over how close he had come to the rare quad.

By the time it was over, Brileyville had a fifteen point win. The margin could well have been in the twenties if Wimbush hadn't pulled the starters with almost five minutes to play.

The Hempstone coach was visibly subdued as he approached Hal after it was all over. "Everything I heard about you indicated you couldn't possibly be as bad as the night we played y'all up at your place," the coach said. "But how come you had to pick tonight to make a believer outta me?"

Hal flashed a grin. "Y'all just got me pissed off," he replied. He shook his head and shrugged. "I dunno. I was just in the zone tonight. When we played y'all, it was like the goal had a lid on it. Tonight, it seemed more like a suction cup."

The Hempstone coach nodded and patted him on a shoulder. "Well, maybe we'll get to play each other again in the regionals," he said.

"Yeah, I wouldn't mind that," Hal said. He chuckled. "With the seedin' format, that'd have to be in the semifinals or finals. Be kinda nice both teams from this district got that far."

"Well, see ya in Lawrenceville," the Hempstone coach said.

Lawrenceville was the home of St. Paul's College, where the regionals were to be played. Hempstone wound up being knocked out in the first round by a low seed from the Richmond area. Brileyville, with Hal continuing to put up all-star numbers, knocked off a team from near Williamsburg which set up a rematch with Winslow.

"Well, I see you predicted accurately," Phil Laughinhouse remarked to Hal as their paths crossed as the two teams were entering the gym for the game.

"Huh?" Hal responded in confusion.

"About us meeting again in the regionals," Laughinhouse reminded him. "You did say we might do that."

Hal vaguely remembered and chuckled. "I was just talkin' then. I wasn't necessarily 'spectin' it," he said.

Laughinhouse's eyes rolled reminiscently. "At the time, your team had a losing record. When I look back on that now, I almost get the feeling you might have known something."

"Well, I didn't know y'all were gonna get here, if that's what you mean," Hal said with a grin.

Laughinhouse's head shook in amusement.

"I kinda figured it, though," Hal went on. "I've heard 'nuff 'bout the history of that program since you've had it, an' I knew y'all were in the runnin' for your district championship. An' I figured we had to start playin' better, too. Shoo, we couldn't do much worse."

Laughinhouse chuckled and patted Hal on a shoulder. Just then, Wimbush approached. "Well, Coach Laughinhouse, you still trying to lure my player away from me?" the Brileyville coach remarked.

"I'd have to talk with someone with the Virginia High School League about changing the rules," Laughinhouse said with a grin. He patted Wimbush on a shoulder. "How are you, Jerome?"

"I'll feel much better if we beat you guys again, but overall, still not bad," Wimbush said.

"I was recalling young McDonough's remark about our two teams meeting in the regionals," Laughinhouse confided to Wimbush. "At that time, it probably would have seemed pretty far-fetched. I was asking him if he was clairvoyant or something."

"Well, we've been playing better basketball of late,"

Wimbush said. He patted Hal on a shoulder. "I won't deny this young man's had a lot to do with it."

"Unfortunately, I'm going to be seeing him for the next two years," Laughinhouse said. He flashed a grin and patted Wimbush on a shoulder. "Unless I can talk to the High School League officials and get those rules changed. I think I'll find out what neighborhood in your town he's in and see if I can extend my jurisdiction to exactly that point."

Hal winced. "I don't think I wanta be ridin' the bus that far."

The two coaches laughed.

"Well, Phil, until you get that jurisdiction extended, he's mine," Wimbush said. He clasped Hal's shoulders for emphasis. "And I've got to get him suited up so we can play a basketball game."

This night turned out to be mostly a Laughinhouse coaching tour de force. He set up a special defense Wimbush had never seen before. It didn't stop Hal necessarily; he did wind up with a game high of twenty-three points. But the passing lanes were cut off so that he couldn't create scoring opportunities for his teammates, and the game was slowed down just enough so that he couldn't ignite a now rather potent Brileyville fast break for easy layups. The Winslow guards did a good enough job of controlling the ball, too, so that he couldn't come up with a lot of steals.

It was a Winslow-controlled tempo. Even so, the game was close throughout, with a dozen lead changes over the thirty-two minutes. Near the end, in fact, with his team up by a point, Hal missed a jumper that would have virtually nailed down victory. Winslow came down and scored, and Ernest turned the ball over on a traveling call on the Falcons' next possession. A couple of desperation fouls to try to get the ball back fizzled, and Winslow wound up with a four point victory.

Hal was more angry with himself than disappointed when the final horn sounded. He kept thinking about that jump shot—for him normally very makable—that he missed with the game on the line in the last minute.

"We coulda beat 'em," Ernest muttered after it was all over and players from the two teams had congratulated each other on a tough game.

"We had it," Hal grunted. "If I wouldn'ta missed that jumper when we were up a point, we woulda won it."

"Hey, man, you gonna miss some shots, an' sometimes you gonna miss 'em when it hurt, but that don't mean you wanna stop shootin'," Ernest consoled him. He draped a long arm over Hal's shoulders. "The team get in clutch situations, you gonna be the one everybody gonna look to to take the shot. That's 'cause they know you the one got the best chance of makin' it."

That wasn't necessarily much consolation to Hal in that moment, but he supposed it was true.

Wimbush gathered his charges together after they all were in the locker room. "I don't want anyone walking out of here with heads down," he told the team. "We had a pretty good run, a lot better than anyone expected us to have. We lost tonight, but don't forget it was to a team that won its district tournament and had a better record. And it was played at their tempo, and we still came damned close to winning. So when you walk out of here, do so with pride. You earned it."

Ernest laid his hands on Hal's shoulders and nudged the white boy to the center of the floor. "I think we owe a big cheer to this boy," he told his teammates. "He come in an' really picked us up when we was just 'bout dead'n buried."

A loud cheer for Hal spontaneously erupted.

"Okay, take your showers and let's get on the bus and go home," Wimbush said.

As Hal was heading back to the bus, he found Laughinhouse waiting for him. "Well, y'all got us tonight," he conceded to the Winslow coach.

"By the skin of our teeth," Laughinhouse said with a shrug. He patted Hal on a shoulder. "I figured I wouldn't stop you completely, but I could keep you from singlehandedly dominating the game. I accomplished that much anyway."

"Yeah, you did," Hal admitted. His lips pursed thoughtfully. "Course that jump shot I missed with us up by a point coulda nailed it for us."

"I was holding my breath on that one," Laughinhouse said. He flashed a grin. "I think any time we're playing you guys and the ball's in your hands, I'm going to be holding my breath."

"Well, I hope next time I'm able to make you eat it," Hal said.

"I'm almost afraid that might happen," Laughinghouse said through a grimace.

The Brileyville team members got on the bus and headed home. The mood was now fairly upbeat. Losing never feels good, but this seemed to be a night that augured better days ahead for the Brileyville program.

"I seen Laughinhouse talkin' trash to you as we was comin' out," Melvin Peebles remarked to Hal.

Hal chuckled. "He's a character. I like talkin' to him."

"I understand he's always that way with star players from other teams," Ernest said. He patted Hal on a shoulder. "But I think it's just kind of a professional courtesy thing with him. His preference definitely seem to be for girls."

Hal broke into laughter. "Well, I'm sure glad to hear that, Ernest," he replied.

29

With basketball behind him until practice started in November, Hal focused on track. The baseball coach had shown some interest in him because of his obvious athletic ability, but he felt that it would take him too long to learn that sport. With track, it was just a question of whether he could run or not, and that he knew he could do well. So all he had to worry about now was conditioning, timing, and technique.

He found track enjoyable more as a sociological experience than a sport. His specialty turned out to be the short sprints—one hundred and two hundred—which in recent years have seemed to become almost completely black owned. He heard more than a few tasteless, though mostly harmless, jokes about his crossing the stereotypical racial line.

One stereotype that never ceased to intrigue him was a supposed affinity between blacks and watermelon. Where that one could possibly have come from totally mystified him. No doubt some blacks do like and eat watermelon, but he didn't think they did so in any greater ratio than whites. He liked watermelon well enough himself, but he was reasonably sure it had nothing to do with how fast he was.

Through all this, he continued to juggle time with Shawna. The two still hadn't told their respective parents, and they were still double-dating on the sly with Trina and Derek whenever possible. That arrangement was at times limiting and awkward, and no doubt Trina and Derek would have appreciated some time alone, too. But it was the best they could manage for the time being.

Hal decided that he had to get a car. He had turned sixteen, and he was one of the few boys in his school who didn't at least have access to a vehicle. Fortunately, the school had a driver's education program that enabled him to get his operator's permit, so it became a relatively simple matter of finding one in a price range that could accommodate him.

Simple in theory.

A thousand dollars to a lot of people is not a lot of money, but to Hal it seemed like a fortune beyond his wildest dreams. And that price range was about the lowest the classified ads seemed to be offering. He found himself cracking frustrated jokes over lines such as *a steal at three thousand* that caught his attention. Yeah, a steal all right. The only way he could get something like that was by stealing it.

Then he found out through the basketball team grapevine that Wimbush was thinking about trading in his second car, a '79 Chevette, for a newer model with an automatic transmission for his wife. Hal had ridden in the Chevette a few times when Wimbush was transporting him to the county rec league and back. The Wimbushes had a newer model with automatic transmission, but Mrs. Wimbush often commandeered it because the Chevette was a stick shift and she preferred an automatic. Hal had learned to drive on a stick, so that part was no problem for him.

"I hear you're thinkin' 'bout gettin' rid of the ol'

Chevette," he accosted Wimbush at school.

"Walls around here must really have ears," Wimbush said. "What? You know somebody that wants to buy it?"

"Me," Hal answered. "Moi. I could use a car for carryin' Mother to the grocery store an' church, an' also it would help after games an' whatnot so I don't always have to be bummin' a ride with somebody."

"Shawna Hanson wouldn't have anything to do with your sudden urge to acquire your own transportation, would she?" Wimbush probed with a smile.

Hal shrugged. "Well, maybe a little bit."

Wimbush eyed him critically. "What about your parents? Have you told them yet?"

Hal gestured in embarrassment. "We're workin' 'round to it. We both been kinda tied up lately, me 'specially with basketball an' now track."

"Well, with track, you're not likely to get your leg broken, and even if you did, it should be healed in plenty of time for basketball season," Wimbush said with a sigh.

"Mother really is my big 'cern," Hal pressed his case. "You ever stop to 'sider how much she pays out in cabfare goin' to church an' back on Sundays an' to the grocery store an' back."

"Well, she could probably save some of the church money by going to the Episcopal church in town instead of the one across town, but I suppose you're right," Wimbush conceded.

"Well, yeah, I'd pick the one in town it was up to me," Hal said. He flashed a grin. "Really, if it was up to me, I wouldn't go to church at all, but it's not up to me. You met my mother. You know what a hardcase she can be."

Wimbush nodded appreciatively. "I also know she won't like it when she finds out about you and Shawna, just as I know Shawna's parents won't like learning that their daughter has crossed the racial line. I don't want to find myself suddenly being cast as the heavy in all this."

"Well, we've awready done it, an' we'll fight the battle

ourselves when the time comes," Hal reasoned. He eyed Wimbush appealingly. "You can always say you didn't know. I'm not gonna say anything different. Neither is Shawna. You don't have to be brought into it at all."

Wimbush was basically sympathetic to Hal's plea anyway, so he finally relented. The two worked out a deal under which Hal paid three hundred dollars. Half of that he paid up front; the remainder would come in weekly twenty-five dollar installments. Hal actually could have paid it all at once, but he wanted some of the money he had saved up to take care of the uninsured motorist's fee. His mother worked for an insurance company and no doubt could have arranged something for him, but he didn't want her involved in any way with the car's ownership. He could imagine her at some point—if she was angry with him over something—using that leverage to wrest the car away from him. She couldn't or wouldn't drive it herself, but she could gain some satisfaction by keeping it out of his hands.

That would be especially true when she found out about him and Shawna. He knew, and so did Shawna, that they could not keep their relationship a secret from their parents forever. Nor were they thinking of trying to. Both intended to tell their respective parents about how they felt and what their status had graduated to. It was just a matter of finding the right time for doing so.

Hal's mother was delighted that he had the car and especially that no apparent financial onus for it fell on her. "It will certainly make going to church and to the grocery store a lot easier," she mused.

"I was thinkin' that when I bought it," Hal agreed. "I got lucky. I found out Coach Wimbush was plannin' to get rid of it, an' I got him down to three hun'ret dollars. He was prob'ly lookin' to get seven, eight hun'ret on a trade-in."

"I must say, for a colored man he does seem to have a lot more class than most," Kathleen McDonough said with a shrug. She lit a cigarette. "I hate to admit it, but I think I like him a little better than I did that football coach. What was his name?"

"Coach Moore," Hal volunteered.

"Yes," Kathleen McDonough said. She drew on her cigarette. "That one seems so crude."

Hal laughed. "He is kinda crude, but I think that's just part of what bein' him's all about."

"Yes, you young people today are always all about something or other," Kathleen McDonough sighed.

Hal finally got around to showing the car to his own girlfriend. "Well, how you like it?" he asked her.

Shawna shrugged. "I would certainly think a buddin' young athletic superstar oughta have somethin' sportier'n this to drive 'round town in," she joked.

Hal laughed. "When I start drawin' a superstar's salary, I will," he promised her.

Shawna didn't really object to the car. And she appreciated the solitude it afforded her and her boyfriend. Hal drove her to a secluded area behind the city park.

"It's kinda nice bein' 'lone with you like this," Shawna murmured as they snuggled together in the parked car.

"I 'gree," Hal said. He grinned and kissed Shawna. "I 'spect Trina'n Derek prob'ly glad to have some time 'lone without us taggin' 'long, too."

"I think I'm glad you were able to talk Wimbush into sellin' you this thing so cheap," Shawna said. She nuzzled Hal's shoulder. "Even if it is kinda ugly."

"It runs good, an' to me that makes it beautiful," Hal reasoned. He kissed Shawna again.

Shawna chuckled. "Well, like they say, it's in the beholder's eye." She returned Hal's kiss. "I'll bet any other school in the country, if I fell in love with the school's star basketball player, he'd be black. How come you ain't black?"

Hal's eyes drifted skyward. "You're gonna have to ask somebody up there 'bout that one," he replied.

30

Some years back, Kathleen McDonough embraced the Episcopalian faith for herself and her son. She had been reared in Catholicism, but now she saw that religion as somehow having deserted her. How much of her choice was driven by faith in a higher being is open to speculation and debate. She probably didn't even really know herself. Certainly snob appeal played a part. At one juncture, when she rubbed shoulders with the Greenwich Village crowd, it wouldn't have. But now a spiritual reversion had set in, and image and status again held great meaning for her. They probably were lost to her personally in this lifetime anyway, but she was determined to immerse her son in them as much as possible.

So every Sunday, as far back as Hal could remember, he and his mother got into a taxi and drove across town to a so-called better neighborhood to attend the Episcopal church there. As Hal got older, he felt a certain embarrassment in being subjected to this. In Brileyville, only the elderly and infirm rode in taxis. It wasn't like New York, where taxis are a way of life for many people.

For a long time, Hal and his mother were at best curiousities, and probably in expressed asides, objects of pity for most of the church's rather well-to-do parishioners. They weren't excluded; they were welcomed to attend services, and Hal went to the Sunday School regularly. But they weren't a part of anything either. Hal suspected that even the rector, who at least made a show of being friendly to them after each service, wouldn't have been unhappy to see this strange mother-son duo pick another place to worship.

A few times Kathleen McDonough said she wanted to expose her son to another class of young people, meaning caucasians. But over time Hal felt even less welcomed by, and less a part of, that group than the blacks in his public school. That was even true in the early days, when he was most isolated and vulnerable and seemingly without anyone to whom he could turn. It definitely was true now that he was an established athletic star and a bright future seemed to loom. He was accepted by his public school peers now, and he had a girl he loved and who loved him. He felt nothing in common with the young whites at his mother's church. To him, they all seemed like nothing more than a bunch of spoiled brats full of themselves because they could attend private schools instead of some institution like Brileyville.

More recently, their mood towards him had begun to change. Athletic celebrity has a way of doing that to groups. Some of the young people who before had scarcely noted his existence were now trying to start conversations with him. He was polite, but he was usually very quick to excuse himself. He had other matters more important to worry about.

The most memorable part of that segment of his young life was Jennie Lee Hudson. Jennie Lee was a pretty blonde on whom years earlier he had a slight crush. She showed nothing close to signs of requiting that passion, so it eventually faded, and over time he had come to view her as empty-headed and shallow and not worthy of his concern. He had almost reached the point of barely noting her existence when he started making headlines in the Gazette-Courier and getting his name mentioned prominently on the area television and radio stations. Now suddenly she was discovering him. She was smiling at him now and trying to initiate conversation and looking at him in a way that seemed to signal possibilities if he wanted to pursue them.

He didn't. He couldn't say for sure that someday he wouldn't leave Shawna for another young woman, but it definitely would not be Jennie Lee.

His mother knew nothing of what was going through his brain at this time. That was merciful in one sense, but in another it brought out an annoying tendency in her. She learned by way of the church grapevine that Jennie Lee was rather smitten with her son and so tried to play matchmaker. Since she was so ill-suited for the role, Hal under most circumstances would have found it comical. But in this instance, since her efforts were directed at him, he was more frustrated than anything else.

"Since you have a car now, Dear, you really should start asking Jennie Lee out," Kathleen McDonough recommended on one occasion as her son was driving her home from Sunday morning services.

"What?" Hal responded. This one caught him off guard.

"Jennie Lee. You know she's attracted to you," his mother said.

"Mother, Jennie Lee is an airhead," Hal groaned. "'Sides, 'til I started gettin' my name in the paper an' on television, she didn't even know I 'sisted."

"I grant you, she's not the brightest girl in the world, and perhaps there is a certain hypocrisy in her sudden mood change," Kathleen McDonough said. She lit a cigarette from his dashboard lighter, which did still work.

"I'd say a whole lotta hypocrisy," Hal said with a frustrated gesture.

"Harold, hypocrisy is a fact of life, just like sex and all those other things you young people seem to be so fascinated by," his mother said. "When you're down, those people don't want anything to do with you. When you gain the sort of area celebrity you seem to enjoy, then they open up more to you. I suppose it's unfair as some might see it, but that's the way of the world. You should learn to use that to your advantage."

Hal heaved a sigh. "Mother, if I figured that was the only way I was gonna get ahead, maybe I would play on somebody like Jennie Lee, but I don't see where my options are that limited right now. Way things look, I stand to get a scholarship to a pretty good school an' all. So I don't need to hang out with a bunch of snotty preppies."

"Harold, Dear, those young people can help open a lot of doors to you socially," his mother rebutted. "And face it, you can stand some more polish. You make good grades, and you seem to be intelligent enough, but you haven't even begun to learn how to speak properly or to understand what people in the better circles view as important or any of those things."

"Mother, if it'll make you happy, maybe sometime I'll ask Jennie Lee out, but now now," Hal sighed. "I still have school, an' I'm on the track team an' all. Right now I just don't have time for that."

"Well, I suppose I can accept that for now," Kathleen McDonough sighed.

Shawna chuckled the following day when Hal told her of his conversation with his mother.

"I'd figure bein' from Boston'n all, she'd pick somebody with a better name 'un Jennie Lee," she said.

Hal flashed a grin. "I think Mother's reachin' right now. Back in Boston, she'd prob'ly look on somebody like Jennie Lee an' that bunch at church as a bunch of rubes. But here she figures it's the best she's gonna get."

"Well, I know what we got may not last forever,"

Shawna said with a shrug. She kissed Hal. "But I do hope if you ever 'cide to dump me, it won't be for somebody with a name like Jennie Lee."

Hal laughed and returned the kiss. "Well, it won't be that Jennie Lee anyway," he assured her.

31

From time to time, Shawna and Hal speculated on when and how news of their involvement might get back to their respective parents before they had a chance to break it themselves. It was something that they hoped wouldn't happen, but every day they put it off increased the likelihood that it would. Generally agreed between them was that if such happened, it would come from a black source. That was because Shawna had taken far the worse of it in abuse from students and teachers of her pigmentation and her parents tended to be more socially active than Hal's mother.

Oddly enough, the revelation finally came from a source to which neither of the two young people had given any thought. A mousy, bookish, not very pretty white girl named Lucille had been in their class since the early grades. Lucille had more than hinted at a crush on Hal back in a time when Shawna didn't seem to know or care if he was alive. Hal appreciated that, but nothing about Lucille excited him enough to want her in any part of his life, so her dreams of a romantic involvement were never realized.

Lucille didn't see it as bitterness that drove her to tell her mother about what was going on between Hal and Shawna. She probably rationalized it as performing a public service. Besides, the thought didn't strike her that her mother would tell anyone else. She knew that her mother worked for the same insurance company as Kathleen McDonough, but it never occurred to her that adults actually talked to one another. Besides, she had heard her mother cracking jokes about Hal's mother. Even the white people who knew Kathleen McDonough considered her out of place in that setting. So it was probably a good private joke around the office about how her son was snuggling up to a black girl, with her knowing nothing about it.

This wasn't something Hal and Shawna would find out about until much later, and by the time they did it didn't really matter. All that did really matter was that Lucille's mother told Kathleen McDonough and no doubt embellished the story to the point that one might almost think Hal and Shawna had been having sex on the cafeteria tables in the middle of the day.

Needless to say, Kathleen McDonough was in an almost murderous fury when she got on the city bus to go home that evening.

She had to wait a while to get at her son. Hal had a track meet at Dunston High, a good hour's drive to the south. But she knew the last name of Shawna's parents and how to check the phone book for their number. She called them to let them know what a trollop and seductress their daughter really was.

Marian Hanson didn't like hearing Shawna described in that manner, but she was no less furious with her daughter than with Hal. After a time, the two mothers calmed down enough to agree that both young people were at fault and time had come to nip this relationship in the bud once and for all.

Shawna could sense her mother's moods, so she had a

feeling something was amiss the second she walked through the door and said 'hi, mama.'

She started to head upstairs and was quickly halted by her mother. "Hold on, young lady," Marian Hanson barked.

Shawna turned and set her books down. She had a feeling that her mother had learned about Hal and her.

"What's this I hear about you and that McDonough boy hanging over each other in school like two dogs in heat? And dating on the sly, too?" Marian Hanson asked.

Shawna shrugged. Well, at least she didn't have to worry about how to go about breaking the news any more. "Yeah, we been out together a few times," she finally said. "Reason I didn't say anything was 'cause I knew you'd react like you're doin' now. I don't like sneakin' 'round on you, but Hal and I like bein' together, an' we didn't want to have to go through a hassle."

"It's more than a hassle you can expect from me," her mother shot back.

"Mama, Hal'n I haven't been doin' anything wrong," Shawna protested. "We haven't had sex or anything like that. What's the big deal?"

"The big deal is you're a young African American woman in a southern city, he's a white boy in that same southern city, and the races don't mix very well that way," Marian Hanson said sententiously.

"Mama, we're not thinkin' 'bout gettin' married or anything," Shawna protested. "An' it's not like we're plottin' some big racial mixin' or anything like that. We're just two people that happen to like each other."

"No, I'm sure you have sense enough not to be thinking of marriage right now," Marian Hanson sighed. She shook her head. "I know you're infatuated with Hal because he's a big sports star now, and being a normal young man, he's going to be looking for female companionship, but it's wrong..."

"Mama, it's not wrong," Shawna interjected. "Maybe it's somethin' a lotta people don't understand or wanna 'ccept, but it's not wrong. Aunt Eunice was married to a white man once, and you didn't seem to think that was wrong . . ."

"Yes, and look what happened to that marriage, too," Marian Hanson reminded.

"Mama, she's 'vorced from a black guy, too," Shawna replied. "What happened to both her marriages is not a question of race. She's told me that dozens of times . . ."

"I think one of your problems is you've spent too much time around your Aunt Eunice," Marian Hanson sighed.

"Not that it matters now, but may I ask how you found out 'bout Hal an' I?" Shawna inquired.

"Hal and me. You're picking up his bad grammar even," Marian Hanson groaned. She gestured in frustration. "If you must know, I got a call from Hal's mother before you came home this evening. She seems to think you might have led her son on . . ."

"Nobody led anybody on, Mama," Shawna sighed. "It just happened. People get 'ttracted to each other. If you never met Daddy, you sayin' you couldn't possibly have been 'ttracted to a white man?"

Marian Hanson scratched herself on the head. "I never thought about it quite in that light, but I suppose anything's possible," she murmured. She heaved a sigh. "I'm sure what you were doing isn't as bad as Hal's mother made it sound or whoever told it to her made it sound."

"I don't think I'd wanna be in Hal's shoes when he gets home tonight," Shawna said.

Her mother nodded understandingly. By now, her anger was starting to ebb slightly.

Hal, of course, had no way of knowing what was going on. He was in the process of winning both his sprints and anchoring a first and second in two relays. It had been a good day for him up to that point.

He didn't get home until eleven that night. The track meet started late and didn't end until after nine, and then he had the long bus ride back to where he left his car. When he came in the door, he was thoroughly exhausted and ready to collapse on his bed.

He was stunned to see his mother still up. It was a week night, and normally she was in bed by no later than nine on those.

"Uh, Mother, what're you doin' up?" he asked her in a confused tone.

"Are you trying to make me the laughingstock of this entire city, hanging all over that Nubian wench at school like you're a couple of farm animals in heat?" Kathleen McDonough screamed at him.

Uh, oh. This was the last thing Hal needed, and the timing couldn't possibly have been worse. "Uh, Mother, I don't know what you've heard, but I can tell you there's nothin' like that 'volved if you're talkin' 'bout Shawna an' I," he responded weakly.

"About Shawna and me. You're even picking up that girl's bad grammar," Kathleen McDonough snapped. She lit a cigarette from one she had just smoked down to the filter; Hal noticed that her hands were shaking badly. "Who in hell else do you think I'd be talking about? We're not in a Wagnerian opera."

Hal shrugged. "We like each other. I'm not gonna try'n tell you we haven't touched or anything ever, but we damned sure haven't been hangin' all over each other like somebody's evidently been leadin' you to believe." His mouth felt dry and craved some water, and he resented the fact that his mother was in the path of his getting some. "We've dated a couple times with some friends of ours, but there's nothin' bad in that. And in case you're wonderin', we haven't had sex."

"You can justify it in your own mind all you want, but that makes no difference," Kathleen McDonough said through clenched lips. "I absolutely forbid you to associate with that girl ever again."

'Forbid' struck a wrong chord in Hal. "Mother, I know you're upset, but there's no way you're gonna forbid me from 'ssociatin' with her," he responded in a voice calmer than what he was feeling.

"I'm still your mother, young man," Kathleen McDonough reminded. She drew on her cigarette. "My God, Harold, listen to yourself. You slur your words like something out of the gutter. That's what comes of association with those kinds of people."

Now Hal was starting to feel real anger. "For what it's worth, Mother, Shawna prob'ly talks better'n I do . . ."

"I don't doubt it," his mother cut him off. "And for that reason, I'm taking you out of that school at the end of this term and enrolling you in that private school, as I should have done last summer when I had the chance."

"No way," Hal shot back angrily. His hands raised defensively; he didn't really want to talk belligerently to his mother, but he couldn't see that she was leaving him any choice. "Mother, I don't mean to sound disrespectful, but you're goin' 'way over the edge on this one. I'm gonna stay at Brileyville, an' I'm gonna keep seein' Shawna for however long she's willin', an' you're not gonna stop it . . ."

"Oh, no? Well, if nothing else, I'll turn this matter over to the court system and see if I can have you put in a home somewhere until you turn eighteen," Kathleen McDonough responded tartly. "You may be a big sports star and all that, but I still have jurisdiction over you until then."

"You have legal jurisdiction, yeah, but that doesn't mean I'm gonna let you tell me who my friends are gonna be an' not gonna be an' who I can date an' not date," Hal rejoined. "I'm gonna keep seein' Shawna, whether you like it or not. You're bein' ridiculous, an' if you try somethin' like that, you're really gonna find yourself lookin' like a fool." He took a deep breath. "An' as for Jennie Lee, she's an airhead snob, an' you might as well stop pushin' me to ask her out 'cause I don't wanta give her the time of day."

The last part came out as a bonus.

"Is that your final word?" Kathleen McDonough asked gelidly, between puffs on her cigarette.

"I guess so," Hal said with a shrug. "I'd like for us to try'n be reasonable 'bout it, but you seem hellbent on not lettin' that happen."

"Well, if it's your final word, I suppose you won't mind looking for other sleeping accommodations tonight," Kathleen McDonough said emotionlessly.

"You're bootin' me out?" Hal clarified.

"As long as you persist in this insolence, you're not welcome in this apartment," Kathleen McDonough confirmed.

"I guess it's okay if I get some clothes, isn't it?" Hal inquired with a shrug. He didn't know how he felt about this new turn. He was already numb from fatigue, so he probably wouldn't be able to put it in perspective until he finally got some rest.

"Yes, get your clothes and get out," Kathleen McDonough grunted.

So Hal shrugged and headed to what had been his room to pack up some belongings.

32

As difficult as his mother often was to deal with, she did represent home, an identifiable place to return to at day's end, for Hal. The timing of the confrontation may have been bad, but it did have one positive note in that it caught Hal when he was too tired to panic or get hysterical. Not that he probably would have anyway; he was not given to panic or hysteria in crucial situations. But he might have worried more over what his next step would be. This way, he just curled up in his own car and went to sleep.

He slept fitfully at best and in snatches. Finally, as the morning light filtered through the car's front window, he decided to head on to school. He knew Wimbush always got in early, so he waited for the coach outside the gym.

Hal was not the neatest guy in the world on his best days, but this was an unusually rumpled look even for him. "Hal, what happened to you?" the coach greeted him. "Even more important, what're you doing here this early?"

"My mother found out 'bout Shawna'n I an' booted me

out," Hal said. "I had to sleep in the car last night. Any chance I can borrow the key to the lockerroom to take a shower?"

Wimbush handed the key to him dubiously. "We're going to have to talk about this," the coach said.

"Yeah, but I hope you don't mind if I take a shower first," Hal said.

Wimbush heaved a sigh and motioned his assent.

The shower felt good. That was one of the luxuries of home that Hal had long taken for granted and now knew he was going to miss. But the school shower was okay, too.

He couldn't help wondering about his mother. Probably almost any other mother he knew would stop short of exiling her offspring. He didn't know for sure what went on between Shawna and her mother, but he had a fairly good idea that it would not include banishment. The Hansons had their code, but they were capable of showing flexibility, too. His own mother was not. At times, she was downright unreasonable. She very well could condemn him to eternal misery and go to her grave feeling justified—just because she didn't like the skin color of a young woman with whom he wanted a relationship.

Shawna finally caught up with him. "I wanted to warn you 'bout what was comin' down," she told him. "But you were out at Dunston, an' I had no idea how to reach you."

Hal shrugged. "Well, it's water over the dam now. My mother booted me out."

Shawna almost choked. "She what?"

"She laid the law down: I was not to see you any more, an' I told her no way," Hal said. He flashed a sleepy grin. "She told me if that was how I felt, get my things an' get out. So I spent the night in my car. I gotta 'mit it's prob'ly the most uncomf'table night's sleep I ever had."

Shawna frowned sympathetically and hugged Hal. "You really did have a night, didn't you?"

Hal nodded. "It seemed so good through most of it, too. I won my two races an' anchored the relay team to a win, an' I was feelin' pretty good 'bout everything. Tired but good. But then I walk in the door, an' I find Mother sittin' there just layin' for me . . . kinda like Melvin Peebles used to do back when we were in the third an' fourth grade. 'Cept it's harder to work 'round your own mother."

"Yeah, how well I know," Shawna murmured. She noticed that two young black women were looking at her critically as she hugged Hal, so she made a face at them and nuzzled her boyfriend's neck affectionately. "Well, we're out in the open now. I guess I don't have to worry 'bout them any more."

"Well, I gotta worry 'bout where I'm gonna stay," Hal mused. He kissed Shawna. "I'm gonna see if I can talk Wimbush into lettin' me use a cot in the lockerroom. I can take a shower there an' whatnot anyway. An' I won't have to go far after a game or track meet."

"I don't think you wanna stay there forever either," Shawna said solicitously.

"Well, least it beats sleepin' in the car," Hal rationalized.

A little later, Hal found Wimbush and handed him the locker room key.

"Well, you look a little more presentable now anyway," the coach remarked with a grin.

"I feel a little bit more human," Hal agreed. "Uh, Coach, uh, I was kinda hopin' you'd let me use a cot down in the locker room 'til I can work out some kinda permanent 'ccommodations."

Wimbush patted him on a shoulder. "You can stay with me until we can get something settled." He heaved a loud sigh. "I hope that's getting your mother to come to her senses. Among other things, I was planning on sending you to basketball camp in South Carolina and Illinois this summer, and I'm going to need a guardian's signature."

"She's pretty set," Hal said matter-of-factly. "An' to be honest, Coach, so am I. The only way I'm gonna stop seein' Shawna is if Shawna 'cides she doesn't wanta see me. An' I'm not gonna let my mother or Shawna's parents stop me."

Wimbush clasped his shoulders affectionately. "I admire your resolve, although I think it might have been better if you had picked another cause to fight for." He took a deep breath and studied Hal. "It might help if you and Shawna kinda cool it for a while, give both your mother and her parents a chance to get used to it. I know Gerald and Marian Hanson quite well. I know they're not unreasonable people at core, and I happen to have it on good authority that they think pretty highly of you."

"That was prob'ly before they knew I was seein' their daughter," Hal murmured.

Wimbush chuckled. "I'm sure right now they're going through an adjustment phase, but they'll get over it. It's not as if you're a serial killer or a child molester or something of that sort."

Hal chuckled. "I think with Mother, those would be a step up from where I'm at right now."

"Now your mother may definitely require some more subtle cultivation," Wimbush agreed sympathetically.

After school that afternoon, Hal drove Shawna to her home. He wanted to clear the air with her parents as soon as possible.

"Before y'all go throwin' anything at me or screamin' for me to get out, let me give my side of it," he appealed to Gerald and Marian Hanson. "Shawna'n I haven't done anything wrong. We haven't had sex, an' even if we did have, we know 'bout AIDS an' condoms'n all that. I respect Shawna, an' I like bein' 'round her. Neither one of us liked sneakin' 'round on y'all, but we knew you'd have a hissy-fit if you found out. We were gonna tell you. I don't know when. We hadn't 'cided that. But we did talk 'bout it, an' we wanted to tell you before you found out from somebody else. We woulda figured out a time, too. I'm just sorry you had to find out 'bout it before we got 'round to it."

"We weren't planning to throw anything at you, Hal," Gerald Hanson interjected calmly. He pointed to a chair. "You might as well sit down."

So Hal sat down. It occurred to him that his spiel of a moment or so earlier must have sounded a bit rambling, and he hoped that he got something of his point across.

"Hal, it's nothing against you—your character as a young man," Marian Hanson told him in well modulated tone. "We don't dislike you. We just feel that you shouldn't see Shawna socially again."

Hal took a deep breath. "I don't mean to sound disrespectful, Miz Hanson, but I think Shawna should have the biggest say in that," he replied.

"Thank you. That's 'sackly what I been tryna get 'cross to her," Shawna told him with a thin smile.

"Shawna's a minor, an' she's under my supervision," Marian Hanson said. "I think I have a right to make decisions relating to her well-being."

"But that doesn't 'clude her choice of friends an' whatnot," Hal rebutted. His hands raised defensively. "Miz Hanson, I'm not bein' disrespectful, but what you're talkin' 'bout is somethin' that was pretty much 'pposed to be out by the end of the nineteenth century . . ."

"Awright! Now we're gettin' the truth," Shawna cheered him on.

"That's enough out of you, young lady," Marian Hanson told her daughter with a baleful glance. She turned back to Hal. "Hal, you're a fine young man. I know you're a star athlete, and I imagine you'll soon be in position to get a scholarship to one of the better schools in the country. You're very popular now in the community because of that. But my daughter is very impressionable, and I don't really think that a relationship with someone like you is what she needs at this point in her life."

"Mama, it's not a question of what I need. You don't know that any more'n anybody else," Shawna protested. "I wanna be with Hal, an' he wants to be with me. We're not all that different 'un a lotta others our age 'cept in one of us bein' black an' the other white. What's the big deal?"

"I'm afraid she does make a valid point, Marian," Gerald Hanson conceded.

"You wanta set curfews for us'n whatnot, I'm not gonna fight you on that," Hal assured Shawna's parents. "I'll go 'long with it. We'll always be pretty much where we're not likely to be havin' sex, so I don't see how that should be a hangup. An' I'm gonna be playin' ball a lot an' maybe goin' off to basketball camp this summer, so it's not like we're gonna be everywhere together."

"Well, I suppose there must be some way we can work out a compromise," Gerald Hanson mused.

"Well, it better not 'clude me not bein' able to see Hal, 'cause I'm definitely not goin' 'long with that," Shawna challenged defiantly.

"Same goes here," Hal backed her.

"Well, I don't want an out and out revolution on my hands, especially when I'm not sure my position is totally in the right," Marian Hanson yielded with a helpless gesture. She shook her head and smiled wanly. "All right. If you two want to date, Shawna's father and I won't try to stop you. Provided, of course, Hal's mother doesn't object."

Hal had to clear his throat. "Well, we got kind of a problem on that one," he said. "My mother kicked me out last night."

Marian Hanson's face contorted in horror. "She what?"

"Booted him out," Shawna confirmed. "Told him to get his clothes and get out."

"Coach Wimbush is lettin' me stay with him 'til we get somethin' worked out," Hal said. "I can't even begin to guess when that might be. You talk 'bout a hardcase, my mother tops the list on that one."

"I'll say," Marian Hanson murmured. She shook her head. "I've been angry enough with Shawna to want to kill her at times, including last night and through much of today, but at no time did it ever occur to me to tell her to get out."

"Listenin' to Hal talk 'bout his mama makes me take back a lotta things I said 'bout you," Shawna told Marian Hanson with a grin.

"I should take offense at that, but I have a feeling it's a phase I've been through, too," her mother sighed. She turned back to Hal. "I sympathize with your position, but still I would prefer that you work things out with your mother before you and my daughter go out together again."

"I think that would be for the best, Hal," Gerald Hanson seconded the motion.

"Good gravy, Mama, Daddy, that may be doomsday," Shawna moaned.

"We won't make you wait that long," Gerald Hanson said. He turned to Hal. "At least try to patch things up with your mother. Will you do that much?"

"I'll try," Hal said with a shrug.

"That's all we're asking," Gerald Hanson said.

As closed as Kathleen McDonough's door had been made to Hal, Velma Wimbush's was comparably open. The coach's wife adored young people. She had grown especially fond of Hal over the preceding months as her husband brought him under his wing. It probably is no exaggeration to say that she might have been willing to adopt him if need and circumstances dictated that course.

Hal adored her equally. He had no real wish to disown or cut himself off from his birth mother, but he wouldn't have minded Velma Wimbush as a surrogate for that role. In some ways, she would be a lot better. She certainly wouldn't be forbidding him to see certain girls because their ancestry was African instead of European or anything like that. And he wouldn't have to spend as much time justifying basically rational decisions he made with her simply because those decisions didn't exactly conform with some mythical code which didn't really apply anywhere except in someone's mind.

The Wimbushes had no children, which accounted in part for Velma's attachment to young people. She had the soul of a mother; unfortunately, nature or God or whatever had seen fit to deny her fertility. So in a sense, part of a need was fulfilled with Hal around the house.

Both Wimbushes also loved dogs, and they had a couple of Shepherd puppies. The two canines took to Hal instantly, and he to them.

Velma Wimbush smiled as she walked into the living room and saw Hal squatting on the floor with the two puppies romping affectionately on him. "They say dogs are good judges of people, so I guess that says something good about you," she remarked.

Hal grinned and moved his head to avoid a canine tongue that was trying to lick his face. "They're just nice dogs period. They'd prob'ly like just 'bout anybody."

"That's not necessarily so," Velma Wimbush said. She sat down and turned on the television to catch the evening news. "We've had some people come around they didn't take to at all. My own sister for one. But they seem to like you."

"Prob'ly that's 'cause they sense a wild streak in me kinda like them," Hal said with a chuckle. "Maybe your sister's too refined for them."

Velma Wimbush laughed. "I hadn't thought of it in quite that light, but you may have a point." She smiled at him warmly. "By the way, I hope you don't mind my turning to the news."

"Naw," Hal said with a headshake. "I get so little time to watch television, I don't even know what's goin' on. I watch basketball when I get a chance, but that's 'bout it. But I don't mind. 'Sides, it's your television . . . go 'head."

"Well, as long as you're in the house, I certainly think you're entitled to an equal say," Velma Wimbush told him warmly.

Hal chuckled. "Hey, that's more'n I get from my own mother . . . or got. I guess that's all in the past now."

"It is a shame that she can't see past that color line someone drew for her so many years ago," Velma Wimbush sighed. She turned on the television, and Dan Rather's face and voice came over.

"Well, to her credit, least she's upfront 'bout it," Hal said with a shrug. He laughed. "I've heard blacks talkin' more'n once 'bout bein' more worried 'bout those whites that hate 'em but pretend to be their friends. At least she's not doin' that."

"True," Velma Wimbush conceded. "Still, I find it hard to sympathize with any woman that can so callously reject her own flesh and blood simply because she doesn't like a person they associate with."

Hal thought about Willard and flashed a grin. "Oddly 'nuff, she'd prob'ly be more understandin' if I 'mitted to bein' a homosexual, long as I was doin' it with a white boy. She's got a cousin. I call him Uncle Willard, but he's not my uncle 'sackly. Anyway, he's a real flamer an' doesn't really try to hide it, but she 'dores him. He lives up in New York an' works for a law firm on Park Avenue."

"Well, I don't believe you should hate those people either," Velma Wimbush said. She turned to catch Tom Brokaw. "I can't stand Dan Rather. There's something about his face that grates on me."

"I can't see a nickel's worth of difference in any of those guys," Hal said with a shrug. He was still petting the puppies, who by now were snuggling up to go to sleep against him.

"But I still think it's a shame what your mother's done," Velma Wimbush sighed.

Hal gestured helplessly. "It's done now. Maybe the coach can work somethin' out with her. I hope so." He heaved a sigh. "Worst part of this whole deal is me puttin' y'all out like I'm doin'."

"You hush that kind of talk right now," Velma Wimbush told him firmly. "It's not an inconvenience or putting us out, as you call it, and I don't want you even remotely thinking of it as that. Now purge your mind of that thought this instant, you hear me?" "Yes, ma'am," Hal acceded gladly.

Kathleen McDonough scanned Wimbush with jaundiced eye as she answered the door to his ring. "If you're here appealing on my son's behalf, you're wasting your time," she told him in a gelid tone and started to close the door in his face.

Wimbush put his arm against the door to prevent its premature closure. "Uh, is it all right if I come in?" he asked.

Kathleen McDonough heaved a sigh and stepped out of the way to allow him to enter.

"I was just getting ready to pour myself a cup of coffee," she said. "Would you care for a cup?"

It had been a long day. "If you don't mind," Wimbush answered. "Black . . . no cream or sugar please."

So Kathleen McDonough went into the kitchen and returned a couple of minutes later with a tray and two steaming cups. She set them on the coffee table and sat down on the sofa.

Wimbush found a chair facing her. He noticed that she had picked up one cup, so he took the other one and sipped from it.

"I suppose Harold has been regaling you with how terrible and inflexible I was," Kathleen McDonough remarked probingly. She set her cup down and lit a cigarette.

"Not really," Wimbush said. He sipped some more coffee and focused on her. "He does think you were wrong. And frankly, Mrs. McDonough, so do I."

Kathleen McDonough drew on her cigarette and shrugged. "Frankly, Mr. Wimbush, I had halfway hoped that you might sympathize with my position. I thought your people disapproved of mixed relationships as much as mine do."

"Well, normally we don't take it quite to the extremes some of your people have been known to, but there is a certain truth in what you say," Wimbush replied. He set his cup down. "It's not something I necessarily encourage. If I had been advising either of them before the fact, I think I would have advised against something of this sort. But sometimes things just happen between two people. I went to a black college, as I suppose you're aware. One of my best friends from those days has been happily married to a white woman for the last fifteen years. I never thought he would meet a white woman in circumstances that would lead to something like that, but he did, which just goes to show you never know."

"Your friend is an adult now, Mr. Wimbush. Harold is still little more than a child," Kathleen McDonough reminded.

"True, I'm not saying the two cases are parallel," Wimbush conceded. He sipped some more coffee. "But your son is starting to grow into manhood, and he has a need for a certain peer socialization process. He and Shawna Hanson became attracted to each other. My own gut instinct, Mrs. McDonough, is that the best way to deal with it is to let it run its course. The two young people will be going separate ways eventually, and it will die of its own accord. The very worst thing you can do is draw the line like you're doing now. That just pushes the two young people farther away from you and closer to each other."

"The way Harold talked to me last night — the insufferable insolence — the farther away he gets from me the better, Mr. Wimbush," Kathleen McDonough snapped.

"I don't think it was insolence as much as the young man standing his ground," Wimbush defended Hal. "You drew the line, Mrs. McDonough. Unfortunately, you drew it at a point he wasn't willing to accept. As he saw it, he couldn't accept."

"As long as he's under my roof, he'll live by my rules," Kathleen McDonough murmured. "If this is an imposition on you or someone else, I'm sorry, but I am not going to put up with that sort of brazen backtalk from him, even if he is a star athlete."

"It's not an imposition on me, I assure you," Wimbush said. He smiled. "In fact my wife, Velma, adores Hal. I almost think she might be willing to adopt him."

"Right now I'm almost inclined to tell her to go right ahead," Kathleen McDonough said.

"I'm not here to fight with you over Hal's custody oranything of that sort," Wimbush said reassuringly. He sipped some more coffee. "My concern is your son. I think he should be back at home with you. And frankly, Mrs. McDonough, I think you should loosen the reins a bit on him. If he wants to see Shawna Hanson socially, don't try to stop him. As I said before, I imagine it will die of its own accord. I had three or four girlfriends in high school, and the woman I finally married grew up on the other side of the state and I didn't even meet her until several years later. So it's not as if it's likely to be permanent."

"Are you prepared to guarantee that?" Kathleen McDonough quizzed.

Wimbush almost choked. "I'm not prepared to guarantee anything. I can't tell you for sure that the sun's gonna rise tomorrow morning. I don't know for sure that George Bush is going to be reelected president. I can weigh the percentages and give you some probability, but I can't guarantee it."

"I don't think right now I could remotely consider settling for anything less than a firm guarantee," Kathleen McDonough said with a cold shrug.

"Well, I'm sorry you feel that way, Mrs. McDonough," Wimbush said.

"I'm tired, Mr. Wimbush. I think I'd like to go to bed," Kathleen McDonough muttered.

Wimbush finished his coffee and rose. "Well, thank you for the coffee anyway, Mrs. McDonough," he said. He started for the door and turned back. "Goodnight."

"Goodnight, Mr. Wimbush," Kathleen McDonough said in an indifferent tone.

Wimbush left with the feeling that he had not penetrated her one whit.

Velma Wimbush kissed her husband as he came through the front door. "Any luck?" she asked.

"I got a free cup of coffee out of it, and that's about it," Wimbush answered with a gesture of disgust. He shook his head. "That is one hard woman."

"I can 'ttest to that," Hal agreed.

Velma Wimbush heaved a loud sigh. "It's such a shame," she murmured. She turned to Hal. "But don't you worry. You've got a place to stay here as long as you need it."

"Yes," her husband confirmed with equal sincerity.

"I 'ppreciate that," Hal said. He closed a book from which he had been studying. "But I still feel bad 'bout puttin' y'all through the wringer."

"I don't want to hear any more talk of that sort from you, young man," Velma Wimbush told him with forefinger extended for emphasis. "You're not a burden, and that's final."

"You don't want to get into an argument with her, Hal," Wimbush said good-naturedly. "You won't win. I've had almost twenty years of experience that qualifies me to tell you that unequivocally."

"I'll take your word for it," Hal said.

Later that evening, the coach and his wife went out to dinner and a movie. Hal had a test coming up, so he stayed in to study. The phone rang, and he picked up the receiver and said hello.

"Harold?" the familiar hoarse female voice on the other end responded.

"Mother?" Hal was equally taken aback.

"I suppose it's all right for you to come home," Kathleen McDonough said.

Hal was surprised in a way, and in a way he wasn't. "You're not going to tell me not to see Shawna any more, I hope," he said hesitantly.

"I think it would be better if you didn't, but I won't try

to stop you," his mother said in a reluctant tone.

"Well, then I'll be home in a little while," Hal said. "I wanta thank the Wimbushes for puttin' me up. They stepped out for a little while."

"I probably won't be up when you get in," Kathleen McDonough said in a weary tone. "I'll leave a spare key over the transom. You know how to get to it."

"Yeah," Hal said. He took a deep breath. "Well, see you tomorrow maybe."

"Yes, I suppose so," Kathleen McDonough said and hung up.

On one hand, Hal was glad to be going home. On the other, he was almost beginning to savor the prospect of becoming Velma Wimbush's adopted son.

34

Religion for whatever importance it held in Hal's young life had heretofore been mostly just orthodox Christianity. His closest brush with the offbeat or mystical came by way of a Beatles tape he picked up once on sale for two dollars. He liked to play the tape from time to time, partly because he was fascinated by the sometimes almost eerie majesty in the Beatles' music but mostly because he felt a strange need to acquaint himself with the decade that ushered his parents into adulthood.

Oddly, neither parent seemed to be a part of the sixties. At some point, *Lucy in the Sky* and *Strawberry Fields* must have touched their souls, but no evidence of it was visible now. Hal couldn't speak knowledgeably of his father. He had only spent a few weeks total with his father over the last ten years, so he couldn't really say he knew what made that paternal figure tick. But it did seem as if his father was more interested in going back to the nineteenth century, and the Beatles, Bob Dylan, and Simon and Garfunkel might as well never have bothered to show up. As for his mother, almost nothing of that period now seemed to appeal to her. She intensely disliked John and Robert Kennedy, or at least strongly conveyed that impression; and her taste in popular music seemed to run more towards Frank Sinatra and Tony Bennett than anything from her own decade.

She did like a couple of post sixties performers: notably Billy Joel and Neil Diamond. Occasionally, she had kind words for *Piano Man, Zanzibar,* and *America.* She didn't like *Only the Good Die Young* or *Anthony's Song.* She professed a fondness for a couple of black performers from an earlier period: notably Dionne Warwick and Johnny Mathis, but she didn't like two of Hal's favorites: James Brown and Aretha Franklin. For some reason, she seemed to find Whitney Houston superior to Aretha. For someone to look at, Hal agreed, but not when it came to singing. As far as he was concerned, no one could top Aretha when it came to belting out a tune.

Hal had come to sense, albeit amorphously, that change is a constant, with its reflection in an era's art, literature, and music. His mother, and evidently his father even more rigidly, seemed to believe that life really should be stuck in a groove, with the line drawn from long before anyone living now was even born as the guide.

Hal accepted the fact that Charles and Kathleen McDonough were his parents, and he never seriously tried to disavow them, nor did he really even feel embarrassed by them. But he couldn't help wondering, from time to time, what mischievous universal force had decided to assign him to them and vice versa.

The divorce arrangement had Hal spending two weeks each summer at his father's apartment in Norfolk. It was an arrangement Hal could have done without. He wasn't really all that sure that his father would have minded terribly if he wasn't around either. But if the latter was true, his father didn't admit to it, and he demanded in full what the court system had granted as his due. So two weeks each summer found Hal stuck in that dreary Tidewater city.

Mostly Hal was bored through the period. That was primarily because he couldn't get away from his father for any extended period. At least in Brileyville, he had only two or three hours of waking time with his mother, and he had basketball and Shawna to keep him otherwise occupied. None of that was available to him in Norfolk.

Eunice visited during the spring, and she made a point on one occasion of calling Hal aside.

"I hear you and my niece have been creating quite a stir the last few weeks," she said.

Hal shrugged. "We weren't doin' anything all that much outta the ordinary, but some folks got a little bit uptight about it."

"I have a feeling you're understating your and my niece's roles in all this, but on the whole I imagine you're accurate in your assessment," Eunice said. She lit a cigarette. "I have mixed feelings about it. I like you, of course, and I adore my niece, but I'm not necessarily sure the two of you are likely to be what's best for one another."

"Uh, Miz Weller, it's not like we're plannin' to get married tomorrow," Hal reminded her.

Eunice nodded. "True." She heaved a sigh. "I guess I was hoping something like this wouldn't happen. Both mothers, Shawna's and yours, expressed concern to me that it would. I kept telling them that they shouldn't worry, that by worrying they were possibly creating a self-fulfilling prophecy. And then it happens, and suddenly my sister looks on me as an evil influence. And I hate to think of what your mother might say if I happen to run into her."

"Well, I'm not tryna get you in trouble. If I did, I'm sorry," Hal assured her.

"I know you didn't," Eunice said understandingly.

Hal's mother at least had reached the point of not trying to stop him from seeing Shawna. That, he supposed, was the best he could expect from her. He could forget about blessings or anything of that sort. He had no idea how long or far his relationship with Shawna would go, but he suspected that his mother would harbor inner opposition to it at every point along the way. He could imagine himself and Shawna twenty or thirty years into the future, happily married and with well adjusted children, and his mother still objecting in her familiarly sniping way.

And she probably would still be trying to play matchmaker for him even then, too. He got that feeling especially when they attended church services and she pointed out some young white woman with whom he might find compatibility if he would just give it a chance. From time to time, she liked to throw out such expressions as *Nubian wenches* as well, with Shawna as the indirect target. Hal didn't really like hearing her talk that way, but he held his rebellion in check for now. He wanted to keep that in reserve for some future date when something more important would be at issue.

School had let out, and that time of year came around again when Hal had to spend the obligatory two weeks with his father. Charles McDonough had a two room apartment near Norfolk's downtown area, in a predominantly black section. Charles McDonough may have preferred living with more whites surrounding him; privately, he expressed some white supremacist views. But he accepted the reality of those neighborhoods costing more than he could (or wanted to) pay. And really, person to person, he got along well enough with the African Americans of his acquaintance.

His main contact with his son came through someone in the court handling the visitations, so he had some idea of what was happening in Hal's life. "I hear you're gettin' to be a hot-shot basketball and football player," he remarked as he picked Hal up at the bus station.

"I dunno. I guess I'm awright," Hal said.

"Baseball was always my sport," Charles McDonough said.

"Yeah, I know. You told me a few times," Hal recalled.

Charles McDonough had his car outside, and they got in. "I never played much basketball. I never thought I was very good at it. I did play football for a couple years. I was a linebacker," Hal's father said as he took the wheel.

Hal could believe that. His father was a little more sturdily built than he. And probably he had been pretty quick back twenty years ago or so.

"I have a hard time picturin' you playin' football," Charles McDonough mused. "At your size especially. And with your build, I'd picture you more a distance runner than a sprinter."

"Well, I run the sprints awright," Hal said with a shrug. He flashed a grin. "An' I'm pretty quick off the mark. I think that kinda threw a lotta guys playin' 'gainst me. They didn't figure a white boy could get down the field like that."

They got back to his father's apartment. It wasn't a bad sort of place. His father tended to be sloppy, but always in one little corner, so the place didn't look totally like a war zone.

"Your mother still doesn't drive, I understand," Charles McDonough said. He sat down on a chair and lit his pipe.

"Naw," Hal confirmed. "I got a car now. I bought it from my basketball coach. So I been drivin' her 'round to the grocery store an' to church an' back on Sunday an' all."

"I recall several times I tried teaching her to drive," Charles McDonough mused. "She just never could catch on to it very well."

The thought struck Hal that the instructor may have been more to blame in those instances than the pupil. Kathleen McDonough was not athletic or a mechanical whiz, but she wasn't remarkably uncoordinated either. His father's rather bombastic method of teaching probably had a great deal to do with her resistance to learning how to drive.

"I reckon your mother still has nothin' good to say about me," Charles McDonough remarked.

Hal laughed. "If she says anything at all 'bout you, it's bad. One good thing: she's not talkin' much 'bout you any more."

"I'm not sure if that's good or bad," Charles McDonough said. "What's the old expression. Love me or hate me, but don't ignore me."

"If you ever heard her talkin' 'bout you, I 'spect you'd think bein' ignored is a step up," Hal said.

Hal's father really was not an unpleasant man to be around. He tended to get rigidly opinionated at times, which could make him quite annoying to someone close to him. But people who knew him just by casual everyday conversation tended to like him. Hal could understand that. He didn't dislike him. In fact, much of the time he felt a certain fondness for the older man. But he also harbored a certain resentment for the heavy-handed way his father dragged a wife and an infant son over half the east coast for no discernibly good reason. It was evidently some vision his father fancied himself as guided or driven by, and Hal couldn't say for sure that he wasn't. But if he was, why did the wife and infant son wind up stuck in Brileyville? And what was he doing in this rather ordinary riverfront apartment?

It totally mystified Hal why his father and mother ever married each other in the first place. Besides having little in common in their personalities, they were poles apart in their respective looks departments. Charles McDonough really was a rather handsome man in his own right, with angular features and thick brown-gray hair that he wore slicked back. Hal at one point thought he used some sort of pomade or oil to get that look, but it turned out that it was greasy primarily because his father only washed it once every two weeks or so. His father seemed to think that might have something to do with why he still had so much of his hair. Hal was no expert, but he had read enough on the subject to have a pretty good idea that his father just happened to be lucky enough to fall into a good genetic line for male hair growth, and he had that much hair in spite of his indifference to washing it, not because.

"How come you didn't drive your car down?" Charles McDonough asked Hal over dinner. He fixed some Polish sausage and sauerkraut, which Hal surprisingly found that he liked.

"When I leave here, I'm goin' to basketball camp," Hal said. "I have to catch a plane. An' I don't wanta leave my car in an airport parkin' lot for two weeks, so I'm lettin' my girlfriend use it."

"Yeah, the guy at the courthouse told me you've been goin' with a colored girl," Charles McDonough said through narrowed eyes. "Is that true?"

"Yeah, she's black," Hal said with a shrug. He pulled out a picture of Shawna he carried in his wallet and showed it to his father.

Charles McDonough nodded appreciatively as he scanned the picture. "Yes, I suppose for a colored girl she's quite attractive," he conceded.

"I think she's 'ttractive for any kinda girl," Hal said with a shrug.

Charles McDonough scanned his son curiously. "Just lookin' at you, I'd figure you oughta be able to find a white girl easy enough," he said.

Hal shrugged. "The white girls in our school are 'bout the scraggliest things you're gonna find anywheres. Gotta couple good-lookin' ones where Mother an' I go to church, but they go to the private school 'round Brileyville—Cedar Grove—an' they're real snobs. 'Sides, I like Shawna. What's the big deal?"

His father gestured indifferently. "I don't think it's a good idea for the races to be mixin' that way."

Hal winced. "How come it's so bad? I've heard you talkin' before 'bout how a lotta blacks got white blood in 'em. That prob'ly came back in slavery days an' through the early part of this century when they didn't have any choice in it. At least with Shawna'n I, it's kind of a mutual thing.

We like each other. It's not like somebody's bein' forced into somethin' 'gainst their will."

"Someday you'll understand," his father responded arcanely. "For now, I'll let it go. I'm sure in time you'll outgrow it."

Hal wasn't sure what it was he would outgrow, and whenever he broached questions of that sort, his father had a way of leaving him even more confused than he had been before. So he deftly changed the subject.

Charles McDonough had to work during some of the days Hal was visiting, so that left the young man alone in the apartment if he wanted to stay there. He fixed breakfast for himself; he had learned how to scramble eggs and fry bacon along the way, and his father always had those items amply stocked in his refrigerator. He liked milk with his breakfast, but his father didn't keep that around. He didn't have a taste for coffee then, so he had to settle for tap water to wash the meal down.

He tried watching television and quickly got bored. He came to feel that one can only take so much *Cosby* and *Designing Women*, and *Geraldo*, *Jennie Jones*, and the body-building shows were even more boring. His father did let him have a spare key, so he could come and go during the days as the spirit moved him. Unfortunately, downtown Norfolk didn't offer much, if any, more in the way of relief from boredom than the apartment.

He got a call from Shawna one morning. He had left his father's telephone number with her before his departure.

"I bet I woke you up, didn't I?" she greeted him in that teasing tone he had come to know and love so well.

"Actually, I was tryna wade through Regis an' Cathy Lee, which leaves me wishin' I was still sleepin'," Hal said with a chuckle. "I hope you're not callin' to tell me you wrecked the car or somethin'."

"Of course not. Do I 'tect somethin' sexist in that remark?" Shawna inquired impishly.

"No, I have every confidence you'll keep the car in real

good shape," came the diplomatic (that is to say, evasive) response.

"You better say that or you're in big trouble next time I see you," Shawna said. "By the way, Mama says thank you for lettin' me use your car. That means she won't have to worry 'bout me buggin' her to use hers—'til you get back anyway."

"Well, maybe she's startin' to warm to me a little bit," Hal said insouciantly.

"Oh, she likes you okay, but you're still not 'sackly what she's lookin' for in a future son-in-law."

"What if she winds up gettin' me as a future son-in-law anyhow? How's she gonna handle that?"

"She'll prob'ly 'ccept it, but she may still go to her grave wishin' you were black."

"Well, I could always paint my face, but I understand y'all don't like that."

"I'm not gonna go rubbin' up 'gainst anything that might rub off back on me. I figure if I wanna put on rouge or mascara, I'll pick my own shade."

"Good, I wasn't figurin' on paintin' myself anyways. I hope you're not closin' the door just 'cause your mother's never gonna 'ccept it with open arms."

"No, if we were both twenty-two an' outta college right now an' you were makin' big bucks playin' pro ball, I'd prob'ly marry you. Course by the time we do get outta college, we mighta gone sep'rate ways. Or maybe some latent gene'll pop up an' make you like your fag uncle."

Hal almost choked on that one. "Not a chance," he rebutted.

"I guess if you were that way for real, I'da picked up some sign by now," Shawna conceded. "How's life with your daddy?"

"Uh, borin' mostly. Nothin' to do 'cept watch television. Couple times I ducked out an' wandered 'round downtown Norfolk, but not much goin' down there. Kinda rough when you don't have anybody your own age 'round."

"Prob'ly a good thing. You might run into a couple floozies an' get corrupted."

"Well, it'd relieve the boredom anyway."

"It's only a couple weeks. It's good for you to be learning some patience at this age. Prepares you for when you get older. Your daddy? He's workin'?"

"Yeah, he's got most of next week off. I'm not sure that's good. I 'member last time I was here. He's got a thing for soap operas."

"You're kiddin'?"

"Nope. He takes the macho thing 'bout as far as Coach Moore in most respects, but he does like soap operas."

"That shoulda put him in tune with your mama anyway."

"No, whatever her faults, least she's got the good sense to see those things as stupid."

"I 'gree. 'Cept maybe for *General Hospital*. I used to like that a little bit when I was real little."

"I never watched any of 'em 'cept when Dad had 'em on. Oh, yeah, speakin' of soap operas, I'm gonna get kinda sappy an' say I love you."

"I love you, too. 'Cept I think it's a theme that goes better with Puccini's music in the background 'un those stupid television shows."

"I don't know much 'bout Puccini 'cept he wrote *Madam Butterfly*. We learned 'bout that in music 'ppreciation class."

"He composed *Madam Butterfly*. Somebody else wrote the story line an' all. He also composed the scores for La Boheme, Turandot—that's my favorite—an' Tosca an' a ton of others I can't think of the names of right off the bat."

"Just outta curiousity, how does a black girl growin' up in a small southern town get into opera an' that sorta stuff?"

"Kinda the same way I guess a white boy growin' up in a small southern town gets into playin' basketball. You get 'sposed to it, an' you find you like it."

Hal chuckled. "Good point." He took a deep breath. "I do love you. Right now I wish I had you here with me."

"You'd prob'ly be tryna do somethin' lewd an' lascivious, an' if you caught me at the wrong time, I might wanna go 'long with it," Shawna said. She chuckled. "I love you. Now I gotta go put some gas in your car."

"It had practically a full tank when I turned it over to you," Hal reminded her. "I know it's not a guzzler. You musta been puttin' some miles on it."

"Been mostly for Trina," Shawna said. She laughed. "Don't worry. I haven't been cheatin' on you."

"I wasn't thinkin' you were," Hal assured her. He chuckled. "Heck, knowin' you, if you 'cided to, you wouldn't sneak 'round 'bout it."

"I like to think I wouldn't," Shawna admitted. She laughed. "By the way, Trina said to tell you hello."

"Tell her I said hello."

"Oh yeah, does your daddy know you're datin' a black girl?"

"Yep. Somebody from the court handlin' the visitation told him. He lectured me a little bit on it, but I showed him your picture an' he 'mitted you're not half-bad lookin'. . ."

"I bet he threw in a not-for-a-colored-girl addendum . . ."

"'Fraid so. He's not very tuned in to what's happenin' today. An' I 'spect it'd take him three lifetimes to make it up to the African 'merican level."

Shawna laughed. "You're talkin' 'bout a couple centuries. By then, blacks no doubt'll wanna be called somethin' else. We seem to change our mood on that every twenty years or so."

"Keep goin' long 'nuff, you'll run outta names."

"Somebody'll prob'ly check out some African tribe an' come back with one no one's heard before, an' it'll catch on, and then you whiteys'll try bein' hip an' imitate it an' look kinda silly."

"Well, lotta whiteys do, that's true. I hope you don't have the notion I'm like that."

"If I did, do you think I could love you?"

"No, I 'magine you'd write me off as a phony," he admitted.

"You got it," Shawna assured him.

Usually in the evenings, Hal and his father went out to eat. Charles McDonough knew a couple of restaurants in the area where the food was reasonably decent. One was within walking distance of the apartment and took them through a park. Hal preferred that route. By evening, he was usually restless enough so that he welcomed the chance to walk and stretch his legs.

Once they strolled past a playground where some young black men Hal's age, perhaps in a few cases a little older, were shooting baskets. One shot clanged off the rim and caromed in Hal's direction. Hal moved quickly to cut it off and tossed it to a young man who was running up to get it.

"Thanks," the young man said. He turned and started to walk back to where the others were clustered. Then he turned back to Hal. "You play basketball?" he asked.

Hal shrugged. "A little bit."

"We need one more guy so's we can get a game up. How 'bout it?" the young man appealed.

Hal turned to his father. "Okay with you, Dad?"

Charles McDonough heaved a sigh. "Yeah, I reckon it is." He pointed to some park benches across a grassy expanse. "I'll be sittin' over there."

"I'm Weldon," the young black man introduced himself as he and Hal walked over to where his friends were gathered.

"I'm Hal," was the response.

A few moments later, Hal was playing and more than holding his own. He was a little rusty because he hadn't played to speak of in a couple of weeks, but he worked it out pretty quickly. He came up with a couple of sparkling defensive plays, and those helped him get the rest of his game flowing.

"You're more'n a little bit good," Weldon told him in an admiring tone as the game ended and the young men were dispersing.

"I played on my high school team back home," Hal

confided. He flashed a grin. "I'm the only white boy on that team, too, so I'm kinda used to bein' outnumbered."

"Anybody play like you do ain't gonna have to worry 'bout whether the others black or white," Weldon said. He glanced across the grassy expanse to where Charles McDonough watched with intermittent interest. "That your ol' man?"

Hal nodded confirmation. "We got—well, him an' my mother got—'rrangement where I stay with him two weeks each summer."

"I know that one," Weldon sighed wistfully. He patted Hal on a shoulder. "My mom'n daddy got the same kind of 'rrangement." He chuckled. "I know one thing: I kinda wish your daddy could get custody so we could get you on our high school team next year."

"I wouldn't mind playin' for your team, but I'm not sure 'bout him gettin' custody," Hal replied with a grin.

Weldon laughed, patted Hal on a shoulder again and headed off. Hal walked over to where his father sat.

"Well, I guess that guy was right about you bein' a good player," Charles McDonough said with grudging admiration. "You were holdin' your own with those colored boys. I thought that was supposed to be their sport."

"You find some pretty good white players comin' 'long once in a while, too," Hal said insouciantly.

"Not very many, it seems," his father replied. He stood and scanned his son. "I still think you might be better at baseball or tennis."

"I'm not sure I wanta play a sport with mostly just white boys to go up 'gainst," Hal said with a shrug.

35

    This summer was a little frustrating for Hal in that it forced several long separations from Shawna. He might have felt better, or at least less bad, about it if he and Shawna had been going together for a couple of years of so. But she was his first real girlfriend, and they had only been an item for a couple of months, so it was a little harder to take under those circumstances.

    He went straight from the visitation with his father to a basketball camp in South Carolina. That was his first time on a plane. He was a little nervous before he boarded; the thought of himself thousands of feet above the ground with only some metal and mechanical parts holding him aloft was somewhat disquieting. But once the plane took off, he adjusted easily enough.

    The camp provided him with a week of instruction in basketball fundamentals. A lot of things he already did well, such as handling the ball, setting up for a shot, and getting out on the fast break, but that was mostly because of his natural physical ability. Wimbush and some of the rec league people (both county and city) had gone over a lot of these fundamentals earlier, but in a much less authoritative and detailed fashion.

"It's like in English classes," one black instructor told him. "Before you write that book report, you gotta know how to make a sentence. To make that sentence, you gotta know what your noun an' verb's gonna be. One thing leads to 'nother. You miss one step 'long the way, the whole thing's gonna topple on you."

It was given as friendly advice, and Hal basically understood that. He also appreciated the value in much of the instruction he received during his camp sojourn. Even so, sometimes he couldn't help feeling that it might be just a little repetitive.

Hal's two best buddies during the week at camp hailed from Tennessee and Georgia respectively. Both were black. One other white boy, from Florida, was in the group, but he sounded almost eggheaded when he talked, and Hal got the distinct impression that he might be thinking of his athletic future in tennis rather than basketball.

"You a little bit different 'un a lotta the white boys I run into at these things," Hal's Georgia buddy, Dennis, remarked to him once. He motioned across the barracks in which they were staying to the young man from Florida. "That boy there gonna have a hard time takin' the poundin' if he 'cide on basketball. You, on the other hand, you don't seem to have no problem with that."

Hal chuckled. "Well, that's 'cause I grew up in conditions a whole lot more like what a lotta y'all are prob'ly used to an' not very much like he is," he replied. He glanced over at the other young caucasian. "'Sides, I don't know how to play tennis, so I can't fall back on it."

He got back to Brileyville, and Shawna was away at a church camp. She returned, and they had two days together before Wimbush had him packing for Illinois.

"You know, I 'ppreciate you gettin' me into these

camps'n all, really," Hal said. He heaved a sigh. "But I was 'way at camp in South Carolina, then I come back an' Shawna's gone. Finally she gets back, an' we get two days together, an' you're sendin' me out again."

"I hope you're not telling me you see all that as a conspiracy," Wimbush replied with a little amusement.

Hal shrugged. "No, I guess not. Still, we only been goin' together three or four months or so, an' I haven't had time to get tired of her. I would like to be able to spend some time with her."

Wimbush patted him on a shoulder. "Hal, I can tell you this right now: If you and Shawna are destined to last as a couple, you'll both be able to get through this separation. If you're not destined to last as a couple, all the time in the world together now isn't going to change that. Take my word for it. You have an opportunity that only a select few boys from all over the country get each year. You get picked for these camps simply because somebody thinks you've got the talent to justify it. It's not because you're a superior human being or because you're being punished. It's because two years from now, you're probably going to be one of the twenty-five or fifty most sought after young players in the entire country. You're going to be getting letters of inquiry from all the major colleges. These camps help you to polish your skills. You do a lot of things well, granted, but there's always room for improvement. The camp helps you improve on all those areas so that if twenty-one months from now, say, Dean Smith or Jim Calhoun is looking at you, they don't have to worry about teaching you how to handle the ball so that you can help break the press in their set offense. You'll already have learned that part."

"I re'lize it's a pretty special thing, but even so I'm not sure I'd mind if you wanted to send Melvin or Lonnie or somebody in my place," Hal said through a moue.

Wimbush laughed. "If I did that, I don't think anybody would ever again take a request or recommendation from me seriously." He clasped Hal's shoulders. "I know how you feel. I used to be young, and believe it or not, it wasn't all that long ago. I still remember it pretty clearly at odd moments. I was hot-blooded, and I enjoyed time spent with my three or four girlfriends through that period. I probably wouldn't have liked being wrenched from them any more than you do, although now, looking back, I wish I had been a good enough player to make somebody think I might be worth the trouble."

"Yeah, I guess you got a point," Hal conceded. He heaved a sigh. "But still, with the summer here'n all, I'd like to at least get a week or so with Shawna."

Wimbush chuckled.

Shawna heaved a sigh. "I just get back, an' you're headin' out again. What's goin' on?" she muttered.

Hal shrugged. "I don't like it any better'n you do, but Wimbush got me into this camp in Illinois. I understand I'm 'bout the only guy not from the Midwest gonna be there. 'Sides, it gets me outta football practice, so I can bypass football season without havin' to 'splain to Coach Moore how come I'm not playin' without him callin' me a candyass'n whatnot."

"If he wants to call you a candyass, so what?" Shawna reasoned. "I know you're not. Ninety-nine percent of the school knows you're not. I just got back, an' I'd like to spend some time with you."

"I want that, too, believe me," Hal said with a helpless gesture. He kissed her. "Hey, look Baby, I've missed you like crazy. Still, like Coach Wimbush tells me, this is a real good opportunity for me. Maybe one percent of the high school basketball players in the entire country get picked for camps like this, an' I'm one of 'em. That's not 'sackly chopped liver, as my mother likes to say."

"I know," Shawna agreed with a sigh. She returned his kiss. "Mama'n Daddy've figured out 'bout these church-run camps just chock full of nothin' but young blacks. They figure I go to places like that, sooner or later I'm gonna forget 'bout you."

"Wimbush told me if we're destined to last, we'll be able to take these kinda separations now," Hal said. He drew Shawna into his arms. "An' he said if we're not, all the time in the world we can spend together won't keep us from splittin' up. I guess you get right to the nub, maybe it's better. I don't like it, but I don't know what to do 'bout it."

"Well, you can always tell Wimbush you don't wanna go to that camp," Shawna told him with an appealing roll of her eyes.

"I raised that idea with him once before, an' he 'minded me college coaches an' scouts go to those camps, an' it's a good way for them to get a look at me up close," Hal said. He heaved a sigh. "When you get down to crunchtime, if that'll help me get a college scholarship a little easier an' faster, I think I'd be a first class fool not to take full 'vantage of it. 'Sides, if I turn somethin' like that down, I'm gonna have to listen to Mother gettin' on my case."

Shawna wasn't totally mollified, but at least she basically understood.

Kathleen McDonough was only too glad to sign the papers enabling Hal to go to the basketball camp. Her only gripe was that she wouldn't have minded it being a longer stay for him.

"You sure you can't get him an extra week or two and some place where he can have some exposure to white girls?" she asked Wimbush in one of her rare attempts at trying to joke.

"Sorry, Mrs. McDonough," Wimbush said with a shrug. "I fear those people are only interested in Hal's basketball playing ability."

"Too bad," Kathleen McDonough said as she signed the papers. "Well, at least this gets him out of town and away from that girl for a little while anyway."

"Well, thanks for the signature, Mrs. McDonough," Wimbush said. He flashed a grin. "At least you'll be spared the agony of your son playing football this year."

"Yes, thank God for small blessings," Hal's mother sighed wistfully. "Of course, I might almost be willing to endure another round of football if Harold would come to his senses and either forget about girls altogether for now, which would be my preference, or get interested in some young white woman in his age group."

"No offense, Mrs. McDonough, but I don't think I'm willing to accept any kind of trade-off if it involves his playing football again," Wimbush said through a grimace.

Wimbush drove Hal to the Richmond airport on departure day with his own wife and Kathleen McDonough along.

"Take care of yourself and try to write, Dear," Hal's mother exhorted her son as the group gathered in the airport waiting area. She punctuated it with a hug.

"I will, Mother," Hal promised.

Velma Wimbush also gave Hal a departing hug. "Don't you let any of those boys at that camp intimidate you," she told him in a mock stern tone.

Hal flashed a grin. "I'll try not to let them know I'm scared anyway, Miz Wimbush."

The coach wound up with the last word. "Some of those boys have had the advantage of playing against better competition, and overall they've probably had better coaching, going back to little league and all, so you might be a little slow getting outta the blocks," he told Hal. "If that happens, don't let it get you down. You have the talent to play with anyone in your age and size bracket. Just listen to what your instructors have to say and utilize it properly, and I think you'll more than hold your own against most of the other young men there."

"It is kinda awesome when I think 'bout it, though," Hal mused. "Goin' up 'gainst guys from Chicago an' Detroit an' places like that."

"Your better basketball players don't always come from places like that," Wimbush reminded. "Remember, Larry and Magic and Michael all came from small towns. Just believe in yourself, and if you happen to have an off-day, don't let it get you down. You can always bounce back. You did it for us during the regular season."

"I won't quit," Hal promised.

"I'm sure you won't," Wimbush agreed. He clasped Hal's slender shoulders. "Just remember, your main reason for going there is to learn. Those guys can teach you a lot to make you a better basketball player. Try to absorb as much of what they have to teach as you can. That will be more valuable to you in the long run than whatever stats you ring up in your scrimmages."

"Course those stats might help 'cide if I get 'vited somewheres next year," Hal said.

"True. You do want to try to play well," Wimbush agreed.

Then the call came that Hal's plane was boarding.

36

One of the flight attendants helped make Hal's flight pass much more smoothly. She was a pretty brunette, and took an almost maternal interest in the young man. They talked for a while about this and that. The exact content of the conversation would not linger in Hal's memory, but the experience itself would. The attendant, Stephanie, had a nice smile and a warm personality, and it occurred to Hal that he might fall in love with her if he was a few years older. She confided to him jokingly, that she she might entertain similar feelings for him under different circumstances.

The plane landed at Chicago's O'Hare Airport. "Go get 'em at that camp, Hal," Stephanie encouraged him as he was preparing to disembark.

"Well, I'll try, Stephanie," Hal called back with a grin.

"Don't try. Do it," Stephanie called back good-naturedly.

As Hal walked down the ramp, the thought kept ringing in his head: *I'm in Chicago.* To some people, that no doubt wasn't a big deal. But it certainly was to a young man from

Virginia whose contact with the outside world had been rather limited.

Hal had read and heard that O'Hare is the world's biggest airport. When he got inside, he could easily believe that. It was one huge expanse.

He understood that he was to meet someone named Mike Lewis near the USAir ticket counter. He found that easily enough; knowing how to read really does come in handy at times.

He carried a sign that read: Hi, I'm Hal! That was Wimbush's idea, and while it looked silly, Hal could see how it made sense. The airport was crowded with people, some of them about Mike's age and fitting his general description. He assumed that Mike would be smart enough to pick him out of the mass or at least to have him paged, but why take chances?

He vaguely noticed a man approaching, a caucasian who looked to be about six feet, five inches and in his late twenties or early thirties. He had close cropped brown hair and was attired casually. Hal had a feeling that this must be Mike Lewis.

"I think I could have picked you out without the sign," the man greeted him with a grin. "Hi. I'm Mike."

Hal's head shook abashedly. "I'm kinda new to this. My coach thought it might be a good way to 'void confusion."

"Well, I have seen you on film before, so I knew what you looked like," Mike said. He picked up one of Hal's two suitcases. "Ready to go?"

Hal picked up the other bag and moved into step with him. "I'm ready." He chuckled. "There was this real pretty stewardess on the plane when I came in. I was almost thinkin' if I coulda swung it, I might be wantin' to take off somewheres with her."

Mike grinned understandingly. "Of course, you know she probably would see you as a little bit too young for her."

Hal grimaced. "Yeah, I know." He flashed a grin. "But like they say, it never hurts to dream . . . long's my own girlfriend doesn't find out 'bout it."

Mike laughed. "She's probably got her fantasies, too."

They continued towards the airport exit.

"I didn't know much 'bout this sorta thing, but I kinda figured I might be part of a crowd you'd be pickin' up at the airport," Hal said with interest.

Mike shrugged. "If you'd arrived earlier, you woulda been. You're the last one to arrive, the straggler, I guess you'd say. Turns out you're the only one from the east coast, too."

That surprised Hal a little. "I knew a lotta the guys comin' here were from the midwest, but I figured you'd get at least a few others from back east."

"In past years we have," Mike said with a matter of fact shug. "But I think a lotta places are gettin' kinda budget-conscious these days. An' you already got camps back east in Connecticut, Jersey, South Carolina . . ."

"Yeah, I went to the one in South Carolina earlier this summer," Hal said.

"I think your coach was a little later in getting his request in for you than some of the other kids' coaches," Mike conjectured.

Hal chuckled. "Yeah, I think when they figured out I might be good 'nuff for somethin' like this, it kinda shocked 'em."

Mike shared Hal's amusement. "It's quite a feather in your cap," he agreed. "It means that the think tank forces out there wherever they are think you're a pretty good player—at least at this stage of your development. That doesn't mean we can't miss someone equally deservin' or that someone else won't catch and pass you before it's all said an' done. But for now anyway, it's a pretty good deal for any young man selected. And if you do well here, there's a fair chance you'll be invited somewhere else next summer."

"Course one thing my coach an' I both like is it gets me outta football practice an' 'way from where the football coach can put pressure on me to be on his team," Hal said.

Mike scanned him curiously. "I wouldn't think you'd be bulky enough for football."

Hal shrugged. "I played last year. I was a wideout. I was leadin' our district in touchdown receptions 'til I got my leg broken in the eighth game. I think the football coach was kinda lookin' forward to gettin' me back this year. But this camp kinda knocks that out for him, an' I can't say I'm sorry."

"Well, we're always happy to oblige," Mike said with a chuckle.

Mike drove a station wagon. He put Hal's two bags in the back of it. The seat was down, indicating that the vehicle had been used a lot for transporting in recent days.

"I can see you're pretty tall," Hal remarked as Mike had the station wagon moving out of the parking lot. "I guess you played basketball somewhere 'long the way."

"I played at it, let's put it that way," Mike said with a grin. He stopped to pay for his parking ticket. "I had a scholarship to Boston U back in the late seventies, and I was a starter one year. We weren't very good then, and I guess I was part of the reason why."

"What position you play? Small forward?"

"Actually, I was recruited as a shooting guard, but I wound up more as a swingman than anything else. That's kinda halfway between shooting guard and small forward. I used to like to compare myself to John Havelicek. You know, hall-of-famer, used to play for the Celtics, helped 'em win a couple championships . . ."

"I've heard 'bout him. I don't think he was as good as Bird."

"At crunch time he was. With a game on the line, he was about as good as anybody that ever played. But overall, Bird was better. I played against Larry once in his junior year at Indiana State. They cleaned our clock."

Hal was impressed. "Did you know you were lookin' at one of the all-time greats then?"

Mike shrugged. "I think everyone knew he was good,

but we didn't think he'd turn out to be that good." He patted Hal on a shoulder. "Which just goes to show, you never wanta take anything for granted. Somebody you don't even think about right now might be the one cleaning your clock someday if you allow yourself to get complacent."

"Well, I don't think I'm gonna get complacent anytime soon," Hal said. He studied Mike with interest. "Whaddayou do now? For a livin', I mean. I know these camps don't run year-round."

Mike chuckled. "True. I coach at a small college in upstate Wisconsin, not too far from Madison."

"I 'member us havin' to learn the state capitals in geography class. Madison is Wisconsin's state capital."

"It is, and it's also home to the so called fighting Badgers."

"I don't think the Badgers are usually very high up in the Big-Ten."

"They haven't been, but I think they're starting to get better. We've tried to get a game with them, but so far they've refused to schedule us."

"It'd be more 'barrassin' losin' to y'all 'un to Indiana an' Michigan, I 'magine."

Mike flashed a grin. "Yes, I imagine it would be," he conceded.

"Boston U doesn't have a bad program," Hal mused. "You musta been pretty good to get recruited there."

"I was all right, nothing special," Mike said with a shrug. "When I got out of high school I thought I was kinda special. I led my team in scoring and rebounding and made the all-state team."

"What state? Massachusetts?"

"Naw. Rhode Island. I was recruited by a couple other schools up in the northeast, an' I finally settled on BU. I wanted to be in Boston. I had been kinda out in the boondocks, an' I thought it might be nice to try big city life for a few years. I wasn't smart enough to go to Harvard, and BC wasn't interested, so I wound up at BU."

"How'd you wind up in Wisconsin?"

"One of my coaches at BU knew of an opening for an assistant. I took the job. Then the head coach got an offer to go somewhere else, and I was hired as his replacement."

"You like Wisconsin?"

"Yeah. It's really not very different than where I grew up. It's real cold in the wintertime. But yeah, I like it. The program I've got isn't a worldbeater, but we're respectable. Usually we win more than we lose, and if we caught the Badgers at the right time, we might have a chance of springing the upset."

Hal laughed. "Maybe someday you'll wanta 'cruit me, an' I can help you beat 'em," he said.

"Well, if you'd be willing to play without a scholarship, I wouldn't turn you down," Mike said good-naturedly. He patted Hal on a shoulder. "Unfortunately, we're only Division III."

Hal winced. He couldn't afford that.

37

    The players were quartered in an old army barracks that antedated World War II. Mike directed Hal there and introduced him to the other young men staying in the barracks. He found a cot and a locker for Hal and then headed out. The young man was on his own.
    Virtually all the other young men in the barracks were black. Hal wasn't really surprised; he had come to recognize that African Americans were numerically predominant in his sport. He spotted one other white face, on the other side of the barracks, but he didn't feel moved to go over and introduce himself. He really didn't mind being a minority as long as the others didn't hassle him unduly.
    "I guess you just got in," a skinny young black man about half a foot taller than Hal said. He was lying on a cot just a few feet away from Hal's.
    "Yeah, few minutes 'go. Mike Lewis drove me in," Hal confirmed. "I guess you know Mike."
    "Yeah, I know Mike," the young man said. He sat up on

his cot and extended his hand. "Hi. I'm Brandon Willis."

"Hal McDonough," came the response as the handshake was completed.

Brandon had a beautiful smile that reminded Hal of Ernest from back in Brileyville. The thought struck him as he shook Brandon's hand that blacks seem invariably to have the best smiles or meanest scowls one can find on a human face.

"I heard you was from back east somewheres," Brandon said as he lay back down.

"Southeast, I guess you'd say . . . Virginia," Hal said. He started putting his belongings in his locker.

"I heard one guy comin' here wouldn't be from the midwest, an' he'd be the last one to get here, an' I guess that gotta be you," Brandon said. "Let me guess. You're a guard."

Hal laughed. "At my size, you're not likely to be a power forward."

Brandon nodded assent. "I figure I'll prob'ly play small forward when I get to college."

"'Cided where you're goin'?" Hal asked.

"I figure next year 'bout this time I'll be gettin' ready to suit up as a Wolverine," Brandon said with that smile again flashing.

"Wolverine. That's Michigan, isn't it?" Hal asked.

"I guess some folks'd see me as kind of a traitor," Brandon answered with a confirming nod. "I live in East Lansing. That's where Michigan State's at."

"I've read an' heard 'bout guys doin' that," Hal said. "Mostly from down in my part of the country. Say like some guy from Tallahassee, Florida 'cidin' to play for Miami or the University of Florida 'steada Florida State or vice versa." He studied Brandon momentarily. "Course I wouldn't figure Michigan State'd be too bad to play for. They did win a national championship not all that long 'go. I know Michigan's won one more recent, but still I wouldn't think Michigan State'd be all that bad."

"Well, with Fisher the program's on the move," Brandon said with a shrug. "An' I think Heathcoat's 'bout run his course at Michigan State. He won that one year with Magic, an' I 'spect a lotta teams coulda won with Magic. Ax the Lakers."

Hal laughed. "Yeah, I don't think they'da won all those championships without him." His lips pursed thoughtfully. "Still, I read somewheres Michigan's got a real top-notch freshman bunch comin' in. I'm not sure I'd wanta take the chance of comin' in with that many good players. You can be good yourself an' still wind up bein' overlooked in that kinda crowd."

"Well, I figure you don't wanna get in the habit of shyin' 'way from tough competition," Brandon reasoned. He flashed that magnificent smile again.

Hal shrugged. He didn't mind the competition part, but he wasn't sure he wanted it to include an unduly crowded selection process for a starting position. Even so, he had to admire Brandon's resolve.

A call to dinner interrupted their conversation. Meals were served in an old army mess hall. The food was surprisingly good, or at least less bad than Hal had anticipated it being. It wasn't as good as his mother's, but it was better than what he got in the school cafeteria anyway.

Brandon had taken a seat across the table from him. He, too, was eating with gusto.

"Not too bad, is it?" Hal remarked.

Brandon again flashed that magnificent smile. "You hungry, you eat. I praise the Lord every day when I can get a meal like this. I can 'member days when me'n my brothers'n sisters didn't have hardly nothin' to eat. That was when my dad lost his job. I was 'bout twelve then. It haven't been so bad lately. Least we been able to eat."

Hal was touched. "Me'n my mother had some tough times, but usually we been able to put food on the table anyways."

"Religion kinda 'portant in my family, an' it help keep

our spirits up when things kinda down," Brandon said. "If you hear me say somethin' like praise the Lord, I hope it don't bother you."

Hal chuckled. "No, it doesn't bother me." He sighed wistfully. "I go to church with my mother. We live in a black section of town, but she feels she's gotta go to the Episcopal church 'cross town where the ritzy white folks live. So for a long time, 'til I found out I could play basketball, I was kinda on the outside of the two groups: the blacks at school that didn't want anything to do with me an' the whites at church that looked down on me 'cause nobody I knew could 'fford to send me to a private school."

"Sound like your ol' lady got a real bad thing for image, an' you kinda got stuck in the middle," Brandon said with a chuckle.

Hal nodded soberly.

Hal and Brandon shot some basketball after dinner. Some other young men joined them, and they split off and got a game going. Brandon and Hal were on the same team, and they wound up winning rather impressively.

"I know one thing: Any time I can choose somebody to be on my team, you gonna be it," Brandon said with a grin as he and Hal left the court.

"Same here," Hal said.

"Man, you got some range on that jumper," Brandon said in an admiring tone. "You sure you only gonna be a junior? Ain't nobody been doctorin' no records to keep you eligible longer?"

Hal laughed. "With the records our team's had, believe me, if they found anybody comin' 'long that could play at all, they'd be rushin' to get 'em in the lineup, not holdin' 'em out," he replied.

It struck him that Brandon looked a lot like Ernest. The two were the same height and weight and had about the same facial structure and, of course, comparably effulgent smiles. But those similarities didn't translate to the basketball court. Brandon was a lot quicker and a better jumper, and his shooting range was considerably superior. Ernest seemed helpless when forced away from the basket, while Brandon was quite capable of sinking the trey. Hal thought Brandon really might be better suited to Rick Pitino's system at Kentucky rather than Michigan, but of course Brandon's heart was set on being a Wolverine.

Hal mentioned the similarities to and differences from Ernest he noted, and that drew a laugh from Brandon.

"Ernest prob'ly the victim of smalltown blahs," he said. "If he growed up where I did, he'da been hustlin' a lot more on the basketball court, an' he'd be learnin' a lotta things he don't know now. That's prob'ly the difference."

"Well, I 'spect it might have somethin' to do with you just bein' born with more to work with 'un he's got, too," Hal rebutted.

Ernest shrugged. "If that's true, it's the Lord that 'serve the credit, not me," he replied.

Hal couldn't argue that point. Talent does seem to emanate from a source beyond any individual's personal merit. As humans perceive, it often falls on people who are not necessarily the more deserving.

A little later, Hal was back in the barracks. He had found an issue of *Sports Illustrated* lying around and was reading that. It was baseball season, and he was reading an article on Jose Canseco. He wasn't really a baseball fan in the sense of having a favorite team or player, but he did have some interest in the sport.

"Well, glad to see there's at least one more vanilla chip in this bowl of chocolate," a voice interrupted his perusal. He looked up and rubbed his eyes. That was mostly because he wasn't sure that what he saw was for real. The tallest human being he had ever seen up close was standing just a couple of feet from his cot. It was a caucasian who looked to be within a year of Hal's age. And like Hal, he had very blond hair and blue eyes.

Hal cleared his throat. "If you were talkin' 'bout ice cream, the chocolate kinda dominates over the vanilla," he responded with a shy grin. "But I'm used to it. I'm the only white boy on my high school team, an' it looks like it's gonna stay that way 'til I graduate or my mother can figure some way to get me in a private school."

"It's 'bout fifty-fifty black and white at my school," the giant said. He extended his hand. "My name's Greg Mason."

Hal's first impression was that Greg had to be seven feet tall or better. Over time, he discovered his actual height to be six feet, eleven inches. Not that the one inch difference mattered particularly. He could get the ball swatted back in his face just as easily from one as the other. Brandon, at six feet, seven inches, could swat it back on him, too, if he didn't use some guile when trying to drive against someone that much taller than himself. Hal instinctively understood as much. That's not to say that he never had a shot blocked, but he was developing moves that kept that embarrassing statistic at a minimum.

"I was thinkin' a couple times I had your shot blocked, an' then you do one them twistin' moves an' get the ball off over me," Brandon remarked to him once while they were playing a game with some other young men. "I don't know how you do it. It don't seem like you go up all that high."

Hal shrugged. "I dunno. I just got this 'bility to see somebody's hand up there, an' I can switch hands real easy." He eyed Brandon with mock severity. "You tryna make some crack 'bout white boys not bein' able to jump or somethin'?"

Brandon flashed a grin. "Naw. I seen a couple white boys could jump pretty good. I played 'gainst one last year. He could outjump me. Lucky for me, he couldn't shoot too good, so I let him jump to his heart's content."

Hal laughed and patted Brandon on the back.

Over the next few days, a bond developed between Hal, Brandon, and Greg. Greg initially had eased himself in because he had an emotional need for another white boy to talk to while he was in camp. But he was a nice guy, too, and

Hal and Brandon found themselves liking him.

They made an odd trio in camp, and some of the other young men remarked on it. A couple of jokes were cracked about Hal looking like Greg in miniature or Greg looking like an oversized Hal or how misplaced Brandon looked in the company of the two white boys. A couple of times the three took a challenge from some other young men for a game in the evening after the instruction part of the day was finished, and what became quickly apparent was that they made a formidable unit. Hal was hard to stop on the perimeter, Brandon could go inside and out very well, and Greg was quick under the basket and had the added dimension of a corner jump shot.

"Three of y'all wind up 'gether on some college team someday, that's gonna be scary," one young black man they played against remarked after one of the games.

"Get these two brothers to join me, we might be bangin' down some buckets for the Wolverines next couple of years," Brandon replied with that resplendent smile. Actually, that didn't appear destined to happen. Greg was semi-committed to attend Iowa when he graduated. Hal was a year younger, and the recruiters had only just begun scouting him, but his mother had already let him know that the only two colleges west of the Mississippi River she was willing to accept were Stanford and Northwestern. Her preference was for a school with a superior academic reputation not too far away, such as Duke or Vanderbilt. If he opted for some school like Michigan, he might never hear the end of her squawking.

The instruction sessions included some scrimmages, and Hal initially had some trouble when he was matched up against a young black man from Detroit named Tyrell. For the first time, he was going against someone who could match him in athletic ability, and Tyrell had the advantage of being a year or so (perhaps even more) older. He also had been playing in one of Detroit's better high school programs, and he had picked up some tricks that Hal hadn't yet had opportunity to learn. So for a couple of days, Hal was getting noticeably the worse of it when they were paired off against each other.

Mike Lewis called him aside on one occasion. "Relax, Hal," he said. "You're as good as Tyrell. Just don't be intimidated by him."

"It's just kind of a shock," Hal said. "I been used to havin' nobody that could play with me one on one, an' now I find myself goin' up 'gainst somebody maybe every bit as good as I ever hoped to be."

"Just between you and me, I think you'll be the better player in time," Mike told him with a shoulder pat. "Now, just go out there and play him hard."

Eventually, Hal got to where he could hold his own with Tyrell. He couldn't say positively that he was consistently getting the better of it. Some days it seemed that he had the edge; others, Tyrell appeared to come out ahead. So over a given period, they wound up just about even. Hal couldn't feel too bad about that. He was giving away age and experience to a quite talented player, so holding his own had to rank as a plus for him.

A couple of times he tried to compliment Tyrell on his skills, but Tyrell's response was terse and not very friendly. Tyrell had no friends among the other young men attending the camp, and he didn't seem to want to cultivate any. He stayed to himself, avoided the evening basketball games the other young men enjoyed and said nothing more than was absolutely necessary to anyone. He didn't make any trouble, so his standoffish behavior was generally viewed with insouciant shrugs.

"What's buggin' Tyrell anyhow?" Hal asked Brandon once. "Just outta curiousity. I've tried to start a conversation with him, an' he just cuts me off an' goes his own merry way."

"Tyrell got a bee in his bonnet, like they say. Don't take it personal. He don't hit it off too good with the brothers here neither," Brandon said.

"I thought maybe it was on 'ccount of me bein' white or somethin'," Hal said.

"I dunno. I don't think he's too keen on white folks, but like I say, he don't seem to like the brothers that much better," Brandon sighed. He patted Hal on the back. "I wouldn't worry 'bout it, man. You ain't did nothin' to him. If he don't wanna talk to you, you ain't missin' nothin'."

Hal chuckled. He supposed that was true.

For tutorial sessions, Hal was paired with a black instructor named Calvin. Calvin was about six feet, four inches and had played guard some twenty years earlier for a black college down in Texas. He now worked as an assistant coach for Detroit University.

Calvin was a strict tutor, and he was not given to massaging youthful egos—Hal's or anyone else's. Through most of the sessions, he was on Hal unmercifully, spotting all kinds of little things the white boy was doing wrong on both sides of the ball.

"You got quick hands an' feet, an' they may get you by 'gainst lower level competition, but when you get up on a higher level, you gonna need more'n just that," Calvin told him once sternly. "Way you position your feet when you dribble, I know slow white boys'd pick your pockets clean. That little juke move you make, a smart defender with less'n half your quickness could draw you into a chargin' call. You gotta learn to think out there, boy. You can't get by on just hustle an' instinct."

By the time he finished his sessions with Calvin, Hal's ego often was deflated, and he almost had the feeling that he might never be able to do anything right. He expressed that thought once to Brandon in a mournful tone.

Brandon chuckled and patted him on a shoulder. "Calvin talk like that to everybody," he told Hal. He shook his head. "Man, last year I went to a camp put on by the University of Detroit, an' he had me thinkin' I had to be 'bout the dumbest thing that every tried to dribble or shoot a basketball. But

Detroit was one the schools sendin' me a letter, an' I understand Calvin had a lot to do with it. An' I wouldn't be a bit surprised if Detroit sends somebody 'round recruitin' you next year."

Hal wasn't sure about that, but he took what Calvin taught him to heart and endured the verbal abuse from the instructor through the remainder of the sessions.

Once Calvin did call him aside. "You think I been pretty rough on you?" the instructor asked.

Hal almost choked. "I hope you're not gonna tell me what you been doin' is patty-cake," he responded.

Calvin smiled. That was the first time Hal had seen him do that. "No, it ain't patty-cake," he admitted. He clasped Hal's shoulders. "You got the tools to be a real good ballplayer. You're maybe not quite as tall as a lotta guards, but you got the ballhandlin', shootin' touch, all that. An' I've never seen any kid your age can crossover dribble like you can."

Hal exhaled sharply. That was an earful. "Way you dress me down, I'd almost figure I can't do anything right," he said.

"I gotta keep you on your toes," Calvin said. He shook Hal's shoulders gently. "I figure right now you need more of the vinegar an' less sugar-coatin'. Maybe someday, if I'm ever coachin' you, I'll see it different. Maybe your confidence will need a boost. Right now, I figure you already been gettin' plenty of compliments, so I just gotta knock you down a peg to let you know you don't know everything or even a very big part of what there is to know."

"You've done that all right," Hal conceded.

"Well, if you think I been rough on you, you shoulda seen me with some other guys," Calvin said.

Hal laughed. "If you been rougher on them 'un you been on me, they oughta be dead by now."

"Well, one of 'em made the all-ACC second team last year at Clemson, an' another made all-Southeast Conference at LSU, so they're a long ways from bein' dead," Calvin said with a chuckle. "I had one boy make the NAIA all-America team; I've had a couple make all-Big-Ten. I'll bet if you axed any of them, they'll tell you in a heartbeat I been every bit as rough on them as I was on you. I 'spect they'll tell you I did it with a purpose, too."

"Yeah, I can 'gree with that," Hal responded sincerely.

38

Greg made a point of inviting Hal and Brandon to spend one weekend the group had off at his home not very far away. Greg had brought his own car to the camp and so was able to drive them there. It was a nice home in a mostly white neighborhood just outside Chicago. That didn't really surprise Hal; he thought Greg probably hailed from a neighborhood a little like something from a TV sitcom such as *Saved by the Bell*—minus some of the zany characters, of course.

Hal was a little surprised to find that neither of Greg's parents was exceptionally tall. Greg's father was about Hal's height: close to six feet. His mother was of about average height.

"I woulda figured, lookin' at Greg, one y'all'd have to be a giant," Hal remarked to Greg's parents over dinner.

Mr. Mason laughed. "'Fraid not, Hal. As you can see, I'm a long way from being a George Mikan. And Lillian here is not exactly as tall as the Burge twins that play for that school down in your part of the country."

Hal laughed. He knew that Mr. Mason was referring to the University of Virginia's women's team.

"What's a George Mikan?" Brandon piped up in confusion.

That was a new one on Hal, too.

"He was top big man back when Dad an' Mom were growin' up," Greg volunteered.

"He was six-eleven. Back then, guy that tall was looked on almost as a giant," Mr. Mason said.

"Still looks pretty tall to me," Hal murmured.

The entire table cracked up. Brandon patted Hal good-naturedly on the back.

"He'd be pretty tall even for today's game," Mr. Mason said. He smiled reminiscently. "I imagine he could play today, but I think Kareem, Wilt, Russell, Walton, Ewing and some of those other guys would be better players. He prob'ly wouldn't be quick enough to stay with them."

"He got with the right team, he might not have to be," Brandon said. He flashed his incandescent smile. "My dad's always talkin' 'bout how Dave Cowens used to play for the Celtics. He was kind of a big lunk, but he helped 'em win a couple championships. Wes Unseld with the Bullets, too."

"Cowens was quick," Mr. Mason said. He chuckled. "He didn't give that impression, but he was mobile. He had to be. He gave away a good three to five inches to most of the other centers in the league."

"Yeah, I think I 'member readin' he was only six-nine," Hal said. "That's shorter'n McHale. 'Bout the same height as Bird."

"Probably the McHale-Bird team was the better of the two championship units," Mr. Mason said. He smiled warmly. "Greg is reminiscent of McHale on offense, but he may fall a little short on the defensive end."

"Well, he'll make anybody tryna guard him work hard 'nuff so you might not notice," Brandon said with a grin.

"You seem a little out of place playing basketball with

the two young men here so much taller than yourself," Mrs. Mason remarked with a smile to Hal.

Hal laughed. "Sometimes I feel kinda outta place, Miz Mason."

"He can handle the ball an' shoot the outside jumper 'bout as good as anybody you're likely to see, though," Brandon supported Hal.

"I know I wouldn't mind having him on my team anytime," Greg seconded that motion. He chuckled. "With him out there, the other team can't collapse on me. If they try it, he'll be lighting it up with three pointers all night."

"Sounds like you might be pretty good for your size," Greg's mother said to Hal.

Hal shrugged. "Well, I don't think anybody just wants to give me that open jumper," he agreed immodestly.

"What I can't figure, lookin' at the two of y'all, how'd this beanpole get to be so tall?" Brandon remarked to Greg's parents.

Mrs. Mason shook her head. "I have no idea, Brandon. It just happened. I don't know of anyone exceptionally tall on my side of the family. Oliver's side had one boy about six-four, but that's about it."

"And no jokes about the milkman please," Mr. Mason quipped. "He's only about five-six or seven."

That one drew a hearty round of laughter.

"Well, you don't know everyone in our ancestry datin' back more than two generations. And when you get right down to it, what difference does it make?" Greg responded in a bored tone.

"One good thing, Greg didn't turn out to be clumsy like a lot of other young men as tall as he is often do," Mr. Mason said.

Greg shrugged. "I think the fact I played soccer and tennis when I was growin' up had a lot to do with that."

"Well, I never played tennis myself, an' 'bout all I know 'bout it is from watchin' it on the tube sometimes," Hal interjected. "But I 'spect you'd be hard to lob over."

That one was also greeted by a good round of laughter.

"Yeah, but those low returns are murder on someone like me," Greg groaned.

The three young men went out a little later and checked out the mall scene in Greg's neighborhood. They drew more than a few stares as they walked along. At one point, someone asked them if they played for the Bulls or DePaul. Hal knew that was primarily because of Greg and Brandon. He knew no one was likely to guess him to be a basketball player on any level at first glance.

"Your parents are neat folks," he remarked to Greg once when the three stopped at an ice cream shop.

"Yeah, they are," Brandon agreed.

"I think so, too," Greg said.

"Your mom's a good cook, too," Brandon said. "Maybe not as good as mine, but still pretty good."

Greg and Hal laughed.

"I still can't get over the size difference 'tween you an' your parents," Hal told Greg.

"I don't know what 'ccounts for it," Greg said with a shrug.

"I'm a lot taller'n anybody in my family I know anything 'bout, too," Brandon said. "My daddy prob'ly ain't quite as tall as Hal here, an' my mama's a little itty-bitty thing. Little in size anyhow. You get her mad, you got a giant on you hands."

Hal chuckled. Images of Shawna's mother and Eunice popped into his brain.

He had previously confided to his two friends the fact that he was dating a black girl steadily. He had broached the fact a little gingerly with Brandon; he understood that many blacks object to white boys getting that intimate with one of their females. But Brandon had no such problem and quickly assured Hal of that fact.

"Prob'ly kinda gutsy you doin' it in a southern state like you doin', but I 'spect it'd take more guts for a black guy to try goin' with a white girl there," he responded insouciantly.

"I never thought of it as guts," Hal said. "Crazy maybe. Funny. I had a crush on Shawna for a long time before I ever thought 'bout makin' a move on her. But I figured it was hopeless an' I didn't even try. Later I found out she'd kinda been feelin' a whole lot the same way."

"When you're an athlete, and especially in your case where you're already the best in the school, that kinda makes girls notice you more'n if you were top oboe player in the school band," Greg said.

Hal laughed. "Oboe player? How you come up with that one?"

"I like to think I know somethin' 'bout life outside of basketball," Greg said with a shrug. "Athletics are a high-profile part of any school's social scene, and your better male jocks draw more fan adulation than your best Broadway singers and actors."

"Plus Hal kinda got the 'vantage over guys like you'n me 'cause of him bein' closer to a height girls can grab hold of," Brandon interjected jocularly.

"Well, we can grab on okay, but even so I'm kinda surprised sometimes how she wound up pickin' me," Hal said wistfully. "She's really not all that big into sports. An' I think her preference overall is for more intellectual guys. I don't think I'm dumb, but I never thought of myself as intellectual either."

"Neither did Brandon or I," Greg quipped.

"Girls kinda funny sometimes what they say they like an' what they wind up turnin' on to," Brandon mused. "Maybe you got some potential you ain't even thought 'bout tappin' into, an' Shawna sense that. Sometimes I really think they can see through a guy an' spot the good as well as bad better'n the guy know hisself."

"You could be called a sexist if the wrong woman happened to hear you sayin' that," Greg reminded him.

"Hey, I been called worse," Brandon said with that gleaming smile.

39

The Hal and Tyrell match-ups were put aside for the time being. The camp's coordinators had decided to put the two young men in different brackets. So now Hal was able to shine more easily against players he was matched up against, and no doubt Tyrell was as well.

Actually, Hal found that he missed going up against Tyrell. He liked the feeling of being tested by a really good player, which Tyrell certainly was. Not that the players he now went up against were bad, but they were less of a match for him in one on one situations. Tyrell forced him to raise his game to a higher level, and he liked that.

Some college coaches from around the country dropped in on the camp and helped with instruction. Jim Harrick from UCLA, Nolan Richardson from Arkansas, Jim Calhoun from Connecticut, and Dale Brown from LSU were among the college mentors checking in on the young prospects. Hal's personal favorite memory was getting a pat on the back and some complimentary words from Bobby Knight.

He chatted with the Indiana coach for a few minutes and was surprised to find that Knight actually seemed like a fairly nice guy. This impression contrasted starkly with the image he sometimes gleaned from television and newspaper accounts.

"I see you'n Coach K gettin' kinda chummy there," Calvin remarked to him with a probing smile.

Hal chuckled. "Yeah. What I read'n hear 'bout him, I almost 'spect him to be breathin' fire."

"Oh, you ever play for him, you'll feel that fire," Calvin said. He patted Hal on a shoulder. "With guys like you, it's sometimes worse. You got a lotta talent, an' that mean with him you gotta produce more. If he think you ain't producin' to your maximum, he'll get all over you like Listerine on bad breath."

Hal winced. "Well, I haven't heard of him killin' anybody yet, an' a lotta his players seem to like him."

"He grow on you," Calvin conceded. "He like to win, an' you play for him, you better learn to like it enough to do what you gotta do out there on the floor."

"Still, with him you got a chance to win a national championship," Hal said with a shrug.

"Yeah, the end reward's prob'ly worth the pain," Calvin conceded.

Hal heard from a couple of other sources that Knight said he combined the best of Isaiah Thomas and Steve Alford. Those were two players Hal could relate to; they were pretty close to the same size as he. Hal thought he probably would be quicker than Alford and pretty close, if not equal, to Isaiah in that department. He had good outside shooting range, as did the two Indiana all-Americans, and he could handle the ball probably as well as either of them at a comparable age.

"I heard Bobby Knight's pretty high on you," Greg said later when they were in the barracks. "He told a couple of people it was a shame you still had two years to go. He could find a place for you in his lineup right now."

Hal chuckled. "I 'spect that's just Knight talkin'. I don't think I'm quite ready for that yet. Still I like to think of myself as kind of an Isaiah type of player. I wouldn't mind playin' for Indiana 'cept for what I'd have to go through with my mother to go there."

"I don't think I'd wanna put up with the abuse Knight throw out," Brandon said through a grimace.

Hal still saw Tyrell from time to time in passing, but by now he had stopped trying to strike up a conversation. Since Tyrell evidently didn't want to talk to him, why bother? No real trouble seemed to be threatened by this status quo. Tyrell just seemed disposed to not being friendly, as opposed to being unfriendly.

Then one evening Hal was straightening out his locker. He had washed some clothes earlier and was putting them away. Part of that process involved pulling some items out and moving them around so that he could put the clean clothes in an organized stack. One of the items he happened to pull out was an eight by ten glossy photo of Shawna. Briefly, he found himself almost tranfixed by that picture. She was pretty. He hadn't forgotten that, but it was something that had passed for a time into his mental recesses. It also dawned on him that he hadn't called or written her, as he had semi-promised before he left Brileyville. Now he felt almost penitent because of that lapse. But more than anything else, he missed Shawna and wished she could be with him that moment.

It just so happened that Tyrell picked that particular moment to pass by on his way to another section of the barracks. He had no intention of speaking or stopping. That changed abruptly when he saw the picture of the black girl in the white boy's hands.

"Hey, what you doin' with a picture of a sister?" he asked Hal in a flat tone that sounded almost like a growl.

"It's my girlfriend from back home," Hal said. He thought Tyrell's tone sounded a little hostile, but he wasn't sure, so he just answered the question simply.

"Fuck you say," Tyrell snarled.

This time, the hostility was unmistakable. Hal was squatting on the floor at the time, and he instantly sensed he was in a dangerous position if Tyrell decided to start a fight. So he quickly rose to his feet. "Uh, you got a problem with it?" he responded.

"You fuckin' right I got a problem with it. You white motherfuckers been takin' everything 'way from us since this country started, 'cludin' our women," Tyrell snapped. He snatched the photo from Hal's hands and spat on it. "Any black girl'd have anything to do with you ain't worth the spit I just put on that picture."

"Hey, Tyrell, ease off. That boy ain't did nothin' to you," a black guy nearby appealed.

"Fuck he ain't. He 'zist, an' far's I'm 'cerned it's more'n he got a right to," Tyrell screamed. He tore the photo into shreds and threw it at Hal's feet. Then he pushed Hal back towards a locker. "What you gonna do 'bout it, white boy?"

"Uh, Tyrell, I don't want any trouble with you," Hal appealed.

"Hey, c'mon, man, leave him 'lone," the mediating young black man pleaded again.

Tyrell ignored the plea. "You fuckin' right you don't want no trouble with me," he snarled. He pushed Hal again, this time hard into the locker.

The push drove Hal into the protruding lock and hurt the lower part of his back. Now his brain was spinning. Tyrell wanted, and was pushing for, a fight, and no one was moving between them to break it up. He hoped for the latter, but it wasn't happening. And he wasn't about to take any more of this. That resolved, he slashed out of the corner Tyrell had him in and started punching. He caught Tyrell upside the head with a right hand and knocked him off balance. He unleashed a barrage of blows that drove the young Detroit man halfway across the barracks. Most of the punches were thrown wildly and weren't connecting solidly, but they were falling on various parts of Tyrell's body and hurting him.

Then Hal semi-tripped over the corner of one of the cots and was off balance for a couple of seconds, just long enough for Tyrell to gather himself and throw a punch back. It caught Hal on the side of the face and stung, but it wasn't hard enough to really stop him. He gathered himself, feinted with his left and came over Tyrell's hands with a right that regained the advantage for him. Again he threw punch after punch after punch; his only strategy was the thought that Tyrell couldn't hurt him while on the defensive.

Finally, he threw a hooking right with some body weight behind it that caught Tyrell flush on the jaw and sent him sagging to the floor. Hal could feel some power coursing through his arm as he landed that punch, and he knew Tyrell had to be hurt. Tyrell was not unconscious exactly, but he was dazed and would not have beaten a legitimate Marquis of Queensbury ten count. Hal didn't have the luxury of a referee to call that for him, so he stood poised to start punching again just as soon as Tyrell got to his feet.

At that moment, one of the counselors (a black man in his forties) burst into the barracks. "What's goin' on?" he shouted.

Hal was vaguely aware that some cheering had erupted from some of the young men watching as he and Tyrell were fighting. That probably attracted the counselor's attention.

The mediating black youth rose and put himself between the counselor and Hal. "Nothin', man, we cool," he said with a reassuring gesture.

The counselor looked dubiously at Tyrell, who was slowly rising to a standing position. "You sure? What's wrong with that boy?"

"Nothin'," the mediator assured him. "He just tripped, that's all. We cool. Ain't nothin' you gotta worry 'bout."

"Well, you better hope you're right," the counselor said. He glanced once more at Tyrell and shook his head. "I don't wanta hear 'nother peep outta y'all tonight, you hear me?"

"We hear you," the mediator assured him.

So the counselor heaved a sigh and departed.

Tyrell made a staggering move as if to attack Hal, and the mediator was quickly in his face. He was a good five inches taller than either of the two combatants and much heavier and stronger. "You heard the man. Ain't gonna be no more fightin' in here tonight," he told Tyrell. He turned to Hal. "That go for you, too. Ain't no reason the rest of us gotta get in trouble on 'ccount of y'all."

Hal was stunned. "How come you pickin' on me?" he responded sharply. "I didn't start it."

"I don't give a fuck who started it, an' I don't care if y'all wanta finish it, but you ain't gonna do it in here, an' you damn sure ain't gonna do it tonight," the mediator retorted.

"You dead meat, white boy," Tyrell grunted to Hal.

The mediator thrust his massive chest in Tyrell's face. "That's 'nuff outta you, too, punk, 'less you wanna try tanglin' with me," he said sharply.

Tyrell knew he didn't want to try taking on this young man, so he slunk morosely back to his section of the barracks. He turned once to toss a threatening glance Hal's way. Hal had a feeling that he had not seen the last of Tyrell.

"Look, you gotta know I didn't start it," Hal appealed to the mediator again as soon as Tyrell was out of earshot. "You were right there."

"Don't matter. Ain't nobody innocent when it come to a fight," the mediator said. "You coulda walked 'way, you know."

Hal almost choked. "He had me in the fuckin' corner, man. No way I'm gonna get outta that without lookin' like a bootlickin' dog 'less I fight my way out. I was kinda hopin' somebody'd come over there an' get between us so's I wouldn't have to fight."

"You got a point," the mediator sighed. He flashed a grin. "I woulda if I figured you was gonna start throwin' punches."

"Goddamn, sunuvabitch hurt my fuckin' back when he

slammed me into that locker," Hal groaned. "You 'spect me to keep lettin' him do that, you got 'nother thin' comin'."

"You right," the mediator conceded. He scanned Hal's right knuckles, still red from the punch that decked Tyrell. "You really hit him that one time. I could hear the crackin' sound. An' way he went down, you got somethin' 'hind that punch."

"Still it woulda been nice if I wouldn'ta had to be in that position to begin with," Hal sighed. "That's how come it'da been real nice for somebody to come between us an' stopped it before it got to that point."

The mediator nodded and patted him on a shoulder and headed off to his cot.

A little later, Brandon came in. He and Greg had gone out shopping.

"Hey, sound like I missed some 'citement," he remarked to Hal as he started undressing to go to bed.

"Well, you wanta call it that," Hal said with a shrug. He was reading a *Sports Illustrated*.

"Couple the guys told me you really decked Tyrell, knocked him cold practically," Brandon said with an excited grin.

"Not cold 'nuff. I got a feelin', like Jason, he's gonna be comin' back," Hal sighed.

For much of the rest of the camp period, Hal and Tyrell were kept apart. Word had circulated on what had taken place between the two young men in the barracks, and camp coordinators tried to keep as much distance between them as possible to avoid another such flare up. Mostly the unspoken concern was for Hal. He had shown in that one instance that he was not helpless, but he had not developed a fighting spirit to the extent Tyrell had. A lot of the guys in the camp were aware that Tyrell could be very mean and nasty, and in a rematch he would try to hurt and perhaps even kill Hal. Hal's instinct would be just to defend himself, and the feeling making the rounds was that such defense might not be good enough against someone like Tyrell.

Hal explained the circumstances leading up to the fight to his two camp buddies. They sympathized with him.

"Shit, I see black guys with white girls a lot, an' it doesn't bother me," Greg said. "I don't know what his problem is."

"I don't think anybody know what Tyrell's problem is," Brandon sighed. He patted Hal on a shoulder. "Watch you back, good buddy. That's one mean brother."

"Yeah, I kinda get that feelin'," Hal agreed.

Hal had no contact with Tyrell again until the next to last day of camp. Then the two were matched up against each other once more in a scrimmage.

At first, Hal was a little worried about a cheap shot from Tyrell, but for a while Tyrell showed no such inclination. He seemed content with just confining himself to basketball, a development which left Hal feeling rather relieved. The two played some good basketball for the better part of a quarter. This was one time Hal might have had slightly the better of it, but only marginally.

Hal found himself relaxing into the basketball flow, and that turned out to be a mistake. At an unguarded moment, he had Tyrell trapped with the ball in a corner. Tyrell feinted as if to move around him. Hal moved with the feint to cut off the dribble. But instead of the ball, he caught a Tyrell elbow squarely in his nose.

A piercing, screaming pain shot through his entire body, and he crumpled to the asphalt in nauseating agony. His hands instinctively moved to cover his face, and he could feel a sticky oozing that he knew had to be his own blood. He could also feel a detachment in his nose that signaled it was broken.

Calvin was the first counselor on the scene. "You're outta this game, an' you're outta this camp, Tyrell," he screamed at the offending black youth.

"Huh? Wha' you gettin' on me for? It were a accident," Tyrell appealed.

"Accident, my ass! Now, you go get your things packed. You're gettin' on the first bus back to Detroit," Calvin snapped.

Tyrell groused and muttered inaudibly, but he didn't challenge Calvin. He turned and headed back to the barracks.

Hal, in severe pain, was rushed to the hospital. Entire galaxies seemed to tear through his brain as the medics tried to keep him calm until a doctor could treat the broken nose.

The nose had to be set; a little while later, the splint and a lot of bandaging left Hal looking like something out of a horror movie. But at least the pain was starting to ease, and he had a doctor's assurance that he wouldn't be left facially deformed.

"Man, you one sad lookin' sight," Brandon greeted him with a grimace as he got back to camp.

"I'm one sad feelin' sight," Hal murmured.

"Well, leastways Tyrell been booted out, so you don't gotta worry 'bout him no more," Brandon said.

"I'm not sure that's good," Hal muttered. "Now I want a piece of him."

"Hey, let it go. He's gone, an' good riddance," Brandon urged him.

"He's gone, an' I got no choice, but he better hope him'n me don't cross paths again," Hal grunted. He meant it, too. He would be just as ready to kill as Tyrell.

"Forget him," Brandon said. He patted Hal on a shoulder. "You 'bove that sorta thing. Don't let you'self get drug down to his level."

"You think you'd be feelin' that way if somebody just broke your nose with a cheap shot?" Hal snapped. He patted Brandon on a shoulder. "Hey, nothin' 'gainst you. You're my friend. But I owe that motherfucker. I may never be able to repay it, but I do owe it to him, and if I get a chance, I'm goin' after him."

"You'll forget 'bout it soon 'nuff," Brandon said soothingly. He draped an arm over Hal's shoulders. "Soon as the nose heal, you'll be awright."

Hal shrugged. He was sure he would deal well enough with the rest of the human race, but it would be a long time before he could find it in his heart to forgive Tyrell.

Not long before departure time on the last day, Calvin came by the barracks specifically to talk to Hal. "If you was havin' trouble with Tyrell, how come you didn't come to me 'bout it?" he asked.

"'Cause I wasn't 'spectin' it to come to this," Hal said, with a finger pointed to his splinted nose for emphasis.

"I heard 'bout the fight y'all had in the barracks," Calvin said. "They shouldn't left y'all where he could get at you like that. I know Tyrell can be one mean sucker."

"He goes lookin' for trouble like that, he's gonna pick on the wrong guy," Hal grunted. He bit his upper lip angrily. "He bumps into me again, you're lookin' at the wrong guy."

"Forget Tyrell," Calvin said. He patted Hal on a shoulder. "You learned somethin' 'bout basketball while you was here, you met Bob Knight an' even got a compliment from him, an' you made some friends. A lotta the brothers really like you. That's what you oughta be carryin' 'way from here, not some grudge that's gonna eat at you 'til you settle the score."

"Well, I do 'ppreciate those other things," Hal said. He tried to grin and winced as the searing pain ripped across his forehead. "I do 'ppreciate 'em really. An' I figure I'll prob'ly never run 'cross Tyrell again, which suits me just fine. If I never see him again, I'll be happy. But if I do, first thing I'm gonna re'rrange his face. That's a promise."

"Well, Lord willin', you'll never see him again, an' that'd be a blessin'," Calvin said. He patted Hal on a shoulder. "I enjoyed workin' with you. I kinda got on you a lot, but that didn't mean I didn't like you or anything."

"Once I got past that part, I enjoyed it, too," Hal said sincerely.

40

Wimbush winced when he first saw Hal at the Richmond airport. "Boy, you really caught one, didn't you?" he said sympathetically.

Hal nodded. "Sunabitch caught me with a cheap shot."

"I heard about what happened," Wimbush said. He grabbed both of Hal's suitcases. "C'mon, let's get outta here."

Hal nodded and moved into step with him.

"Calvin Peters told me about what happened last night," Wimbush said as the two walked along. He flashed a grin. "Well, least one consolation, you're not on crutches."

"Yeah, I can move okay," Hal agreed. "But it hurts when I try to talk, eat an' stuff like that."

"I heard the boy that did this to you was booted outta camp," Wimbush said.

"Yeah," Hal confirmed. "Good thing for him. If I see that slimy asshole anywhere, anytime, I'm goin' after him . . ."

"Let it go, Hal," Wimbush urged solicitously. "What he

did was wrong. But you harboring this festering desire for revenge isn't going to do you any good."

"It prob'ly doesn't matter," Hal said with a shrug. "He's from Detroit, an' I don't 'spect I'm ever gonna see him again. That's all for the good, I guess. But if I ever do see him, watch out."

"I can understand you feeling angry," Wimbush told him with a pat on the back. "Just don't let it eat at you."

Hal shrugged assent. He didn't intend to dwell on the bad memory.

His mother recoiled in horror as he walked through the apartment door. "My God! What happened to you?" she exclaimed.

"An elbow full force in the face," Hal said. "Guy was swingin' 'round, an' I just happened to be in the way."

"For someone who's supposed to be so graceful and quick, you seem to have the darnedest knack for stumbling into all sorts of physical problems," his mother sighed.

"It will go 'way, Mother, an' I understand my face will look pretty much like it did before," Hal said.

"I certainly hope so," his mother responded.

After he unpacked and got settled back in, Hal took the bus over to Shawna's to pick up his car and to see Shawna. He understood that she should be getting back from summer camp just about now.

Marian Hanson's face contorted in horror as she opened the door and saw his bandaged face. "Boy, somebody sure did a number on you," she said.

"Cheap shot. Guy 'cided he didn't like me an' gave me an elbow in the face durin' a scrimmage," Hal said with a shrug.

"I thought basketball was supposed to be a non-contact sport," Gerald Hanson chimed in.

"This guy 'cided he wanted to be like Bill Laimbeer, 'cept he's black an' 'bout my size," Hal muttered. He glanced around the Hansons' home. "Shawna back yet?"

"She's down at Nags Head," Marian Hanson said. She

handed Hal the keys to his car. "She left these for you. Her father and I made sure the gas tank was filled."

"What's she doin' at Nags Head?" Hal asked dubiously.

"She met this young man while she was at camp, and his family invited her to spend a few days with them," Marian Hanson said.

Hal's eyes narrowed. He didn't like the sound of what he was hearing. Especially the *young man* part.

"The young man, Brian, and his family live down there," Gerald Hanson said. His tone was sympathetic, even though he probably did prefer the new status quo. "He and Shawna became quite friendly at camp. At your age, that's likely to happen."

"I wouldn't know. All I had 'round me was a buncha sweaty guys an' one that wanted to make hamburger outta my nose," Hal murmured.

Marian Hanson patted Hal on a shoulder. "You'll find someone, Hal, don't worry," she said in a kindly tone. "I imagine you're feeling a little hurt now, but you'll get over it. I expect this pain will pass more quickly than that broken nose you're carrying."

Hal winced. "Don't 'mind me of that," he appealed. He heaved a sigh. "I'll get on with my life. When you see Shawna, tell her I said hello."

"We will," Gerald Hanson assured him.

Hal wasn't really surprised to learn that Shawna had found another young man. She was certainly pretty enough, and the camps to which her parents sent her no doubt provided a chance for contact with black males more interesting than the ones she knew in Brileyville. Besides, he had always supposed that their relationship might not be forever, that eventually the two of them would part company and go in different directions. Even so, it still hurt. The pain in some ways was more excrutiating than the one from his broken nose.

Shawna's parents had not been unsympathetic to him. He realized within himself that they didn't dislike him and, indeed, would always be friendly to him as long as he gave them no cause to behave otherwise. Still, he could sense almost a glee they felt because their daughter finally was socializing in an amorous way within her own racial group. He could understand that. He could understand why his own mother would prefer to see him dating white girls. Line crossing is not something with which a lot of Americans even now feel comfortable. He supposed in any one of their places, if he had a son or daughter, he would probably prefer seeing that young person showing an opposite sex interest within his or her own group, too.

He wondered about this Brian, evidently Shawna's new beau. That was the name Gerald Hanson had thrown out. He didn't know much about Nags Head except that it was in North Carolina and people who had homes there were generally rather well-off. Brian probably came from a rather well-to-do black family, at least comfortably middle class—rather like Shawna's parents really. Brian might be a little older, perhaps a rising senior by now. He no doubt spoke with some polish and had an interest in life that transcended what Shawna was accustomed to. Hal knew that Shawna's basic preference was for intellectual men, and right now he fell well short of that. He might rise to that level someday, but that would take some time in college and exposure to other social elements to which so far he had been denied access. If Brian already was well on the road to that, he could see how Shawna's head might easily be turned.

His wanderings took him by the rec center and the outdoor basketball court, where he had a feeling that he would find some of his schoolmates playing basketball. Some things in life are still predictable.

"Good Lord, man, what the fuck you run into?" Wesley greeted him with a wince.

"An asshole motherfucker throwin' a cheap shot," Hal sighed. He took a deep breath and shrugged. "I get this. Then I come home an' find out Shawna's taken up with some guy at her summer camp an's spendin' some time with him down at Nags Head. Her mother says they're with his family, but I know how some of you guys are 'bout pullin' the wool over your parents' eyes, so that one I'd have to see to believe."

"Shit, man, you better off without her," Melvin told him consolingly. "She's got her head up in the clouds somewheres. Don't worry 'bout it. They's a lot better fish'n her in the ocean."

"Shit, you get 'way from here, you gonna have white girls crawlin' all over you for you to fuck," Lonnie agreed. "No reason you gotta put up with her bullshit."

"Not a case of puttin' up with bullshit or anything," Hal sighed. "We had a good thing goin', or least I thought we did. If she found somethin' that suits her better, more power to her."

"Yeah, now you can shop 'round, or maybe tap into some that white stuff where your mama take you to church," Wesley told him with a pat on the back.

"One thing I gotta say: If you gonna say the other guy look worse, I damn sure don't wanna see his face," Melvin joked.

The entire group broke into laughter.

"No, not yet, but if I catch him 'lone someplace, I'm gonna do my darnedest to change that," Hal said. He shook his head and shrugged. "But I'd have to go to Detroit to find him, an' I don't figure I can swing that. An' even if I could, I'm not sure it's worth that much trouble."

"Well, one thing sure, he couldn't leave you lookin' much worse," Thurlow Carter said.

Hal chuckled and took the basketball from Thurlow's hands and drove in for a layup. "Let's play some hoops," he said.

Hal later saw Trina and came away with little if any more insight into what was happening with Shawna. "All I know is she was gushin' like crazy over this guy named

Brian, an' then his family 'vite her down to Nags Head," Trina told him.

"Well, too bad I didn't have a chance to line somethin' up before she dumped me," Hal semi joked.

"Sound like you got a case of the brittle ego bigtime," Trina said in a scolding tone. "'Sides, how you know Shawna dumped you?"

Hal laughed. "Trina, I know I'm not the smartest guy to ever come down the pike, but give me credit for some common sense."

"I still say you shouldn't go jumpin' to no conclusions 'til you hear what Shawna gotta say 'bout it," Trina said with a shrug.

"Well, since she's not rushin' to get back, I don't know when that might be," Hal said with a frustrated gesture.

Hal wasn't sure what to believe about Shawna, but he didn't think that she intentionally set out to hurt him. He wished she had given him some warning, but then perhaps she wasn't able to. Over several months, he had come to know Shawna rather well, and certain character traits shone through rather vividly. She was at her worst headstrong, impulsive, often thoughtless, but she was not evil. She didn't especially take delight in hurting other people, although at times she also failed to calculate how something she did or said might be received by someone else before she launched into it. And while the romantic feeling for him might be dead, Hal didn't think she would take it so far as to dislike him or not want to at least be friends. If she did, he would definitely want some explanation for why she felt that way. He didn't think he had done anything to merit her dislike, but he couldn't discount the possibility that she misinterpreted something or someone else told her something about him that was wrong.

Well, c'est la vie.

He didn't plan to let the void in his life linger very long. He was already plotting how to fill it through the school months. One of the black girls in his class, Melba Johnson, had been tossing occasional signals his way through the recent months. Melba wasn't quite as pretty as Shawna, but she had a marvelously filled out torso that looked rather appealing under a tight sweater or sweatshirt. He thought he might try to see if he could get something going with her. In fact, he called her up that very evening and asked her out to a movie, and she assented.

Melba's mother may have harbored misgivings about her daughter dating a white boy in the same manner as Shawna's parents, but she didn't convey that impression. In fact, she was quite friendly to Hal as he waited for Melba to finish dressing.

"I been hearin' quite a lot 'bout you," she remarked to him at one point. "Seem like every time I open the paper or turn on a TV, I see your picture."

Hal flashed a grin. "Those guys gotta do somethin' to keep busy."

"Well, when you score points like you been doin', you gotta figure you gonna get wrote up," Mrs. Johnson said. She glanced at Hal's bandaged face and chuckled. "Course you don't want 'em takin' you picture while you lookin' like you do now."

"Yeah, you're right 'bout that, Miz Johnson," Hal agreed.

Melba came out. She glanced at Hal's splinted nose and bandaged face and grinned. "I hope that ain't permanent. I used to think you was kinda cute."

Hal chuckled. "No, I understand 'fore long I'll look pretty much like I did before," he said.

"That's good," Melba said. She clutched his arm. "See you later, Mama."

Her mother nodded and refocused on some knitting she had been working on before Hal arrived.

"I was 'pposed to have a date tonight, but he called early today an' cancelled," Melba confided to Hal when they were in his car. "I was a little bit 'prised when you called. I thought that snooty Hanson girl had a ring in your nose."

"Well, what I hear, she's taken up with some guy from

summer camp, an' she's shacked up with him at Nags Head," Hal said with a shrug. He flashed a grin. "I don't know if the ring's still there or not, but she's not pullin' on it."

Melba laughed.

They watched the movie, and then Hal drove Melba by the burger hangout where most of the Brileyville students liked to go in their spare time. All his basketball buddies were there, as they very often were on summer evenings.

"Well, look like you done got you a even hotter squeeze," Melvin made a point of telling him when Melba left for a moment to use the restroom.

Hal shrugged. "I dunno. I get the feelin' she could be. I know one thing, way her titties stick out in those tight sweaters she wears a lot, I wouldn't mind bouncin' my head on 'em for a while."

Melvin laughed and patted him on the back. "You awright, dude," he responded.

A little while later, Hal took Melba home and tried to kiss her goodnight. They got passionate for a moment, and then a wrong tilt jerked his splint and sent a sharp pain searing through his face and forced him to pull back.

"It's this thing," he told Melba, pointing to the splint. "When you turned, it hit this thing an' hurt like hell. I 'spect I'm not gonna be much good 'til I get this thing off."

Melba nodded and gave him a brush kiss on the mouth. "Well, you got off to a good start anyhow," she told him. She grabbed him by the hand. "C'mon, you can walk me to the door."

So he walked her to the door and kissed her gingerly one more time. Her crotch was pressed against his, and his penis was getting hard, and he knew she knew it, and he was glad of it.

Melba's hand rubbed across his penis and she smiled slyly. "I'm glad you 'vailable now," she cooed. Then she quickly kissed him and went inside.

Hal was still a virgin, but he had a feeling that if he went out with Melba a few more times, that would change. So in a sense, he saw something positive in not having Shawna occupying that part of his life any more. Not that he wanted to lose Shawna—frankly, he still would like to have her back. But if it wasn't to be, it wasn't to be. And Melba definitely was ringing his chimes right now.

His mother found out from Marian Hanson about her daughter's new beau, and needless to say Kathleen McDonough was ecstatic. "You'll see, it's all for the best, Harold," she told him in almost a smug tone.

"Okay, I'll take your word for it, Mother," Hal said with a shrug.

"A girl like that isn't for you," Kathleen McDonough said. "She belongs with her own kind, just as you do."

"Well, I 'spect an alien comin' down from 'nother planet would look at blacks an' whites an' Asians an' see us as kinda the same thing, just like we look at a couple of cats of different colors," Hal said philosophically. "But if it's better for her, I'm happy, an' I'll get over it."

"Of course you will, Dear," his mother assured him. She lit a cigarette and a gleam rose in her eyes. "I think now is the perfect time for you to try to establish something with Jennie Lee. Why don't you give her a call?"

Hal really wanted to try Melba out some more, but that would pretty much have to wait until he had the splint and bandages taken off his face. So, he reasoned, why not? His mother helped him find her phone number, and he called her up and asked if she would like to go out to a movie. He rather hoped she had other plans that night, but as it turned out she didn't, so he had another date.

He did warn her about the nose splint before he started over to her place. He didn't want her to be recoiling in fright at the first sight of him.

"A girl such as Jennie Lee can help open a lot of doors to a young man like yourself," Kathleen McDonough told him before he departed. "You should try to cultivate her."

"I'll keep that in mind," Hal said as he walked out the door.

He didn't think he had any such intention. Besides, he felt confident that soon he could be opening a lot of those doors by himself. But he wasn't disposed to arguing with his mother at that juncture.

Jennie Lee's mother was quite friendly to him when he arrived. She was still rather pretty in an aging cheerleader sort of way, and he had a feeling that Jennie Lee would look somewhat the same twenty years or so into the future. In fact, Jennie Lee would probably hold up in looks better than Melba. Melba's mother was not ugly, but a certain roundness of body and features had set in. Melba probably would be susceptible to the same process if she didn't exercise and diet to keep herself fit. She would never be slender like Jennie Lee or Shawna, but she might be able to keep herself from turning to fat if she worked at it—but only if she worked at it.

"Must be interesting going off to basketball camp like that with the best young players in the country," Jennie Lee's mother said. She eyed the splinted nose and winced. "If you don't get all broken up, that is."

Hal chuckled. "It's a good feelin', Miz Hudson. I'd like to keep my nose intact, but even that you figure you might have to deal with somewheres 'long the line. I hope this is my quota for a lifetime."

"It is a little unsightly, but I suppose that's part of what being a man is all about," Jennie Lee's mother said with a shrug.

Jennie Lee came down. She was dressed nicely. "Well, you were right about your face being a mess," she greeted Hal.

"I did warn you," Hal reminded her. "But it's 'pposed to go 'way pretty soon. I oughta be able to take the splint off in a week or so."

"That will certainly be a relief," Jennie Lee said.

So he and Jennie Lee went out. He took her to a nice restaurant across town. He had enough money saved up from his rec center job to afford that. He didn't think she was ready for the burger joint and his black friends. More to the point, he wasn't ready to show her off to them. Right now, the desire uppermost in his mind was to have sex with Melba, and Jennie Lee might spoil that. He wouldn't mind flaunting Jennie Lee in front of Shawna once or twice to let her know that two could play that game, but since she wasn't in town now, that gesture would be wasted.

He took Jennie Lee to a movie in the county mall after dinner and then home. It wasn't a bad date. It turned out that she shared some of his taste in popular music. They both liked the Rolling Stones, and he happened to have a Stones tape, which he played on his car's casette. When he got her home, he kissed her goodnight, gingerly.

"I do have to be careful," he said. "Turn the wrong way an' hit this thing, it hurts like crazy."

"I can imagine," Jennie Lee said. Her nose crinkled. "I won't deny I'll be happy to see it off."

"Not half as happy as I will," Hal told her with a grin.

While they were kissing, Hal's penis again got hard, and Jennie Lee ran a hand across the outline of it on his trousers. He had a feeling that she wasn't a virgin either. By instinct and breeding, she was a snob and a social climber, but she had a bit of the alley cat in her as well.

A Billy Joel line—*you're no stranger to the streets*—struck him as he drove home. It occurred to him that Shawna probably did him a favor. Now he could explore some other options.

Hal finally crossed paths with Shawna just a couple of days before school was ready to start again. He was in the burger place, sharing a table with Wesley, Melvin, Thurlow,and Lonnie when she walked in with her new beau.

The young black man accompanying her was tall and slender and rather nice looking. The thought struck Hal that his features and movements looked a little effeminate, but he was also gracious enough to admit to himself that it just might be a personal complex on his part.

"Look like your ex-squeeze done settled in with that brother," Thurlow observed.

Hal shrugged. "It's a free country. If that's what she wants, far be it from me to try'n stop her."

"I think that guy's a fag," Melvin muttered.

That remark took Hal slightly aback. "God, Melvin, you don't even know him. How come you're sayin' that?" he responded.

"Yeah, c'mon, Melvin, give the brother a break," Wesley agreed.

"I'm not sayin' it to be critical of the dude or nothin' like that," Melvin defended himself with a double handed gesture. "It's just, you know, like I told you, I got a older brother that hang out with that crowd, an' that dude look like he'd fit right in. You get so you can spot the type."

"He doesn't look outta the ordinary to me," Hal said with a shrug.

"Me neither," Thurlow concurred.

"Shit, what I hear now, fags look an' sound kinda like anybody else," Wesley said. "Only thing different 'bout 'em seem to be they like suckin' dicks 'steada gettin' pussy."

"Well, I bet you right now, if that girl marry that dude, she gonna walk in on him an' catch him in bed with 'nother man someday, you mark my words," Melvin told his friends with a straight face.

"It'd serve her right for bein' such a snooty bitch," Lonnie said. He patted Hal on the back. "You a thousand times better off without her, man, take my word for it."

Hal shrugged. "I got my own feelin's on that, but I don't wish her anything bad. I sure don't wanta see her get hooked up with some guy an' find out he's a fag."

"I bet it'd be funny as shit, though," Wesley said.

Hal laughed. "Yeah, I 'spect it might be," he agreed.

Hal noticed Shawna and Brian talking animatedly on the other side of the diner. He thought about going over and saying hello to her but then abandoned the idea. It was better to wait when he wouldn't be intruding on something.

Before she and Brian departed, Shawna made a point of stopping by the table where the basketball players were gathered. "Mama told me 'bout what happened to you," she remarked to Hal. "It's too bad. A good thing got spoiled 'cause of somebody's idiocy."

"Well, I wish I could say it doesn't feel as bad as it looks, but I'm 'fraid that wouldn't be true," Hal said with a grin.

"I heard you're quite a basketball player," Brian told Hal. He had an almost effeminate quality to his voice.

Hal shrugged. "Shawna's aunt helped open that door for me. If it wouldn't been for her, I might still be out on the sideline an' the class wallflower."

"Well, it could stand to get you a scholarship to one of the really fine universities," Brian said. "So you look at it that way, it's a good thing."

"My mother likes playin' with it better'n I do right now," Hal said. He flashed a grin. "I think whatever school I wind up pickin' 's gonna be at least halfway to 'ppease her."

"His mama's a real snooty one," Shawna told Brian. "I told you 'bout her comin' from a well-to-do Boston bankin' family."

"Well, nice meeting all of you," Brian told the group with a nod. Then he nudged Shawna with an elbow, and they departed.

"Well, nice meetin' all of you," Melvin mimicked Brian's parting words. He snorted. "Goddamn, that boy got fag wrote all over him."

"Hey, man, he ain't Clint Eastwood, but I don't think he sounded any more like a fag'n any of us really," Hal defended Brian.

"He's a fag, I'm tellin' you," Melvin said.

"Melvin, just 'cause you brother's one don't mean you gonna spot every fag in the world," Lonnie rebutted.

"I spotted that one. I'll bet you you check in a few years, you gonna find I'm right," Melvin said.

Hal doubted that Melvin had that kind of special insight, but he didn't think it was a point worth arguing either.

"Course I know one thing, that bitch called my mama real snooty, I'd have throwed some real choice words back at her," Lonnie told Hal.

"Well, Lonnie, in the case of my mother, I'm afraid she hit that nail right on the head," Hal responded.

Hal understood that sooner or later he and Shawna would cross paths in school, and they would talk. He wasn't sure what would be said. His intention was to let Shawna dictate the course. He didn't think she would get hostile with him, but if she did, he would respond accordingly. If she remained civil, so would he.

On the first day, he was walking down the hallway to a class when Shawna came along behind him. He slowed down to let her move into step with him.

"How come you didn't call me over the weekend?" she asked him with an impish grin.

That one really knocked Hal for a loop. He tried to respond and found the words choking in his throat. "Uh, wha...wha...wha...?"

"I heard you dated Melba Johnson last week," Shawna said in a teasing tone.

Finally Hal's voice cleared. "Goddamn, Shawna, you go runnin' off with that Brian guy an' you're surprised?" he shot back.

Shawna giggled. "You thought I dumped you for Brian?"

Hal looked at her in a bemused manner. "Didn't you?"

"How come you thought that?" Shawna queried mischievously.

Hal's head shook and his arms extended in a thoroughly frustrated gesture. "Uh, Shawna, your parents told me that, Trina told me that, everybody 'round seemed to think it. An' you got the gall to ask how come I got that idea? I think I'd have to be real dumb not to get it." He heaved a sigh. "I saw the way y'all were talkin' in the burger joint the other night. If he's what you want, fine, but don't play fuckin' games with me."

"So Mama told you I was goin' with Brian," Shawna said with a chuckle. She clutched Hal's arm. "You wanna know the truth, Harold Nelson McDonough, you'd be more likely to find Brian competin' with me for you 'un with you for me."

"Shawna, I'm not in the mood for riddles," Hal said testily.

Shawna kissed him on a cheek. "Hal, what I'm tryna tell you is Brian's a fag."

Melvin's words of the other night came back to Hal. "What?"

Shawna's nose crinkled impishly. "He didn't say it outright, but he ninety percent told me he was. His preference is for boys. I 'spect in a few years he's gonna be hangin' out with people like your uncle."

Hal shook his head in bewilderment. "Melvin told me the guy was that way, he swore it, almost like he'd bet the family farm on it, but goddamn I had no idea in this world he could possibly be right."

"Oh, the signs are there, if you look close," Shawna said. Her arms went around Hal's neck. "He's a fag. Trust me. He hung in with me 'cause he didn't want his parents knowin' it yet, an' I hung in with him 'cause it was a good way to keep the other guys at camp from hittin' on me. You see, most of the guys at camp 're 'bout as big a bunch of bozos as what you find 'round here."

"Okay, I understand that part, but how come you practically flaunted it in my face?" Hal countered.

Shawna shrugged. "Mostly 'cause I figured you needed to be taught a lesson. You told me you were gonna call or write when you were 'way, an' you didn't do it."

Hal exhaled sharply. "I meant to, but I got tied up an' forgot 'bout it. You get a lot goin' on at camp. It's not always easy 'memberin' things like that."

"Well, you gonna hang in with me, you better get in the habit," Shawna told him. She brushed his mouth with a kiss.

"Looks like I got back just in the nick of time. What I hear, you were tryna get somethin' goin' with Melba Johnson."

"Well, you gotta fill up the empty space with somethin'," Hal reasoned.

"Well, the space ain't empty any more, 'less you're dumpin' me," Shawna said.

A moment later, they were sharing a passionate kiss. The space really wasn't empty for Hal, and Melba and Jennie Lee were once more relegated to some far corner.

41

Marian Hanson was not exactly pleased with her daughter at this moment. "I think it was a rather cruel hoax to go playing on anyone," she said angrily. "It was bad enough your doing it to your father and me. But I feel even worse for Hal. It disturbs me a little that you seemed to feel this compulsion to play some sort of headgame with him."

Shawna grinned. "Y'all were askin' for it, really. You keep pushin' me to go to these camps an' whatnot just so I'll meet black guys..."

"We're doing what we think is best for you," her father interjected.

Shawna shrugged. "Like they say, the road to Hell is paved with good 'tentions."

"That still doesn't explain your jerking Hal around like that," her mother said. "I grant you Hal is not what I would envision for a son-in-law, but he is a nice young man and deserves something a little better than that kind of treatment."

"If I were in his shoes and you did that to me, I'd probably dump you," Gerald Hanson expanded. "I couldn't blame Hal if he did."

"We patched things up," Shawna said. She chuckled. "I gotta 'mit I was a little bit antsy when it came time to get back with Hal. I know he's got some pride, an' I kinda thought I mighta carried that thing with Brian just a teensy bit too far. Brian kinda told me the same thing."

"Well, if Hal had done what would certainly be understandable from almost anyone's point of view, that would have taken care of one worry anyway," Marian Hanson mused. "In a way, I'm almost sorry he didn't."

Shawna heaved an exasperated sigh. "Mama, just gettin' rid of Hal doesn't automatically guarantee I'm gonna fall in love with a black guy down the road," she countered. "An' me goin' with him right now doesn't mean I won't fall in love with a black guy down the road. It doesn't mean I will either. Maybe it'll be 'nother white guy comin' 'long. I know you'n Daddy mean well, but why can't you 'ccept that whatever I do is gonna be my choice? It's not like back in olden days when people 'rranged marriages an' whatnot."

Marian Hanson started to say something and found the words wouldn't form for her. At her core, she knew that her daughter was right.

"Right now, what Hal an' I got goin' isn't hurtin' anybody," Shawna went on. "I know some people don't like it, but that doesn't mean it's bad. Why can't you just relax an' let it run its course? If that means we split up 'ventually, fine. If it means we wind up gettin' married five or six years down the road, well, that's life, too. Say what you will, you could do a lot worse for a son-in-law'n Hal."

"It disturbs me hearing you throw out a thought like that," Marian Hanson sighed. "Even so, I suppose you make a valid point."

"Of course I do," Shawna said. She kissed her mother on a cheek. "We're a long ways from gettin' married or anything of that sort, so you don't really have anything to worry 'bout right now. It's just a high school girl and boy thing. It's not like it's the end of the world or somethin'."

"High school girl and boy things have a way of getting out of control at times," Marian Hanson murmured.

"Well, Hal'n I are not outta control type people, so that oughta ease your mind somewhat," Shawna reasoned.

Marian Hanson's lips pursed thoughtfully. She supposed that was true enough.

Kathleen McDonough was nonplussed. "You mean she was keeping company with a boy who is homosexual just to remind you not to take her for granted?" she said through a moue.

Hal flashed a grin. "Yeah, that 'bout sums it up."

Kathleen McDonough lit a cigarette and sighed loudly. "That tells me that you should be severing relations with that girl posthaste. It sounds like she's devious and self-willed."

"Mother, she's prob'ly not half as devious as somebody like Jennie Lee that you keep pushin' me to go out with," Hal sighed. "I gotta 'mit I was kinda ticked off, an' I don't like somebody playin' headgames with me, but when I think 'bout it, it was kinda funny. An' it's not like I didn't have it comin', at least a little bit."

"A real man would tell her where to get off in a heartbeat," Kathleen McDonough groused.

Hal chuckled. "Park benches're fulla real men, as you call it. My dad thinks he's a real man. An' they never have any women 'round."

"Your father is not a good example," Kathleen McDonough countered sharply.

Hal shrugged. "I don't wanta be like him. I'm just pointin' out that guys like that like to throw out the real man line a lot, an' they wind up 'lone. I don't like what Shawna did, an' she better not do it again, but that doesn't mean I oughta dump her right now."

"Harold, she's no good for you, I'm telling you for your

own good," his mother pleaded. "Why can't you come to your senses and break off with her as you should and start focusing on your real life?"

"Right now she is a part of my real life," Hal reasoned. "The no good part is in your mind, Mother. It has nothin' to do with Shawna or what kinda person she is or anything like that. Why don't you just 'mit it an' let it run its course? We're not hurtin' anybody, an' it's not like we're dumpin' babies off on the world or anything like that."

"Heaven forbid that you even think of something such as that," his mother muttered in disgust.

Hal laughed. "Mother, we're not thinkin' 'bout it. Last thing either of us wants is somethin' like that. C'mon, I throw out somethin' just as a joke, an' you gotta pounce on it like I just 'spressed some wild, radical thought. I just said that 'cause how you been rantin' . . ."

"I'm not ranting, I'll thank you to note," his mother said sharply.

Hal shrugged. "Okay, you're not rantin', but you're not really makin' any sense either. You don't like me goin' with Shawna, an' you gotta throw out some line 'bout her bein' no good for me every time you turn 'round. I'm not gonna tell you not to do it . . ."

"You'd damned well better not," Kathleen McDonough told him sternly.

Hal gestured resignedly. "Mother, if you don't like it, that's your right. I'm not sayin' you have to," he sighed. "But just 'cause you tell me she's no good for me is not nearly 'nuff reason in an' of itself for me to drop her."

"I have had the advantage of a few more years to gain some understanding of life and people," Kathleen McDonough said sententiously.

"You can't understand 'em if you don't talk to 'em an' get to know 'em, I don't care how wise you are," Hal rebutted. "You haven't 'schanged ten words with Shawna in all the months I've known her. You don't know what kinda person she is or whether she's good for me or not. Talk to her, get to know her. Then if you have to, form a 'pinion."

"When I want your advice, I'll ask for it, Harold. Until then, I think you would be well counseled to experience a bit more of life and people before you go telling me how I should or should not judge others," Kathleen McDonough said.

Hal heaved a sigh. This was hopeless.

As the basketball season neared its start, Shawna decided on a whim to try out for the cheerleading squad. She didn't really want to be a cheerleader, but a couple of people noted that it was a good way for her to get closer to Hal, and she had some amorphous notion of that as something people in love, as she fancied herself to be, might do. Besides, she didn't expect to make the squad. She wasn't that well liked by the returning cheerleaders or, indeed, many of the other students. In the past, she had made passing references to cheerleaders as inane and braindead, with no appreciable concern over whether they heard her or not. So she calculated that she would be turned down for the squad out of spite, and she could throw out the fact that she had gone out for it as her way of showing that she at least tried.

"You don't have to do this, you know," Trina told her solicitously. "Hal's crazy 'bout you. He know you ain't big on doin' cheerleadin' routines an' whatnot. 'Sides, it ain't like the two of y'all gonna be doin' some heavyduty makin'-out on the bus to an' from the games."

Shawna gestured in frustration. "Instant I turn my back, ol' Melba Johnson's tryna stick her big tits in his face. An' Cynthia Pruitt, too. Cynthia's on the squad already. I can see it now, with me not 'round, she'll be ploppin' down on the seat with Hal an' prob'ly unzippin' his pants an' God 'lone knows what else."

Trina laughed. "Shawna, you got less to worry 'bout from Hal on that score'n prob'ly any boy in this school. I'm tellin' you. You don't have to ride on the bus with him or nothin'. You'll be the one he look for when he get back,

355

believe me, 'less you got him thinkin' you dumped him for somebody else like you did over the summer."

Shawna nodded soberly. "That's partway how come I 'cided to do this," she muttered. She shook her head and smiled wanly. "Well, least I figure I'm prob'ly gonna get turned down, which is good. 'Less a couple those girls figure out I really don't wanna be on the squad. If that happens, they're prob'ly gonna be pullin' strings to get me on just to make me miserable."

Trina laughed.

Shawna ran into Hal a little while later. By now, the splint was long removed from his nose and he looked pretty much the same as he had before.

"What's this I hear 'bout you goin' out for cheerleadin'?" he asked her.

Shawna shrugged. "I just 'cided to do it on a lark. Maybe to show I care or somethin'. I dunno. I think I lost my mind."

Hal laughed. "You musta. Last time I heard you sayin' anything 'bout cheerleaders at all, you were callin' 'em inane an' braindead."

Shawna winced. "I 'spect a couple of 'em'd love nothin' more'n makin' me eat those words, too."

"Well, for what it's worth, you didn't have to do it on my 'ccount," Hal assured her. He punctuated it with a kiss. "The bus rides're no fun. I can tell you that right now. I like it 'cause I like playin' basketball, but I don't think I'd be wantin' to do that if I wasn't playin'."

"I guess maybe I'm scared of what might happen when I'm not 'round," Shawna murmured, her head buried in Hal's chest. "I've seen Melba an' Cynthia comin' on to you. I 'spect Cynthia might spread her legs for you right on the bus just to spite me if nothin' else."

Hal laughed and kissed Shawna. "I don't think so. Not with a whole busload of people around, an' a couple of 'em teachers," he reminded her.

"Well, I'm already committed to tryin' out for the team,"

Shawna sighed. She kissed Hal. "I guess I'll go down and go through the motions. I know most of those girls don't like me, so I'm sure they'll wanna keep me off the team."

"Well, if you called me some of the names I've heard you call them, I prob'ly wouldn't like you either," Hal said. He kissed Shawna. "Good luck. If you really don't wanna make the team, I hope you get your wish. I love you anyway."

"I love you, too," Shawna said in returning his kiss.

Unfortunately, Shawna wasn't riding a good luck cycle at that juncture. It was true that she wasn't well liked by the other cheerleaders, and most of them didn't want her on the squad. But Hal was both well liked and respected by virtually everyone associated with the unit, and everyone was aware that she was his girlfriend. Besides, she was a long way from uncoordinated. She had some acrobatic ability and she certainly was appealing to the eyes. Those factors wound up outweighing her unpopularity with the other girls, and she was among those finally selected.

"Well, I guess you didn't blow it 'nuff," Hal remarked to her sympathetically when she ran into him again.

"I kept thinkin' what stupid thing can I do to look like the biggest klutz in the world? An' then I figured it didn't matter, 'cause those girls all hate me an' they're gonna get me booted off anyway. So I play it straight, an' I wind up on the team," Shawna sighed.

Hal draped an arm over her shoulders. "Well, you can always tell 'em you don't wanta be on the squad," he reasoned.

"Hah! An' wind up lookin' like a quitter? No way," Shawna snorted. She nuzzled Hal's neck. "'Sides, least this way I know that she-cat Cynthia ain't gonna be unzippin' your pants on the bus or anything like that."

Hal laughed.

Not long after he and Shawna were officially back together, Hal ran into Melba Johnson in the school hallway.

"Well, look like you ain't got rid of the ring yet," Melba said in a teasing tone.

Hal was momentarily puzzled. Then he recalled part of their conversation on the one night they dated and shrugged. "No, I guess not," he conceded.

"I was kinda hopin' me'n you could get somethin' goin'," Melba confided with a sly grin. "I got a feelin' if you ever got it on with me, you'd like it."

Hal would remember that remark for a long time. Occasionally, too, when Melba's ample bosom was vividly outlined by a tight sweater or t-shirt, the thought struck him that it was something he might not mind trying out. Of course, then the thought of facing Shawna after he had done so fell like water on his inner fires. That didn't mean that the fires went out. It just meant that he wasn't ready to follow up on those urges.

42

The big question mark hanging over the Brileyville team's pre-season was exactly how good the Falcons would be. It was a given that Hal would be a superstar. He had already established himself as that while only a sophomore, and almost certainly he would continue to improve through his junior and senior seasons. But a new face at three of the other four positions left the rest of the team suspect. The only returning regular (not counting Hal) was Sammy Williams; he would play one forward slot. Wesley would play center, Lonnie the other forward and Melvin the off-guard. They were as talented as the people they replaced, but their lack of varsity experience was expected to be a handicap for a while.

Two starters from the junior high team, Thurlow Carter and Earl Wilson, would be on the bench. The irony in that was remarked on a few times, although by now no one really griped. Obviously, Hal would be one of the starting guards, which meant that either Thurlow or Melvin would have to accept a substitute's role. Of those two, Melvin had the edge. Earl would be a starter by his senior year, but right now Coach Wimbush preferred Sammy's experience.

In pre-season interviews, Wimbush admitted that he had no idea how good his team would be. The Falcons were co-favored with Hempstone to win the regular season championship, primarily because of Hal's presence in the lineup, but he wasn't sure that they deserved that high a ranking. He thought they might develop into a really good team near season's end, but he was braced for some early stumbles as the new players groped for identity.

Surprisingly, the Falcons roared out of the gate, winning their first seven games by convincing margins. That included a nineteen point victory over Hempstone on the latter's home court, the first time a Brileyville team had won there in seven years.

"We cruisin', Baby," Melvin exulted to Hal with an accompanying hug after the Hempstone victory.

"Yeah, beatin' the 'fendin' reg'lar season champs on their home court ain't half shabby," Hal agreed.

Hal had been the main catalyst in all the Brileyville victories. He led the team in scoring, assists and steals and was second behind Wesley in rebounds. He was the player who had to rise to the occasion if his team hoped to move up to the next level, and he was doing it. But he was far from the entire story. Wesley was developing into a force in the paint. Melvin had found a nice medium-range jump shot that could ease some of the pressure opposing teams tried to apply to Hal on the perimeter. And Lonnie and Sammy were capable on given nights of scoring in the low-doubles in both points and rebounds. So a genuine team chemistry had formed, and Wimbush was pleasantly surprised.

The chemistry wasn't fully consistent, of course. In game eight at Blanchard High, it broke down. Hal had an off-night, the rest of the team played below form and the Falcons lost.

"In a way, it's good," Wimbush told the collectively

disconsolate team after the game. "You probably needed a game like this to make you realize you can lose. When you're riding high like you guys have been, sometimes you lose track of your own mortality. This brings you back to earth a little bit and hopefully will make you a better team in the end."

"I dunno what he sees as good 'bout it," Hal groused to Wesley as the players headed for the bus to go home. "I stunk the place up."

"We all stunk," Wesley said sympathetically. He patted Hal on a shoulder. "They're comin' up to our place in a couple weeks. We'll get 'em then."

Hal nodded, and his eyes gleamed resolutely.

Wesley noted the intensity in that gleam, but he didn't think about it until after the Blanchard rematch. Hal was a demon that night on both sides of the ball and wound up setting school records for points: forty-two, and assists: nineteen. He completed the triple-double with fourteen rebounds and just missed the quadruple with nine steals. The rest of the team played well, too, and Brileyville won by thirty points. The margin would have been in the forties if Wimbush hadn't shown a kind heart and put the reserves in early in the fourth quarter.

It was also learned after the game that Hal had broken the district single game scoring record which had stood for almost twenty years. That surprised him a little. He had never even thought to ask what the record was, and no one else considered it important enough to mention until now. It might have gone unnoticed that night, too, except for the fact that the record holder was a Blanchard player who now happened to be coaching his old alma mater.

"I think we made the mistake of makin' that McDonough kid angry by beatin' y'all down there," the deposed record holder remarked to Wimbush afterwards. "Man, I've never seen a kid all over the court like he was tonight."

Wimbush couldn't argue that point. "Yeah, I understand

it was your record he broke," he responded.

"I could take that, as long as we could win the game," the Blanchard coach said. He shook his head and tried to smile. "I figured my record had to be broken sometime. I'm kinda surprised it's held up this long. But way that kid broke it, he's gonna be rewritin' all the record books before he's done."

"He's quite a gifted young man," Wimbush agreed. "And there's a certain inner drive that helps push that along."

"Back about halfway through the second quarter, when it became obvious we weren't gonna win the game, I found myself almost fixated on that kid," the Blanchard coach sighed. "He had a bad game against us down at our place, and it was almost like he felt he had to prove something."

"I think in large measure that's true, although I don't really think he understands it," Wimbush said thoughtfully. He looked across the gym to where Hal was talking to a couple of sportswriters. "He has incredible natural ability, but I think what really sets him apart from some other players is something much deeper. The junior high coach in our town wouldn't even play him, and I think subconsciously he may still be trying to make up for that and prove himself beyond all doubt. When you beat us at your place, and he didn't play well, it struck a nerve. Not that I'm apologizing, mind you. I'm glad he's on our side instead of yours. And I'd far rather be on the long end of a performance like he had tonight instead of the short end."

The Blanchard coach laughed. "In your place, I'd enjoy it, too," he conceded.

Later, in the locker room, Wesley recalled that strange glint that flashed in Hal's eyes as the two left the Blanchard gym after the team's loss there. "It didn't strike me none 'til after this game was over, but I never seen nothin' like the way this guy's eyes flashed outta his head awmost while we was gettin' on the bus down at Blanchard," he related for Melvin's and Lonnie's benefit. "I think 'bout it now, the signs was all there. They hurt his pride, an' he were gonna get even. An' boy did he ever. I don't think them boys know what hit 'em yet."

"Kinda like he done last year 'gainst Hempstone," Thurlow interjected. "They beat us, an' he had a bad game, an' then he turn 'round in the district final an' set a new school scorin' record."

"Tonight he set a new scorin' record, too, an' it turn out to be for the whole district," Earl Wilson said.

Hal shrugged and grinned sheepishly. "Well, no way I can tell y'all I planned that one. I didn't even know what the district record was 'til the scorekeeper from Blanchard told me," he said.

"Well, every time you break it from now on, it's gonna be you own record goin' down the tubes," Melvin reminded him with a chuckle.

"Well, then that just means I don't have to worry 'bout anything 'cept us winnin' games," Hal responded good-naturedly.

The state high school ranking system was slow catching up with the Falcons, but gradually they eased into the top five and stayed there. They were as high as number two at one point, then fell to number five after a loss to Piney Grove near season's end, then got back up to number three. Markham from Virginia Beach was number one and had been all season. The Seabees (Markham's nickname) were led by a six foot, nine inch center named Tyrone Sloan who was rated the state's best player along with Hal.

Hal was drawing considerable attention these days from scouts, coaches, and sportswriters. Eunice found and clipped an article in *Newsday* that listed him among the thirty best underclass high school prospects in the entire country and sent photocopies of it to Shawna to distribute as she deemed fit. Hal didn't know how anyone could come up with a reliable formula for narrowing the select list down that precisely, and he wondered how people who probably had never seen him play could determine that he belonged on it. Still, he had to admit to himself that it felt pretty good to see his name appear in such a prestigious faraway publication, even if only on one line.

"Aunt Eunice told me to tell you if you go gettin' swellheaded on her, she's gonna come down an' personally box your ears," Shawna told him impishly.

Hal chuckled and glanced again at the line that Shawna had underlined in red. "I can't get swell-headed 'til I figure how they came up with my name."

"Well, they had to fill up the page with somethin'," Shawna said jocularly.

Later, Hal cornered his coach and showed him a copy of the story. "I'm not knockin' it," he told Wimbush with a grin. "I'm just wonderin' how they pick my name up like that."

"The college basketball recruiting network is one of the most efficient, well-oiled operations in the world," Wimbush replied. "You might be able to sing like Mario Lanza and be totally missed. But anyone who can play basketball the way you can will be spotted. Scouts have been in the stands checking you out for quite some time now. It's a network set up, and all the major college and pro programs use it. The instant you started showing signs of excelling, someone from here called someone else probably in Richmond or Raleigh or Baltimore, and that person in turn called someone else in New York or Los Angeles or wherever, and on and on down the line . . ."

"You mean people been checkin' me out all this time? How come you never told me?" Hal asked.

Wimbush shrugged. "I didn't want to put any more pressure on you. I didn't want you to start playing to impress them or anything like that."

"I wouldn't. Shit, Coach, you know I could prob'ly score ten, twenty points more a game if I just wanted to show how good I am," Hal said with a shrug.

"I'm aware of that," Wimbush said. He clasped Hal's

shoulders. "I'm not worried about you. It's just I don't want you to be looking up in the stands all the time wondering who up there is taking notes on your strengths and weaknesses."

"I figure if I just play a normal game, that's all I have to worry 'bout," Hal said. He laughed. "If I can play good when I know Shawna's aunt's gonna be up in the stands watchin', you know nothin' else is gonna shake me up that much."

"Well, now you know, they are looking you over," Wimbush told him with a grin. "I think by this time next year, you'll be able to write your own ticket. Duke, Kentucky, Chapel Hill, UCLA, Arizona, Arkansas, Kansas, UConn, St. John's, Georgetown, you name 'em. You'll be a hotly pursued young man. I hope you're up to handling it."

"It's more my mother I'm worried 'bout 'un that," Hal sighed.

Wimbush nodded understandingly.

In the Piney Grove loss, Hal played well enough, but the rest of the team fell a little flat. A couple of other times during the season he was a little off form, but the other players raised their games enough to make up for it. Overall, as the season wound down, the team had four losses in twenty-three games, by far its best regular season showing in Wimbush's tenure and the school's best in almost four decades. Someone dug up some statistics showing that the last Brileyville High team to do this well was from the segregated fifties, when the school was undefeated until it got to the state semifinal round and was knocked out. The first scoring record Hal broke while still a sophomore was set in '62, again while the school was all white. Some irony was noted in the two top single game scorers in Brileyville High's history being white boys, although no one seriously compared them as players. Hal had established his marks with and against black players, whereas the other white boy's came in what now would more resemble preppie private school competition.

Oddly, Hal got a letter of congratulation from the fellow whose record he had broken three times already several months after the fact. He found out that the fellow was now a middle-aged executive with the telephone company out of Richmond and had played college ball for Hampden-Sydney. He still had relatives in the Brileyville area and evidently was kept abreast of this new phenom lighting up the scoreboards for his now desegregated alma mater.

"I 'spect that dude when he was playin' here then didn't have no idea in hell thirty years down the road, his lilywhite school'd be almost coalblack," Lonnie remarked as Hal showed the letter to some of the other players while they were practicing one afternoon.

"Well, you got least one vanilla chip still," Hal said with a grin. He folded the letter back into the envelope and slipped it into a shirt pocket.

"Pernell? Seem like I heard that name before," Lonnie said. "My daddy work for some guy name Pernell. He say he still got kin 'round here. I'll bet that guy my daddy work for's 'lated to him."

"I dunno," Hal said with a shrug. "Shit, whites 'round here kinda make themselves scarce. Almost like they're 'fraid of you guys or somethin'."

"'Fraid we might fuck they daughters, more like it," Melvin said with a grin. "An' even more'n that, they 'fraid they daughters might like it."

The entire group cracked up over that one.

"Well, if Hampden-Sydney the best he can do, obviously he ain't no way in you class," Earl Wilson told Hal sincerely. "Shit, I 'spect you mighta been able to take that team he played on all by you'self awmost."

"Well, I wouldn't go that far," Hal said. He chuckled. "I figure I'd need at least a couple you guys 'long to keep 'em from just makin' a circle 'round me so I couldn't get through."

"That's 'bout the onliest way they gonna stop you," Wesley said. He patted Hal on the back. "I figure if some the brothers we go up 'gainst can't hold you down, no way that bunch could hope to."

"Well, they didn't have a shot clock then, so they could freeze the ball an' slow the game down an' maybe figure on puttin' me to sleep," Hal said with a chuckle.

A special time for Hal every season now came when the Falcons played Winslow. This time the game was being played on Winslow's home court.

"Well, I've been hearing and reading a lot about you the last few months," Phil Laughinhouse remarked to him as the team entered the Winslow gym. "Looks like you boys are getting some of the state recognition some of my teams used to get a few years ago."

Hal grinned. "Most part we been doin' awright. For my part, I guess it's just 'cause those guys're bored an' just grabbin' at anything they can find to write or talk 'bout."

"Oh, I think it's a little more than that," Laughinhouse said with a chuckle. He patted Hal on a shoulder. "I would wish you good luck, but not tonight."

"Well, tell ya the truth, Coach, I prefer to make my own luck as much as possible," Hal said with a grin.

Winslow had knocked Brileyville off in last year's regionals with a special defense designed to slow the game down and cut off the passing lanes to Hal. Wimbush hadn't forgotten that, so he worked out a couple of special plays to use if Laughinhouse tried it again. And he was sure Laughinhouse would; the Winslow coach had a history of using offensive and defensive ploys until someone figured out a way of beating them. In this instance, Melvin was the focal man. He would post up behind a Lonnie screen just inside the circle, and when the defense moved with Hal, he would get the pass for a medium range jumper. He didn't have Hal's three point range, but for this he didn't need it. He just had to knock down a few twelve to fifteen footers, so that someone had to move over to pick him up and then a lane would open up.

Wimbush guessed correctly about Laughinhouse's strategy, but his plan seemed to have momentarily backfired when Melvin missed his first shot badly. A case of nerves had hit him. Then Hal patted Melvin on the back and told him not to worry, just to take the shot, and Melvin rattled home five in a row. That disrupted the Winslow defense, just as Wimbush had calculated, and soon the lanes opened up for Hal to penetrate and dish off to Lonnie, Wesley, and Sammy and to score from both inside and out himself. Down the stretch, the Falcons had things pretty much their own way and wound up winning by eighteen points.

Hal, as usual, was high scorer, but everyone agreed that Melvin's baskets had helped open the game up so that he and the other players could operate at peak efficiency.

"You outcoached me tonight, Jerome," Laughinhouse conceded to Wimbush after it was all over. "We had it all figured out to stop McDonough or at least slow him down enough so he wouldn't beat us all by himself, and then you cross me up by havin' that Peebles kid hittin' those little jumpers. That blew my whole game plan outta the water."

"Well Phil, I remembered the last time in the regionals you were leaving that position almost totally unguarded, and I knew Melvin could hit that shot, and tonight he happened to be on target," Wimbush said with a grin. "If he'd been off, my great plan woulda turned to mush in a hurry. My heart really skipped a beat when he missed that first shot. But then when he hit those five in a row, I had a feeling we were gonna beat you guys."

"Well, your guys deserved to win. I won't deny that," Wimbush said. He patted Wimbush on a shoulder. "But you couldn't have pulled something like that off without a player of McDonough's caliber on your side."

"I'm aware of that, Phil," Wimbush said. He chuckled. "But I had to endure those three years when you had that seven-footer, the one that wound up going to Nebraska, so I feel that I have every right to bask in the luxury of having Hal to throw back at you."

"Well, like they say, it all goes in cycles," Laughinhouse said. "See you later, Jerome, maybe in the regionals."
"I wouldn't be surprised," Wimbush said.

43

The one worry Wimbush had as tournament time came around was that his team might experience a letdown. If it had to happen, the district might be the best tournament for it. After all, by winning the regular season championship, the team already had a regional berth sewn up. But Wimbush had a theory about momentum, and at no point after the post season started could he see a loss as good. "We proved we had the best team in the league for the season, but don't forget Hempstone proved the very same thing last year, and they wound up losing in the first round of the regionals after we knocked 'em off in the district tournament," he reminded his players. "This is where you really need to start picking it up a notch. The farther we go, the tougher the competition we'll be going up against and the better you guys are going to have to be. And if you lose a game now, even one you can afford to lose, that can take some of the edge off your momentum. So stay focused. You've beaten every team in this field at least once this season, and you've beaten the second highest ranked team twice. There's no reason you shouldn't be able to do it again. Just stay focused and do what you have to do, and you should win this thing."

The team did stay focused and breezed through phase one of the post season. In three nights, the Falcons beat Dunston, Piney Grove, and Hempstone by respective margins of twenty-three, twenty-seven, and thirty-two. In those three games, Hal scored twenty-nine, thirty-five, and twenty-six points respectively. He provided the victory cushion in each game and gave the scouts in the stands something more to think about.

The regionals were again being played at St. Paul's College. The Falcons went into that competition with momentum and a genuine feeling that they might well have a chance to go all the way this time. They were hungry, too; they wanted to give their school something to take pride in. Plus they were such an off-beat unit in so many ways that they almost had the feeling that destiny demanded no less than a championship of them.

Their first round opponent would be a team from the Newport News area. They didn't know much about this team except what little their coach could glean from scouting reports. Not that this ignorance bothered them particularly. They had a genuine feeling that they could beat any team in their class if they played to their capabilities.

Hal and some of the other Brileyville players were walking through the doors leading to the St. Paul's gym when they encountered most of the team they would be playing this night. One of the other team's players, a black guy just a shade taller than Hal, smirked as he spotted the white boy among all the Brileyville African Americans. "What y'all doin'? Bringin' you mascot 'long?" he taunted Wesley and Melvin.

"I think he mean you," Melvin remarked to Hal with a grin.

"Yeah, I'm the team mascot," Hal told the taunting black guy with a shrug.

Someone confided to the Brileyville group that the taunting black guy was Ernest Slocum, a returning second team all-state player. Slocum had figured to move up to first team this year but was denied that because of Hal's emergence. He was hurt and angry and determined to show that Hal wasn't as good as some people were proclaiming him to be. He might have succeeded, too, except that he struck a raw Hal nerve when he called him a mascot. Now he had Hal's adrenaline flowing.

"I see y'all lettin' you mascots take the floor with y'all," Slocum remarked to Wesley as the two teams lined up for the opening tap.

"Uh, I 'spect that's one mascot you gonna have you hands full with, fool," Wesley told him in an admonishing tone.

Slocum found that out firsthand mere moments later. The first time Hal got his hands on the ball, he deliberately went at Slocum. Slocum had a reputation as a tight defender, and he was not afraid of the challenge, but he also was not up to stopping Hal. Hal showed a stutter-step dribble and went around Slocum easily for a lay-up.

"Not bad for a mascot, huh?" Hal taunted as the teams headed back to the other end.

That got Slocum pumped up. He got the ball and went straight at Hal and tried to return the favor. As he quickly discovered, this white boy was also a very good defensive player. Hal stripped him of the ball in mid dribble and left him watching helplessly as he cruised downcourt all alone and scored on a pull-up three pointer.

"I coulda told you, that's one dude you don't wanna get stirred up," Wesley told Slocum with a thin smile.

By this point, the game's tone was set. Slocum was completely out of rhythm, and Hal methodically punished him and his team for the rest of the first half. Hal scored against Slocum virtually at will, both inside and out; and when he wasn't putting the ball in the hole himself, he was dishing off to his teammates for equally easy baskets. By a certain point, he was almost playing with Slocum. On one occasion, he pump-faked three times, and Slocum, now very gun shy from all the times he already had been beaten, flinched on each. Finally, Hal just went up and calmly drilled another trey and topped it off with a you-asked-for-it smirk.

Slocum was thoroughly frustrated and irritated. Hal didn't know how much until a couple of minutes later when he trapped the Newport News player along the baseline and was about to draw a five second call and Slocum threw a punch at him.

Fortunately, Hal saw the punch coming and easily danced away from it. He had learned that much from his battles with Tyrell at camp. He assumed a fighting stance, more to defend himself if necessary than to actually get into a slugfest with Slocum. Instantly, Lonnie and Melvin grabbed him; they wanted to keep going in post-season play and they didn't want their best player thrown out of the game and possibly disqualified for the rest of the tournament. A couple of Slocum's teammates did the same with their man.

Slocum, unlike Tyrell, was not really a mean-spirited young man. The swing had come more from frustration than any real desire to hurt Hal or anyone else. He instantly recognized that he was wrong and mumbled an apology to his teammates and the referee. That didn't stop the referee from calling a technical foul on him. What had to hurt was seeing that Hal, Brileyville's best foul shooter, was the one selected to shoot the free throws. Hal sank both, and then on the automatic possession, he rubbed salt in the wound by drilling another three-pointer.

By halftime, Slocum was a thoroughly humbled young man, and Brileyville held an incredible twenty-nine point lead over an opponent expected to be quite competitive.

Wimbush had sensed what was going on out on the court, and he was more than a little angry with his star player.

"Hal, you're deliberately trying to humiliate that kid," he said when he finally got the young man alone in the locker room. "I don't like that."

"Damn, coach, you shoulda heard the trash he was talkin' to me before the game," Hal defended himself.

"Players do that. You're gonna have to get used to it," Wimbush told him sternly. "The kid's hurt. He was second team all-state last year, and now you come along and keep him from moving up to first-team. How do you think you'd feel under those conditions?"

Hal shrugged. "Prob'ly hurt an' angry an' wantin' to take it out on somebody," he admitted.

Wimbush patted him on a shoulder. "Bullseye. I think it's safe to say it was a bitter pill for him to swallow." He rumpled Hal's hair. "You're a better player than he is. Everyone in the gym knows it by now. Coaches all over the country knew it long before tonight. I want you to go out there to win, but I don't want to see you deliberately going out of your way to embarrass another player. That's unhealthy. It doesn't do you or anyone else any good."

"I guess I did get a little carried away," Hal admitted soberly.

Wimbush patted him on a shoulder. "Well, at least one consolation: I probably won't have to leave you in very long the second half." He chuckled. "I get cold shivers when I see someone wanting to take a swing at you. I don't wanta lose you for the rest of the post season."

Hal grinned.

Hal played only a few minutes of the second half, just enough to make sure the cushion wouldn't evaporate once Wimbush put the subs in. In fact, the bench played the entire final quarter. A thirty-two point lead was cut to fifteen by game's end, but that wasn't close enough to make Wimbush nervous.

"I don't blame you for rubbin' it in on Slocum like you done," Melvin told Hal as the two sat on the bench and watched the final minutes being played out. "I'm just glad you didn't get in a fight with him an' maybe get disqualified for the rest of the tournament or somethin' like that."

"Well, I did kinda make it a personal thing," Hal said with a shrug.

"Yeah, I heard Wimbush gettin' on you," Melvin said. "If he heard how Slocum was talkin' to you, he mighta felt different."

"Naw, he was right. I went outta my way to put Slocum down, an' I shouldn'ta," Hal said with a shrug. He thought about it for a moment and flashed a grin. "But I gotta 'mit, it sure felt good."

Melvin laughed. "I bet it did," he agreed.

Later, after Hal was showered and in street clothes, Slocum made a point of approaching him. "Sorry I took that punch at you," he said, almost timorously.

"I'm just glad you didn't hit me," Hal said. He flashed a grin. "I got a broken nose at basketball camp last summer. I'm not ready for 'nother one of those anytime soon."

"You're some player," Slocum told him sincerely. "You're the best I ever went up 'gainst by far. I didn't think it was possible for a white boy to be that good, but you definitely are."

Hal emitted an almost embarrassed chuckle. "I 'spect watchin' basketball on TV an' all, I'm not sure I believe it either sometimes," he replied.

"I figured when I heard you was bein' moved up 'head of me for first team all-state, it was 'causea you bein' a white boy," Slocum said. His lips smacked thoughtfully. "My coach'n teammates let me know prob'ly the worst thing I coulda did was get you riled up like I done, an' they was right." He smiled wistfully. "I'll never make that mistake again."

"Well, I gotta 'mit I didn't 'ppreciate bein' called a mascot, but now I think 'bout it, it seems kinda funny," Hal said with a grin.

"Well, you goin' on, an' I'm goin' home. In you place, I'd feel better, too," Slocum said. He extended his hand. "I think we gonna be on the same team for the east-west all-star game this summer. If it's awright with you, I'd like to bury the hatchet permanent."

Hal shook the proffered hand. "It's awright with me," he responded.

The bus ride home that night took about an hour and a half. Most of the bus was jubilant. Shawna was grousing a little, but everyone by now was used to that. She didn't take well to the bus rides and losing sleep and study time.

"Look like we might be on a collision course to play Winslow 'gain in the finals," Melvin remarked to Hal from across the bus aisle. "They beat Hempstone tonight, an' they play that team from the Williamsburg area next. I watched a little bit of their game. They ain't nothin'."

"You don't ever want to start thinkin' like that," the voice of the team's coach rang out from some unseen dark corner. "Any team in this competition might be capable of knocking us or Winslow or anyone else off if we don't go into the game in the right frame of mind."

"Ah, why don't y'all pipe down an' let me get some sleep?" Shawna moaned. Her head was rested on Hal's chest. "Worry 'bout that game 'morrow night."

Hal gestured helplessly and grinned for Melvin's benefit. "I'm not arguin' with her," he said.

"You better know it," Shawna murmured sleepily.

The Falcons and their coaches and cheerleaders had to be back on the bus early the following afternoon. The semifinal game was with Kimberlin High from a district down near the Carolina border. Kimberlin was virtually all white, the first team of that composition Hal had seen since that one summer when he played rec league ball against his now teammates.

"Hey, don't you belong over here?" one of the Kimberlin players shouted to Hal as the teams came out onto the floor for their pre-game warmups.

"You try grabbin' this white boy, you gonna be drawin' back a nub," Lonnie yelled back good-naturedly.

Kimberlin was not much of an opponent. It was the kind of game the Falcons could win even playing substantially below form. Fortunately for them, they had that bad a game to get out of their collective system. Hal was only five of twenty-one from the floor, and the team as a whole shot only about thirty-five percent for the game. Even so, they won by eighteen, simply because Kimberlin didn't have nearly enough firepower to exploit their off night.

"I got a feelin' you're better'n you looked against us tonight," the Kimberlin center told Hal after it was all over. He thought about what he had just said and chuckled. "I know you are. I saw what you did to Slocum last night. We played them up at their place in January, an' they beat us by twenty-two points. I thought Slocum might play you pretty close to even."

"I was better last night," Hal agreed with a shrug. He patted the Kimberlin player on a shoulder. "Nice game."

The Brileyville players stayed long enough to watch the first half of Winslow's game against the Williamsburg area team. This was not a vintage Winslow team in the sense of having a lot of player talent, but everyone understood that as long as Phil Laughinhouse coached there, that program would be competitive. When the Brileyville players left, Winslow had an eleven point lead in the type of slowdown game that made that margin look almost like thirty.

"I figure the onliest way we gonna lose to Winslow is by us havin' 'nother game like we had tonight," Wesley remarked to Hal when they were on the bus.

"We could beat Kimberlin playin' like that, but we're not gonna beat many other teams," Hal agreed.

"Hold that thought! Freeze it! Carry it into the game with you tomorrow night," Wimbush called out from his unseen corner.

Hal and the team did. The result was probably the best total effort the players combined on for the season. Hal again set a new school and district record with forty-six, and Brileyville won by a whopping forty-nine points. The

Falcons grabbed the lead early, with five three-pointers from Hal sparking the spurt, and kept pouring it on both offensively and defensively until Wimbush finally put the subs in late in the third quarter. Hal had twenty-two assists and fifteen rebounds to go along with his game high scoring, and again he barely missed the rare quadruple with eight steals.

"One these days you gonna pull off that quad," a bespectacled stat-keeping African American named Lennie told him admiringly after it was all over.

Hal grinned and patted Lennie on the head. "Too bad I'm not a few inches taller so maybe I could think 'bout goin' for the quintuple double," he said.

Laughinhouse walked over to Hal as he was being mobbed by Brileyville teammates and school partisans. "You guys did a job on us tonight," the Winslow coach sighed.

Hal grinned. He couldn't argue that one. "We had it together tonight," he agreed. "We were hittin' on all cylinders."

"I figured it was too much to expect you to have another off game like the one you had last night," Laughinhouse said. He patted Hal on a shoulder. "Good luck in the state. Bring some honor back to our region."

"I'll give it my best shot, Coach," Hal promised.

The ride home was a very happy one. The school had its first regional championship in almost forty years, and the players and cheerleaders would be able to get a full night's sleep or two and recharge some physical and emotional batteries and not have to worry about these long bus rides to and from the regional games in the middle of a school week for at least another year.

"We goin' to state, Baby!" Melvin crowed to Hal and complemented it with a high-five.

"Yeah, on to Charlottesville," Sammy Williams called out.

"All the way! We goin' all the way!" Lonnie chimed in.
"Ah, shut up an' let me get some sleep," Shawna murmured.

44

The state championship tournament was to be played in Charlottesville, at the University of Virginia. This time the Falcons had hotel accommodations for however long they kept winning up to and perhaps through the Saturday night championship game. They weren't guaranteed a victory at any point along the way, but at least they could figure on being well rested.

"I'm glad we don't have to take that stupid bus ride to the game an' from the game three straight nights like we had to last week," Shawna murmured. Her head rested on Hal's shoulder as the bus headed up Interstate 64 to Charlottesville. "I was thinkin' a couple times it might almost been worth it for y'all to lose so we wouldn't have to go through that any more."

"Hush, girl, you don't even wanna think somethin' like that," one of the other cheerleaders called out to her.

"I didn't really wanna see y'all lose," Shawna assured Hal with a grin and a kiss. "I was just gettin' tired of spendin' so much time on that bus."

Hal laughed. "I coulda done without that part, too," he admitted.

"Well, it should be a little more pleasant this time," Wimbush interjected. "We've arranged for you folks to get a tour of Monticello and a chance to see some of the sights around Charlottesville. It's really quite interesting, and a few of you might even find it educational."

"We might take in some them great waterin' holes I heard 'bout," Lonnie piped up.

The entire bus cracked up.

"The only watering holes any of you will be taking in are the ones that provide non-alcoholic beverages," Wimbush told him good-naturedly.

"Course you know, talkin' 'bout Monticello, ol' TJ was rumored to have sired some children by his African 'merican mistress," Shawna said with a bored shrug. "Somebody on this bus could be descended from him."

"Well, I don't think it's me," Hal replied.

"Uh, Hal, you ain't 'zackly African 'merican," one of the cheerleaders reminded him.

The entire bus cracked up over that one, too.

"Well, y'know, they say all life began in Africa, so's that means I prob'ly got some African blood in me somewheres you go back far 'nuff," Hal reasoned with a grin. "An' you never know. Maybe somewheres I came from somebody that looked white 'nuff to pass for white, an' that person married a white, an' the children kept comin' out lookin' white."

"Be kinda hard in a line like that for the African part to not pop out somewheres 'long the way," Lennie, the team statistician, said. He reached over and patted Hal on a shoulder. "You kinda play basketball like a brother, but I think you'd have a hard time passin' for one."

Again everyone who heard broke into laughter.

"Well, anyway, whatever I came from, I don't think it was TJ," Hal said with a shrug. "Only prominent person of that time I know 'bout I'm kin to is Aaron Burr. I'm a distant cousin. I had a great-great-great-great . . . I dunno how many times great-uncle that married a cousin of Aaron Burr's."

"Female, I hope," Shawna quipped.

Again laughter.

"I don't think same-sex marriages were comin' off then like you find 'em now," Hal said. "Yeah, it was a girl, a woman. They moved out west. That was back in the early 1800s. I got some ancestry datin' back to Virginia from the real early days, but as far as I know, none of it was connected to Jefferson or any of those guys."

"Too bad," Shawna said. She kissed him. "TJ had a lotta class."

"My dad calls him the most vile man that ever lived," Hal said. He laughed. "I never have figured out how he came up with that one."

"Well, I think he get a little bit overrated sometimes," one of the cheerleaders remarked. "He was 'pposed to be a big libertarian an' whatnot, but he owned slaves."

"A lotta people owned slaves then," Shawna said with a bored shrug.

"Shoo, girl, you sound awmost like you 'fendin' him ownin' slaves," the cheerleader shot back testily.

"No I'm not 'fendin' it," Shawna replied, her tone now also getting a bit sharp. "But way things were then, if he didn't have 'em, somebody else'd prob'ly figure out some way to grab 'em up, so maybe he saved some of our people from a worse fate."

"Course I'm not sure I like the part 'bout him havin' all them kids by his black mistress," Melvin chimed in. "That sound awmost like takin' 'vantage of a good thing or somethin'."

"From everything I've read, she prob'ly was a willin' participant, if that's what happened," Shawna said. "You don't know what went down 'tween those two people. I don't think anybody today really does. They mighta loved each other. Or maybe she was playin' him for what she could get outta the situation. When you're in a bad scene, you use your brain if you're smart. Some y'all prob'ly'd go mouthin' off to somebody an' get that person pissed off an' make things worse for yourself. Maybe she figured you could catch more flies with honey 'un with vinegar."

"Sound to me like she just figured out how to make life more cushy for herself," someone from a far corner remarked. "I can't see what she done for her people."

"Well, she couldn't do much for her people, as you call it, if she couldn't do somethin' to raise herself," Shawna argued. "An' you don't know. Maybe she put a bug in ol' TJ's ear to make things easier for some of your folks 'long the way that nobody ever told you 'bout. Some of the other slaves might have just seen she was cozyin' up to the white master. They didn't even try to understand that she might be tryin' to help them."

"An' maybe all she was tryna help was herself," Lonnie countered.

"Yeah, maybe," Shawna conceded. She nuzzled Hal's neck. "Just goes to show one more 'zample of a dimension you find in blacks every bit as strong as you find in whites."

"If you think it's somethin' to brag 'bout, I'll take your word for it," Hal said.

"It's not somethin' to brag 'bout or bitch'n'moan about," Shawna reasoned. "It's just a fact."

Hal shrugged concession. That made sense.

The visit to Thomas Jefferson's home was a first for Hal. He recalled several times when his father declared Jefferson to be the most vile man who ever lived. Hal himself wasn't sure how Jefferson's character could be assessed accurately as either bad or good by anyone living today; and left to his own devices, thoughts of any kind about Jefferson would be quite infrequent and impersonal. Yet his father had a way of bringing Jefferson's name up in regular conversation, punctuated with venomous sounding denunciation.

Shawna on the other hand found Jefferson fascinating. She didn't attempt to assess him as good or bad; she supposed he had mixed the two pretty much like most other humans. But he struck her as interesting, which to her made up for a lot of other qualities many might perceive as deficiencies. She might have viewed the Sage of Monticello differently had she known him intimately, and since her beliefs on the spiritual side included reincarnation, she was not altogether sure that at some historical juncture she hadn't.

"You ever get the feelin' you been some place before, even though you know it hasn't been in this life?" she asked Hal as the Brileyville group was touring Monticello.

Hal didn't know how he should respond to that. "No, I can't say I have," he said. He looked around the opulent, well preserved Colonial surroundings. "I'm kinda familiar with this place from readin' 'bout it an' whatnot, but I know I haven't been here in this life an' I don't think I was here in any previous life."

"Could be your 'ssociation with it wasn't vivid 'nuff to carry over to a future life," Shawna said. She smiled wistfully. "But as we were walkin' through this house, I just had this really eerie feelin' like I'd been here an' lived here an' really knew the place like I know my mama'n daddy's house back in Brileyville."

Hal paused to help Shawna up a step as they were following the tour guide around the mansion. "Course, you do know if you were here back when TJ was 'live an' some of the stories 'bout him are true, it could be you were his mistress," he said.

Shawna grinned and kissed him. "Well, that'd just go to show ol' TJ had good taste, an' I wasn't 'fraid to try livin' an interestin' lifestyle," she responded.

45

Brileyville's first game was against a team from near the West Virginia line. This opponent had a lot of blacks, but none of them were outstanding athletes. The Falcons weren't particularly sharp that night; Hal was off his game, and so were the other players. But they did manage to win by sixteen points.

"Man, we play like that again, we gonna be in big trouble," Wesley moaned as the bus carried the team back to its hotel.

"Well, least it seems we're havin' our worst games 'gainst teams we can 'fford 'em on, so maybe that's good," Hal sighed.

"No, it isn't," Wimbush chimed in. "You catch one of those teams on a night when they're playing about ten thousand miles over their head, you could be in a lot of trouble. Now of all times is when you have to stay focused and concentrate on what you know you have to do."

Actually, Wimbush wasn't that displeased with his

players. He realized that they had a collective faculty for bouncing back impressively after a bad outing. He didn't know what caused it, or how to explain it, but he had seen it enough to know that it existed. He had a feeling that the team would play well in its next game.

It turned out that he was right. The next night, a much tougher opponent from just outside Washington was the unlucky target. Hal was on fire, the other Brileyville players performed well, and the Falcons won by twenty-five points in a game that really wasn't that close.

"Wow, just from watching your boys last night, I wouldn'ta had the slightest inkling we'd be in for something like this tonight," the losing coach remarked to Wimbush after it was all over.

"Well, I was sure we'd play better tonight than we did last night," Wimbush said. He looked over to where his players were still celebrating and hugging each other and the cheerleaders. "We have a disturbing tendency to play down to the opposition."

"You're also capable of playing up to it," the other coach said. He shook Wimbush's hand. "Good luck in the finals."

The team stuck around to watch the second semi-final game, matching Markham from the Tidewater region and a Richmond area team. Markham had the state's other marquee player. Tyrone Sloan was a six foot, nine inch junior and, like Hal, a consensus all-state selection. Hal knew about Sloan, but this was the first time he actually had seen him play.

Hal couldn't help mentally comparing Sloan to Greg Mason from basketball camp. Sloan was an inch or two shorter. He might have had a slight edge in mobility, although Greg was no slouch in that department. He probably blocked shots and played defense better. Greg was more versatile on offense; he could shoot the corner jump shot and put the ball on the floor better, and he had better hands for catching the ball down low. Overall, Hal thought Greg was the better player, although not by a great margin. That would be of little comfort to Wesley, of course. He would be helpless against either Sloan or Greg in the post.

"Man, watchin' that guy give me goose pimples," Wesley remarked at one point, almost as if reading Hal's thoughts. "He's a monster."

"Yeah, if we beat 'em, we're not gonna do it by stoppin' him," Hal agreed.

Markham won the game easily. Whatever Sloan's shortcomings by college recruiting standards, no Virginia high school team had the manpower to exploit them. He was going to score a lot of points in the paint, from offensive rebounds if nothing else. Probably what Wimbush would do was try to have Lonnie or Sammy front him and perhaps have Hal prowl the inside on defense and try to steal the ball if Sloan put it on the floor as he sometimes did. Something like that might slow him down and keep him from totally dominating the game. But stopping him cold or holding him to under twenty-five or thirty points was probably too much to hope for under the best of scenarios.

"We're gonna have to put some points on the board," Wimbush remarked to Hal as the game was winding down. "I hope you're on target with your jump shot. We're gonna need it."

Hal's lips pursed thoughtfully. He agreed.

The Brileyville team was in the process of leaving the university gym when Sloan, still in uniform, walked up to Hal. "So you're the great white hope I been hearin' 'bout all season," he said.

Hal almost choked on that one. "I dunno 'bout that. I am white, but I don't 'sackly see myself as anybody's hope."

"That ain't 'sackly true," Lonnie said. "You're our team's hope."

Sloan laughed and slapped Hal on a shoulder. "I heard a lot 'bout you through the season," he said. "Kinda fittin' the two best players in the state go at it for the state championship."

Hal shrugged. "I'm glad to be goin' for the championship.

I think I might rather be playin' that team y'all just beat."

Sloan grinned and slapped Hal again on a shoulder. "See ya tomorrow night," he said and departed.

"He seem like a nice 'nuff guy," Lonnie mused as the Brileyville players and cheerleaders headed for the team bus outside.

"Watchin' him swat balls down that guy's throat tonight, he ain't half nice 'nuff to suit me," Wesley groused.

That remark drew a nice collective laugh.

"I hope I live long 'nuff to see the day when a white boy good in some sport like basketball or boxin' comes 'long, he doesn't have to be called the great white hope," Hal said casually.

"Well, how you think it makes African 'mericans feel to be called the first black this or first black that?" Shawna countered.

Good point.

"I have to wonder if some of y'all guys were 'round back in Colonial times, how y'all'd manage to get 'long without basketball?" Shawna teased Hal once the group was on the bus and seated.

"How come you think so many blacks joined the Indians?" Lonnie countered. "They had a kinda basketball. Not like the game we play, but it was still sorta put-the-ball-in-the-hoop thing."

"Mighta found some white boys joinin' the Indians, too," Hal said with a shrug. He draped an arm around Shawna. "I dunno. Maybe we tried toppin' GW in throwin' silver dollars 'cross a river or somethin'. Life without basketball. That is scary."

The sportswriters' pre-game stories for the championship tilt were played mostly from the marquee matchup angle. Both coaches threw out the reminder numerous times in interviews that the eventual winner and loser would be decided by what the other four players on each side contributed. Still, it could come down to how the two superstars performed. If Sloan had a sub-par game and Hal sparkled, Brileyville would win. If Hal played below his norm and Sloan was dominant, Markham would win. If both stars were at peak performance, it probably would go down to the wire, perhaps decided by which team got the last good shot.

Markham was slightly favored. The Seabees were a more established state power; Brileyville was the proverbial new kid on the block, and the fact that the Falcons actually were in the state championship game still took some getting used to.

Early on, Markham appeared more poised and the Falcons a little nervous. Hal missed his first four shots and even turned the ball over a couple of times, and the Seabees got out to a ten point lead. But Hal discovered something while getting the feel of the game: that the Markham guards couldn't contain him if he was hitting his shots. He finally got the range on his long jumpers and knocked down four in a row at one juncture and had helped pull his team within a deuce by halftime.

"Awright, we're in it, we've got a chance, and momentum seems to be swinging our way," Wimbush told his players in the locker room. "Only sixteen more minutes. I think we can beat this team. But you've got to keep playing hard. Don't let up. This is it, the big enchilada, for all the marbles. You've got all day tomorrow and even after that to rest. You don't wanta let up now."

The Falcons had no intention of letting up. They moved out to an eight point lead in the third quarter, mostly behind Hal. He dribbled through the Markham guards virtually at will and scored with a couple of long treys, one from probably behind the NBA line, and a couple of nifty drives, including one around Sloan.

But Markham wasn't going away. Sloan blocked a Hal layup and triggered a fast break that ended in a three point play when Hal committed a foul trying to stop the shot. The momentum swung back the other way, and by the middle of the fourth quarter, the Seabees were up by six.

Hal wasn't going away either. He hit one trey, then stole the ball from a Markham guard and hit another three pointer that tied the score. Markham went back in front on a Sloan turnaround; then Hal followed with yet another trey to regain the lead for his team.

The lead changed hands five times over the next three minutes or so, until Hal drew Sloan out and fed Wesley underneath for a bank shot that put Brileyville ahead by a point with thirty seconds remaining.

Markham called time out. Then the Seabees worked the clock and the ball around until with five seconds to play it wound up inside in Sloan's hands for an easy turnaround.

Wimbush called time outs twice; he wanted the ball in Hal's hands. But every time it was inbounded, Hal was surrounded. So Lonnie wound up taking the last shot from about twelve feet and seeing it rim out. Markham was state champion.

Hal's heart sank when the shot failed to go in. He knew it had been a good game, and he certainly had nothing to be ashamed of in his performance. Even so, it hurt to have come this far and close and not win the game.

"Man, that other boy hit that shot, it'd be me with the hangdog look an' you all smiles," Sloan told him consolingly. "One thing we all 'greed on in the huddle: You wasn't gonna be touchin' the ball. I'd rather have that other boy tryna beat me from twelve feet 'un you with the ball an' a chance to win it from thirty."

"It was a helluva game," Hal said with a resigned gesture. "It hurts to lose, but somebody had to. You're a helluva player. Tyrone, isn't it?"

"Yeah. An' you ain't half bad either, Hal," Sloan told him with a shoulder pat.

Wimbush gathered the team together in the locker room. "I don't want anyone walking out of here with their heads down," he told the players firmly. "It was a great game. We lost, but we we took 'em down to the wire. You guys have nothing to be ashamed of. You hung in there with a pretty damned good bunch of players and you came within a whisker of beating 'em. I'd say you have every reason to feel a lot of pride right now."

"Right now, I feel lower'n whaleshit for missin' that last shot," Lonnie confided to Hal.

"Don't," Hal said. He patted Lonnie on the back. "You had to get that ball, set and fire right away."

"Yeah, but I think you mighta made it if we coulda got the ball to you," Lonnie murmured.

"I don't know that. Not really havin' time to get set," Hal said. He punched Lonnie on an arm. "You were on target. The ball just 'cided to come out on you. I miss 'em, too. That wouldn'ta been a guarantee for me."

"They had you surrounded tighter'n a drum," Lonnie sighed.

"We'll get 'em next year," Hal said with a shrug.

46

The heartache that followed defeat had pretty well departed within a few days. Life had to go on, and basketball tends to have lingering importance only to those with enough talent in the sport to anticipate a livelihood from it. Even the latter have other considerations, especially when they are under eighteen and still in high school.

Hal had to attend a banquet when his selection to the first team all-state squad was officially announced. Also announced was that he had been named to a couple of high school all-American teams. His personal stock definitely was rising, and he was starting to understand that losing one basketball game is not necessarily the end of the world.

The banquet provided another face-to-face encounter with Tyrone Sloan, this one of a friendlier note. It seemed odd to Hal to see Sloan in a suit and tie ensemble. He realized that basketball players don't necessarily have to be slobs, but a suit on someone as tall as Sloan struck him as almost ludicruous.

"I never thought 'bout how you might look all duded out," he remarked to the Markham center. "I think the one image I'm always gonna carry of you is you swattin' the ball back in my face a couple times."

"'Lieve me, if I coulda got outta wearin' this outfit, I woulda," Sloan said. He checked out Hal's attire, also suit and tie. "Kinda hard to drill them treys in them togs, too, ain't it?"

Hal chuckled. "Yeah, sure is," he agreed.

The big question hanging over the banquet was who would receive state Player of the Year laurels. Everyone supposed it would come down to Sloan and McDonough, and the eventual honoree seemed like a veritable tossup. The close voting reflected as much. The honor eventually wound up going to Sloan by a very slim margin. The reasoning for most who voted for him was that his team had prevailed in the championship game.

"If it'd been up to me, you'd have been the man," one of the black coaches from another Tidewater school confided to Hal. "Sloan's got size, but you're a better all 'round player."

Hal shrugged. "Well, I'm not gonna spend forever worryin' 'bout it," he reasoned. He thought about it and realized that he was much less disappointed over not receiving top-player honors than losing in the championship game. "I think I was up there, but you come right down to it, only one can win, an' I can't really say I 'served it more'n Tyrone did."

By coincidence, a Brileyville home track meet happened to be held on a day when Eunice was down visiting family. Now, in an odd sense, she almost numbered Hal as a family member, at least by proxy. So she made a point of going to see him run. She wasn't disappointed; he won both the sprints and anchored two winning relays. His times were not exactly world class, but his lack of proper training and facilities considered, they weren't all that unimpressive either.

Eunice's thoughts drifted back to that day a couple of years earlier when she happened on this lonely little boy shooting jump shots all by himself. She thought she detected something special. Now she was almost surprised by how correctly she had gauged his potential.

"It's almost like I'm seeing someone else," she murmured.

"Huh?" her sister responded in surprise.

"It's Hal," Eunice said. "Watching him beat those other young men in that race and seeing him get all-American recognition, I keep thinking about that lonely little boy with a puppy dog kinda face I spotted out behind the Hilton school. It's almost like I'm seeing two different people."

"Well, I think my life might have been quite a bit easier if you'd left him out behind that school," Marian Hanson sighed. "My anxiety level and risk for a stroke or heartattack would be considerably lower anyway."

"I don't really think you mean that," Eunice said in a semi scolding tone.

"Well, I'm glad Hal's future's looking up, of course," Marian Hanson said. She heaved a loud sigh. "But why did my daughter have to become infatuated with him?"

Eunice laughed. "Marian, deep in your heart, you have to know that it wouldn't be the worst thing in the world even if Shawna someday marries Hal."

"Well, Hal's a nice enough young man," Marian Hanson sighed. She draped an arm over her sister's shoulders. "But deep down, wouldn't you rather see your niece choose a young black man as a life's mate?"

"Deep down honestly, sister dear, I just want Shawna to be happy, and if Hal is part of that equation, I'm not going to argue with it," Eunice reasoned.

At that moment, Shawna was approaching with Trina in tow. "Well, Aunt Eunice, what'd you think of Hal's performance?" she asked.

"Actually, I'm kinda glad to see a young white man do well in a sport that seems to be the sole property of African Americans even more than basketball," Eunice said. "I don't think any sport should be labeled any group's sole property. It's possible that Hal will encourage some younger white boys to compete in those events in the same way Arthur Ashe paved the way for blacks to play tennis."

"I think it's a little extreme comparing Hal to Arthur Ashe," Marian Hanson rebutted sharply.

Shawna laughed. "I'm not sure Hal really counts if you're talkin' 'bout him as a role model for white boys. I'm not sure he even really knows he's white anymore."

"He'll be getting plenty of reminders of it, don't worry," Marian Hanson assured her daughter.

Just then, Hal was approaching. Just the slightest hint of a smile indicated that he felt good about his day's performance. "I didn't know you were a track buff," he greeted Eunice.

"Oh, I like all sports," Eunice said. She greeted Hal appreciatively. "And I must say you ran very well today. And I deliberately avoid the 'for a white boy' addendum. You seem to be pretty fast for any group."

"Well, I'm not gonna be throwin' out any challenges to Carl Lewis or Leroy Burrell anytime soon, but I guess I can outrun a lotta guys," Hal said with a shrug. "I got a decent shot at winnin' the district next week. It's prob'ly gonna come down to me an' the guy from Blanchard. He beat me once, I beat him once, an' our times been pretty competitive, so's I guess it's just gonna come down to who's better on that day."

"Oh, by the way, I haven't had a chance to congratulate you on making high school all-American," Eunice said. "You've come a long way in a very short time."

Hal nodded thoughtfully. "Least once a day, too, it 'ccurs to me none of it mighta happened if it wouldn'ta been for you," he responded. "I coulda slipped through the cracks real easy. I might be watchin' somethin' like this from up on top of that hill an' not have any idea in this world I might be good 'nuff to be down here runnin'. When I think 'bout that, it kinda makes me 'ppreciate what a lot of y'all had to go through over the years."

Eunice was genuinely touched. "I think hearing you say that just now might be my greatest source of pride if I contributed anything to what you've developed into," she said. She draped an arm over the young man's shoulders. "Let's go get something to eat. I'm starved."

"Here, here," Shawna seconded the motion.